A NOVEL BY

Leonard
Harris

The

Hamptons

Wyndham Books
New York

This novel is a work of fiction. Names, characters, places and incidents are either the product of the author's imagination or are used fictitiously. Any resemblance to actual persons, living or dead, events or locales is entirely coincidental.

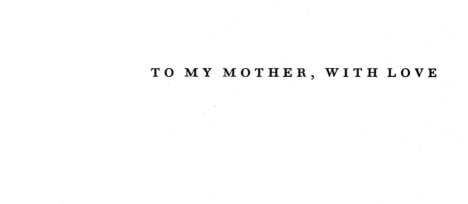

TO MY MOTHER, WITH LOVE

December, 1976

IN ANGRY disregard of the off-season, the storm, half-white half-gray with snow and sleet, tore apart the December calm of East Hampton, its winds whipping the winter ocean to a frothing frenzy. For twenty-four hours before the storm's arrival, radio and television stations had been broadcasting warnings and the local police had been suggesting —not ordering—that Hamptonites within a half mile of the ocean leave their houses for a while.

Bea Fletcher knew none of this.

In Nashville she would have known it, because there she'd been a housewife, her daily routine performed to the sound of the radio— music, news, commercials. In Washington she would have known it, because there she'd been a journalist . . . well, a gossip columnist, but still she'd had to read the papers and watch the news carefully.

Now she was a novelist, or trying to be, and pleased with it, proud of it, lost in it. And lost in the quiet of her rented East Hampton cottage near the dunes. It was not *hers*, but she loved it, and in the off-season could afford it. Some days she never left it except to go to the beach, where she'd walk or jog or sit and watch the ocean; she wouldn't even go to town to pick up the *Times*.

The storm was a surprise to her; the first she knew of it was the rising wind driving through the stunted evergreens around the house. The sound, the movement, excited her. Much as she loved the house and the season and being by herself, with Staunnie and Amanda gone off to boarding school, she had to admit she sometimes grew a bit lonely. Never bored—there was always too much stewing in her brain, about her life and her characters' lives—but lonely. The storm was company arriving.

The rising wind, the darkening sky, were exciting and cleansing; they made her feel that she and everything around were being aired, cleaned of the complications and the mess she'd lived through for her first thirty years. They made her feel clean and simple, like the house and the double dunes around it and the sun setting behind those dunes on these quiet, cold evenings when the Hamptons themselves were purged of the plague of chic that infested them all summer.

When the wind hit forty, then fifty miles an hour, the excitement was joined by fear, but still delicious. Then an unhooked shutter tore loose from a second-story window, went crashing to the brick patio, and the excitement waned as the fright grew. Then the sleet started, fine, wind-driven at first, growing fiercer and denser, while the wind picked up and the skies darkened.

The house began to groan; Bea had trouble concentrating on her reading, so she went to her electric typewriter, determined to use her mood, hoping the energy of the machine would keep her company. She moved the bar to "on." Nothing happened.

"Oh shit!" She said it loudly, as if to calm herself with the companionship of her own voice. She fidgeted with the plug, hoping that would solve the problem, knowing it wouldn't. Quickly, almost desperately, she walked to the lamp nearby, turned the switch. Nothing happened. She got up from her desk, left the den, went into the dining room, flipped on the light. Nothing happened.

At a run, she reached the kitchen, picked up the wall phone, got a dial tone.

"Oh, good! Oh, thank God!" Again it was for her own ears, but this time the words were more encouraging. She didn't know whom to call. It was a Friday in December; perhaps someone who didn't have to stick to an office all day might have come out early for a long winter weekend.

Harry Majors would probably be here—God knows he didn't worry about an office!—but their "relationship"—the one she thought was going to be the love of her life—was coming apart. No Harry.

Johnny Wainwright, president of the publishing company his family had started. Yes. She looked up his number in the little book near the kitchen phone, and dialed it. Three rings, four, five; he had a big house, she'd give him some more. She'd *will* him to answer. But he didn't. She put the phone down, looked out the window; it was getting darker, the wind attacking, the house groaning in pain. Who else? With a tightness growing in her chest, she riffled through the phone book, saw it open to the letter K, saw the name Freddie Kohl. No, not Freddie. She didn't like him, but he might be out here, he was rich enough and powerful enough to come out early on Fridays if he felt like it. Hell, he was rich enough and powerful enough to stay out here all week—all the rest of his life—if he felt like it. She dialed his East Hampton number, let it ring three, four, five times, half hoping he wouldn't answer, half hoping he would. On the sixth ring he answered.

"Freddie, it's Bea Fletcher."

"Well, hello, my dear, how are you? Holding up amid this storm?" Freddie was not American born and though he had a brilliant mind and a richer English vocabulary than most Americans, he often sounded strained when he was trying to sound easy and idiomatic.

"Barely, Freddie. I'm scared. The power is out here, it's dark. I wish I weren't such a coward. Do you have lights?"

"No. I'm in the dark. It's dreadfully inconvenient. But we've got some candles and flashlights, and we're managing."

Of course, she said to herself, you're not all alone, you've got staff—paid company. And flashlights and candles. Almost as if he'd read her mind, he asked: "Do you have any emergency light at all?"

"I never thought to get any. Electricity is not supposed to fail; this is 1976, for Christ's sake!"

"I'll be right over, with some light."

"Oh no, Freddie, don't be silly." Ordinarily she would have meant the no. This time she was hoping he'd push through her protest. He did.

"Nonsense! A beautiful lady in distress. I'll mount my white charger and be coming over at the gallop." Freddie's white charger was a powder-blue Rolls Corniche, which she thought ostentatious—and gorgeous.

Again, another time she would have assured him she was on her way somewhere. This time she just said, "Oh, Freddie," weakly enough, she hoped, so he'd override her again.

He did. Thank God, she said to herself.

"I insist. I'll be over in five minutes."

She hung up, began to feel a lot better, headed for the living room to put a record on, remembered she couldn't because she had no power, started to feel just a little worse, when the phone rang. She ran for it, anxious for the voice, hoping it wasn't Freddie changing his mind.

"Hi! I'm worried about you. Is that allowed?" The pleasure at the sound of a voice was overridden by a stronger feeling—pain, love, remembrance. The voice was Harry's . . . barely audible over the howling, shrieking, voice of the wind and the rising drumbeat of the rain.

She covered herself in the cloak of flippancy. "Yeah, it's all right. I'm so scared I'm even glad to hear you."

"Your effusiveness is underwhelming. Makes me almost glad I almost didn't call."

"Sorry, Harry. I am so scared I won't even ask what that means. And I *am* glad you called. How much worse is this thing going to get?" The wind drove the cottage to a kind of moaning echo of her question.

"A little bit worse, not much—according to the radio. Your house should stand. I won't have to offer you squatter's rights on my estate." For years, Harry had been renting the same small bungalow on the dunes. But that was soon to end; the owner wanted to sell it—for $300,000, which Harry couldn't afford.

"How come you have a radio working, with all the power out?"

"A mystical power source, kid. Called batteries. Is the unflappable Bea really scared?"

"I'm talking to *you*. Doesn't that prove it? I don't like being alone, in the dark, in a storm, worrying about the house coming apart. Any *one* I could handle. Maybe two. Three, I doubt. Four, definitely not. I don't know why I feel scared; but I do. So scared I called Freddie Kohl, who gallantly offered to hop into his Rolls and bring me candles, flashlight, and company. So scared, I accepted."

Harry was a little hurt; she could hear it in his voice. "So he gets the nod ahead of the old Saint Bernard in a storm, eh? Even with the cask around my neck."

"You don't mean that, do you, Harry? Surely you know the difference—he merely offends me; you upset me. I'd rather be offended."

"I'll be right over; I hate the idea that in a crisis, you're relying on that . . . man, rather than on me."

"Harry, you . . ."

But he hung up before she could finish. A ferocious burst of wind and sleet, which rattled the old glass panes in her windows, made her glad he hadn't listened to her.

She phoned Freddie, to call him off. His housekeeper, Sophie, said he'd just driven away. So she'd have both men there.

A few minutes later she saw a car's headlights through her living room window. She ran to the door, expecting either the tan of Harry's rented Ford or the light blue of Freddie's Rolls. It was neither. She saw instead Johnny Wainwright's white two-seater Mercedes 450 SL. His tall lean frame unfolded from the seat, and he came toward her, jeans and an Irish sweater showing beneath a yellow slicker, an old-fashioned kerosene lantern in hand.

"Thought you might need a hand, little lady," he said, grinning, as he walked up to her.

"Little lady sure as hell does, come on in." He entered via the kitchen, which was the door next to her driveway, and therefore the one everybody used. The glow of the lantern gave the room a mysterious, warm look. She felt a lot better, smiled as Johnny took off the dripping slicker, put it on the floor in a corner. "You were the first one I called, Johnny. Only you didn't answer, so I had to go to my second string."

"I just drove out from the city. The storm was bad and getting worse when I was about to start, so I went down to the basement, got a couple of old lanterns and thought I'd check on a few friends on the way out. You're actually the third stop. Hope you're not hurt by that."

"Hurt? I think it incredibly gallant of you. I couldn't be hurt by it any more than you'd be if I told you you were the third one to offer to come to my rescue—and the first to arrive."

"Am I really the third?"

"Yup. First I called you. When there was no answer, I asked myself who might be out here this early. I tried Freddie. He was home, and he volunteered to rush to my rescue. He's on his way now."

Johnny looked at her curiously. "Freddie before Harry, eh? My, my!"

"You say it as if it's pearls before swine, but you've got it wrong.

Freddie and I are definitely not an item for Liz Smith or Suzy. I called him because I was in trouble, and looking for help. I call Harry when I need help looking for *trouble*. See the difference?"

Johnny grinned at her. "Yes, subtle, but I think I've got it. Harry is a no-no."

She had to laugh. "Not exactly. Harry is on his way over. He called me; the dear considerate thing was worried about me, and nothing could dissuade him from coming over. I suppose I didn't try too hard."

Harry and Freddie pulled into the driveway together, and ran to the door, Freddie carrying a big electric torch, a small flashlight and a box of candles in a plastic bag, Harry carrying nothing.

The hellos were jovial, and Bea never doubted they were meant. These four people, the Middle-European moneyman, the Jewish comedy writer, the Wasp Ivy League publisher and the Southern "lady," were about as far apart as neighbors could be, yet with the snow and sleet trying to beat down the roof and the wind trying to lift it off, they all were united.

"I suddenly feel so snug and safe with all of you here, as if no storm in the world could touch me," she said. "By the way, are we about to be obliterated? Because if we are, I think we'd better have a drink first."

"Alas, I think we're going to survive," Harry said. "But we could always pretend we weren't. For drinking purposes."

"Wonderful," Bea said. "Let's drink to . . . the storm. Do they give names to winter storms?"

"No," said Freddie. "Only to hurricanes."

"That doesn't mean *we* can't name her," Harry offered.

"All right," said Bea. "But what?"

There was a pause, then Harry came up with something, as she knew he would.

"Shirley."

"Shirley?" Bea asked.

"Why not?" said Johnny with a grin. "The weather's the one thing left the Jews don't control."

"So far," said Harry. "Which is why you get things like this storm. If we did . . . *when* we do . . . it'll be Malibu everywhere."

"That'll be just great for us skiers," Johnny replied.

"Oh hang up your jock, Wainwright," said Harry good-humoredly. "At your age it begins to be embarrassing. And oh so Gentile!"

Bea began pouring from an open bottle of red wine. "All right, all right. If Moshe Dayan and Yassir Arafat will each take a step back, we'll all drink to . . . Shirley." She handed each of them a glass, and raised hers.

"To Shirley," she said.

"To Shirley," they echoed.

After a sip, she spoke again. "You know, I wasn't kidding about being glad you're here, about thinking what a lovely thing it is that you should come out in this storm to help me. Makes me feel like I belong someplace, like I have a home. I haven't really felt that before, not for a long time, since way back in Nashville. Certainly never in Washington."

Johnny nodded. "I guess I'm the senior citizen in this room; I've spent more time than any of you out here. I've seen it happen. The South Fork has what they call a sense of place. People who come out here catch it. It becomes a neighborhood for people who've never had one before, not in New York or wherever they're from. People who, in the city, might damned well close their windows to shut out a neighbor's screams, out here will ride for miles through a storm on the chance someone might need help."

"Very well said," Freddie Kohl offered eagerly. "*I* should like to be thought of as part of this neighborhood. As someone who can be counted upon when needed in a storm."

As if cued, the wind picked up with a howl, tore at a shutter, which clattered in protest.

Bea shuddered. "You certainly *are* all needed. The force of that beast out there makes me feel tiny and fragile. And in need of neighbors."

"They're always available out here. That's the way it is," Johnny said. "Perhaps it's because there aren't so many people out here— they're fewer, farther apart, more precious. Perhaps it's the presence of that big brute of an ocean out there that makes us feel so tiny we huddle together for shelter."

"And . . . *perhaps* . . . it's the old school tie that binds," Harry said.

"Oh, hell!" Johnny replied. "You know what you are? The worst, most bigoted kind of inverted snob. Here we are, the four of us, as different as we can be, come together to help one of us. You make it sound as if we were trying to get a quorum for the Maidenhead . . ."

Shirley hurled another blast of wind, driving the snow and sleet with a slashing fury against the clapboard. Again, Bea shivered.

"Should we all be bracing ourselves against the wall to keep the old manse from collapsing? Are we and this old place going to make it?"

"Is your insurance paid up?"

"The federal government insures you against hurricane and flood," Johnny said.

"I meant life insurance, not house insurance," Harry replied.

"Harry, I'd forgotten how little I missed your humor," Bea said. "Thanks for reminding me. Johnny, is my little house in any danger?"

The publisher shook his head. "Those farmers knew what they were doing when they built their houses. They knew what storms were, too, and they lived with the power of nature—remember they had that ocean in their backyards every day, not just on summer weekends. They had nowhere to go where they could snuggle in a big safe apartment house, surrounded by other piles of brick and steel, to keep safe. After all, how bad can a storm get in the city, where the environment is nine-tenths man, and only one-tenth nature? No, this farmhouse was the only home its owner had, and it was built by a man who *respected* the elements. It'll be all right. We'll be all right. Now, the beach—that's something else. I hope we've got some left after this blast. Don't worry about the house."

"Which is not to say we should get cocky or anything, and stop drinking." Harry emptied the wine bottle into their glasses.

"And will the basement flood?" Bea asked. "Will the roof leak? How do I turn the heat back on? It's getting so cold in here. Who'll get a blaze going in that fireplace for me? One of the blessings of a husband —maybe the *only* blessing—is having someone to look after things like that."

"Tell you what," Johnny said. "You open another bottle of—whatever that was—I'll start a fire and check the house."

"It's a new Beaujolais, cheap but not bad," she said. "And you've got yourself a deal." She pulled another bottle from a wine rack standing in the corner of the kitchen.

Harry got to his feet. "Well, I'm not about to check your leaks. It's beyond my area of competence. But when it comes to uncorking wine, nobody does it better. Here. Let me."

Bea handed him the corkscrew. Freddie also stood, feeling a need to contribute to the commonweal.

"And I'll provide the atmosphere." He began lighting the candles he had brought with him and placing them around the kitchen.

Johnny started a fire, checked the house and was back in ten minutes, during which Bea and Harry had worked their way through half the new bottle, with Freddie sipping to offer a bit of help.

"The house is as sound as a dollar, or as a dollar *used* to be," he announced. "No damage, no water in attic or basement. But the heat won't go on. I've checked the furnace, and nothing seems wrong, except it won't start. Did you have it on before?"

Bea looked at him, shrugged. "I don't know. Isn't that pitiful? I don't *know* if the heat was on. I just know it wasn't cold before, and now it is."

"It's *His* fault," Harry said. "Take care of *Him* in your book."

"Don't be a smartass," Bea snapped. "Fix the heat, if you're so damned smart."

"I *am* fixing the heat," Harry replied, holding up his glass. "We'll all be warm as toast—as long as the wood and the wine hold out."

"There's more, Harry, don't get upset. In fact, why don't you uncork another bottle—I know you know how to do *that*." Bea handed him the corkscrew. Harry got to his feet.

"It is one area where my expertise is legendary," he said. He'd just pulled the cork, when they heard a rap on the kitchen door.

"Who was it said help is hard to find?" Harry said. "You're one damsel who's going to be distressed by how much you're getting. Especially if they drink wine the way we do."

"What they say, Harry dear," she replied as she started toward the door, "is that *good* help is hard to find. The kind that knows how to turn my furnace on."

"Surely you don't mean that metaphorically," he said.

"Don't get fresh!"

She opened the door; the wind almost tore it from her grip. A stocky man of medium height stood there, protected against the storm by a yellow slicker and sou'wester. Beneath the hat his face was square-jawed and beefy. He didn't look like anyone Bea knew or was supposed to know.

"Can I help you?" she asked.

"Detective Stanley Wisniewski, East Hampton police," he said.

"Come in," Bea told him, "before we all freeze or get blown away."

"Thank you, ma'am." He stepped inside, helped Bea pull the kitchen door shut. The detective took off the sou'wester, tried not to let it drip on the floor. Hat off, he seemed younger. His eyes were a light blue, his hair straw-colored and cut as if for Army basic training, medium length on top, shorn almost to the skin on the sides. At 5 foot 9, he looked like an undersized Notre Dame football player.

He also looked deferential and uncomfortable, trying to twist and squeeze the hat to keep it from dripping, until Bea said, "Here, give me that," and took it from him and stood it on the counter next to the sink.

"You got here just in time, officer," she said severely. "These are your men"—she looked toward the three at the table—"lock them up and throw away the key. I charge each of them with impersonating a rescuer—and doing a lousy job of it, at that."

The detective smiled at her, his face crinkling at the eyes and mouth. "They put us all on duty, to check on residents who might need help during the storm. I saw all the cars and figured there'd be people here, so I decided to give it a look-see."

A look-see. Bea didn't think people said that anymore, not anyone as young as he. "I didn't know detectives did that kind of work," she said.

"We don't," he replied pleasantly. "But we're a small department, ma'am, and . . ."

"Well, then, who's out investigating the homicides?" Freddie asked, patronizingly.

"We don't have any to investigate at the moment, thank goodness." If he heard the condescension, Wisniewski ignored it.

"If there were one, wouldn't they call in the FBI?" Freddie asked.

Again the detective smiled placidly. "In order for the FBI to be brought in, there must be a presumption of an interstate crime." He said it as if reading from a text. "Of course, we can use their technical help, if we need it—their labs."

"You mean thair Labrador retrievers?" Bea asked.

Still, he gave no sign he knew they were teasing. "Their laboratories. You hardly ever need dogs; there's never any tracking to do. Out here most homicides are committed by people who know their victims, not by outsiders or strangers. Of course, in the city . . ."

"Ah yes, the city," Harry interrupted. "They'll kill you there without so much as an introduction. I've always said our problem in New York City is not so much violence as it is bad manners."

"Detective Wiz . . ." Bea began, and then hesitated.

"It's spelled W-I-S-N-I-E-W-S-K-I," he said, "and pronounced Wizz-

NEFF-ski, which is a bit the Polish way of saying it, and a bit the American way." Bea saw him staying polite and restrained in the face of their wisecracks, and she admired him for it.

"Detective Wisniewski," she said. "I think you should be introduced to these people who are asking you so many questions. I'm Bea Fletcher. This is Johnny Wainwright. Freddie Kohl. And Harry Majors." The detective reached out with a broad, thick-fingered hand to shake their hands.

"It's my pleasure to meet you, folks," he said. "I'm happy to answer any questions, but if you're all right, I've got many stops to make, and . . ."

"We do have a real problem," Bea said. "We can't seem to turn on the heat. I know it's not exactly in your line . . ."

"My brother-in-law's in plumbing and heating," Wisniewski said.

"Oh," she answered. "Can you give me his phone number, or call him for me?"

He smiled again. "I didn't mean that. I'll take a look at it. How do you get to the basement?"

"Practice, m'boy, practice," Harry said. Bea stared angrily at him; he seemed a little drunk. The detective looked puzzled.

"It's a bad joke about someone asking a musician how to get to Carnegie Hall," she explained. "He has a limited repertoire, Detective Wisniewski, and one has to be with him only a short time to learn it. You, luckily, will be spared that experience. Let me show you how to get to the basement." She walked him to a door in the far corner of the kitchen. From the big pocket of his slicker he pulled a flashlight, shone it on the walls inside the basement door until he spotted a switch, checked that it was on.

"Of course you understand the furnace won't work till you have power . . ."

"Oh," Bea said blankly.

"The switch is on, so as soon as the power goes on, the furnace will." He said it simply, with no condescension.

"You are wonderful, sir," Bea said. Then she turned to Harry. "You see, he does what *he* does a lot better than you do what *you* do."

"Whatever *that* means," Harry replied.

"It means, m'boy, that *you* should practice. And Detective Wisniewski, you should sit down and have a glass of wine with us."

He shook his head and smiled. "No, thank you, ma'am, I'm just glad

I could help." He walked to the sink, picked up his sou'wester. "I've really got to be going. There are a lot more houses to check."

"Not that have cheap Beaujolais," Bea said.

Another placid smile. "Thanks anyway. Goodbye, Mrs. Fletcher. Mr. Majors. Mr. Wainwright. Mr. Kohl."

The four of them murmured return goodbyes. He'd gotten their names perfectly, and they all realized it. As soon as he was out the door, Johnny said: "Well, Ralph Waldo Emerson once said, there's something to be learned from everybody—or words to that effect. He said it when a humble dairymaid showed him how to lead a calf out of the barn by putting a finger in its mouth, imitating the teat of the mother."

"Sounds like a good imitation," Harry offered. "Do you suppose she did Bette Davis too?"

"Oh shut up, Mr. Show Business," Bea said. "And all of you, you're shameful, the way you tried to put that man down. Why don't you all get drunk and try to be pleasant."

"For me, the latter is impossible," Harry replied. "And I'll keep trying the former till I get it right."

"You're known for it, Harry," she said. "The former, that is." It was growing dark, which seemed to subdue the storm by cloaking the ferocity of its driving sleet and glowering gray clouds. Johnny lit his lanterns, put one on the sink, one on a far counter. Freddie lit three more of his candles and stood them on the table.

Bea looked around her and grinned. They all smiled back. "This light does wonders for us. None of you looks a day over thirty, and I'm sure I must look . . ." She hesitated.

"Twenty-five," Johnny said.

"Twenty-one," Freddie underbid him.

"Fourteen—and not looking it," Harry said.

"For that, the wine keeps flowing." She refilled their glasses, raised hers.

"To my rescuers, my neighbors, my friends. To the Hamptons, which I love so. To the storm, which brought us together."

They all raised their glasses and sipped.

"To the next bottle of Beaujolais," Harry said.

"It's ready and waiting," Bea responded. "And the one after it, and the one after that. As many as you want, my dear pals."

Johnny raised his glass. "To *this* port, in *any* storm." They drank.

Then Freddie raised his glass, his black eyes darting around the table. "Hear, hear! And to Bea, who brought us together. To Bea and her new book. May it bring us all health, wealth and happiness!"

And with that the spell was broken, the communality shattered, the single common purpose split into four, each forming its own head and tail and wriggling off in its own direction. They all remembered who they were, what they were after, who was in their way.

April, 1977

Now SHE had her own house. Hers, not rented, and Bea luxuriated in it, breathed it in through her pores as she dropped onto the chaise on her patio and stretched her long slim legs out in front of her. She felt satisfied, pleased with her Sagaponack farmhouse, her patio, her chaise and her legs. Everyone said it was criminal that a woman of forty who never exercised should have such legs. To which Bea replied: "Nashville women have *always* had perfect legs. And they have *never* exercised."

"Are you ready?"

"Yes, dear," Irv Schnell replied. "I'm ready."

For none of his authors but Bea would Irv Schnell sit still and be read to. Not even for Heinemann, whose paperback sales were beginning to challenge the Bible's. Not for any of the others, despite their National Book Awards or Pulitzers.

Bea was special. Irv, who was sixty-one, short, round, widowed after thirty-three years of happy marriage, had a crush on Bea. Nothing sexual, or romantic, but a real crush. In the publishing business, Irv was an undersized tiger. With Bea, he was an oversized pussycat.

"You don't have to, unless you really want to."

"I want to, I want to! Go ahead."

She lifted the manuscript. "Now remember, this is just the pro-logue . . ." Then she enunciated the word "prologue" as if reciting a poem at school. Irv grinned. He thought everything she did was enchanting.

"By the time of the American Revolution, the string of villages we now call the Hamptons had been settled for more than a century, and today many of the names of the seventeenth-century English settlers can still be found there, borne by descendants of those early farmers and fishermen. Later, Polish names and many others joined the English ones, but farming and fishing remained the principal occupations, and the people of the Hamptons, nestled in the small villages, or living out on the flat potato fields, remained light-years away from the metropolis which stood only one hundred miles to the west . . ."

"You're writing this for public television?"

"Irv, I don't want you to say another word unless it's to switch from white wine to hemlock. I'm nervous enough baring myself before one of the two or three greatest literary agents in the free world."

"Two or three?"

"I'll change it to five if you don't shut up and listen! This is *not* for public television. Was 'WashingtonShock' for public television? This part will be every bit as bitchy; believe in me, will you? Now I'm going to try to continue . . .

"By and large these communities which nestle up to the endless white barrier beaches of the South Fork have English names, East Hampton, Southampton, Bridgehampton, Water Mill, Wainscott, with a smattering of Indian: Sagaponack, Amagansett, Montauk. The ones I'll be talking about stretch eastward from the Shinnecock Canal. I *could* include certain other villages, such as Westhampton and Quogue, but since the essence of the place is exclusiveness, why should I allow any place *in*, when I can leave it *out*?

"In any event, the natives are no longer exclusively farmers and fishermen. They've discovered a more lucrative area, the service trades. They are the plumbers, contractors, electricians, carpenters, shopkeepers, pool vacuumers . . ."

"I'm sorry, Bea, they're not called pool vacuumers . . ."

She threw Irv an exasperated look. "Did you interrupt Tolstoi because he got the name of a battle wrong?"

"No, sweetheart, Swifty Lazar was Tolstoi's agent. I was hoping *you'd* be my Tolstoi."

"And I was hoping *you'd* be my Swifty Lazar! Now may I go on?" Without waiting for an answer she resumed reading.

". . . Pool vacuumers, lawn mowers, house watchers, real estate agents, and on and on—people who cater to the needs and share the wealth of the New Class in the Hamptons, the summer people. Or weekenders, or vacationers, or second-homeowners. Call them what you will, what I mean is, they're not native and they don't depend on the Hamptons for their living. By the way, the rubric, The Hamptons, is used only by the newest of this New Class. One will never hear the natives refer to 'The Hamptons,' and very soon after he looks around him, even the summer person realizes it is definitely *nouveau* to use the term, and he stops at once.

"There is, of course, a hierarchy of summer people. At its very bottom stands the grouper, who, from Memorial Day weekend to Labor Day weekend, shoehorns himself into a rental house shared with others, usually several more than the house can hold, and spends the summer battling over who owns the wine, who does the dishes and who has the guest privileges.

"Next stands the single renter who, by himself, with loved one or wife and family, *rents* a house for the season at a figure one customarily associates with the *purchase* of a house for ever and ever. Imagine a $35,000, $50,000 rental for a *summer?*

"Then, on top, is the owner, who if he is not a snob when he buys, has snobbism conferred upon him with his down payment and first mortgage. But who among us does not have a bit of the snob lurking within, waiting to break out? Who does not have the temptation to pull the ladder up behind him, once he's climbed up where he wants to be? As if to say, now that *I'm* here, the place is crowded enough! No room for any more! Which is why a friend, walking along a crowded Amagansett beach, could look down his nose and say, 'I didn't know the *subway* came out this far!' I happen to know that once upon a time this man took the subway to the beach himself, and was damned glad it went there. Now he gets to his beach house by Mercedes, and the devil take the subway crowd!

"Well, you can't get to the Hamptons on the subway; which to its summer people is part of its charm. In fact, sometimes I think you can't get here at all. The Long Island Rail Road is a disaster . . ."

"Wait a minute," Irv interrupted.

Bea reached for his glass. "You *will* switch to hemlock?"

"Stop it, Bea!"

"I told you, hemlock was the only reason . . ."

"Suppose the Long Island is all fixed up by the time the book comes out?"

"I know I'm supposed to be writing fiction, but this is ridiculous! How long have you been coming out here, Irv? Ten years?"

"Fourteen."

"In all that time have you ever known the track bed to be smooth, the ride fast, the train clean, the toilets usable? In short, the Long Island Rail Road to be *fixed?*"

"No, but they're supposed to make improvements . . ."

"And *with* the improvements, do you know how fast the ride is going to be? Let me tell you. *With* the improvements they hope to get the train out as fast as it got out here in *1903!* Nineteen-oh-goddamn-three! Now, dear Maxwell Perkins, do I get to go on? Are you interested in getting to the climax? Or do you want to turn this into a read-us interruptus?"

Irv blushed. "OK! OK!" He was a prude and Bea loved to embarrass him.

"Even in a $30,000 Mercedes the ride can take four hours on a Friday afternoon. Someone has suggested a special Mercedes lane on the Long Island Expressway. You know, like the bus lanes? But there aren't enough Mercedes owners for that—thank goodness. If only the Governor had to get out here by car, it might be different. But he comes by helicopter—which is the only right way! Even a regular plane won't do, because it means a cab ride to LaGuardia, which can be a pain on a Friday afternoon. Yes, a helicopter is ideal, signifying as it does affluence, distinction and ease—but then those three usually do go together, don't they?

"By now you're probably wondering who *I* am to be making all these pronouncements about the Hamptons"—Bea paused, looked up, sipped her white wine—"and indeed you are right to, so let me introduce myself. My name is Barbara Forrester, and . . ."

Irv burst in. "I said it before, I'll say it again! It's too close! Bea Fletcher! Barbara Forrester! Too close!"

"Irv, don't be such an old maid. It's supposed to be close—the initials are *supposed* to be the same! That's the fun of it. Hell, you can be sure I'm not going to sue myself! As for the other characters, I'll get just as close as I can, until the lawyers tell me to stop. It worked for 'WashingtonShock'! Want more wine?"

She brought her knees up to flex her legs, stretched them out again, looked off into the potato fields behind her house. The afternoon was sunny, not too warm, the air still. The summer was months away. How lucky, she thought, to be able to earn money, and *lots* of it—the success of "WashingtonShock," the serialized first part of her book, made her believe that—while sitting out here and doing what she loved. Writing. And playing God. It sure beat working for a living, she told her family down in Nashville.

"No more wine, thanks, Bea. Go on reading."

"My name is Barbara Forrester, and I came to the Hamptons' literary scene from the South, via Washington, D.C. I came to it late, which may be a blessing, because I'm able to see with an outsider's eye the indigenous lunacy which so many of the local lunatics think perfectly normal.

"There are many characters and many stories in the Hamptons, some as interesting or perhaps more interesting than the ones I've chosen. Of course, I'd like to claim mine are the best, the most significant, the most representative. But I can't. I can only say they are stories and characters *I* know and find interesting. Some of the people I even *like!* Some. Some, I detest.

"Fritz Kane, for example, may be the richest man in the Hamptons, a superlative that's not easy to come by. He may also be the most insecure and tortured, which is even harder to come by. Now some of those closest to him—I shan't make the mistake of calling them his friends—would quarrel with that. They'd say he doesn't *suffer* the most pain, he *inflicts* it. Perhaps they're right. What fascinates me is how his money has failed to buy him generosity, or ease, or surcease from pain. How he must still grab and manipulate and corrupt. And *get no enjoyment from it*. Or from anything else. How his eyes are always darting around, like a cornered animal's.

"Senator Marty Hogan is an example of a good man corrupted by Fritz. In my Washington chapter I mentioned him when he was still an idealistic young Congressman, and promised I'd tell more about how he went off the deep end. I'll keep that promise.

"Then, Bobby Rourke, another noble man marred by a tragic flaw, or two or three. They're the most interesting, aren't they—unless you happen to be married to one. Ask Cathy, Bobby's super-wife—super ex-wife, now—mother of their two children. She watched her handsome war hero go from hot-shot executive and family man to drunkard and philanderer. And so her rise, *deserved* rise, to Queen of Television News is spoiled. So is her marriage. Wonderful Cathy deserves better, but then I'm biased 'cause she's my best friend. Barbara and Cathy, the Damon and Pythias of the Hamptons! I realize that analogy leaves something to be desired. I'm working on it. Besides, it's only my first book!

"Jamey Warner is a publisher, one of the last nice guys in a business that used to be full of them. But that's changing. Will Jamey change with it, or go under, flags flying? A rotten choice for a nice guy to have to make.

"The new rules—or should I say no-rules—in publishing were made to order for Suzy Miller. That tough little cookie thrives on back-alley fighting. Alas for her, and for her ex, Hank, both balls in the Miller marriage went to the wrong partner. . . ."

Irv couldn't let that go. "Wait a minute, Bea. You'll make enough enemies, in any event. Don't you think that dig is kind of personal, and small? And bitter?"

She snapped at him, something she hardly ever did, something no one else could get away with. "Shut up! You're right, but shut up anyway. I let Harry get through to me. I must remember not to do that again. Besides, if I don't get to do a little personal pissing and moaning, why write a book?" Quickly, she answered herself. "For the money, that's why. I'm almost finished, Irv, so be patient. . . ."

She started reading again. "Then there's my agent, Ike Schwartz . . ."

"Ike? Bea! Ike? Do you have to?"

"Oh vanity, vanity! Irv, I told you I wanted all the initials to match! Would you prefer Izzie? Iggy? If you come up with something better and I like it, I'll change it."

"One more thing."

Bea shook her head. "What is it?"

"Is . . . Barbara Forrester . . . are *you* . . . going to be the heroine of your own book?"

She smiled her dazzling smile. Bea had beautiful teeth. Johnny Carson had once said she had the only set of pearly fangs he'd ever seen. "What makes you think there's going to be a hero or a heroine in the book? I know you keep asking for one, but you should know better, sweetheart. Didn't I say it was about the Hamptons? Didn't I say it was going to be *true?* Doesn't leave much room for heroes or heroines, does it? Now, I'm practically finished!"

She resumed reading.

"Then there's my agent Ike Schwartz, and a slew of supporting characters. But the book is less about these people than it is about the Hamptons. What life is like there. What sparks are struck as the literati rub shoulders, and God knows what else. Despite the orderly, manicured facade, despite the protests of Hamptonites that their weekends are for calm and rest, there is a turbulence to the place. Of course it would be easy to say the people, not the Hamptons, cause the turbulence. And it would be true, but not the whole picture. It's an interaction. Maybe the people started it, but now the place itself is like a maelstrom, and though you enter it with serenity, staying there and staying serene is another matter."

Bea looked at Irv, as if she knew what he was thinking. "Worry not, agent mine," she said. "The public television stuff doesn't go on. We're right at the windup."

She looked down to her manuscript.

"Finally, I want to answer the question: Is the book true? Are Fritz and the Senator and Cathy and Bobby and Jamey and Suzy and Hank and of course, yours truly Barbara Forrester, real people? The answer to that is yes. And no. Certainly I hope the book is full of truth, true observations about human beings and the way they act and think. True conclusions about their essences. Certainly, individual traits I've borrowed from living people. But none of my characters is supposed to be an actual person. *I've* given them life. They are *my* people, and no reader should go through the book asking, is Fritz really so-and-so? Is Cathy really so-and-so?

"However, if the reader finds some comparisons, and is turned on by them, well, why not go on thinking so, and having fun? As they say . . . anything that gets you through the book!"

She stopped reading, put the manuscript down, looked up, shrugged at Irv, had another sip of wine.

"Amen! And may lots of people get through the book! Lots and lots of people! By Labor Day I'll have it finished, Irv. So it can come out next spring. Perfect timing."

"You're not worried?" he asked.

"About what? That it won't sell?"

"No, sweetheart. That you'll antagonize powerful, desperate people.

Buster Reilly, for example, who'll know Bobby Rourke is him. Buster, don't forget, is supposed to have strangled people with his bare hands during The War, and gotten medals for it. And Freddie Kohl, who'll stop at nothing—*nothing*—to get what he wants. Johnny Wainwright, who will not be pushed out of this business without a fight. The Governor, whose eye is on the White House, and will use a lot of muscle to keep anyone from getting in his way. These are all people who will not be fooled by your fictitious names. These are all people who can hurt you. In many ways. Including physically.

"Will it sell is the least of your problems. And by the way, it *will* sell!"

She leaned to Irv, squeezed his knee. "*That's* what I want, *that's* what I care about. I'm not scared of any of the rest, as long as this book makes me rich. I want to be able to put in a pool. I want to be able to enclose the deck with glass. I want to set the table for my dinner parties with Baccarat crystal and Porthault linen. That's what I want to happen. Make it happen, Irv!"

The little agent looked at her. "All right, let's say no one harms you. And let's say it sells, and if it's as good, as bitchy, as the Washington part, it can't miss. And let's say you get the pool and the enclosed deck and the Baccarat and the Porthault linen. Let's say all those things happen. Then, once the book comes out, what you'll have to worry about is, Who'll swim in your pool? Who'll sit on your deck? Who out here will accept your dinner invitations?"

Bea clapped her hands delightedly. "Oh Irv! Fourteen years, and how little you understand the Hamptons! *They'll line up!*"

Labor Day Weekend, 1977

MIKE HUGHES strode quickly from the helicopter toward the powder-blue Rolls Corniche waiting for him halfway across the tiny East Hampton airport. He was a lot trimmer, fitter and younger than his round, florid face and white sideburns made him seem on TV; in fact his faithful shadow, Warren Daniels, who at twenty-eight was nearly twenty years younger, had trouble keeping up the pace.

"Jesus, Warren, I hate having to pretend I'm glad to see the guy!" Hughes threw the line over his shoulder. Daniels wanted to say, well, then, why do you? But he knew the answer.

Freddie Kohl got out from behind the wheel of the Rolls and scurried to meet Hughes. "Welcome, Mike, welcome!" He grabbed Hughes's hand, pumped it up and down. "Great to have you. Going to be a wonderful Labor Day weekend! I'm only sorry you couldn't be here yesterday at the start of it!"

Mike threw a big smile—he was a great smiler. "Thanks, Freddie. Great to be here. We'll just have to make up for lost time."

"Hello, Mr. Kohl," Warren Daniels said, but Freddie, his right hand still clutching Hughes's, his left hand on Hughes's shoulder, had half turned away from the younger man, and barely managed, a "Yes, hello." Freddie never could remember his name; Daniels was used to that by now.

The three men climbed into the Rolls, Freddie at the wheel, Hughes in front with him, Daniels in back. In the Hamptons, Freddie did his own driving, an ostentatiously humble gesture to the informal beach style he was trying to master. Harry Majors had called it a "Uriah Heep o' humility." Freddie didn't really feel that someone worth $100 million *should* drive his own car, but he tried to fit in.

Freddie smiled—the way he usually did, only with his mouth, while his eyes remained hard and distracted. "Yes, a wonderful weekend. Good weather. Good everything. We'll have dinner at Bobby Van's tonight, then tomorrow there's the softball game and Ernst's big bash."

Every season, the famous novelist Ernst Heinemann threw a huge party on Sunday of Labor Day weekend. He invited everyone, even people he barely knew.

Mike nodded, took a beat, then asked the question that had been on his mind since he stepped from the helicopter.

"What about the book?"

Freddie's hard smile widened. "Her agent has not said no to me; nor has he said yes to anyone else, which is easy to understand, since my offer, it is fair to say, is the most astounding in the history of publishing."

Mike had to laugh at that. "You're too modest, Freddie. I just hope it works."

The Rolls crossed the highway, went down Georgica Road, along LaForest to Apaquogue, then to West End. On these roads even the most modest bungalows cost over $150,000, and a big beach house was out of the question for less than half a million. Freddie had bought his only a year ago for $700,000, a steal for a 16-room house with pool, tennis court, guest house and garage, on six acres starting at the dunes and sweeping to the road in a long, sloping lawn.

The asking price for the house had been $950,000, and the owners were prepared to take $900,000, but Freddie knew they were in a hurry to sell, and he worked out a deal that would save them a lot of taxes. He stole the house—Freddie was expert at that.

"Sophie will show you to your room." Freddie barely looked at Daniels as he spoke to him.

Hughes softened the snub by saying, "Go for a swim, Warren, have a drink, relax. Freddie and I have a few things to talk over."

Sophie was a strapping woman, six feet tall, weighing perhaps 180 pounds. She seemed to be around forty, and she served Freddie as a housekeeper and confidential assistant—some people said bodyguard. Other people said other things about their relationship, about what kind of hold she had over him, or he over her. No one ever saw them really talk to each other, but then Sophie was one of the enigmas of the Hamptons merely because she never said *anything*, and so visitors were free to read into her blank brown eyes, her powerful frame, and her presence, anything their imaginations supplied.

This time she did not acknowledge Freddie's words, did not say anything to either guest, just stood there until Warren Daniels looked at her, and then began walking in the direction in which she wanted to lead him, which was to the east side of the house, where he'd be given a room far from his boss's.

Freddie walked upstairs with Mike. "I have a little surprise for you."

"The surprise I'd like to hear is that you got hold of the book—and the right to burn the damned thing."

"Be patient. I'll *get* the book for you."

"For us, Freddie. For *us!*"

Freddie said nothing to that, just led Mike up the carpeted stairs along the hall to the huge bedroom in the southwest corner of the house. The room's outside walls were all glass, through which the setting sun was flooding in and nothing could be seen but ocean and dunes.

On the east wall hung a bright, modern geometric tapestry, commissioned by Freddie. The north wall was mirrored, floor to ceiling. Against the south wall was a king-sized bed, which faced the mirror, not the ocean.

"As I said, I have a little surprise for you." Freddie opened the door for Mike, but did not go in with him. The room was dazzlingly bright, and it took Mike's eyes a moment or two to adjust. When they had, he saw the girl on the bed. She was naked, lying on her back, propped up on her elbows, her breasts gleaming white, a startling contrast to the brown of her nipples and golden tan of the rest of her body. Also white was a small triangle on her abdomen, the outline of the tiniest of bikinis. Her legs were slightly spread.

"Hi!" she said.

"Well, hello there," he replied. "What's your name?"

"Lolly." She didn't offer a second name; nor did she ask his name.

"How old are you?"

"Eighteen." She was twenty-two, but on this and everything else, she'd been briefed carefully by Freddie. And paid extravagantly.

He walked to the bed, stood over her.

She smiled up at him. When he didn't speak, she asked, "What would you like?"

As soon as Mike was in the room, Freddie closed the door, raced downstairs, found Sophie.

"Where is Daniels?"

"Swimming," she said, nodding toward the pool set in back of the dunes to the east of the house. "Out of the way." She looked straight at him, her face expressionless.

"All right, then." Freddie spoke a kind of shorthand with her, but always respectfully.

Sophie just nodded, turned, walked quickly upstairs, headed toward the southwest bedroom. She opened the door next to it, which led to a large storage closet. In it was an 8-mm movie camera on a tripod. A small part of the mirrored wall in the big bedroom was a one-way mirror, and it was through this the camera stared. By now Sophie knew the speed and the f-stop needed to shoot with the available light in the bedroom. The camera was already loaded with a 1000-foot magazine of the fastest black-and-white film available. Sophie looked through the viewfinder to check the focus; then she turned the camera on, to record Hughes's answer to Lolly's question, "What would you like?"

As Sophie walked upstairs, Freddie went into the kitchen, poured himself a glass of Perrier. Then he picked up the phone, and dialed Bobby Van's restaurant in Bridgehampton.

"Hello, this is Freddie Kohl. No, not Cohen! K-O-H-L. Is Bobby there? Well, he knows me. Tell him I'm coming for dinner tonight—at nine. I need a table for five, out on the porch." Freddie wanted to make sure the table was right. "Tell Bobby I'm bringing Carlotta Reilly with me.

"And Mike Hughes. *Governor* Hughes."

He hung up. "Please" and "thank you" were words he seldom used, for he'd long ago given up on getting anything through good will. He'd found another way: money and power. You got a good table at Bobby Van's not because he liked you, but because you brought people like Governor Hughes and TV anchorwoman Carlotta Reilly with you. You stayed close to the Governor not because he liked you but because you supplied money to feed his political appetite and women to feed his sexual appetite.

Bea's favorite way to work on warm, sunny days was to set her old portable typewriter up on a chaise on the deck behind her house, and sit there and think, and type, from time to time looking out over the Sagaponack potato fields—now selling for $65,000 for the minimum acre-and-a-half subdivision—and say to herself, *this* is what I'm doing it for. For this house, and these fields, and the sky and the serenity.

She always made sure the phone was unplugged; otherwise it was too easy to call and be called, too easy not to work.

Bea was sticking to her resolve to complete the book by Labor Day, and was right on schedule, which meant she was virtually finished. Occasionally she'd read parts to Irv, whose combination of approval and embarrassment meant to her she was hitting the right notes. The storytelling was over; now she needed an ending, a way to take all the scandal, all the characters, all the stories, and tie them up, sum them up, bring them to a climax. Tell what it all meant. That she didn't have. Not yet.

The phone on the deck was plugged in this Saturday morning of Labor Day weekend, because Irv was there, and he had, always, to be in touch with the rest of the world. When it rang, he picked it up; it was Carlotta, someone Bea would *always* talk with.

"Hi!" she said, only it came out more like "Hah!" Bea used her Southern accent for emphasis. "How *are* you?"

"Better, this morning," Carlotta replied. "Last night I didn't think I was going to make it. You would never have *believed* the traffic!"

"For goodness sake, Carlie! Friday of Labor Day weekend! What did you expect?"

"Leaving at 7:30? I expected it would have thinned out. But the *tunnel* was tied up! The Long Island *Expressway* was tied up! The Montauk *Highway* was tied up! Manhattan to Montauk, bumper to bumper! It took four hours. I got out here at 11:30; all I could do was fall into bed."

"Drive out alone?"

"Yup."

"Plans for the weekend?"

"Sunday, the usual, softball game, Ernst's party. Today, not much . . . I . . . told Freddie Kohl I might have dinner with him and the Governor . . ." Carlotta tried to make it sound casual. ". . . I like to keep in touch with potential Presidents."

They both knew the real reason for the dinner. Carlotta wanted to put in a good word for her ex-husband, Buster, should Freddie get the rights to Bea's book. Buster wanted to produce the movie—*had* to produce the movie. It might be his last chance to salvage the wreckage of a career.

But neither woman said it. Both left a lot unsaid about Bea's book, and not only the question of film rights. They never mentioned how Carlotta and Buster would be treated in the book. Carlotta feared Buster would come out badly. Bea knew all about his drinking, his screwing around. She knew Bea resented the way Buster had hurt her; that Bea might want to chop him up—for *her* sake.

Almost more than that, Carlotta feared that Bea would paint her as a heroine, and the better she came out, the more Buster would resent her. Especially she was afraid Bea would reveal the way she was using her clout as anchorwoman to support Buster's faltering career at the network. Bea knew all about that. Bea had come to know everything, and everyone, in the Hamptons.

"No wonder you're a star, Carlie," Bea said. "Anyone who could stomach dinner with Freddie deserves to be an anchorwoman!"

Carlotta responded with a mellow laugh. "So there's no point asking you to join us, to make things easier for me, is there?"

Bea laughed back. "Climb Everest for you? Run the marathon for you? Try me! But Freddie Kohl? No way. I was going to ask you over for a piece of broiled fish, a salad, some local corn and a couple or three glasses of soave. I've got Irv hanging around, looking absolutely edible —in fact, we could have him for dessert. If I'm left alone with him this evening, there's no telling what may happen, so if you care for his purity . . ."

"I've got a better idea," Carlotta said. "Why don't you and Irv go to Bobby Van's for dinner, and sit nearby, so I can use you as my escape hatch, maybe come over and sit and dish awhile. And if I find out anything at the head table, who knows, I might give you something good for the magnum opus."

She might indeed, Bea thought. She might even come up with an ending.

"What time are you going to be there?" Bea asked. "We might do that. You know the only way I dare be left alone with Irv is with salt-peter in my drink."

"Nine, I suppose. God, I *hope* you'll be there! Make a reservation, will you?"

"Don't need one, Bobby's wife has a terrific crush on Irv." Bea said it loudly, so Irv could hear. "Probably see you. Bah!"

Some people said Irv was the biggest literary agent in the business; no one rated him below the top four. His income was close to a million dollars a year; adversaries were now honest with him because they'd long ago given up trying to outwit him. He knew everyone, and had few friends. Irv was involved in a perception gap. Others saw him as a formidable, legendary figure, and were in awe of him. He saw himself as what he had been, a kid from the Bronx, son of impoverished Russian-Jewish parents.

Only Bea, being new to the book business, was not awed, and went crashing through the barriers his reputation had set up. Irv loved her for it. Not that he represented her any differently from any other author. There, he was a pro. Had he represented Nixon—whom he had turned down—he'd have given him the same total effort he gave Bea, whom he loved. Bea sometimes feared his affection was hindering her career.

"For God's sake," she'd said to him, "stop being my father and my conscience. Just go out and make me *rich*, as if I were an ordinary client you weren't nuts about."

"I want to see you become something wonderful," he'd replied. And then knowing what she was driving at, had added, "Someone like Freddie Kohl won't do a thing for you there."

She'd snapped back, "Rich *is* wonderful, Irv."

"Sweetheart," he'd replied, "if you think my caring for you gets in the way of my being a good agent, there are other top people. I'll intro-duce you to them. It's true that in your case, if I had to choose, I'd rather be your friend than your agent. Because I've got lots of impor-tant writers, and very few friends. But I *don't* have to choose. You've got a book there which is going to make you a millionaire, whether we take Freddie's offer or not. What I'm trying to get for you is something *more* than money, not *instead* of money. Do you understand?"

Bea had walked to where Irv was sitting and kissed the top of his head.

When Harry Majors got to the East Hampton station, he was amused to see Buster Reilly. He figured Buster was there to meet a date, too. And he was right.

"We're like a couple of college boys on a football weekend," he said, smiling.

Buster grinned back. "Who's the lucky girl?"

"I was going to ask you the same question. Mine, you never heard of. A young clothing designer named Nellie Brandon. Not yet a household name, but working on it. Has all the necessary raw material, and twice the ambition. The mind of a Machiavelli in the body of a Cheryl Tiegs. Your turn."

Buster's grin became a laugh. "My turn. You can say that again. I'm waiting for Betsy Shore."

Betsy, an actress who'd just edged past thirty-eight while trying to hold on to twenty-eight, was known for her appearances in TV productions and even better known for her appearances in producers' beds. Harry, who'd been out with her and in bed with her, had once, in a cruel moment, said, "That's one shore no one ever had trouble landing on."

The joke of the summer was that the one person who hadn't landed on her was Freddie Kohl, which was the reason she was Buster's date. Desperately wanting the film rights to Bea's book, believing Freddie might be in a position to give them to him, Buster decided to invite a woman Freddie wanted. He had little else to offer; his status as a UBC executive was shaky, he had no money, his recent track record on acquisitions was weak. He was a drinker.

Once he'd been a football star and a war hero, but that was thirty years ago, and he hadn't done much lately. Now he had two assets left. One was his glamour and his attractiveness to women. He was big, strong, handsome, with jet black hair and sharp blue eyes. But the past year, with all its alcohol, had not worn well on him. The booze was beginning to show, around the eyes, around the middle.

The second asset was his ex-wife Carlotta, whose career at UBC had waxed as his waned. She now had power at the network, and though she and Buster were divorced, she still cared what happened to him, and let it be known.

Carlotta's help infuriated Buster. He wanted to manage on his own, yet hardly knew how. He didn't really think Freddie would swap the film rights for Betsy Shore; he did think that appearing with her would give him a psychological edge in dealing with Freddie. And he needed any edge he could get.

Harry's appeal was entirely different from Buster's. Harry was laid back, determinedly unaggressive and unambitious in a world of relentless aggression and endless ambition. He was a first-rate comedy writer who did not want to be a screenwriter, playwright, director, producer, or rich. He did not take anything or anyone seriously, least of all himself.

He was a big man, at six foot two, taller than Buster, with none of Buster's athletic grace or strength. Harry detested exercise. He claimed to have founded an organization called Athletics Anonymous, into which he admitted only beautiful women. "Every time one of them feels like exercising, I lie down with her until the feeling goes away. And of course they're prepared to do the same for me. Only I never *feel* like exercising. Once in a while, however, I fake it to give them the practice. Like a fire drill."

Although he and Buster had gone out with many of the same women, Harry felt no sense of rivalry. He'd once compared their styles: "Buster swashes. I buckle." Women were a bond between them. The two they'd loved and lost were the closest of friends; for Buster it was Carlotta. For Harry it was Bea Fletcher.

"Well, here it comes," Harry said. "The Cupid Express bearing its cargo of bliss. And only twenty minutes late. For the Long Island that's like being twenty minutes early."

"Do they ever arrive on time?" Buster asked.

"Oh sure!" Harry replied. "Happened once a couple of years ago. The 4:20 arrived exactly on time, to the minute. Everyone on the platform cheered. The engineer stuck his head out of the cab and shouted, 'Thanks! But this is *yesterday's* train!' "

"No!" said Buster.

"No. People tell me I ought to try writing comedy."

"Don't listen."

"Oh, sharp, Reilly. Very sharp. How'd you like it if I took up tennis? Or got to Betsy ahead of you? There she is now. Want to race?" Harry looked toward Betsy, getting off the train with the help of two conductors, who could not take their eyes off her bosom.

Betsy Shore was a flashy, platinum blonde with a model's face and a

Playboy centerfold body. Her long legs and perfect behind were poured into a pair of skin-tight bluejeans and her famous bosom barely contained by a flimsy man-tailored shirt unbuttoned almost to the waist. When she stood straight, the outline of her breasts was clear through the shirt, nipples prominent. When she twisted or leaned, the shirt would gap, which made it tough for a man not to look her in the bosom. The shirt never gapped by accident; Betsy was master of the tease.

She approached Buster and Harry. "The two best-looking men in the Hamptons waiting for me!"

She leaned to Buster, then to Harry to kiss and be kissed, each time shrugging open her shirt. "What did I do to deserve it?"

"Unbuttoned your shirt." Harry tried to make it sound kind, but knew it wasn't.

"You mean I don't turn you on anymore, Harry? Are you getting old?"

He wondered why he was feeling so cruel. He was tempted to reply, No, but you are. He stifled it, said instead: "Why is it when you shrug your shirt open, it's always the right one you show?"

Buster broke in on the sparring. "All right, Harry, you only get to be clever with your own date."

"Never mind," Betsy said. "I can take care of myself. I happen to be equally well built on both sides. I do it to keep a little mystery, Harry!"

"Oh Betsy," he replied, "don't you know the old saying, when you've seen one tit you've seen 'em both?" He leaned forward to kiss her forehead. "And they're both fantastic!"

Then he saw Nellie walking along the platform, looking lost. "Hey listen, I'm going to run! See you later." He hurried off; he wanted to skip the introductions.

Nellie was twenty-eight, slim, blond, freckled, beautiful, with over-sized brown eyes. She was as tough and knowing as she seemed fragile and innocent. Harry took the Louis Vuitton bag she was carrying, and gave her a hug.

"Hi, beautiful!"

"Hi! What an asshole-ian train ride!"

Harry laughed. "Not familiar with the term, but know the ride all too well. So what else is new? Well, from here on, things improve rapidly. Dinner at Bobby Van's. Big softball game. Big party. Big bloodbath."

❖ ❖ ❖

Johnny Wainwright and Sally Majors drove out together late Friday night in Johnny's white Mercedes, talking shop all the way. They were a handsome couple, but no glimmer of romance or sex had ever flashed between them. Their relationship represented two tides in the publishing business, Johnny's ebbing, Sally's at the flood. Johnny, a blond ex-Marine with a strong, austere face, was the president of Saxon, a distinguished house founded by his father. Two years ago, it had been sold to a conglomerate. Now Johnny was just an employee, highly paid, but with no ownership interest. His job was in danger; the conglomerate felt Saxon was overstocked on prestige and short on profits. Johnny was being edged out.

Thirty-two years old, Sally was editor-in-chief of an aggressive paperback house named Greyhound. At twenty-two, she'd married Harry Majors, at twenty-three divorced him. She'd been ambitious enough for two; he not enough for one, which infuriated her. At thirty, she owned a house in East Hampton. It was north of the highway; the next one wouldn't be.

Driving out, the lateness of the hour having cut Labor Day traffic, Sally put her head back on the leather seat and listened to Johnny worry.

"Sometimes I think I'd rather bow out a gentleman than fight these new battles with these new weapons—germ warfare, dirty bombs."

Sally laughed. "Spoken like a true Marine, Johnny."

"You mean that as an insult. It's not, Sally. I take it as a compliment."

"Well, damn, you shouldn't! The Marines are an organization that trains to kill people. To make them *dead!* Now if I tell you a better, faster way has been found to do that, why should you be proud to stick to the old way? They're no less dead that way!"

"First of all, Sally, you're just wrong about the Marines' mission. They're out to win battles, not kill people. If they could take their objectives without the loss of a single life, that would be fine! But even if the end result *is* the same, the way you accomplish it makes all the difference! As Lord Keynes said, in the long run, we'll *all* be dead. What you do on the way from here to there makes a hell of a difference, even though we all know where *there* is."

"A Geneva Convention of life, is that it?"

"You bet!" Johnny said it vehemently. "Playing fair. Fighting fair. Living fair. Living by the rules. You bet, that's it! If you're waiting for me to apologize for that, you've got a long wait!"

"That's shit, Johnny! Do you know why? Know why John van Rensselaer Wainwright—what is it, the Third? . . ."

"The Fourth."

"OK, the Fourth . . . Do you know why he loves the rules? Because he was born on top. And the rules are designed to *keep* him there. To protect the status quo. Under the rules, *he* plays on the grass courts of the Maidenhead Club, while others are kept off. So sure he loves the rules. Sure he thinks they're fair. Can you see, John the Fourth, why some Puerto Rican might not think the rules were so fair?

"Or some poor Polish-Irish kid born in the shadow of the slag heaps of Scranton, P-A? Which happens to be me, Johnny. Bright kid, father worked in a steel mill. Know what my future was, as a bright kid? Maybe with luck, schoolteacher. My mother wanted me to be a nun. Know why? Because she was so religious? Nope. Because it was clean work. Respectable. You didn't have to slave all day in a primitive kitchen. And try to get a grimy house clean that would never really come clean. And get jumped on periodically by a man, with nothing in it for you but six kids. Know when my mother dressed up, Johnny? For mass on Sunday mornings. Aside from that, never put on decent clothes. *Never*, day after day, year after year. Yeah, being a nun looked good to her."

She turned to stare at Johnny. "You think I'm pretty? Most people do. My mother was *really* pretty, you should have seen her. Only I never remember her looking young. I remember her when she was thirty, looking forty-five. Gorgeous pale skin, dark brown hair, blue eyes, the most beautiful kind of black Irish. Only faded, tired, worn out at thirty."

Sally had the dark hair, pale skin, blue eyes. But in her eyes, there was steel. Her publishing house too was owned by a profit-minded conglomerate, but in it she saw no danger, only opportunity. She saw in it a chance to trade the editor-in-chief's job in for a vice presidency, her $90,000 house north of the highway for a $300,000 house near the beach.

Johnny looked over at her briefly, then his eyes went back to the road ahead of him. "But somehow you managed to get where you are, didn't you, Sally? The rules let you do it! You didn't rob any banks, forge any documents, commit any murders, yet you're *not* a nun and you're *not* a schoolteacher. All I'm talking about is fair tactics as opposed to foul. Are you opposed to that?"

"Clawing is how I got where I am," she answered heatedly. "The

rules didn't *let* me do anything. I did it despite them. And your blessing on my struggle touches me, Johnny! Thanks for the permission!
Noblesse oblige! You're not interested in the fairness of the rules,
you're interested in them as barriers. You're interested in making sure
the grass courts of the Maidenhead never get too crowded, not in
whether access to them is awarded fairly or unfairly! Tell me how
many Jews use the courts, Johnny? How many blacks? How many
Puerto Ricans? Dammit, how many women? Not as wives, but on their
own? Tell me how many *you* championed? Tell me why Freddie Kohl
was turned down—aside from the fact that he wasn't well-born. How
does one make oneself well-born, Johnny?"

He shook his head, smiled one of his tight, muscular smiles. "Oh,
Jesus, back to the Maidenhead. What do you want, Sally? Do you
want to see some Puerto Rican get in? Or do *you* want to get in? I'll
put you up; honestly, I will. Yes, dammit, the club *is* discriminatory, I
know it. It just so happens I've pushed for more Jewish members;
we've got some already, you know. And yes, I like the grass courts. I'm
not going to pretend to be a social crusader. Suppose I quit, do you
think it would change anything? I must tell you I happen to believe in
the principle of the private club, in people who get along well with
each other, and who can afford certain privileges, choosing whom they
wish to associate with. I have nothing against compatible people in the
club who are Jewish, black, Puerto Rican, Greek, Eskimo, or anything
else.

"But if you ask me would I like to see a horde of ghetto blacks
swarming over those grass courts, the answer is a resounding no. Nor
would I like to see them in the clubhouse—or in my own house. But
my answer would be the same about a horde of hillbillies from Ap-
palachia, and they happen to be the purest English stock in the nation.

"As for Kohl, I find him a most objectionable man. I do not want him
in my house, or in my club, whether he has a hundred million dollars
or nothing. Whether he is a Jew or of the House of Windsor."

"Would you like to see him denied admission to the Hamptons entirely?" Sally asked.

"I would like not to have to associate with him. If that's your way of
making the case that I'm a snob, so be it. If you're trying to get me to
say I regret certain changes in the Hamptons, consider it said. You
may be damned sure I do. I don't like the mobs on summer weekends,
I don't like the loudness of a lot of the people, or their flashy clothes, or

the bourgeois pushiness of the whole scene. If you expect that feeling to change, or me to apologize for it, you've got *another* long wait."

Sally nodded. "And how about doing business with Freddie to get hold of a book?"

"Not if I can help it. And I . . . *we* . . . can help it, if we hold firm, stick together. Irv Schnell would rather do business with us than with Freddie. If we stand together, we can do it."

"*I'm* holding firm. *I* won't be the one to cave. I told you that." She stared at him. "Don't worry about *me!*"

But Johnny was worried. She had, after all, confessed—no, *pro-claimed*—that playing by the rules was passé. Which meant she would stick with them, with *him*, only as long as it suited her. But if she could do better by deserting him . . .

Sally was worried, too. Johnny had seen his best days in publishing. He was approaching obsolescence. Could he adapt? Did he want to? His old-fashioned statement of ethics sounded fine for the headmaster of a boarding school, but not suitable for a high-stakes battle with Freddie Kohl. Johnny might choose to go under, reciting the rules of the Geneva Convention, but she was damned if she'd go under with him.

About the time they reached the Southampton bypass, both fell silent, until they reached Water Mill.

"God, it's past midnight," Sally said. "I'm glad I have a ride to my door."

"My old-fashioned principles," Johnny said with a smile.

She laughed. "I knew they'd be useful for *something!*" When he said nothing, she added, "Want to have lunch tomorrow?"

"Can't," Johnny answered. "Got a doubles game at one. How about dinner?"

"Fine. Love to."

"Where shall we go?"

"Uh . . . I don't know," she said. "Let me find out where Bea's going."

Labor Day Weekend, 1977; Saturday Night

HARRY AND Nellie clinked glasses. Being twenty-eight and au courant, she had a kir in hers; being forty and a drinker, he had vodka in his.

She looked around at Bobby Van's porch. Bare floors, checked table-cloths, lighting rotten, not enough of it and what there was, harsh, bouncing off the polyurethane sheeting that kept out the wind and the rain. Ordinary-looking people, no one she recognized, although there were several empty tables; perhaps the famous were yet to come.

"So this is the Hamptons!" she said.

"Not your first time, is it?"

"Uh-huh."

"Can't be. Nobody comes here for the first time."

She laughed. "There's a first time for everything."

"You would think so, wouldn't you? But not for *here*. People go somewhere else for the first time."

"What are you talking about, Harry?"

"I'm not sure. Maybe I'm saying this is not 'the Hamptons.' This is the porch at Bobby Van's. It's not for anybody's first time. If you want to go somewhere for the first time, go to the sweaty part of the Hamptons. Go to Asparagus Beach where the single girls wear gold chains around their waists, to show either how much chain they have, or how little waist. Go to the discos, where every square yard you rub up against three guys who think they're John Travolta. That's for the first time.

"Or go to the stodgy part. To the Maidenhead, in Southampton, to play on green courts with gray people in white shorts; a girl with obvious Wasp credentials like yours should have no trouble getting invited. *That's* for the first time.

"Or if you like flash, go to Westhampton, where everybody looks like a big Chevy dealer. Go to a motel in Montauk, have the lobster dinner at Gosman's. Only don't forget to take off the bib. Or you can even stand at the bar right here at Bobby's, and look for famous writers.

"But this dingy little porch is not for the first time. It's like the number one room at Grenouille or '21,' like the tables along the right-hand wall at Elaine's. The place to be. God knows why, or how it got to be that way. But it is. It's where the most interesting, most political, most talented, most nervous people come. Like the four coming in right now."

Nellie looked up, saw two couples coming in, one man sixtyish, short and plump, the other younger, tall and strong; one woman a young, intense brunette, the other with streaked, gray-blond hair, taller, older. They sat at a table perhaps ten yards away.

"At the moment," Harry explained, "she's what it's all about, the eye of the storm. The one with the streaked, fluffy hair and the beautiful legs—well, you may not be able to see how beautiful they are in those pants, but take my word for it. She's Bea Fletcher."

"You mean the Southern woman who's so funny on the Carson show?"

"Yup, that one. She's writing a novel about the Hamptons, a *roman à clef* that's aroused a lather of fear and greed thick enough to shave the entire male population of Italy—and a lot of the women, too. The short man with her is Irv Schnell, her literary agent. The big man who looks like an ex-Marine, *is* an ex-Marine, Johnny Wainwright, the head of a publishing house. And the woman, Sally Majors . . ."

"Same name as you?" Nellie looked surprised. "Don't tell me . . ."

"Nope," he said. "Wrong! She's *not* my sister. Not my wife, either. Not anymore, anyway. She's the hottest young thing, professionally speaking, that is, in paperback publishing at the moment. A kind of genius. The only mistake she made in recent memory was to marry me. And she corrected that in a hurry!"

"Is that bitterness I hear?"

"God, no! It should sound like gratitude. If we were still together I'd be chopmeat by now. I knew there was something wrong when the guy who married us said, I now pronounce you woman and husband."

"Harry, why do you always hide your feelings with jokes?"

"Maybe I don't *hide* them with jokes; maybe I *show* them with jokes. Maybe if I didn't, the tablecloth would get too soggy to eat on. You're a terrific lay therapist, Nellie, but a therapist is not what I'm after. About the other part . . ."

She slapped his hand gently.

"As I was saying," he continued, "Sally Majors is after Bea's book. In fact, everybody is. Except me. And even *I'm* not so sure."

"I'm not after it, Harry."

"Honey, I told you, *you're* not here. Nobody's here for the first time. Next time you'll be here, and by then you too will probably have worked up some reason to want the book. Or hate it. Or both."

As Bea sat down, she said to the other three, "For God's sake, let's pretend to be human, instead of in the book business. There is to be no shop talk in my hearing. I expect all of us to stick to that, until the first drink arrives, anyway."

"Am I allowed just to ask how the book is going?" Sally said.

"Yes, you are, but I don't have to answer until I get a glass of white wine. Now why don't you turn and wave to your ex-husband, who's sitting there with a gorgeous girl young enough to be your daughter. And my granddaughter."

The two women turned and waved and smiled at Harry, who smiled back.

"She seemed to show real affection for you," Nellie observed.

"Which one?" Harry asked.

"I meant your ex-wife, but actually both did."

"In the case of my ex-wife, I wouldn't call it affection. More like relief—with a *soupçon* of contempt and pity. In the case of Bea, it was

"I'm sure you could," he replied.

"It would mean so much to me to get that part. It would make a big star of me, you know."

"Yes, Betsy."

"Don't forget, I'm pretty well known now. Don't kid yourself. You have no idea how many people stop me on the street because they recognize me from a soap or a TV series. But Bea's book could really put me in a class with Dunaway or Fonda. Believe me, it's ninety-nine percent breaks."

"I know it would mean a lot to you to get that movie." He squeezed her hand. "It would mean a lot to me, too, and I'm going to give it my best shot."

"I'll help in any way I can," she said eagerly. "Just tell me what to do." They both knew what she might be called upon to do. Betsy was not squeamish; nor did she play hard to get. Her refusal of Freddie had come because his crudeness had violated even her minimal need for gallantry.

On a Saturday six weeks earlier, Freddie had invited her to his house for lunch. After a drink, Betsy had said, in good spirits, "What's to eat?" and Freddie—"Mr. Delicacy," Harry had dubbed him—had replied, "This!" and lowered his swimming trunks.

Offended, Betsy had said only, "Freddie!"

And he'd responded, "How about five hundred dollars?"

"What the hell do you think I am, a hooker?"

"All right," he'd said, "I'll make it seven hundred and fifty."

"Fuck off!" she'd yelled, and stormed off to Johnny Wainwright's, where she spent the weekend doing with Johnny, for nothing, what she'd refused to do for Freddie's money. But then Johnny was a gentleman. And she had a crush on him. Besides, he might get hold of Bea's book.

And what Betsy would not do with Freddie for money, she would for Buster and for a chance at that role. If she could help Buster merely by being with him so he could show off, she would. If it took more—well, she might do that, too.

Harry pointed to Buster and Betsy with his eyes, and Nellie looked over. "That's the couple I was talking to at the station when I picked you up."

"Oh boy!" she said. "Is he glamoroso! A little old for me, but oh boy! Who is he?"

"Buster Reilly, star of tennis court, gridiron and World War Two. Ex-husband of the well-known TV woman Carlotta Reilly. Among his other credits are lush and lecher. Abandon hope, all ye who are entered there. The demure blond bombshell with him is a TV actress named Betsy Shore, who has been around—personally and professionally."

"I thought her face looked familiar."

"Looking familiar is her best number."

"You're mean, Harry."

"You think I'm mean? Wait till Bea's book comes out. Then you'll find out what mean means." He picked up his glass, signaled to the waitress for another drink. "Yeah, Bea has the will. She's also got the way. How she finds out so much about so many, I don't know. I guess it's because people out here love to gossip. But Bea gets it all. And she knows how to tell it! Nobody is safe; anyone she goes after, she can leave in shreds. Did you read the two-part series in *Scope* magazine called 'WashingtonShock'?"

"Nope."

"It will be the first part of Bea's book, and it does to Washington what she intends to do to the Hamptons, namely, bloody it, or at least a lot of its leading citizens. Get hold of a copy—I'll lend you mine. You'll stop wondering who the meanest of the mean is. You'll notice the corpses lying around, but if you don't know Washington, you may not be able to tell one from the other without a program. So let me give you a quick rundown. One cabinet member resigns 'for personal reasons' and then is divorced by his wife. A promising young Senator and three Congressmen decide not to run for reelection. Five marriages are broken up, and that's the good news! It was devastating. And by now she knows the Hamptons as well as she knew Washington. And the Hamptons are juicier. . . ."

Harry paused as he saw five people walk in. "And here are the juiciest of them all." Nellie looked toward the entrance. She saw three men, one middle-aged, white-haired, florid-faced; the second younger, smaller, dark; the third quite young, tall and rangy; and two women, one about forty, tall, good-looking, gray-haired. The second very young and flashy.

Harry gave her a rundown. "The red-faced man is the Governor of our state, Michael Hughes. The young man is his press secretary, Warren Daniels. The broad who looks like a hooker, holding Daniels' arm as if she were his date, *is* a hooker. But she's not his date. She's the Governor's . . . *date* . . . if I may use the term loosely."

"And the gray-haired woman is Carlotta Reilly!" Nellie burst in excitedly.

"Yup, *the* Carlotta Reilly, Buster's ex-wife. And the little charmer with her is *the* Mr. Nice Guy, the well-known hundred-millionaire political fundraiser and procurer, Freddie Kohl."

"You mean Friedrich Kohl?" Nellie asked. "He's supposed to be a financial genius."

"Yes," Harry answered. "He's well known for that, too. But don't accept any invitations over to his place without putting on your pick-proof chastity belt . . . I said *pick*-proof. The other kind wouldn't hurt either."

"Oh dear, poor Carlotta Reilly! Why is she with him?"

"She's probably asking herself the same question. I guess because she thinks Freddie might help Buster. It means a lot to Freddie to be seen with people like Carlotta; he's pushing hard to join the 'in' crowd out here. He has trouble understanding why, just because he's slimy and obnoxious, people don't take to him. He's so used to buying whatever he wants, he thinks he can buy his way into the Hamptons. He thinks that with mere money he can get classy, glamorous, high-minded types like Bea and Irv and Sally and Johnny to do business with him."

"Can he?"

"Of course!"

"Is it worth so much money to be in?"

"When you've got enough of it, sure," Harry replied. "Some people devote their lives and fortunes to it. Freddie always tries for double value. If he gets the book, he is not only buying his way into the literary crowd, but at the same time he's protecting his reputation, and his friend the Governor's. He thinks when he gets control of the book he can clean it up, or delay publication until November '78, when the Governor has been re-elected—and long before he'd have to make a move for the Presidency. Then the Governor would owe him a hell of a lot."

Harry shook his head. "The slimy, obnoxious creep thinks that by suppressing the truth about the Governor's sexual kinks, someday he might get to be Secretary of State."

"And can he?"

This time Harry laughed aloud. "Of course!"

Warren Daniels smiled at his "date" and helped her sit, then he took the Governor's arm and whispered, "Let me get her out of here. She can pretend to be ill. You're nuts to have brought her!"

Mike Hughes just smiled at him. "I'm doing it for you, Warren. You're never seen with a woman, and people are beginning to think I've got a gay press secretary. It's getting so I'm afraid to be seen alone with you." He sat on the other side of Lolly, slid his left hand under the table and squeezed her thigh. She took the hand and lifted it a little higher.

Resignedly, Warren sat down at Lolly's left. On his other side was Carlotta Reilly, who'd been helped into her chair with conspicuous solicitude and familiarity by Freddie Kohl. He wanted everyone to see he was having dinner with the famous TV newswoman. Then he sat between Carlotta and the Governor, completing the circle.

Carlotta tried not to let her loathing for Freddie show, but when he turned away from her for a moment, she grabbed the chance to look to her right and start talking to Warren Daniels. She'd much prefer that Freddie not get hold of Bea's book, but if he did, she'd try to do something to help Buster. And she could not dismiss Freddie as a leading contender. She knew Bea liked him as little as she did; she also knew how Bea felt about money—the feeling of a divorced woman who'd once been penniless and powerless.

Carlotta also knew the real insecurity was not the money, but the standing alone, after a lifetime of thinking you had to stand together with a man. She knew that was an insecurity no money could assuage —even when you were making a half-million dollars a year. You were still alone; the half-million could end tomorrow, and where would you be without a man? She hated to think that, hated to want to be in someone else's hands. She looked down at her own hands, with their workmanlike fingers, short, untinted nails. She wore no wedding band, and it would be a long time, if ever, before she would.

Yes, she knew exactly how Bea felt.

"Carlotta, dear, what will you have to drink?" Freddie said it loudly; he wanted to make sure everybody heard it. She would not, could not bear to, return that intimacy. Yet she couldn't afford to offend him. Adroitly, she turned her response toward the Governor.

"Oh my! In the presence of our chief executive I dare not have anything stronger than a chaste white wine." Only then did she turn back toward Freddie to say, "Please, sir!" thus avoiding having to call him by his first name. Then as quickly as she could, she engaged Warren Daniels in conversation.

"I like your friend," she said, smiling. Daniels, tall, earnest, just a few years out of Columbia Journalism, and fresh off *The New York Times*, had been picked by Hughes because he was smart, loyal and respectable. He was not about to concede the blonde was not his date. But for fun, Carlotta would try. It beat talking to Freddie, anyway.

"She is attractive, isn't she?" He said it with an utterly straight face. "Known her long?"

"Actually, no. We'd met a couple of times but this is our first date."

"How interesting! I didn't catch her last name." They both knew it had never been offered; she'd been introduced only as Lolly.

Warren looked stricken, but only for a moment. Then, not trying too hard, he said, "Lolly Jones . . . from a Welsh family."

Carlotta didn't want to let him off easily. "Jones, eh? That's funny, because she bears so strong a family resemblance to people I know, I thought she might be related to them."

"Oh, isn't that a coincidence?" Warren had expected worse; he was relieved.

"Yes, maybe you know them, the Smiths. I was sure you were going to say Lolly Smith."

She couldn't get him to crack a smile. He's all right, she said to herself. "How do you know her? Is she a journalist?"

"No. I met her through a mutual friend."

"She's kind of flashy," Carlotta said. "Do you think a public figure should be seen out with her?" Suddenly he looked startled. "I mean, Warren, you *are* kind of a public figure, being the Governor's press secretary."

"I don't consider myself one," he answered, "but I do believe a public figure is entitled to a private life which is nobody's business, as long as he does his job well. And I think I'm doing a good job for a Governor who's doing a great job, and that girl sitting there is irrelevant."

Carlotta couldn't help teasing him. "Aren't you worried about making the Governor jealous, you with a sexy blonde, he all alone? He really must miss Rosemary. By the way, where is she?"

"With a couple of their children going off to school, she had so much work to do, packing and all that, he couldn't persuade her to come with him for the entire weekend, but she will be in tomorrow for Heinemann's party. And yes, he *does* miss her."

"I'll bet Miss . . . Smith . . . over there is looking forward to the party. It must be exciting for a journalist to rub shoulders with so many famous writers."

For the first time, Warren smiled. Even smiling, he had an austere seriousness to his lean face that reminded her of a birdwatcher; none of the restless glitter of the Hamptons about him. "She's not a journalist at all . . . you said that, I didn't. She's a model, who's studying to be an actress, actually. She's really talented. And it's *Jones*."

"I'll bet she's talented."

"And though she'd love to stay for the party, alas, she's got to be back in the city in the early evening, so she's catching the 3:18 train."

"Too bad. Then you'll be lonely at the party."

"I was hoping you might save a dance for me, Carlotta."

"At least one. Some day I'd like to have someone as loyal to me as you are to the Governor. Whether I deserve it or not."

Freddie had been engaging the Governor in furious conversation, until Mike saw, out of the corner of his eye, that Lolly was sitting there, unattended. He turned away from Freddie to interrupt Warren and Carlotta.

"Hey Warren, your friend . . . uh . . ."

"Lolly Jones, sir," Warren offered. Carlotta tried not to snicker.

The Governor ignored her. "Yes, of course. Miss Jones is not going to think well of this administration if my right-hand man takes her to dinner and then spends the entire meal talking to the woman on the other side of him, however fascinating she may be."

"Of course, sir." And dutifully, Warren turned to Lolly, wondering what in hell he was going to say to her.

Mike leaned across Freddie toward Carlotta. "A lot of people out here are worried about Bea's book."

"Not those with clear consciences."

Mike made believe he hadn't heard that. "Why does she want to do that? These are all her friends. It's like fouling your own nest."

"Ah, but *she's* not fouling it, Governor. She's just *naming* the ones who are. At least, that's what people say. No one's actually read any of it, you know. Not from what I hear."

"But remember the part about Washington! In *Scope* magazine!" When Freddie got excited, an indefinable trace of a European accent crept into his speech.

"Yes, I guess that did upset our best and brightest, didn't it. You were down there then, Governor, you must have seen that."

Carlotta knew she was being cruel. The Governor, then a Congressman, had more than seen it. "WashingtonShock" had spoken of a Congressman Marty Hogan, of how he loved to splash around in the super-sized tub of a certain financier because there were always two or three young ladies splashing with him. *Very* young ladies. One in particular was only thirteen, although in justice to Congressman Marty, Bea had written, she looked more like sixteen. But what made her age all the more embarrassing was the fact that she was the daughter of a very important Pentagon general.

Bea had entitled it "Congressman Marty and His Rubber Ducks," and promised she'd be telling more about the man and his hobbies in the Hamptons part of her book. Of course Bea had elevated her Congressman Marty Hogan not to Governor but to Senator, but from the blunt fact of his initials, his sexual habits, his visits to the Hamptons and his financier friend, it was hard not to connect Marty and Mike.

Mike Hughes was a man of intelligence and humor, essentially principled and compassionate, who'd been corrupted sexually, and rationalized his position by saying that as long as he did his public job well, his private sexual habits didn't matter. He argued it convincingly, without ever convincing himself.

Now, talking with Carlotta, he was expert in presenting his position. "I think 'WashingtonShock' was a terrible invasion of people's privacy; it served no purpose. It hurt people's careers and lives, entirely without regard to what kind of job they were doing in office, how well they were serving the American people!"

What Carlotta wanted to say in reply was: A man who's a cheat in his private life, who pretends to be the model family man while sloshing around in tubs with thirteen-year-old girls, is immoral—a fraud and a liar. He's also blackmailable by creeps like Freddie. She wanted to say that. She didn't, because the Governor was getting upset, his face getting redder, and because she was a journalist who didn't want to indulge her morality now and pay later. She had to be able to deal with him, to interview him. He was Governor; some day he might be President. Besides, if she were to antagonize every politician who was a crook, liar or lecher, that would leave her with virtually *no one* to interview.

She did ask, "Moral issues aside, Governor, don't you think certain private activity leaves a public figure open to all sorts of pressure and blackmail?"

Hughes handled himself well under fire, but she could see his tension in the red of his face and the whitened knuckles of his hand as he squeezed his glass. "All right," he said. "Let's leave the morality aside. I never argue morality with a saint, it puts the rest of us at too much of a disadvantage. Let's talk about blackmail. Since virtually everyone in Washington—for Christ's sake, everyone *everywhere*—is vulnerable, there's an unwritten law against public reference to one's . . . *private* life. So nobody tries to blackmail anybody."

"I think you both miss the point." Freddie had been swiveling his head from side to side following the dialogue, but he couldn't stay silent for long. And he had never studied Dale Carnegie. "The real point is that Bea could write a *marvelous* social history of this part of the world we know and love. Instead she is cheapening the Hamptons and herself with petty gossip. Much of it false—you know that and I know it. But most readers won't. So good, innocent people will be hurt, and Bea will be hurt worst of all. She's too talented to waste herself that way. I will give her a chance to show *all* her talent! On this book and books to come! And false modesty does not prevent me from saying, although I know the Governor has already heard this, that the deal will probably be the most important in the history of the book business."

Freddie looked at them both; what he saw did not please him, but he went ahead. "Bea and I can work together, I know it, and the result will not only be a book she can be proud of, but a huge paperback sale and a wonderful motion picture. Perhaps a TV series after that. Of course I shall be needing people to work with me in all aspects of the deal, editing, publishing, film, TV." He looked Carlotta straight in the eye as he said it.

Subtle, she thought. Really subtle. Be a good girl, Carlotta, get your buddy Bea to clean up the book, to sell it to Freddie, and he will throw Buster a bone. Whatever the qualities which had yielded that unpleasant little man a hundred million dollars, subtlety was not one of them, she told herself. She watched his eyes darting about, wished she didn't have to be sitting there, wished she could tell him to fuck off. For Buster's sake she couldn't, she mustn't. She wanted to help her ex-husband if she could. He needed help; he was in bad shape, worse than anyone could tell. *She* could tell, from the flaccid skin of his face, the glazed eyes, the defiant set of the head.

"Well, Freddie," she said, "if I can help with any suggestions, I'll certainly make them. You can be sure of that." Even civility was a strain for her, but she was at least satisfied her answer was as ambiguous as it could be without putting him off.

The differences between her ex-husband and her dinner partner dismayed Carlotta. Buster was such an attractive, graceful man—and fallen so low. Freddie was such a pushy creep, and risen so high, powerful enough to manipulate a man like Buster—and therefore a woman like Carlotta, as much as her queasy ethics and stomach would allow.

"I hope so," Freddie said. "I'll count on it."

"All right," was all she managed to say aloud. Where's the justice in this world? she asked herself.

Nellie looked at Harry with awe after he'd told her about Bea's book. "All these people," she said, "circling, like animals around a juicy carcass."

"Precisely," said Harry. "And they never know if the next carcass is going to be theirs. Do you find it exciting?"

"Uh-huh! Especially to be close to the finale. How soon will it all be settled?"

"Soon. Very soon. If Irv is smart, and Irv *is* smart, he'll want a big publicity splash to announce the deal—at '21,' or Elaine's, or The Four Seasons—right after Labor Day, when people are settled back in the city again. In order to do that, he'll want to nail the deal down soon, maybe over the weekend."

Harry sighed. "Over the weekend. In just a few days, the Hamptons will be so quiet, so peaceful again. Their soul will be like their exterior: calm, orderly, restful. Now the place looks beautiful, but inside it's a rat's nest. That might be a good title for Bea's book, *Rat's Nest*."

"What *is* the title?"

"As far as I've heard, there is none yet. I've made a few suggestions. One is *Greed*. Then I offered *Lust Story*. Or *HamptonSchlock*. For some reason Bea hasn't grabbed at any of them."

"What's schlock?" Nellie asked.

"Oh, it means cheap, shoddy, tacky. The pushcart merchandise behind the Tiffany's window. Because, you see, behind the great houses, the Mercedeses, the chic clothing and the perfect privet hedges of this place, its soul is schlock."

Labor Day Weekend, 1977; Saturday Night (continued)

THE BAR was so packed with singles and gawkers Irv had trouble pushing through the fringes of the crowd to get to the men's room, and Freddie, waiting for what he thought was a suitable interval after Irv's departure, was able to walk in right after him.

Irv was at the urinal. Freddie walked to the washbasin next to it and went through the motions of washing his hands.

"We can conclude our deal?" Freddie asked. "Draw up a contract? It will be a glorious announcement. Merely the biggest sale in the history of publishing—that's all."

Irv was startled. "Is this your office, Freddie? Or are you under the impression it's my office? Or are you waiting to pee?"

"My office is wherever there's a good deal to be made. Isn't yours?" Freddie was combing his gleaming black hair.

Still at the urinal, looking straight ahead, Irv said, "You know, when I was a kid in the Bronx, they used to write on toilet walls, 'This is the only room in the place where everybody knows what he's doing.' What are *you* doing, Freddie?"

"Don't be funny."

"I'm not. Somebody walks in and sees us standing around like this, not finishing our business, and I don't mean book business, and he'll think we're a couple of *faygeles*. And we're not *faygeles*, are we, Freddie?"

"What is a *faygele?*"

"That's right, you don't know. I forgot you weren't Jewish. It means a gay, a queer, the kind that stand around in bathrooms to do their business."

Freddie would not get upset, and Irv didn't really want to try too hard. Not that he cared for Freddie; rather he owed it to Bea to listen. You could learn things at the most unexpected times in the most unexpected places. And when a man said things like five million dollars, you really should pay attention to what else he had to say.

"All right then . . ." Freddie wiped his comb on a paper towel, put it in his pocket. "Let's have a drink at the bar."

"Only if I pay. I can't let my clients think I'm being bought off."

"How could you be bought off for a drink?"

"I don't know. Never having been bought off, I have no idea how low my price might be." He stepped away from the urinal, moved toward the sink. "Now let me wash my hands."

Freddie stepped back. Irv looked at him through the mirror. "You know, I'm not accustomed to performing bathroom functions under scrutiny. I don't think I like it." He dried his hands, started out.

Freddie, right behind him, grabbed his arm. "All right, Irv, let's have a brandy; you buy."

He held on to Schnell's arm and half accompanying, half leading him, forced a way through to a corner of the bar, and somehow, Irv could not be sure how, got the bartender to pay attention to him at once, so he could order two brandies. Irv shoved a ten at the bartender, who took it and gave them change.

Freddie began with a blockbuster. "Look, I know what Wainwright and Sally Majors offered. You're not going to let $2.3 million stand in the way of $5 million, are you?"

Goddammit! How had he heard about the $2.3 million? He wasn't supposed to know! Irv said it only to himself. Should he deny it? No point. Should he ask Freddie where he heard it? Again, no point.

"A 2.3-million-dollar offer could very well compare with a 5-million-dollar buy-out. You know numbers well enough to know that."

Who in hell had told him? Irv wondered. It had to be one of three: Sally, Johnny. Or, and he hesitated even to say it to himself, Bea. They and he were the only ones who knew. And whoever told Freddie was, in effect, negotiating behind his back. And therefore not to be trusted.

Johnny? Hard to believe. He personified what was left of the honor of the industry. Yet . . . Johnny was a desperate man. Irv knew the situation at Saxon well enough to know that.

Sally? She may not have been a moral bastion, but she was smart enough to know that a bad name would kill her chances for this book, and hurt her, perhaps kill her in the publishing business. Of course, if Freddie could promise her enough . . . Or if she could find a way to shift the blame . . . She was smart enough for that, too.

Then there was Bea. That he couldn't believe. How many times had he warned her to keep her mouth shut and let him do all the negotiating? But Bea was sassy; maybe she thought she could do a little dealing on her own, talk to Freddie in confidence, force his price up, and then say to Irv: See how clever I am! I got more money than the great Schnell could! Not realizing, of course, that Freddie was planning some way to grind her to chopmeat.

"Yes, I know numbers," Freddie replied. "Between 2.3 million and 5 million is 2.7 million. Where is all that money going to come from? I also know that 2.7 million dollars represents an agent's commission of $270,000. Where is *that* going to come from?"

"You heard of TV, Freddie, haven't you? You've heard of motion pictures?" Irv half whispered; the noise of the crowd was some protection, but you never could tell if some reporter, or somebody in publishing, might be standing right next to you.

"Come, come," Freddie said. "You know and I know there's no 2.7 million there. And what's more important, there's none of the impact. You announce a 5-million-dollar package—with a half-million-dollar commission—and you're making publishing history. You'll be the biggest! Every top author in the business will be on your doorstep."

Neither was a big man, and with Freddie still clutching Irv's arm, the two were being jostled, pressed together, pulled apart, pushed around like small boats in rough waters. Neither noticed; both were caught up in the feverish moment, Irv's fever being detestation and resentment, Freddie's, the desire to win.

"There are some who think I'm the biggest now."

"After this, they'll *all* think so."

A plump blonde in a white sweatshirt pushed by them, her outstanding bosom driving Irv into Freddie. Irv just looked around dismayed; Freddie did more.

"Watch it," he hissed. "Be careful where you are going!" She gave him an angry look, turned to her boyfriend, who was right behind her.

"Whatsa matter?" asked the boyfriend.

She looked at him as if she'd been molested, and he stared at Freddie. Freddie glared back.

"I said she'd better watch where she was going!" There was a force to his voice and his look that was intimidating, despite his lack of size. Freddie was surprised at his ferocity. So was the boyfriend, who, although he was much bigger and younger than Freddie, didn't want to take on all that anger.

"Oh, come on!" he said to the girl, and instead of pushing through the two older men, they made a path around them.

What surprised Irv was not only Freddie's ferocity, but his fearlessness. Clearly, he would not back down—both Irv and the boyfriend had seen that. Kohl was not soft, Irv told himself. Arrogant, rude, a bully, a lot of other things—but tough, and not a coward. Irv would have to remember that.

When he turned to Irv, Freddie had already forgotten the whole incident. "I could make out a check, right here, right now, for five million dollars; it would be something, wouldn't it?"

It would indeed, Irv had to admit—to himself. To Freddie, he said: "Don't write it unless you've got a very big bar bill."

"Very funny. How often do you think such an offer will come in your lifetime? Or Bea's?"

"So I salute you for it. It doesn't mean I have to accept it."

"Listen . . ." Freddie got conspiratorial, put his head closer to Irv's, which was hard to do because they were already jammed together. "Not being a publisher, but another kind of businessman, I'm in a position to make you a slightly different kind of offer. To make *you* the offer." He poked the lapel of Irv's tan jacket. "I'm in a position to offer you a finder's fee, above and beyond your agent's commission. A finder's fee, let's say, of $500,000. In short, you'd make a million dollars on this. Has any literary agent—or any other kind for that matter— ever made as much?"

Irv gave him a quizzical smile. "Let's see now. With a finder's fee I'd be making a million while Bea made 4.5 million, so in effect my commission would be nearly 20 percent, when it's only supposed to be 10 percent. I'm Bea's agent, and I'm supposed to be looking out for her welfare. You're asking me to become *your* agent, too, and go behind her back to make a deal. Tell me, Freddie, do you regard that as ethical? How do you explain it—to yourself?"

Freddie was a hard man to put on the defensive. "Is that against the ethics of your business? You know, different fields look at things differently. In many places a finder's fee is perfectly ethical, done all the time. If you do not regard it as so, the answer is simple: give the additional $500,000 to Bea and take your 10 percent of it. I'm here to learn about this industry, goodness knows, Irv, not teach it."

And you're full of shit, too, Irv thought. Freddie knew damned well what he was doing, Irv said to himself, and was totally unembarrassed at being caught at it. But he was offering Bea a lot of money, too much for Irv just to say no. Freddie had *bought* his silence, and he hated having to admit it.

Irv also hated having to admit that Freddie was successfully creating dissension: Who'd told him about the 2.3 million? Sally? Johnny? Bea? The last possibility worried him most of all, and he began to get furious with her at the thought of it.

He brought himself up short. Hold it! She hasn't done anything!

Then he realized Freddie was trying to tear things apart, and doing a hell of a job. He had to be stopped.

"All right, you want to learn about this business? Here's the first lesson. The agent does all the negotiating for his author, and in full consultation with the author. Neither tries to work behind the other's back. Nobody should try to deal with one behind the other's back, to get one to undercut the other."

"Of course, of course! I plead guilty!" Freddie said. "Guilty to coming from a business tradition far less genteel than that of publishing. And as I said, I am here to learn your ways."

"Good," Irv answered. "There are still some gentlemen in the ranks of publishing and one more is always welcome. Now, I'm going to push my way through this mob and get back to my dinner, and my author. Before you and I talk again, she and I will go over the situation very carefully." He tried to make it a warning against dividing and conquering, but he knew it wouldn't slow Freddie at all.

"Hope you liked the brandy," he said as he was walking away.

Neither man had touched his drink. When Irv turned to look, Freddie was already several steps behind him.

"Are you coming?" Irv asked.

Freddie laughed. "Believe it or not, now I do have to pee. See you later. And, oh yes, thank you for the brandy."

As soon as Irv was gone, Freddie headed not for the men's room, but for Johnny's waitress, who was standing at the bar waiting for a drink order.

"Do you know Mr. Wainwright, the man with the blond hair, sitting at the table for four with Bea Fletcher?" As he asked, he took a five-dollar bill out of his pocket.

She looked at him, down at the money, at him again. "Yes, I do."

"Would you go and tell Mr. Wainwright there's a phone call for him at the bar?" He extended the bill.

"All right." She took the five dollars.

Freddie waited at the phone, smiling. He was beginning to see rents in the fabric; he got a kick out of tearing things apart. When Johnny got to the phone, Freddie's smile widened.

"The call was from me, Johnny. Can I buy you a drink at the bar?"

"No, but I'll buy you one. What do you want?"

Freddie shook his head, amused. "Why are all you people so allergic to having a drink bought for you?" He didn't have to say anything about Irv; Johnny knew it from the length of time both men had been gone. Freddie *wanted* Johnny to know, wanted him to wonder what the two had been talking about, agreeing on.

"Maybe because it sets the tone of the conversation."

"Then I definitely should be buying, Johnny, because I'm the one who's going to do the asking."

"All the more reason I should buy—makes it easier for me to say no." Johnny smiled but they both knew he meant it. "What'll you have?"

"Oh, a brandy."

Johnny signaled the bartender. "Tommy, a couple of Hennesseys, and will you put them on my dinner check, please?"

When the snifters were put in front of them, Johnny lifted his and took a tiny sip; Freddie didn't even touch his glass.

"What is it you're asking, Freddie?" Johnny could not afford to get too angry with Freddie. He knew Freddie was a director of WTI, the conglomerate that owned Saxon; he also knew he might need him. Like

Irv, Johnny could not do what he wanted: tell Freddie to fuck off. Freddie was pleased.

"I can appreciate," he said, "that you resent me as an arrogant outsider in your business. You are understandably sensitive to that, and I don't blame you. But in my case you are wrong. I approach publishing respectfully, wanting to learn, to contribute whatever acumen I have acquired in a not altogether unsuccessful career."

"Uh-huh." Johnny liked the fake humility in Freddie even less than he liked the arrogance. "What can I do for you?"

"You can help me understand publishing, earn its respect, perhaps even become a worthy part of it." Freddie paused for the kicker. "We might even work together in some way." He watched Johnny and again was pleased, because in his face he saw what he'd seen in Irv's a few minutes earlier: interest, grudging but genuine. It beat affection anytime.

"Really?" Johnny made it noncommittal, but Freddie wasn't fooled. He looked at the publisher, big, strong, with aquiline nose, light blue eyes. A blond, a jock, the kind of man Freddie envied and hated. Social, too, to the Maidenhead born. And now he had to stand and pay attention to Freddie. It beat membership anytime.

"I don't understand," Freddie said, "why anyone would think twice before grabbing a five-million-dollar buy-out. It sets the writer up for life. Tell me, Johnny, what am I lacking? There is no question I have the money. Is it because I do not yet have any publishing credentials? What is it?"

"It could be a question of personalities. It could be a preference for dealing with known quantities. It could be a wish to begin a continuing relationship with a publisher that will serve fruitfully for many books, as opposed to dealing with someone who may just be in the business for a killing, and will cash in his chips and never be seen again."

"You mean if I were Johnny Wainwright, my offer would be grabbed?" Freddie smiled.

Johnny's return smile was forced. "If you were Johnny Wainwright, you wouldn't have made that offer. But yes, if I made it, it would be grabbed. As soon as they checked my sanity, of course."

Freddie laughed a shade too broadly. "A lovely combination, then," he said, "would be my money and your reputation."

"Neither one would hurt."

Freddie shrugged. "We would have been perfect. Perfect, for this deal. Of course I respect your commitment to Sally, I'd never try to break it up . . . you see . . ." His eyes opened wide, Freddie tried to sound earnest. ". . . I *am* learning the modus operandi of your business. Ah well, a deal is a deal. As long as you and Sally are partners, I would never . . . perhaps on another book, at another time."

"Perhaps," Johnny said.

That was enough for Freddie; he'd said what he wanted to, let Johnny know that if something went awry with Sally, he'd be waiting. Freddie figured if Johnny got desperate enough, he'd *make* something go wrong. And maybe Freddie *would* be waiting . . . and maybe he wouldn't; maybe if he broke up the entente between Sally and Johnny, he wouldn't need either of them; it would be enough to neutralize the alliance.

"I'd better get back to the table," Freddie said. "But first, I must visit the men's room."

Johnny wondered who Freddie would summon next, was just as glad not to be seen walking back onto the porch with him.

Actually, this time Freddie *did* have to pee.

When Irv left Freddie at the bar and returned to his table he found only Sally and Johnny there; Bea had gone over and plunked herself down in the chair vacated by Freddie and was busy talking with Carlotta. No sooner had Irv sat down than the waitress came to call Johnny to the phone—which suited Irv perfectly, because he wanted to talk to Sally alone.

"Either you've got a serious bladder problem, my dear," Sally began, "or you were doing more than just peeing all this time. *Meanwhile*, Freddie's out there somewhere. *Meanwhile*, Johnny is suddenly called to the phone. What's going on?"

Irv didn't like that kind of unfeminine talk from a young woman, but he had to admit she was very astute, and she got down to business right away, which he admired. He wanted to talk business, too. Someone had revealed the $2.3 million offer to Freddie. He most strongly hoped it hadn't been Bea, but even if it had been Sally or Johnny, that still meant there was someone around who couldn't be trusted, who had to be watched.

"Freddie followed me into the men's room. His motives were indecent, but not the usual men's-room-indecent, they were the usual Freddie-indecent."

"You don't have to tell me. I know *exactly* what he tried to grab:

Bea's book. And to think, he'd operate in a location that's off limits to me! Wait till ERA passes! Irv, want to come into the ladies' room?"

He smiled. "No. But what you really want is to go into the men's room. Don't you?"

"Uh-uh, no headshrinking. I pay sixty dollars an hour for that kind of thing. Twice a week, for three years. I've given the good doctor another six months either to grow me a penis or make me stop wanting one." The grin disappeared from her face. "Freddie didn't get the book, did he, Irv?"

"No. But I'll tell you what he got—and not from me. He got the figure 2.3 million—the one that was supposed to be a secret." He waited, watching for a reaction. He got nothing. So he went on.

"One of three people has told. Bea. Johnny. Or you."

"Why three?" she asked. "How about four? Why leave yourself out?"

"What would my motive be?"

"Simple. The same as Bea's. To get Freddie to raise his offer. What would mine be?"

Irv had to laugh at the symmetry. "The same as Johnny's. To dump your current partner and carve out a new deal with Freddie. Or to move first because you thought Johnny was about to dump you."

Meanwhile, both noticed that Johnny's phone call was taking unusually long; both noticed that Freddie hadn't returned either. Both surmised, correctly, that Freddie was trying to divide and conquer.

Maybe Freddie's working the wrong half of the partnership, Irv said to himself. Maybe *she* will be the first to defect. Yet Johnny was the one in trouble; Johnny was the one who wouldn't trust the new breed of publishing executive. It might not be hard to convince him that *she* was going to desert him, and *he'd* better move first. And if anyone could play upon that, Freddie could; Freddie *would*. He needed Saxon's prestige more than he needed Greyhound's money. Irv realized the Marquis of Queensberry rules were out the window. Not only could you not tell where the next punch would land, you couldn't even tell who'd be throwing it. You couldn't turn your back on anyone. The only thing that couldn't be hurt in this free-for-all was the price of Bea's book. As for a rooting interest, Irv was no longer sure whom he wanted to win; the only certainty was whom he wanted to lose: Freddie. But even that was merely personal. He might be rooting against five million dollars, while his author was cheering hard *for* it.

Irv wasn't sure if Sally knew why Johnny and Freddie were both missing; it wasn't long before she let him know.

"Amazing how the tension over Bea's book is affecting people's toilet habits, isn't it? Will you excuse me?" She got to her feet.

Irv stood too. He smiled at her. "Not to mention their telephone habits."

Sally headed straight for the bar and walked up to Johnny and Freddie just as they were breaking up their meeting.

"Can't stop. On my way to the men's room!" Freddie said good-naturedly, and kept on going. He wanted Sally and Johnny to have some time to accuse each other, to shred their entente.

Sally stood facing Johnny, legs apart, hands on hips, looking a bit like Wonder Woman.

"So how was the phone call, Johnny?"

"There was none. The message was from Freddie and it was delivered in person."

"No!"

"Yes. Want to know what it was?"

"Want *me* to tell *you?*"

"Why don't you? I'll get you a drink first. What would you like?"

"Just a Perrier, please."

Johnny signaled the bartender, who, again, responded quickly.

"How do you do that?" she asked.

"Do what?"

"Get that instant service in the teeth of the mob."

He smiled. "Class will tell."

"I just knew you'd say that. Did it ever occur to you, it might be big tips?"

"Do you think Freddie could get that service?"

"If he leaves big tips, as soon as the bartender gets to know him, of course! Look, I'm not against class—just don't count on it too much, or you'll end up awfully disappointed."

Johnny towered over her. She seemed so tiny to be so fierce. "You're a tough gal," he said admiringly.

"*Woman.* The tough are taking over this game. I had to make a choice: either play tough or not at all. You've got to make the same choice. And soon, before someone beats your brains in."

"I suppose I've got to learn the new game. I tell you my heart isn't in it, but I'm trying."

"And was your first move to tell Freddie about our offer?"

"What?"

"Careful. Better learn to walk before you try running. Freddie knows about the 2.3 million."

"And you think *I* told him?"

"You're the logical choice."

"The mistake you're making, kid, is to think that because I'm not as ruthless as you, I'm not as smart. The logical choice for selling out is *you!*"

"Damn, that makes me mad! Furious!" Her face was tight with anger, but she kept her voice down. "One minute I'm blamed for being the Lady Macbeth of the piece. Next I'm blamed for selling out to the enemy, for being the . . . the Mata Hari. Look! There are four major possibilities: Irv, Bea, you and I. *Irv* might want to heat up the competition. *Bea* might want to pull a smartass trick behind Irv's back to show how bright she is. *You* have never been hot on this deal. After all, dammit, Freddie *is* on WTI's board of directors. *I*, more than anyone else, want to fight Freddie and win! Why in hell would I be the one to tell him?"

"The trouble with you is you think nobody before you ever solved any problems, ever showed any cunning. You think everything you do, you've invented, and that it's going to take us old folks by surprise. You're almost insulting about it. Yes, you want to beat Freddie, but my guess is, you want the book more than you want to beat him. And my guess is, if you had to join him and dump me to get the book, you'd do it. And believe me, Freddie knows just how to take advantage of that."

"That's what the shrinks call projection, fella. You're putting *your* thoughts into *my* head. *You've* been out here talking to Freddie. He knows how shaky you are at Saxon—don't look at me that way, Johnny, the whole industry knows, there are no secrets. If Freddie promised to save you, you might cave in."

Johnny stared down at Sally, and to her looked a little frightening. "In fact," he said, "that's what he just offered, and what I just refused, old-fashioned though it may have been. Sorry to disappoint you."

"OK, so he's planted the seed. You may yet think differently about it."

"What are you trying to do, Sally, convince yourself I'm trying to dump you so you can justify dumping me?"

She came close to sneering at him. "We can keep going round and round on this, can't we? What I'm trying to do is quite the opposite. I'm telling *you* to screw your courage to the sticking point, as Lady Macbeth told *her* partner."

"Yes. Of course." Johnny nodded vehemently. "And you know what happened to Lady Macbeth. And to her partner, for listening to her."

He turned and walked off; Sally followed.

When Freddie, having left Sally and Johnny at the bar, got back to the porch, he saw Bea occupying his seat, so he walked to the table where Irv was sitting alone and began talking with him, about houses, property, the weather, zoning, inflation, anything but the book. Johnny, returning to his table, saw Freddie already there, and changed course. Grabbing a chair from a nearby table, he sat down with Buster and Betsy.

"How's Big Bill Tilden?" he asked.

"He always asks me that," Buster said to the woman. "Tilden was gay, and Johnny is indulging in some closet fantasizing. That's why he wants to play me, even though I keep beating him. He hopes he can catch me in the shower. But I always outwit him."

"Yes," Johnny answered, jovially. "He never *takes* a shower." He looked at Betsy. "And how's the sexiest woman in the Hamptons?"

"Fine, Johnny! How are you? You look wonderful. Handsomer than ever." Glittering Betsy had a crush on John Wainwright; he was a kind of Gregory Peck-James Stewart figure to her—upright, responsible, attractive. Husband material. With Johnny, and only Johnny, she was the ingenue. She had less chance of winning him than of getting the lead in Bea's book. Even she knew that.

Like most men who'd slept with her—and most men had—Johnny paid little attention to her at other times, although he was more gallant than most. He patted her hand, squeezed it, kissed her cheek; then he and Buster focused on each other as if she weren't there.

"How does it look, Buster?"

"Oh, I'm not playing much these days, Johnny. Haven't been over to the club hardly at all lately, which explains why you're the king of the hill, fella."

"I didn't mean your tennis game. I meant generally, and at the network."

Buster was operating in that gentle alcoholic glow he'd become so adept at reaching and maintaining, and his answers were easy. "Oh, you mean in the game of life? Down a couple of games—but I've got the big serve going for me."

Johnny liked Buster and felt for him.

"Big serve coming up, eh? Glad to hear it."

Buster raised his glass to just below eye level. The eyes were blood-shot, their look bemused yet defiant. He glanced at the Governor's table. "Yeah, big serve. Sitting right over there."

Johnny turned to look, turned back. "Big book the big serve?"

"Yup. Here's to it." Buster took a swig of his martini.

"Network going for it?" Johnny asked.

Buster waggled his open hand. "Or some other way," he responded.

The "or some other way" made Johnny think, because the only way open to Buster, other than his network, would be through Freddie. And would Freddie be parceling out film rights unless he had the book all sewed up? Or would the film rights be part of a *quid pro quo* between Bea and Freddie? Possibly. Freddie would get his buy-out, provided he'd assign film rights to Buster—maybe even help Buster to raise the money to produce the movie. It made sense. Bea wanted to help Carlotta, her dearest friend, and the only kind of help she needed was for her ex-husband. So Bea would give Freddie the book, and Freddie would give Buster the movie.

Was the deal already set up? No, Johnny told himself. Why not? Because Sally would know about it if it were—that girl knew every-thing. Suppose she knew it—was, indeed, part of it—and was keeping it from him? Suppose she were going to handle the publishing for Freddie!

Johnny began to fear he was growing paranoid, told himself to relax. But he knew what a rotten business it had become. You couldn't really relax, ever. It was no longer *his* business; *his* antennae were no longer properly tuned. He didn't even want to be fighting the battle over this book; yet he felt he had to if he wanted to keep Saxon, to fight another day.

Of course there were other publishing houses, but they weren't Saxon, and they didn't have the inside track to Bea's book. He and Sally were fighting Freddie for that, and there was little chance any-one else could win it. The offers were too big and the time too short; Irv wanted to announce a deal soon. Maybe Sally and Freddie were conspiring to push him out!

"You thinking about it for theatrical release or TV?" he asked Buster.

"Either one. Perhaps both."

Obviously, Buster wasn't going to say more; perhaps he had no more to say. Johnny started to rise. "Well," he said, "I've got to get back to that table, keep an eye on those others." He made it sound light, but he meant it. To Betsy, he said, "See you, good-lookin'." To Buster, "We may yet be holding hands on this thing."

Buster reached his hand to Betsy's. "I'd rather be holding hers," he said with a grin.

"And who can blame you? I was young once myself. I'll leave you two kids alone."

He went back to his table. Prestige was what he had to offer, and he didn't know if it would be enough. He looked at Irv and Sally, and at Freddie, who was still in Bea's chair. "All right," he said. "What have you been cooking up behind my back?" All four of them smiled— cautiously.

When Bea left her table to take the seat next to Carlotta vacated by Freddie, the first thing she said was, "Where else could all this be happening?"

"Nowhere," Carlotta replied. "All this intrigue and sand 'n' surf, too. Does it make you uncomfortable to be the center of it?"

"Oh honey, if I said I *didn't* like to be in the spotlight, you know I'd be lying. That part of it I like. The chance to be rich, I love. Writing rough things about people bothers me, but hell, if any group deserves it, this one does. And more, God knows! Just look at them!"

She looked across the table, lowered her voice. "The Governor of our fair state, sitting there with a hooker. Just charming! And poor straight-arrow Warren Daniels is probably being warned about getting her out of here tomorrow. Freddie's scuttling around, turning brother against brother, and against sister, and from the looks on some of the faces, doing a good job of it. Sally and Johnny, for example, probably don't know whether to worry more about doing or being done to. And Buster, wanting to do, not knowing how, or to whom." Bea wanted to say more about Carlotta's ex-husband, decided not to.

"And how about me?" Carlotta asked. "What part am I playing?"

"The part of my dear friend and confidante." Bea hesitated, went on "The part of a faithful, loving, *dumb* woman, dying to help a man who doesn't deserve it."

"You're so cynical."

"Guilty, as charged. But how can one not be cynical? Just look around! And Carlotta, dear, how can I not be cynical about Buster's ability to make a film or a TV series of the book?"

Carlotta was stung. "Oh Bea, how wrong you are! He is a smart, resourceful producer. He has such good taste. He could do a wonderful job, he really could! He knows the people, the place. And it would mean so much to him!" She stopped herself short, and said, "Shut up, Carlotta! I'm sorry, honey, I'm presuming, and I'm putting you in a tough spot. I shouldn't. It's just that I . . ."

Bea interrupted, put a hand over her friend's. "No, no, no, it's you in the tough spot, Carlie. And I can't help you with it. You know it won't be in my power to name a producer, anyway; I'm so sorry."

Harry was enjoying the scurrying.

"It's a vipers' nest," he told Nellie. "Just look at them: rich, success-ful, good-looking, smart, and so caught up in their wheeling and deal-ing and screwing—and I don't mean the sexual kind, alas—that they can't enjoy their brains, money, looks or fame. Not to mention their hunks of turf in one of the beauty spots of the world. What a bunch! A Governor who might be President someday, a super-rich banker, two top publishing people, a glamorous sexpot, a network news star, a big TV executive, the top literary agent, and . . . and . . . Bea Fletcher. Running around like rats in a maze. Only they *know* where the food is, and they *know* where the exit is. So why don't they get out? What the hell's it all for, Nellie?"

"You're so smart, Harry. And you're not so smart. Maybe they *like* running around in a maze. They *like* having other rats to push and shove and race. It's what they've trained to do all their adult lives, it's what they do best. What else could they be doing, Harry? Reading poetry? Taking pensive, windswept walks along the beach? Birdwatch-ing? Hardly. Thank God for the maze!"

"They should be grateful, huh? Then how come they're so miser-able?"

"Who isn't, Harry?"

"I'm not."

"How do you spend your time, O Wise One? I didn't notice any bird-glasses or copies of Roger Tory Peterson around your digs."

"I like to curl up with a good book. And a good drink. And a good woman."

"In that order?"

"Saving the best for last."

"And how many of *them* will get laid tonight?" Nellie asked.

"Let's see. The Governor will. He should, Freddie is paying enough for it. Irv, no, but he's over sixty, past caring . . ."

Nellie objected. "My parents are older than that, and they still make love. How can you be so mean?"

"I can be so mean because I'm only forty. All right, my wrist is slapped, and you get a merit badge for helping Irv cross a street he didn't want to cross. Do you want me to continue my answer?"

"Yes. Unless you want to wait while I sew on my merit badge."

"I'll ignore the obvious comment on where you can sew it. Carlotta won't; Freddie, Johnny and Sally won't, of course; their minds are on other things. Buster and Betsy, yeah. You don't keep her around for conversation."

"That's cruel too . . ."

"OK, for the first time in Bobby Van history, two merit badges in one evening. I may sew the second one on for you. Now I shall proceed. Warren Daniels, no. He used to be a *Times* reporter, and I understand they're all altered, so they'll keep their minds on their work. Which leaves Bea. She better not!"

"Then there's us," said Nellie, looking Harry straight in the eye.

He looked straight back. "Oh, promises, promises!"

Then he saw Nellie's eyes look across the room, and he turned. Freddie had gotten up from his own table, and gone to Bea's, where he was bending over, talking, smiling, gesticulating. In a couple of moments, he straightened up, slapped Irv Schnell on the back and walked to Buster Reilly's table.

"OK," Nellie said, "you're my all-knowing guide to Hamptons life, what's going on? What's the meaning of it?"

Harry watched for a moment, as Freddie spoke, then slapped Johnny's back—and started toward them.

"We'll soon know, kid," Harry told her. "He's coming toward us."

"Harry, my boy!" Freddie said jovially, and stuck his hand out. But even as he was shaking it, his eyes moved toward Nellie.

"Nellie," Harry said, "this is Freddie Kohl. Freddie, Nellie Brandon."

"Pleased to meet you!" Freddie said, beaming. "I'm having some people over tonight after dinner, for a nightcap around the pool, and I hope you two can make it. All our friends over there"—Freddie turned his eyes toward the other tables—"will be coming. Bea, the Governor, everybody."

"Why, thanks," Harry said. "We wouldn't miss it for the world. Would we, Nellie?"

"Not for the world," she echoed.

"You know my house," Freddie said.

"But of course," Harry replied.

"Good, we'll be leaving soon. See you any time you want to get there."

"Fine, thank you."

Freddie slapped Harry on the back, looked toward Nellie. "Glad to meet you. I'll look forward to seeing you at my house."

"He seems jovial enough," Nellie said, when Freddie had walked away.

"Oh yes. He shakes a good hand. Did you count your rings?"

Startled, Nellie looked down at the signet ring on her right hand. "Oh, come on! Then why did you say we'd go over there?"

"Because it will be interesting. All the gladiators, and the lions, in one ring."

"No Christians?" Nellie asked.

"You can be the Christian. But don't be disappointed if they're too busy with each other to tear you apart."

"How boring that'll be!"

"Oh, I'll be there with you, providing the bite-by-bite commentary. I'll tell you who's getting laid. More important, who's getting screwed."

Labor Day Weekend, 1977;
Early Sunday

IT WAS after midnight when Harry and Nellie drove up to Freddie's magnificent shingled beach house off West End Road. They parked and walked to the kidney-shaped pool nestled behind the dunes.

Looking at the cars in the parking area, Harry figured he and Nellie were the last to arrive, and yet no one was in view.

"Everyone's lost," he said to Nellie, "and this is the perfect place to get lost in." Freddie's house stood on six acres, a big lot for an East Hampton beach house, and it butted up to the dunes, which gave it a limitless backyard. On this warm September night, a guest could be anywhere, pool, lawn, garden, guest house, dunes, beach, ocean, or the sixteen rooms of the house itself.

From the pool, which Freddie kept heated to over 80 degrees, 15 degrees warmer than the night air, wisps of steam rose, and through them Harry saw outdoor chaises and armchairs, empty and in disarray.

"Looks like hell on a slow night," he said.

"What does hell look like on a slow night, and how would you know?"

"I know because I live there. It looks a little like this—steam, and all the chairs out of line."

"My God, Harry . . ."

"Can I get you something to drink?" Sophie startled them. She'd walked silently from the open doors of the sun room and gotten to within six feet of them without their seeing her. But it was not only her proximity that was startling, it was her size. In a pair of rope-soled sandals, she seemed to Harry virtually as tall as he and he was over 6 foot 2. She wore a sleeveless summer dress, and her shoulders looked broader than his, her arms bigger. Yet she didn't seem flabby, in fact Harry suddenly found her sensual: well-formed, big-bosomed, yet out of scale. A pro basketball player might really go for her, Harry thought. He wondered about her and Freddie; he knew everyone else did, too.

"Another kir?" he asked Nellie. She nodded.

"A kir for the lady, and . . . do you have Stolichnaya?"

"Yes sir." Sophie's face remained blank.

"Thanks, Sophie."

She walked off without replying. Nellie went to the pool, knelt, touched the water. "It's like a warm bath. I think I'll go for a swim."

"I'm sure Freddie has a complete set of bathing suits somewhere— probably there." Harry looked toward the poolhouse.

"Don't be silly." Nellie just pulled the shirt over her head, unbuttoned her jeans and slipped them and her underpants off. Her breasts were small and pale-nippled, her body not quite as rickety as it had appeared in jeans. She stood at a three-quarter angle to Harry. She held out a hand. "Come on."

"Go ahead. I'd rather watch. Besides, Sophie's going to be back with the drinks, and I'll be damned if I'll be naked in front of her. She's probably used to giants."

She waved the hand she'd been holding out. "Older men are so modest!" Then she turned and walked to the edge of the pool, poised briefly before diving in.

As Harry watched her swim easily across the pool, Sophie approached with the drinks on a small tray. A few steps behind were Freddie, Carlotta, the Governor, Daniels and Lolly.

"Ah, there you are!" Freddie called. "And where is your . . ." Then he saw Nellie in the pool, and couldn't stop staring. "How nice!" She turned at the far end and started back, saw them all, showed no sign of embarrassment.

"Isn't anyone going to join me?" she shouted.

Freddie looked around. "No one? How about you, Lolly?"

"Oh, I don't think so, it's kind of chilly . . ."

"Oh no," Freddie said, with an edge to his voice this time. "It's warm. You'll enjoy it."

"OK," said the young blonde, sounding businesslike. She took her blouse off. Her breasts were big and full; they swayed and shook as she reached down and with some difficulty peeled off her tight white silk pants and the bikini underpants beneath. Then she walked to the pool, touched the water with her foot, and slid delicately into the warm water.

Harry kept watching her. While Freddie and the others could see her, she remained pleasant, but as soon as her back was to them, so much hatred came over her face, Harry almost felt sorry for Freddie. He wondered if anyone cared for him, if there was anyone who knew him who didn't detest him.

Harry's eyes went to Freddie, whom he caught watching the two naked women in the pool with undisguised hunger. He'd never seen Freddie reveal himself that way before and he realized why: Freddie was drunk. Harry had never seen that before, either.

As Harry watched the others, Carlotta turned silently and went quickly back into the house. The Governor and his press aide stood there, looking sullen, uncomfortable. Freddie seemed not to notice the evil feeling around him.

"Does wonders for a pool to have two gorgeous women in it with no clothes on, doesn't it?" he said loudly.

No one responded. A couple of moments of silence followed. Poor Freddie, Harry thought again. He wondered if the man had any idea how much resentment he aroused, how much hatred and anger were radiating through the night air. Harry felt uneasy; the night, the steam rising from the pool, the two women in it, the anger, reminded him of what he'd said earlier about hell. Except it was no longer on a slow night.

He wondered if Freddie felt any of it. As if to answer, Freddie said, "It's times like these that make all the work worthwhile! To have a beautiful home. And a pool. And friends. This is what it's all for!" He stretched his arms out wide; to Harry he looked as if his body were slightly out of control. "How wonderful!" Freddie almost shouted it.

Still no one replied. Harry was embarrassed for him, wondering if he could really mean all those things, really not see, feel, what was going on around him. Finally, Harry couldn't take any more silence. "Where are all the others?" he asked, for lack of anything better to say.

Just then, the Governor decided on an exit. "I need a minute with you," he said to his press secretary. "Excuse us, will you?" And Hughes grabbed Daniels by the arm and walked him back into the house.

Freddie stood there watching the women in the pool, saying nothing. Harry figured, what the hell, why should he try. Soon, Nellie and Lolly got out of the water, headed quickly for the poolhouse. Then Freddie turned to Harry, swaying slightly, planting his feet as hard as he could on the flagstones to steady himself.

"Ah, and just as I was about to join them!" He looked around. "Isn't it beautiful? Isn't it a wonderful place? And all these wonderful people! I'm a lucky man!"

"It's a beautiful night," Harry said, tangentially, and worked his way back to his earlier question. "Too bad the others aren't out here enjoying it. Where are they anyway?"

"Your ex and Bea and Irv and Johnny are in my library and, would you believe it, talking about books! You'd think they'd want to forget that for a while. I just got tired of listening," Freddie said.

You poor fool, Harry wanted to say, they did that to get rid of you! "Too bad they're not out here enjoying the night," was all he said.

"Then let's go in and break up all that shop talk," Freddie said.

Harry was not in the mood to enter a room holding both his former love and his former wife. What he should do was get Nellie and drive home, but there was something so morbidly compelling about this night he couldn't bring himself to do it. "No," he told Freddie, "I'll let you handle that one alone. Where are Reilly and Betsy Shore?"

"Oh, they grabbed a couple of glasses and a couple of bottles of the bubbly, and went for a walk on the dunes," Freddie replied.

A couple of bottles of the bubbly, Harry repeated to himself, amazed that anyone still used the expression. He wondered if they too had whiffed the hellishness of this place and wanted a little distance from it; he wondered if they were any more at peace out on the dunes than the people were here.

Holding the two bottles of Dom Perignon in one hand and the glasses in the other, Buster led Betsy along a path through the dunes until he spotted a trough of sand amid the dune grass. It was perhaps twenty feet across at the top and its sloping sides met in a pocket that was eight to ten feet deep at the center.

He handed the glasses to Betsy, sat down on one of the sloping sides and shoved one bottle into the sand. He twisted the other open rather than popping it, so that he wouldn't lose any of the precious wine.

Betsy started to touch her glass to his, but Buster began drinking the moment his glass was filled and almost immediately refilled it. She just sipped from her glass.

"How much of Bea's book have you read?" she asked.

"As much as you have." He was snappy with her. Lots of men were. She didn't like it, but no one, at least none of the men she spent time with, seemed to offer her anything else. They were courtly until they'd been to bed with her, then most of them were either offhand or rude, if they talked to her at all. Some of her friends said she should hold back more, but Betsy felt men had to be kept interested, and the men she knew were so high-powered and successful, she didn't know any other way to hold them than to go to bed with them. Most of the time it was not even as if she enjoyed it.

"But I haven't read any of it!" She said it nervously; she could tell he was annoyed.

"You mean you haven't read the part in *Scope* magazine?"

"Oh yes, I read that, everybody did. I meant the rest."

"*Nobody's* read that." Irritation oozed from his voice.

She looked over at him, saw the sagging jawline, the puffy eyes, the lines in the thick neck. Buster was beginning to look like an old man, an old man who drank too much. She felt sorry for him, yet frightened at not being able to say the right thing.

"If nobody's read it, then why is everybody after it so?"

"If *you* haven't read it, then why are you so damned anxious to play the lead?" He took another swig of the champagne.

"Why do I make you so mad?" she asked. "Am I that dumb? If you can't stand me, why did you invite me out here for the weekend, anyway?" Adversity hadn't hardened Betsy; the tears began to well up in her eyes.

He put his hand to the top of her platinum hair. "I'm just an irritable son of a bitch who drinks too much and gets mean. Sorry, honey. Let me answer your question. They know from the 'WashingtonShock' segment that Bea can write, and write *mean*. They know the Hamptons are a snake pit, and Bea knows every snake. They know she's out to make a buck and a name for herself. That she's got the best agent in the business, a man who would not go for the big dollar if the manuscript were not hot. It all adds up to something big. Now have some more champagne and enjoy the moonlight." Though she had barely drunk any, he poured some more in her glass. Then he leaned to her and kissed her.

The tears which had begun with his abuse now poured forth with his kindness. She turned her face away, tried to hide her crying.

He patted her hair, then his own knee. "Come on, honey, sit here." Betsy slid around toward him; he opened his legs so she could sit between them, her back to him.

"Can I ask you something else, Buster?"

"Sure, honey, anything." Both his hands lay on her thighs. He stroked the right one.

"Are you going to produce the film?"

He reached for his champagne glass, propped in the sand, took another swallow. "Looks good," he said. He slid his hand along her right thigh.

"Oh, I'm glad!" She wanted to ask more: why it looked good, when he'd do it, for whom. But she was afraid.

"Yeah, it's really something," he replied. He turned her face to him and kissed her.

"Can I ask something else?"

"Sure, anything, I told you." He began to undo the small pearl buttons on her blouse.

"Would you really consider me for the lead? I mean, I'm not asking you to guarantee anything. But would I have a fair shot at reading for it?"

"You'd have a fair shot." He finished unbuttoning her blouse.

"It hasn't been promised to anybody yet, has it?"

"No. Don't be silly. Lean forward." She obeyed, and he slipped the blouse off. He touched her nipples, cupped her breasts with his hands.

"I can do a Southern accent, you know. Y'all will be truly surprised at how much lahk a No'th Ca'lahna girl I can sound."

"Wonderful," he said. He didn't tell her she sounded like a black field hand, or that Bea came from Tennessee, not North Carolina.

"I'm so happy!"

"Of course. Stand up and let me look at you."

She got to her feet, faced him. Betsy had beautiful breasts, full, pointy, with the beginning of a sag that made them even sexier. She was proud of them. She knew that soon they would no longer be sexy, just saggy, but she wouldn't hesitate to have a silicone treatment when that happened. To be able to stand before a man this way and feel proud was very important to her.

"Take your jeans off, everything off."

She pulled down her zipper, kicked off her high heels. Delicately, quickly, she slid jeans and panties down and stepped out of them. She knew that bending over that way revealed some drooping of the bosom and abdomen, and experience had taught her how best to conceal it. She stood naked before him; she stood proudly.

"It's too bad the Bea Fletcher character wouldn't get to do any nude scenes. You're sensational. Especially in the moonlight."

"You like me, Buster?"

"Sensational!"

She was pleased; she felt she had the talent, as much as many of the big stars. She just hadn't been in the right place at the right time. This was such a crummy business!

"I'm glad you like me, because I know I can do it. I never got the breaks. This time it's going to be different. You're going to be proud of me, Buster."

"I'm proud just to sit here and look at you, you turn me on." She did have a magnificent body, creamy-skinned, with none of the hair on forearms or thighs that turned Buster off. Even her pubic hair, a pale reddish-blond, was almost invisible. Her thighs, hips, abdomen were still full and smooth, although he figured she didn't have too many years of that left. But this was now.

"Do I turn you on? I'm happy."

"Touch yourself, Betsy. Let me see you touch yourself."

She put her hand between her legs.

"Oh yeah, that turns me on," he said. "Does it turn you on?"

"Oh yes. Oh yes!" Men always wanted that reaction and so she faked it for them.

"Want to see how it turns me on, Betsy?"

"Yes, oh yes!" Her breathlessness was the top of her acting art.

He spread his legs flat on the sand. She came and knelt between them.

"Go on, look."

She unzipped his pants; he was indeed turned on. She looked up at his face to make certain what he wanted her to do and when. She saw the answer. Here. Now. She took his penis into her mouth.

Buster sighed, tilted his head back, closed his eyes, put a hand on her blond head, just as he had earlier, when he was comforting her.

Despite her expertise, it took awhile, for he was not young, and he was a heavy drinker. Then she stood up, looked down at him. He opened his eyes, looked back.

"God, you've got a luscious body!" he said. After the initial fondling of her breasts, he hadn't touched her. She wanted to tell him so, only she'd never dream of saying a thing like that to a man. She reached for her clothing.

"No. Don't," he said. "Just sit down the way you are." She obeyed.

He took another sip of champagne. "You've got just about the sexiest body going," he said.

"I'm glad you like it, Buster. Buster?"

"What?"

"When am I going to hear something?"

"About what?"

"About the part!"

"There are so many steps before that, it pains me to mention it. How in hell can I tell you now about the part?"

"I thought you said you had the movie rights sewed up?"

"When did I say that? What in hell are you talking about?"

She'd taken him to a sexual peak, then over the top; now he didn't want to have to bother with her. He was tired, drunk, irritable, no longer interested in being helpful, or even polite.

"I just asked you a couple of minutes ago if you were going to produce the movie, and you said yes!"

"I didn't say anything of the sort! I don't know what you're talking about, which makes *two* of us. You've got to stop thinking with your snatch, kid, and start using your head."

"What a filthy thing to say! What a vile thing to say! Why do you do this to me, Buster?"

"Do *what* to you, for Chrissake!"

"You said you'd consider me for the lead. Am I dreaming all this?"

"I wish *I* were! Look, nobody has any rights to that book yet, and people are throwing big money around, money I don't have a smell of. Now I'm gonna try, understand? Do you want a written guarantee I'll make you a star? Get off my back, will you?"

"You didn't say that a few minutes ago!" She was putting on her blouse.

"A few minutes ago, I *liked* what you were doing and where you were, and it wasn't on my back. Now why don't you go to bed and leave me alone?"

She struggled into her jeans, losing her balance, righting herself, shouting. "You lied to me, Buster! Why did you lie? To get me to make love to you?"

"*Make love to me?* Is that what they call a blow job these days? Tell you what, let me pay you for it, so we can cut the bullshit. What's the going rate?—you ought to know. But not a movie lead. Not for a blow job. Uh-uh, that's too high."

"You bastard! You rotten bastard!" She was sobbing as she shouted. Stumbling, neither buttoned nor zipped, she headed off across the dunes, not sure where she was going, until she tumbled over the edge of the dunes onto the beach.

Johnny didn't mind drinking the champagne, and rather liked sitting in the sumptuous library talking shop with Bea, Irv and Sally. But he couldn't take too much of the host, and when Freddie walked in and sat down with them, he stuck it out for five minutes for the sake of courtesy, then asked, "Who's for a moonlight walk on the beach?" knowing no one would accept.

And when no one did, with relief, Johnny headed for it alone—for the beach he loved, one of the rare places that hadn't been contaminated in the past ten years. Sure it had changed in shape, shrunk in many places, grown in a few. But that change was natural, eternal—unchanging change. He crossed the dunes in a walk so fast it was almost a run, and burst into a grin as he ran down onto the beach, headed straight for the water.

He'd gone only halfway when, in the moonlight so bright figures cast sharp shadows, he could see Betsy about thirty yards off.

"Johnny!" she screamed when she saw him. "Johnny!"

She ran toward him, tripped, fell, got up, fell again. He got to her, sat in the sand next to her.

"What's the matter, Betsy, honey?"

"Buster, that drunken bastard! He lied to me, Johnny! He humiliated me! He treated me like dirt!" Johnny took her hand; she seized it with both of hers and pressed it to her bosom. "Men are such bastards! I don't mean you. Why are they such bastards?"

He wanted to say, because you're such a natural victim, Betsy, you invite it. But he didn't, it was too late, it would only hurt her more. "It's OK now, Betsy, OK." He put his arm around her. "Everything will be all right. Tell me what happened. You and Buster have . . . been together . . . before, haven't you?"

"Yes, but . . ." She was sobbing too hard to talk.

"Easy, honey, easy."

"He lied to me! He said he'd produce the movie of Bea's book. He said I'd have a chance to play the lead. But after I . . . made love to him, he said he couldn't do *anything!* Then he said some terrible things to me!"

"Calm down, Betsy," he said. "I'm sure he didn't mean the terrible things. Maybe he expects to get the book, but just isn't sure, and he's worried about it. You shouldn't let it worry you. The night is too special, the moon is too bright, you're too beautiful, to spoil it with those tears and those red eyes. Just sit here now, and relax."

"I can when you're here, Johnny. You make me feel protected. Let me lie here with my head on your lap." He was sitting and she stretched out and put her head on his thigh near the hip.

"Do you feel better, beautiful?"

"Do you really think I'm beautiful?"

"Yes, I do," he said patiently. "Everyone does."

"And do you think I'm a good actress?"

Lying did not come easily to Johnny. "I never watch TV, you know that. But lots of people who've seen you tell me you're marvelous." Actually, Johnny had seen her in one episode of a comedy series, and had not thought her marvelous. But then her part was really too small for him to tell.

"Well, I am, really talented. I know my faults and I know my strengths—I am a good actress. I *could* play the lead in Bea's book. If you helped me get it, you'd never be ashamed of me."

"I'm sure I wouldn't, Betsy. Now just calm down."

"Would you, then?"

"Would I what?"

"Help me get the lead. You're an important person, Johnny. You could do it."

"I'll do what I can." He tried to make it sound as noncommittal as he could without hurting her. He didn't want her to misconstrue it; she did.

"Oh, thanks, Johnny! I knew you would. You'll be proud of me, you will!" She put her hand under her head and on his crotch.

"All I said was, I'll do what I can. That's not much to thank me for. It's a long way from getting you the role."

She kissed his thigh through the pants. He was amazed that despite his pity for her, his contempt for exploitative men, he could feel so aroused by her kiss, the touch of her hand.

"You *are* going to publish the book, aren't you?"

He was in a spot. He had to sound confident, like a winner—Betsy talked to everybody.

"There's no deal yet," he said, "but it looks good for us. As the saying goes, we've made them an offer they can't refuse." Of course, Johnny knew, they could.

"Oh that's wonderful! I know you're going to do it! *You're* wonderful." Her hand on his crotch was stroking him. She was kissing his thigh, higher and closer to her hand. "I love touching you there," she said. "I love kissing you."

He liked the feel of her, but he hated leading her on about the book. "Getting hardcover rights is a long way from casting the film, you know."

"You'll have a lot to say, Johnny. People like you, they respect you. They want to please you. I want to please you, Johnny. I always have, you know that." She reached up to unzip his fly.

"No!" He pulled her hand away. "For God's sake, Betsy, I can't get you that part! How can you be so dumb?" His vehemence startled both of them. She sat up as if he'd pinched her.

"Johnny, don't say that!"

"But it's true! How can you not know it? What in hell are you doing? What kind of dream world do you live in? How can you not know that a hardcover publisher has nothing to say about casting the film? You close your eyes to what's really happening, and go around screwing or blowing"—he loathed the word so much, he used it on her—"everyone who's a second cousin to some producer—or tells you he is! Wake up, you poor dumb bitch!"

"How dare you talk to me that way!" she shouted. "You'd think I was a . . . hooker!"

Tired, angry, Johnny let go. "You *are* a hooker, don't you see that? Only you don't even get paid—you settle for worthless IOUs! You fuck Buster, who can't do a thing for you, not a damned thing! You try to fuck me, and I have no way to get you in that movie, even if I do publish the book! At least a hooker gets her hundred or two hundred or five, whatever they're getting these days!"

She began punching and pummeling him with both fists. Because she was sitting and had no leverage, she was unable to hurt him, until her right fist caught his left eye. Then Johnny got angry, swung his left arm in a wide arc and, with his forearm and biceps, knocked her flat on the sand, without hurting her. Still she kept punching at him until he jumped on top of her, straddled her and pinned her arms to hold her still.

There was no sexuality to the press of their bodies. Her face was blotchy, distorted by strain, tears, anger, humiliation. Her ugliness, her abjectness, made him furious.

"If you're going to be a rug, dum-dum," he shouted, "at least lie down for the right people! The one man in all the Hamptons who could do you some good is the one man you pull your virginity act on!"

She stopped flailing and writhing. "What? Who the hell are you talking about?"

"Don't play dumb, for Chrissake! Who's the only man in the Hamptons you ever said no to?"

"Oh, you bastard! I said no to a lot of people!"

"You know what I mean."

She paused a moment, thought. "You mean Freddie?"

"That's right, I mean Freddie. He's the front-runner, he's the number one possibility for getting you a part in the film."

"Oh, no!" All the fight, all the life seemed to ooze out of her. He could feel her body beneath him go limp.

"Let me up, Johnny. I want to go." She said it quietly, almost docilely.

He climbed off her, lay on the sand alongside her. Quickly, calmly, she sat up, got to her feet, brushed sand off, walked away.

"Betsy, good night," he said. When she didn't answer, he said more loudly, "Good night, Betsy, I'm sorry." She didn't speak or look back.

He lay there, unsure whom he hated more, her or Freddie. He decided on Freddie. The son of a bitch, he said to himself, is pulling the strings even when he's not around. We're all playing his game.

Betsy stumbled back to the house and began searching for Freddie. In the big sitting room, she met Sophie, looking mountainous in a white terrycloth robe.

"May I help you?"

"Where's Freddie?"

"Wait here," Sophie said, and turned and left the room.

Betsy started to sit in a wicker rocker, then on a sofa, then didn't sit at all, just wandered around, looking at books, lamps, pictures, without seeing them. In a few minutes Sophie was back.

"Come with me."

She led Betsy to an upstairs bathroom, where Freddie was waiting in a silk paisley robe.

"What do you want?"

"When they make a motion picture of Bea's book, I want to play Bea."

"You've come to the right place."

"What do I have to do to get it?"

He opened his bathrobe; he had nothing on under it. He pointed to the carpeting in front of his feet. She looked over to Sophie, who gave no sign of leaving. She looked back at Freddie, asking with her eyes. More decisively, he pointed to the floor.

"In front of her?"

"Make up your mind, quickly!"

She got to her knees, took him into her mouth. He just stood there with his hands on his hips, let her do all the work. When she was finished, she stood, looked at him as if to ask, will that be all?

He turned to Sophie. "Get the other one."

Silently, the big woman left, returned almost at once with Lolly, who looked as if she'd been asleep.

"Betsy," he said, "have you ever made love to a woman before?"

"Oh, no!" she replied. "I mean yes, but . . ."

"In less than a week," he snapped, "I will own the rights to Bea's book. *All* the rights. Film. TV. All of it. I can do whatever I want with the book. Do you understand?"

"Yes, but . . ."

"What did you come here for?" He spat the words at her.

"You know what," she said.

"All right then."

"All right," she echoed.

"Take your robe off," he ordered Lolly. She obeyed. Under the robe she wore a short black see-through nightgown which was crumpled from being slept in. "Take that off, too." Lolly lifted the nightgown over her head. "Now undress Betsy."

Betsy stood there, as Lolly walked to her and began unbuttoning her blouse. The blouse came off, Betsy neither helping nor interfering. Lolly unzipped her jeans, slid them and her panties down to her ankles, and Betsy acquiesced to the extent of lifting one foot, then the other.

Still on her knees, Lolly kissed Betsy's thighs, then her pubic hairs.

She stood, pressed her body against Betsy's, put her hands on Betsy's buttocks, rubbed her body from side to side across Betsy's.

Betsy just stood there, hands at her sides, neither resisting nor helping.

"Kiss Lolly as if you cared," Freddie ordered. "Put your arms around her neck."

Betsy did as she was told.

Lolly began to lead her back toward the bed. "No, no, not here," Freddie said. "Wait. I'll come back for you."

He started from the room, then stopped, turned, looked at Sophie.

"I need you." Sophie hurried after him.

"Yes."

"You have some filming to do. Is everything set up?"

"Yes. It's always ready."

"Then hurry, get going!"

"I'm going." In her bare feet, she went into the small room between the two west bedrooms, closed the door.

Gently, Freddie knocked at the Governor's door, opened it, walked in.

"Who is it?"

"It's Freddie, Mike. Sorry to wake you, but I have a little surprise for you, something you might enjoy. May I turn on a light?"

"Yeah, all right. Not too bright."

Freddie flicked on a small lamp on the dresser near the door. Then the Governor turned on his bedside lamp. "What time is it?"

"A quarter to two. Believe me, you'll thank me."

"Believe me, I hope so. I hope it's better than sleep, 'cause that's what I want right now."

"You'll change your mind; you'll like this better."

"We'll see, we'll see. OK, I'm up now, what happens?"

"Go on into the bathroom, leave the door open a crack, and watch. You'll see a performance that will delight you, I promise."

Mike got the picture. "How about audience participation?"

"Whenever you feel like it."

"Well, OK, what the hell!" He got out of bed, put on his robe, went into the bathroom, closed the door, leaving it only two inches ajar. Freddie turned on all the lights in the room. In case the Governor was wondering about that, he said loudly, "You'll want to be able to see *everything*, Mike!"

And we'll want to be able to film everything, he added, to himself, as he moved quickly out of the room to where the two women were waiting.

"All right," he said to them, "come with me. Someone's going to be watching you, that'll be quite a turn-on, won't it?" Neither woman said anything as they followed him into the glare of the Governor's bedroom.

"There you are, girls, enjoy yourselves." And since Freddie knew the Governor wouldn't want him watching, he went into the small filming room, where he could watch through the one-way mirror.

Lolly, though the younger of the two, was more experienced in this kind of scene. "Let me do you first," she whispered to Betsy. And she put her hand on the small of the older woman's back and led her to the bed. She put Betsy down on her back near the foot of the bed. Then she knelt on the floor between her legs.

"May as well enjoy this, honey," she said, and she started to kiss the insides of Betsy's thighs.

Slowly, she worked her way up—she knew audiences liked a build-up—taking her time before her tongue began touching the lips of Betsy's vagina. Then, slowly, she moved to Betsy's clitoris.

Betsy had made love with a woman before and liked it. But not with someone watching. This time she was at first nervous and embarrassed. Then, despite the embarrassment, despite the awareness of a spectator, it began to feel good again. Here was someone paying attention to *her*, making love to *her*, knowing how to arouse *her*.

When Lolly, without taking her mouth away, got her body up on the bed, and swiveled it around so Betsy could reciprocate, Betsy was happy, eager, to do so.

But before she could climb all the way to the peak, she was aware of a naked man standing over them. The fun was over and once again the servicing was about to begin.

In the little dark room on the other side of the one-way mirror, Freddie was watching, Sophie was ready, and the filming was about to begin.

For a while after Betsy had gone off across the dunes Buster just lay there. "Silly bitch!" he said aloud after a time. "Goddamned stupid bitch!"

He was offended at the idea that a woman would offer her body and in return expect anything more than his. Buster Reilly, war hero, football hero, glamour boy, big shot, should be prize enough. God knows, the women had always lined up; it had honestly never occurred to him that anyone would ever want a *favor* in return for her favors.

He was truly surprised at Betsy for being so dumb as to expect that kind of swap, *and* for taking seriously his blustering about Bea's book. God, that broad was stupid! You'd think she'd have fucked enough people in this business to have learned—if only by osmosis—the difference between facts and bullshit.

He took a swig from the champagne bottle. You had to *sound* like a winner—although in his case it was taking a hell of an acting job. If only he *did* have the film or TV rights! If only he *could* offer his body for them, he'd be damned if he'd complain! If only they *were* paying off on being a swordsman, he'd be president of the goddamned network!

Buster thought about it, and saw the problem: There were no women in positions of power to fuck! Well, almost none. Too bad! The idea of fucking his way to the top amused him. What a way to go!

If only he could fuck his way to the film rights for Bea's book! But who? He took another gulp of champagne, thought about it.

Why, Bea, of course!

He laughed aloud; the idea was funny. Bea. He thought some more. Maybe it wasn't so funny. Why not? He and Bea were a natural! Sure, he'd never considered it before because Bea and Carlotta were such friends—but why not? He and Carlotta were split, definitely and irrevocably. He and Bea were both unattached, they knew each other well, they knew each other's friends and lifestyle; they could fit together without missing a beat.

Did he find her attractive? He'd never really thought about it, had never allowed himself to. But again, why not? Why shouldn't he? She was slim, delicate, beautifully shaped. Yes, she was attractive.

But what did she think of him? Buster assumed *all* women found him appealing. That was his rock-bottom strength. When he looked at a woman, he never doubted he could go to bed with her if he wanted. When he looked at a man, he never doubted he could beat him as a tennis player and as a lover. Usually, he was right. An adolescent set of superiorities to fall back on, he told himself when he was depressingly sober.

When he was not sober, he was proud of them, as he was of his football record and his war record. They were more important than the minuscule achievements of his new network bosses. He thought himself the kind of man he wanted to be, was proud to be—especially when he was drunk.

Now, with each gulp of champagne, the idea of using his strengths to advance his career seemed better and better. Was it prostituting himself? Not half as much as kissing the asses of his pygmy bosses—*that* was prostitution. Offering himself to Bea was dealing from strength. It might work. It might be fun! It might be the start of a beautiful . . . something. And profitable, too.

He stood up, tossed the empty Dom Perignon bottle off into the dunes, grabbed the full one, popped it open, watched the cork leap into the moonlit night. He poured a little into his mouth, started back toward Freddie's house.

When he got to the pool, the only people he saw were Harry and Nellie, sitting and talking.

"Hi! Have you seen Bea?" Buster tried to stand straight, sound sober, knew he wasn't doing too well.

"Everybody's somewhere," Harry replied. "Try the library."

That sounded kind of silly; Buster wondered if Harry was as drunk as he. He waved and headed toward the house, walked into the sitting room, out the far end, into the hall, where he saw Sally and Carlotta coming out of the library.

"Seen Bea?" He tried to avoid Carlotta's eyes. He didn't need any more of her disapproval.

"Just left her in the library," Sally said. Carlotta said nothing.

"Thanks." He walked by without looking at either.

Bea sat alone in the library, writing on a small pad.

"Scribble, scribble. The writer's work is never done. I thought you'd about finished your book by now."

"Just about," Bea said. "The 'just about' is the hardest part. All I need is an ending, and I'm trying to let my characters write it for me."

"Uh-oh, I'd better watch it."

"No, please don't. The worse you behave, the better my ending." She smiled at him.

"Got some time to talk?" he asked.

"Sure. What about?"

"Nothing in particular. It beats going off to sleep."

"The extravagance of your praise could turn a girl's head."

He thought he detected in that a come-on. "I can be a lot more gallant."

"Let's hope so," she said. "Yes, let's talk. For you, it beats sleeping; for me, it beats writing."

"Want a swig of champagne?" He extended the bottle.

She took it, held it in both hands, tilted it to her mouth. "Yum. Now, what shall we talk about?"

"Your book. The film rights. Us."

"Some agenda," she replied. "Not surprising. *And* surprising."

"Which is which?"

"Not surprising that you'd want to talk about the book and the film rights. Surprising that you'd want to talk about 'us.' There is no 'us,' Buster."

"Up to now there couldn't be," he replied. "Up to now there was you and Harry. There was Carlotta and me. Other us's. Now there are no more us's."

"That doesn't make an 'us' of you and me."

"True. Only we can make an 'us' of us. I don't think that would be so hard. I think maybe there was an 'us' there all the time."

"Do you think so?" Bea was beginning to be put off, yet was also curious. "Are you sure you want to say this? Aren't you worried about a little trickle of disloyalty running through your conversation?"

"Yes, I'm sure. No, I'm not worried. While Carlotta and I were together, I would never *think* about it, let alone talk, or do anything about it."

"How about while Carlotta and *I* are together, as friends?" Bea asked.

"Look, there's no way you or anyone else will get us back together. It makes no difference who I go out with, Carlotta and I are finished. Totally. Forever."

"What makes you so sure?"

They were sitting on opposite ends of a long wicker sofa; he gesticulated with the champagne bottle. "What in hell is this? Do you ask for an affidavit of non-attachment from every man you're contemplating a liaison with?"

She didn't like that—at all. "What makes you think I'm contemplating a liaison with you?"

"Well, why don't you?" He stared at her with the Irish blue eyes which had once hypnotized women. Now all she could see was how bloodshot they were. Simultaneously she felt indignation and a kind of contemptuous pity for this man. She could see he was trying to be seductive, compelling, and wasn't even coming close.

"A liaison? What's in it for me?"

"Me," he said.

"Oh? And what's in it for you?"

"You."

She smiled at him. "Even-up swap, huh?"

He grinned back. "Yup."

"Aren't you forgetting something?" She tried to keep the smile, felt her mouth tighten.

"What?"

"My book."

His grin disappeared. "You're a cynical woman. I feel sorry for you."

"Oh, come on, Buster! You're being insulting. How dumb do you think I am?"

"Not dumb. Just suspicious, insecure. Why can't you believe I'm interested in you just for you? I'm quite willing to believe you're interested in me just for me."

"Let's be brutal about it. That's *easy* for you to believe. *Necessary* for you to believe. What else have you got to offer but you?"

"That *is* brutal, it sure as hell is. Also untrue. I happen to have a list of TV credits as long as one of your beautiful legs. I'm a producer, and a damned good one."

"And you *don't* want to produce the film of my book, right? You're just after me for *me*, right?"

"Those are two separate questions. I am after you for you. And I *do* want to produce the film."

"Would you take one without the other?"

"Sure. Which are you offering?"

She managed a tight smile. "You'd like it to be the film, wouldn't you?"

"I'd like both. I'd rather have one than none, though."

"Suppose you had to choose one—me or the film?"

"But I *don't* have to choose. Except as part of this nasty little game you're playing."

She stared at him; no more smiles. "I won't say who's playing a game. Let's just say I have it in my power to offer you one or the other . . ."

"Or both," he interjected.

She nodded. "Or neither, for that matter. But for the moment I don't choose to offer you both. Or neither. I choose to offer you one. Which one?" She underrated the daredevil in him.

"You," he answered.

Suddenly she found herself furthering a flirtation with this aging child. Drunk, immature, outrageous, he had, for the moment, outplayed her.

"Your choice is made," she said, "on the clear understanding that it loses you the right to produce the film."

He grinned; he could see he'd gained an advantage. "Sure. Provided *you* understand I reserve the right to charm you into changing your mind."

"You mean *fuck* me into changing my mind, don't you, stud?" She was angry at his arrogance and her loss of the upper hand.

Buster tried not to let himself get angry back. "Whatever works," he said.

"Let me ask you something. How old are you, fifty-six, fifty-seven?" It was too high a guess and she knew it.

"Only fifty-three; give me a break, will you?" He *wouldn't* let himself get riled.

She kept after him. "Is that all? Well, all right, let's say fifty-three. What in hell makes you think I'd be turned on by a man that old? You know, I'm thirty-nine . . ." For effect, she knocked a year off her age. "Do you think a *man* of thirty-nine would be tantalized by a fifty-three-year-old *woman* offering herself to him? You aging Don Juans have a lot of nerve! And *you*—you're not even a well-preserved fifty-three! You drink too much and you're getting paunchy. What the hell have you got to offer? I'm near my sexual peak. You're thirty years past yours. You've got a lot of *nerve*, but I don't know how much else you've got."

"Haven't had any complaints so far." He wanted to keep it light, but he was getting annoyed. "However, that's not really the point, is it? The point, the game, is: get Buster. I don't know what I did, but it must really have been something. Want to tell me?"

She glared at him; the only thing she felt for him now was cold anger. "Uh-huh. Yes. I do want to tell you. First there's what you did to one woman, Carlotta, who loves you more than you deserve. Then there's what you do to women in general, the way you humiliate them, debase them, and then think you're doing them a favor. You're one of those perennial locker-room types who sit around boasting about their scores! Just once I'd like to see you have to *take* it, instead of dishing it out. So when you made your splendid offer of that aging, alcohol-soaked body, I thought this was my chance to let you see what it's like the other way around. To put you in the role of the hooker, someone like poor Betsy, offering your body for small favors somebody powerful might throw at you—and might not."

Buster shrugged. "You want my body, you can have it. I told you that right off. You want my balls—you can't have them." He got to his feet unsteadily; she was afraid he was leaving, and she didn't want the game to end yet. But he was only going to find a glass.

"Want some champagne?"

"No, thank you."

He walked over to the bar, picked up an old fashioned glass, filled it, started back to the sofa. He could feel his shakiness and, trying to correct it, ended up with the stiff dignity of the drunk—he could feel that, too. Before he could reach the sofa, Bea stopped him with raised hand.

"We've known each other about, let's see, two years," she said. "You've gained some weight, haven't you? How much?"

"Not much."

"How much, fifteen, twenty pounds?"

"Oh no, maybe seven or eight. What's the point?"

"No, no, no, more than seven or eight—definitely. You've got what looks like a real pot there, fella."

"What's the *point?*" His voice was sharper.

"The *point,*" she replied, just as sharply, "is that you think you're making me an offer I can't refuse: Your body for my film rights. And I'm wondering just how big your offer is."

"My my, what crudeness lies within the classy lady. Who would have dreamt it?"

"Crudeness? Hardly. Just call it truth in packaging. The same kind of inspection countless women have been put through for years and years by countless macho types like you—who then have a big laugh afterwards, as if humiliating a woman were a joke. So, let's see what you've got, Buster. Come on! Maybe I'll take you up on your offer. Maybe, on the other hand, the girls and I will just have a laugh over it."

He stood there and looked at her. "You're serious, aren't you?"

"You mean about inspecting the merchandise? You bet I am."

"Goddammit, Bea, you're really out to get me. You must have it in for me to want to humiliate me this way."

"Humiliate you? You guys are always having naked women paraded before you. How come you never say you're humiliating *them?* How come?" She paused; he said nothing; she went on.

"Besides, it all depends on what you look like naked. If you've got a good body, you're supposed to be proud of it. Aren't you? Isn't that what you tell women about their bodies? Well, then, come on! Yes or no? You made the offer, I'm calling you on it. If I like what I see, who knows? After all, I do have what you want!"

"Oh shit, Bea, I've stood naked in so many places, in front of so many people, you think I give a damn about one more? If I say no, what is it supposed to prove—that men have exploited women since the beginning of time? You know as well as I do that the minute I start to undress you'll tell me to stop."

"Will I? Why don't you try it and see?"

"Want to fake me out, huh?"

"No, Buster, I think *you* want to fake *me* out. Go ahead and try. Let's see who's doing the bluffing."

He was wearing a red Lacoste tennis shirt, white ducks and a pair of loafers with no socks. He pulled the shirt over his head. Buster's shoulders were big and still solid, the trapezius muscles running out from his neck still thick and strong. But his chest muscles were flabby, his waist larded with fat, his biceps going soft.

Bea stared at him. "What did I say? Fifteen or twenty pounds? I was about right."

"Don't worry about it, kid," he replied. "I'm not charging you by the pound." He stared back at her. "Waiting for the humiliation? For the blush of shame to creep up my face? Waiting to cry vengeance is thine? For the ghosts of exploited sisters past to come back and cheer? Forget it. When you call the score in to *Ms.* magazine—if they're still in business—you won't be able to report a big win on this one. And let me tell you something else, kid, I'm *not* the enemy. Not unless you identify the enemy merely by genitalia."

"I haven't seen any yet. Quit stalling. Are you going ahead, or are you trying to talk your way out of it?"

Decisively, he unzipped his pants, lowered them and his undershorts, stood naked before her. "Now it's your turn," he said.

She ignored him, just sat there staring, unflinchingly. At least she hoped it would look that way.

"Ordinary. Very ordinary. And not at all turned on. Limp. Very limp."

"Nothing to be turned on about yet."

"Never mind. A younger man, someone, let's say, *my* age, would be standing out. And you are *not* outstanding at all. Freddie told me you couldn't get it up. I assumed he meant the money to buy the film rights. Now I see he meant *both*. Sorry about that, old man."

"Now it's your turn," he said, again, and took a step toward her.

"Stay where you are, you disgusting *old* lecher!" She shouted it, her voice venomous. "Who the hell do you think you are, that I would be interested in *that* as payment for my book! Oh, how I hate you! I hate you for the misery you caused Carlotta—she doesn't know how lucky she is to be rid of you! I hate you for the misery overgrown children like you caused me, and other women. You're disgusting! You're a drunk and a lecher! You've got the morals of a rattlesnake! And you've got the ego of . . . of . . ." She spluttered, groping for words damaging enough. "Dammit! If your cock were half the size of your ego, you'd be half the stud you think you are!"

He just stood there, still limp. He did not find this experience arousing. "You got a lot to learn about turning a man on," he said.

She ignored that. "Carlotta's always telling me what a great guy you are. What happened to it? Where did it go? She *needed* you. All she ever wanted was for the Reillys to be happy, and you fucked it all up. Fucked up your home, your wife, your kids, your career. And you end up trying to fuck her best friend—and thinking you're doing *me* a favor, to boot!"

She was standing, voice tense with anger but not loud, eyes blazing, no longer concerned with his nakedness.

"You're like this place, Buster! This manicured cesspool! I thought Washington was the pits—the Hamptons are no better, just fancier. Like you: classy on the outside, spoiled rotten on the inside. Maybe the Hamptons are worse than you are, because at least you're beginning to *look* like what you are—decaying. *Decaying*, do you know that, Buster? You're not fooling anybody anymore, your outside is starting to look like your inside. At last, in spite of yourself, you're starting to look truthful! Like a lush—the veins on the nose, the bloodshot eyes! Like an old man, with the droopy neck and the pot belly. Like a has-been, with the limp cock.

"You look like what the Hamptons deserve to look like! Like Dorian Gray! If Freddie's estate looked like his soul, it would be Bedford-Stuyvesant! The South Bronx! But no! It looks like Kew Gardens, Versailles, a damned national park, a place where poets and philosophers should be walking across the lawns talking about truth and beauty! Instead Freddie uses it to drop his pants, so poor slobs like Betsy will suck his cock! How's that for truth and beauty? Tell me, Buster, did you get her to go down on you? What did *you* offer? A part in the movie you don't have the rights to?"

He looked startled. "I hit it, Buster, didn't I? I can tell! You know, sooner or later I find out everything. There are no secrets in the cesspool; gossip, uncontrollable diarrhea of the mouth, is one of the many rottennesses of this place. Of course, treachery—screwing your buddy —is another. Makes it hard to count on a confidence around here! That's why it amuses me the way you all hate Freddie. You think he's different from you? Nonsense. He's just *better* at it."

Buster looked at her, tried to regain his advantage. "Are you going to get undressed *before* you get all the self-righteousness out of your system, or after? Do I first have to say how impressed I am by your grasp of the folkways and mores of the Hamptons? OK, I'm impressed. Now will you take your clothes off?"

Deliberately, she stared at his genitals. She sneered. "For that? Buster, you couldn't touch me with a ten-foot pole—something, I notice, you are a long way from having."

"Too late for flattery," he said as he stooped to put on his pants. "I am hurt more by your put-down of our fair community than I am at any personal insults." He zipped up his fly. "Sorry you no longer adore this little oasis of tranquillity the way you once did; it means of course you'll get no sexual satisfaction from *me*."

"Oasis? Tranquillity? This South Fork sewer? I sure have had a tough job holding on to my adoration. The problem was, I found out what it was really like, and that changed the adoration ever so slightly —to loathing."

He stood in front of her without putting his shirt on. "I should think you'd have a little more affection for the place you're using to make a quick buck—*many* quick bucks. I should think you'd want to say: Thanks, Hamptons, for putting all that nasty little gossip into my nasty little head and then into my nasty little book. For you to put down the oasis just reeks of ingratitude. You're one of *us* now, Bea. No false modesty! You *belong*."

"Don't flatter yourself," she shot back. "The one who turns the rock over is *not* the same as the crawling creatures underneath. Though they may not like her revelations, she is *not* one of them. Not even if she gets rich doing it. And believe me, I'd love to get rich. To zap all of you and make some bucks doing it sounds just dandy. Although they're not *quick* bucks, let's get that straight, they're bucks worked long and hard for."

He slipped his shirt over his head. "Zap. *And* get rich. And be Mizz Self-Righteousness, too. Sounds like you've got it all—and sainthood just around the corner."

"Well, if you don't mind, I'll skip the sainthood. I'll take revenge instead, against the men who fucked me over, the men who exploited poor Betsy, the man who destroyed Carlotta's family and happiness. Which is why it was such a treat to have you stand there and offer your body to me, the way so many women have had to do to you. A treat. Not much of a *body*, but a real treat."

Suddenly Buster leaned over and seized her wrist. "With a film or a TV deal, I could make a lot of those wrongs right, Bea!"

She pulled her arm away and shouted, "A whore right to the end! Well, I'm not buying. You laid it on the line, baby, and it wasn't good enough!" She jumped to her feet and raced out of the room.

"Yeah, give me the lecture, bitch!" he yelled at her back. "And then sell your book to Kohl, the worst bastard of them all! *He'll* get it, that loathsome fuck! That bastard doesn't deserve to live!"

He took another gulp of champagne, put his head back on the sofa. He should have gone home. But Buster Reilly was never the first to leave a party.

Labor Day Weekend, 1977;
Sunday (continued)

STANLEY WISNIEWSKI had lived in his small white colonial house for nearly a dozen years without ever quite getting used to it. It was too cramped, too suburban, too close to other houses, too dominated by pavement—the concrete of sidewalks, the asphalt of roads and driveways—for a farmer's son who'd been raised amid the flat potato fields of Bridgehampton. But this house on a village street in East Hampton was home for him—and Lee and the kids—and he worked to make it as good-looking as he could.

Sunday for him was invariably a day of house maintenance. Today it was going to be exterior painting; he never could get over how much clapboard a house this size had and how often it needed painting. He got out his brushes and roller, paint, turp, rags, ladder, wondering as he did how far he'd get before the desk would call him. It was a talisman—he figured if he thought about the call, it wouldn't come. Sometimes that worked. This time it didn't.

He climbed the ladder, poured paint into the pan, dipped the roller in—and the phone rang. He put roller to clapboard, hoping that would make the ringing go away—or make it something unimportant. That didn't work, either; in a few moments his wife was out of the house.

"Stanley. The desk calls you."

Goddammit, he said to himself, twelve years and when is she going to learn to speak English? Then, still to himself, he apologized to her. He was angry at the message, not at her.

"Did you say I was here?"

"Yes, I said."

"Tell them I'm in the middle of something and I'll call back as soon as I can." He rolled the paint on, still pretending it would all go away, knowing now it wouldn't.

In another few minutes, Lee was back. "Very important! It must be right now."

"Who's on the desk?"

"Larry." She had that confusion of the "l" and "r" sounds many Orientals did. Wisniewski used to think that was cute. He painted a capital F with the roller, put it in the pan and started down the ladder with them. Larry was the sergeant and if he thought it important enough to get Wisniewski off the ladder, he wouldn't be painting again real soon.

Wiping his hands on a rag he hurried into the house. Another thing he didn't like about his house was that it was just off Newtown Lane, about a half mile from police headquarters—so old Stan Wisniewski was easy to reach. It was always "Call Wiz" any time of day or night.

He picked up the phone. "Hey, Larry. What have you got?"

"How you doing, Wiz? We got a man floating in his pool. Face down."

"You mean you got a body."

"That's right, a body. Dead body. The name is Kohl. K-O-H-L. He's rich. He *was* rich. Very rich. The house is on Lily Pond, near . . ."

"I know, my brother-in-law does a lot of work for him."

"OK. It's all yours. Foster and Steeves are out there now."

"Did you talk to the chief?"

"Yup."

"He say it was mine?"

"Yes, he did."

His heart gave a little jump in his chest. He was a detective; after all the minor accidents, and domestic disputes, and petty thievery, this was the kind of case he was supposed to want—that he *did* want—a possible homicide, the victim rich and important. Yet he was nervous —eager, but apprehensive.

"I'm on my way."

"Want me to call Riverhead?"

"Not yet. I'll call 'em if we need 'em. We don't know what it is yet. Do we?"

"Looks like he drowned, but could have been a heart attack. Don't know if he fell, or was pushed, or hit his head, or what."

Wisniewski knew the Suffolk County police were available to help in a case like this, and usually were called. He also knew they usually ended up doing more than helping, they took over. Of course that would be the easy way for him. But he wasn't ready for it yet.

"Let's hold off on Riverhead."

"OK, Wiz."

"OK, Larry, I'm on my way. Talk to you later."

He hung up the phone, checked to see if there were any paint stains on it. Lee liked things spotless. He walked out of the house where she was hosing and scrubbing the Toyota. She looked up and saw him when he was still about ten yards away. For a few seconds they stared at each other. She looked so small, slender, a wave of tenderness surged through him for her, and he disliked himself for the resentment he often felt. He'd known what he was getting into when he married her—well, not all of it, but he had an inkling—and it certainly had changed his life. He knew you didn't walk in on that tough potato-farmer father of his with a Vietnamese bride and expect the old man to hold his arms out to embrace her.

But he hadn't been ready for the full fury of it. Stash Wisniewski wouldn't have anything to do with either his son or his bride. He pronounced her name contemptuously, as if it were "lye," even after Stan told him that Li was pronounced "Lee." Soon the old man wouldn't mention her at all, or talk to his son. And soon after that, the son was disinherited, which was no small matter, because old Stash's potato fields were growing into a couple of million dollars worth of real estate.

That was twelve years ago; two years ago his father died without ever having spoken to his son Stan again—and without leaving him a cent or a square inch of land. Stan missed those potato fields; he hated looking out of his window—into someone else's. But he had no regrets about being a detective, or about marrying Lee—they'd decided to re-spell her name rather than having to explain all the time that Li was not "lye."

She kept looking at him. He wondered what she was thinking; he'd probably been sold a bill of goods on Oriental inscrutability, he knew, but often he felt mystified by what was going on in her mind, even after all these years.

"What is the matter?" she asked.

"Some rich guy drank half his swimming pool."

"I don't understand."

Twelve years and still he sometimes forgot the language gap that opened when he used slang. She'd never picked it up. Mostly he re-membered to speak straightforward English, but sometimes, after work, or after he'd spent some time at the bar at Sam's or had been on the phone, he went on talking the same way, and usually she missed something.

"One of the rich men who live on Lily Pond Lane was found dead in his swimming pool. I've got to go over there." He pronounced his words a little too slowly, too precisely, and Lee heard it. She looked at him, showing she heard, but showing no reproach, either at his condescen-sion or his going to work on Sunday of Labor Day weekend.

When he was in a mood to be bothered, that bothered him, too—he'd wish for a wife who'd say: make sure you're home for dinner! When he was in other moods, he revered her docility, thanked God he wasn't saddled with one of the overweight, loud-mouthed local girls most of the other guys had latched on to—or been latched on to by.

"I'll try to be home for dinner, sweetheart."

Then he ran into the house, up the stairs to their bedroom, opened the locked bureau drawer which was off-limits to Lee and the children. Two guns lay there; he picked up the .25-caliber Beretta he preferred to the heavier police special. He grabbed a clip, snapped it into the butt of the gun, made sure the safety was on. He looked down at his pants, faded gray, stained with paint. They wouldn't do. Neither would the old shoes. Quickly he got out of them, put on a pair of rust-colored checked double-knits and his new brown boots. They were too warm and heavy for this summer's day, but they were the best he had.

He took his belt halfway off, threaded it through the slot of the holster, put it on again, raced down the stairs, reached into the closet alongside the front door for a jacket. He did not want the people on Lily Pond Lane laughing at his clothing. The jacket was light blue with a dark blue stripe. He looked down, wondering if it went with rust pants. Well, hell, he thought, it was too late to worry about that now.

Lee was wiping off the car as he got in, finishing the front windshield, as if he were in a car wash.

He smiled at her through the open window. "I'll be home for dinner." As he backed the car out of the driveway, he looked at his watch: five after ten. He damned well should be able to get back in time.

When he parked in Kohl's driveway he saw two police cars, a Rolls Corniche, a Chrysler station wagon and a jeep with big beach tires. He parked next to the station wagon, got out, sniffed at its engine, put a hand on the hood: it was still warm.

He walked up to the pool, saw Jack Foster and Billy Steeves standing near a lumpy shape covered by a soggy sheet. Kohl. Or what used to be Kohl. Kohl. Kohl. Why did he know that name? Sure, he'd seen it in the papers, the East Hampton *Star, Newsday*. The guy gave money for the library, for all the environmental causes, for everything. But there was something else. Wisniewski let it perk in his mind. Kohl. Kohl. Yeah . . . the dark-haired man at that writer's—Bea Fletcher's— house the day of the big blow last winter. He was pleased with himself, tried to dredge up some more. There were two other men in her kitchen that time—four people in all sitting around the table. One was Johnny Wainwright; that was easy, everyone in East Hampton knew him. The other he couldn't remember, but maybe if he heard the name, or saw the face . . .

"How are you doing, Jack? Billy?" he greeted the two officers.

"How are you, Wiz?" Foster replied. Steeves smiled at him.

"OK." Wisniewski walked over to the pile under the wet sheet, pulled back the top of it. Kohl looked so pale. Death certainly kills a man's tan, he thought. "How long you been here?"

"Maybe twenty minutes," Billy Steeves replied.

"Anyone else around?"

"Yeah, a woman who works for him."

"Where is she?"

"She asked us if we wanted coffee. She's getting us some."

"Go get her, will you, Billy?"

"You guys lift him out of the pool?" he asked the other cop.

"No, she did."

"That couldn't have been easy for a woman."

"Wait till you see her," Foster answered.

"Did you call for medical assistance?"

"Dr. Ryan was here when we got here. He left five minutes before you came. She called him."

"What did he say?" the detective asked.

"He said by the time he got here, Kohl had been dead for a number of hours."

"Anybody coming for the body?"

"Yeah, apparently she called a New York funeral home."

"Uh-uh, no good. We're going to have to do an autopsy. It's got to go to Southampton Hospital or to Riverhead."

Goes to show you, Stan said to himself, how experienced I am at handling suspicious deaths. Not even sure where you send the body. He kneeled and pulled the sheet all the way back. Kohl was wearing a shirt with an alligator on the chest, a pair of expensive linen pants. He had on a pair of loafers, but no socks. Both the loafers and his belt had a pair of G's on them.

A sound made the detective look up, and he saw Steeves approaching from the house with a woman who carried a tray with three cups of coffee, cream and sugar. Wisniewski hadn't gotten around to asking what Foster had meant about the woman. Now he knew. She seemed a shade taller than Steeves, who was a couple of inches taller than Wisniewski. Her shoulders were decisively broader. He'd bet she weighed 180 pounds, yet she didn't seem fat.

"I'm Detective Wisniewski, of the East Hampton police," he said, and reached his hand toward her. She took it in a hand that was easily as big and strong as his.

"I work for Mr. Kohl," was her only answer.

He had to ask, "What's your name?"

She hesitated, replied reluctantly, "Sophie." As she spoke, her face never changed from its look of alert remoteness.

"Can you tell me what happened?" he asked.

"I looked out my window this morning . . ."

"About what time?"

"An hour or so ago. About nine. I saw something in the pool. I ran down and could see it was Mr. Kohl. I jumped in and pulled him out, I tried to revive him. But it was no use . . ."

"How? Mouth-to-mouth?"

"Yes."

"For how long?"

"Five minutes. Perhaps ten. It's hard to say. When I saw nothing was happening, I called Dr. Ryan. Then the police."

"Did you drive anywhere this morning?"

She hesitated. "No."

He started to ask why the station wagon engine was still warm, decided not to. "Did *anyone* go anywhere this morning? Is there any-one else here?"

"Yes, the Governor and his press secretary. But they didn't go any-where. At least I don't think so."

"Governor *Hughes?*"

"Yes. He and Mr. Kohl are close friends."

"And that's all? The Governor and his press secretary?"

"As far as I know." She shrugged.

"Was there anyone else here last night?"

"Yes. Mr. Kohl went out to dinner with some people, and a number of them came back here for a drink afterwards."

"Can you tell me who they were?"

"No. I didn't see them. I was in bed. I heard the cars and the noise. But I didn't get up."

"So you can't identify *any* of them?"

She shook her head no.

"Does Mr. Kohl have any other help?"

"No."

Then who waited on his guests last night? he wanted to ask. He looked around. And who cleaned up after them? He figured this woman was lying to him. That could mean merely that she was being loyal to Kohl. Or that she knew something more about his death.

"Who were his close friends out here?" Wisniewski asked.

"Close friends? He didn't have any. He knew lots of people, though. Almost everybody."

"OK, how about enemies?"

She shrugged again. "Not that I know of."

Wisniewski looked up into her gray-brown eyes, which were small for the size of her face. Her hair was brown, too, with a bit of gray, and cut short. Her neck was thick and strong. He didn't ever want to go to the mat with her, he thought. "Rich, successful men usually pick up a few along the way," he offered, to jog her memory.

"I suppose so." She didn't even go through the motions of pretending to think about it.

"Did he have any hobbies, outside interests?"

"He liked to collect wicker. The furniture in the house and stored in the basement is the best collection in the Hamptons—at least that's what *he* said."

"Did he play golf? Tennis?"

"No golf, a little tennis."

"Was he a member of any clubs out here?"

Just for a moment he spotted a flicker of interest in her eyes; then the mask took over again. "No, he was not a member of any clubs."

Labor Day Weekend, 1976

THE UNDERPLAYED elegance of the Maidenhead's library was almost shabby: old white wicker chairs, old black-and-white pictures of club champions in tennis and golf, shelves of old books, on the sea, on Long Island, on the Hamptons. Lots of old novels.

Five men sat easily in the room, as if they belonged. They *did* belong, and they decided who else was to belong. They all wore variations on the club uniform, boxy traditional blue blazers—not a European suppressed waist among them—and bright pants. Spence wore canary yellow pants and held a gin and tonic; Chip, beige pants, with a gin and tonic; Brad, green pants, Scotch and soda; Parker, green pants, vodka and tonic; Clint, red pants, vodka martini.

All were comfortable, relaxed, smiling, except for Parker, who was tense and defensive.

"You've got to understand the position I'm in," Parker said. "I work for the sonofabitch; I *need* him. And the man is totally ruthless. He demands your *blood.*"

Chip, the joker, smiled. "Well, you tell him he can have his pound of flesh, but no blood."

Spence laughed appreciatively. "Hey, that's good, Chip!"

Parker didn't feel much like laughing. He twisted his Princeton ring nervously. "For what it's worth, the man insists he is *not* Jewish."

"Yes, and the Pope is *not* Catholic," Chip replied.

"Perhaps he'd build us a new clubhouse," said Clint.

"Probably would," Parker offered, but not with any hope it would help.

"He'd have it all to himself," Chip said. "Who else would want to use it?"

"Look," said Brad, turning serious. "Why are we wasting time? Whether the man be Jewish or not, does anyone want to present the man to our membership?" He looked around.

Spence shook his head.

"Only if he promises not to marry my daughter," said Chip.

"No, of course not," Clint said. "I wasn't serious about the club-house."

"Well, then, there's no need to spend any more time on this," Brad said, unfolding his lanky frame and rising. "Tell the *gentleman* we cannot put him up before our membership."

"*Tell* the gentleman," Clint added, "that there are certain types our members do not want to associate with, and we would no more have them in our club than in our homes."

"No, don't tell him that," Brad corrected.

"*Tell* the *gentleman*," Chip said, "that our menu would not suit him. We don't serve Chinese food."

Brad finally cracked a smile. "Don't tell him that, either."

Parker looked worried. His handsome young face was tight, the muscles in the square jaw clenching and unclenching. "I hope you understand the pressure I am under . . ."

"Of course we do," Brad said, and Spence nodded. They were all standing now, looking like minor variations of a form shaped in a single mold, their frames lit by the setting sun pouring in over the dunes through the big french windows.

"It hasn't harmed you here at the club at all," said Brad. "Nor will it."

Chip walked over, grinning, and clapped Parker on the shoulder. "Sorry about the rest of your life!"

Even Parker had to smile at that.

"Let's have lunch tomorrow, Parker," said Brad. "And let's talk about your future." Brad was president of a major investment house, and Parker was pleased at the suggestion.

"I'd love to," the younger man said eagerly.

"Fine."

"Chinese food?" Chip asked, and they all laughed.

"Now, shall we join the ladies?" Brad asked.

Freddie Kohl sat on the patio of his Southampton beach house and heard the bad news from Parker the day after the decision was made. Then he looked out at the ocean. The surf was high but not riled up; waves breaking with a tranquilizing regularity. The sun was low in the west, the beach deserted except for a teenage girl and her golden retriever, their shadows elongated in the late afternoon light.

In this serene moment Freddie was agitated; he fidgeted with a vodka and tonic without drinking much of it. His left hand clutched the arm of his deck chair; he glared at Parker Lipscomb, who was sitting tensely in a director's chair facing him.

"They can't do this to me. They *cannot* do this to me!" Sweat beaded below his fine, slender nose and on his forehead. His straight black hair, slicked down and curling a bit at the ends, glistened, as it always did. His dark eyes narrowed, fastened on the young Kohl and Company vice president. "I can buy and sell those people!"

He paused, pushed his wiry body forward in his chair. "What happened, Parker? Am I not good enough for them? Do they think I'm Jewish? I'm not Jewish, Parker. Do they know that? Did you tell them that?"

He caught the young man in the middle of a gulp of his drink, and Parker nodded furiously until he could swallow and speak. "I told them you unequivocally denied being Jewish, Mr. Kohl."

"What do you mean you told them I *denied* it? Do *you* think I am? Tell me, Parker!" Freddie got to his feet and stood threateningly over the seated Parker. His physical aggressiveness was almost amusing, for Freddie was five foot nine and weighed less than 150 pounds, while Parker, a former tight end at Princeton, was six foot three and weighed over 200.

"I believe you are what you say you are, Mr. Kohl." Parker was flustered. "That is, I believe you are *not* what you say you aren't. Why should I doubt you?"

Kohl went back to his chair, but decided against sitting, instead paced back and forth on the patio. "Then what happened? I asked you to see to it that I get into the Maidenhead Club, and you couldn't deliver. I was counting on you, and you couldn't deliver. Can I count on you or not, Parker? You're twenty-eight years old and last year you made $82,000. Should I be able to count on a man I am paying $82,000, or not?"

"Look, Mr. Kohl. I do a good job for you. I've never let you down. But this is a social thing. They don't know you at the club. Membership at the Maidenhead is mostly a family affair, anyway, passed from parents to children. It's hard for an outsider to come in, not knowing anybody; it's unfair to him. Perhaps in a few years, when you've made more friends in the community out here . . ."

That was a lie, and they both knew it.

Freddie dropped into his chair. "The fact remains, Parker, that I asked you to do something, and you couldn't. Or didn't *want* to . . ."

Parker was worried. "I did the best I could, Mr. Kohl. I warned you that there would be problems, I told you it was not within my power to get you into the club singlehandedly. Surely you can understand that."

Freddie's eyes burned into the young man's. He pointed a finger at him. "Parker, if it had been up to you, and only up to you, would you have taken me into the Maidenhead?"

Parker hesitated only a moment. "Yes, Mr. Kohl. Yes, I would have. Please believe that!" He would brood about that answer for a long time afterwards, chastise himself for cowardice. But at lunch earlier that day with Brad, he'd learned that $82,000 a year was far more than anyone else would pay him. "Perhaps $45,000 now," Brad had said, "and in three to five years . . ." And Parker had not wanted to go from $82,000 to $45,000.

Freddie did not believe his young vice president, which was why he was all the more pleased with his response. The fact that Parker would lie proved that Freddie had bought him, had found his price and paid it. He looked at the blond, hulking young man sitting there, and said to himself: He's mine. I own him.

Only when you bought something was it really yours—Freddie believed that. He didn't trust loyalty based on feelings; he'd never given or received it. He could count on purchased loyalty, because he knew that anyone who paid *his* price could count on him—at least until he was offered a higher price. Freddie understood that. He saw nothing wrong with it.

What he could not understand was why he couldn't buy his way into the Maidenhead. That he'd have to find out about. If he couldn't, well, he was in the wrong place. He'd have to look for a soft spot in the social fabric of the Hamptons. If the Maidenhead didn't prove to be the spot, to hell with it. He'd find another way. And he'd get rid of that big dumb ox, Parker Lipscomb the Third, or Fourth, or whatever he was. He overpaid him, anyway, and if Parker couldn't deliver on those few items where Freddie really needed him—like the Maidenhead—he wasn't worth his salary.

Parker began to worry about the way his boss was sitting there, staring, face tense, fingers clutching the arms of the deck chair.

"Mr. Kohl. Mr. Kohl? Can I get you a drink?"

Freddie clapped a hand on his knee, and exclaimed, "So that's it, then, Parker; the club doesn't want me, it doesn't want me. Did you tell them about my charitable contributions? No, no, never mind; it doesn't want me, that's that."

"Perhaps next summer, Mr. Kohl, as early as that, we can try again. You see, being in the community is *so* important. They respect your charitable work, you may be sure of that, but the feeling of neighborhood counts first. People say we have no blacks in our club, and very few Jews. Well, I answer, there are no blacks in our *neighborhood* . . . and very few Jews. The club didn't create the neighborhood; the neighborhood created the *club*."

Again Parker misunderstood Freddie's mood. "Why are you telling me about blacks and Jews?" Freddie was trying not to shout, his dark face flushed. "Do you think I'm a black or a Jew? I'm not interested!"

"Mr. Kohl, I didn't . . ."

"I know, I know, you didn't mean anything." Freddie seemed to calm quickly. "Yes, yes, all right, we'll try again next year. Go home, Parker, I don't want to take up any more of your weekend. I'll see you on Tuesday."

Parker took the dismissal as a burst of thoughtfulness, and was startled by it. He was wrong; Freddie just wanted to get rid of him in a hurry. Parker was equally anxious to go; he got to his feet quickly.

"Well, thanks, Mr. Kohl, I appreciate it. Samantha's waiting for me; we're going to the . . . beach . . ." Parker had been about to say "club," caught himself just in time. "I hope you understand the situation, I really do. And you know, our invitation to dinner tonight stands. Samantha would love to have you; she specially asked me to try to talk you into it."

"No, no, I can't. Tell her I said thank you." Freddie wanted him to leave. He owned Parker. Freddie said it to himself with satisfaction. The question was, did he want to any longer? He didn't for a moment believe the young ox about trying again for the Maidenhead. And what other use was there for him? As a banker, he was mediocre, stodgy, a young fuddy-duddy who could be replaced easily. Freddie looked at the broad shoulders of young Lipscomb moving away from him and made up his mind quickly.

Lipscomb folded his long muscular legs into his MG two-seater and expelled the air from his lungs with a whoosh. He'd gotten out of a tough situation better than he thought he could. He'd taken a lot of heat about the club, but it could have been worse; he'd actually been worried about losing his job. Then there was the gaffe he'd almost made about going to the club. That would have really been rubbing it in! But he'd caught it at the last moment. And the dinner invitation. Samantha hated Freddie Kohl; she'd met him a couple of times and found him "repulsive" and "oily" and "pushy."

"If you make me invite him," Samantha had said, "you'll be sorry. You'll be good and sorry!" Which usually meant she slept at the edge of the bed with her back to him.

"Sam, for Chrissake, he won't come! After all he *is* my boss; he pays me damned well. And he's desperate for acceptance. It's pitiful. We've got to at least *look* like we're making the effort! I tell you, he won't accept."

"He'd better not," she'd replied. "If he does, don't you come near me!"

Parker pulled into the driveway of the shingled bungalow Samantha's parents had given them as a wedding present. He jumped out of the car, ran around to the back, where she sat leafing through *People* magazine. "OK, we're home free!" he shouted. "I made it, and he's *not* coming to dinner. He says thanks for inviting him."

He leaned over and kissed her on top of the head. She had blond, shoulder-length hair, which for tennis was tied back with a blue ribbon which matched her eyes. In tennis shorts and Lacoste shirt she looked like she belonged in a Coke ad—with Parker.

"Praise the lord!" she said, rolling her eyes upward and shaking her open hands in a revival-meeting gesture. "Did he give you a hard time—that horrible man?"

"It could have been worse. I thought he'd try to hit me, though, every time I mentioned the word Jew as if I thought he was one."

"Well, isn't he?" By now they were both headed toward the car.

"Is the Pope Catholic? Come on, we don't want to be late for the court."

The next Tuesday morning Lipscomb was fired.

"Goddamned little Jew," he told Samantha over the phone. "Can you imagine *him* at the Maidenhead!"

"It's the best thing for you, dear, to get away from there," she told him.

"I suppose," he said. "But by God I'd like to get that bastard some day."

A week later he started work at Brad's banking house, at $45,000 a year.

The Maidenhead rebuff was not Freddie's first, yet he had a hard time accepting it; a couple of weeks after Parker Lipscomb broke the bad news, Freddie called his friend the Governor and asked for his help.

Mike Hughes had no intention of wasting any clout on Freddie's aspirations to the Maidenhead—and was secretly pleased at Freddie's rebuff—but being a politician, he instinctively replied, "Let me see what I can do." A few days later he called Freddie.

"No way. The original immovable object. Don't waste your time or your money, Freddie. Once you get a no, forget it."

Freddie wouldn't forget it. Maybe the Governor didn't *want* to help him. If he had a chance, he could start a campaign, use money, use contacts, put on some pressure. *If* he had a chance. Otherwise he was wasting time and money. He needed the advice of a real Hamptons expert, and started asking around to find one. From several people he heard that Bea Fletcher, whom he'd met several times, was becoming *the* authority on Hamptons society, a combination of de Tocqueville and Liz Smith.

One morning he picked up the phone and called her. "We hardly know each other, Mrs. Fletcher, but I hear you're an expert on life in the Hamptons, and I'd like to pick your brain. May I take you to dinner?"

They hadn't even had the first sip of their first drink at "21" when Bea leaned toward him and said, "You know you haven't got a Chinaman's chance of getting into the Maidenhead. I suppose I could pick more hopeless ethnic groups, but you get the point."

He was startled and discomfited. "How did you know?"

"When someone is embarrassed out there, the news travels fast. Especially if the someone is rich and powerful. Now, I suppose you're buying me dinner because you want to know why you were turned down."

"Not quite. What I really want to know is how to reverse it. What sort of campaign I might start in order to get in."

She shook her head. "Why, in God's name, do you *want* to?"

"Why does anyone want to?"

"A lot of reasons. Some want to because their friends are in. Or because their family has *always* joined. Some want a sterilized, Saran-wrapped romper room, free of such irritants and undesirables as Jews, blacks, Puerto Ricans, intellectuals, leftists, the poor and other lesser creatures. Some because it gives them a prefab social life; some because it will help them in business; some because it will elevate them socially, because it's the 'in' thing to do. Some want to use the grass courts, which are a rarity and becoming rarer all the time. Of course, that's part snobbism, too. Some want the golf course, which is one of the dozen best in America. Some, believe it or not, want to join so their kids can have an activities program during the summer. And believe me, if it got my two off my hands I'd be tempted, too—*if* I could get in, and *if* I could afford it.

"Most join for a mixture of reasons. And they lie about which are the important ones. Now in your case I know it's not family, or friends, or kids. And I don't think it's golf or tennis or business. And since they've already turned you down, it *can't* be you're looking for a ready-made social life, because they've let you know they don't want you to be part of their social life.

"So it's got to be social climbing. You want to join the 'in' crowd, right?"

Freddie was not used to being talked to this way. He didn't like it. She grinned at him. "If you want my expert opinion, Freddie, I have to know all the symptoms. Think of me as a doctor. I have to prescribe, don't I? So open your mouth and say ah. Or something. This won't hurt."

"Anywhere I travel, I have learned to travel first class," he began. "Anywhere I stay, I stay first class. As a child, I made too many bus trips to St. Louis and Chicago ever to imagine that any place is worth getting to that way. Now I either go first class and stay first class, or I don't go. That is, or I go somewhere else. To me, first class in Southampton is the Maidenhead. There's your answer."

"In other words, you want to join the 'in' crowd. And I *am* right."

"No, not quite. Originally, yes. Now, after their refusal, I know very well the *crowd* doesn't want *me*. Yet I still want to join their club."

"I find that hard to understand," Bea said. "Join a club where nobody will have a drink with you at the bar? Where no one wants to have dinner with you? Where you won't play golf, and your tennis game isn't good enough to make you a desirable doubles partner, even if they liked you? Yes, I know all that, too . . . I'm afraid I *don't* understand."

"It doesn't matter whether you understand. It makes sense to me, and that's what counts. You're right, I'd have no friends, I'd never play golf, hardly ever play tennis, perhaps never eat a meal there—except to take friends to lunch once in a while—yes, to show off. Yet I want to join just to show *I can do it*. Like getting my citizenship papers to Southampton, becoming a first-class citizen, no longer a foreigner. Tell me how to get those citizenship papers, Bea, and I'll meet your price."

"I'll do more than that, Freddie," she replied. "And at no charge. No IOU, no return favor, no nuthin'. I'll tell you to save your money and your blood, sweat and tears. Don't try. You won't get in. The very effort defeats itself. The harder you try the more you show them you're not their kind. The essence of being a Maidenhead Wasp is never to sweat. The final test there is you're put in a sauna, and allowed only one drop of sweat, on the upper lip—it's called the Richard Nixon memorial bead. Any more than that, and you're out."

He looked puzzled; she shook her head. "No, that's not for real. But let me tell you what is. You won't make it, Freddie. You can't push your way in, or pay your way in, or power your way in. Forget it!

"Because you see, what's more important is that you shouldn't *want* to get in. The Maidenhead is passé, it's no longer the key to the Hamptons. It's no longer anything but a place to play tennis and golf and see your stodgy friends. As the 'in' place, it's dead, has been for five years, and those twitches are the final spasms of its involuntary nervous system, the last leaps of a headless chicken. The Maidenhead is no longer where it's at. Southampton is no longer where it's at. Anybody who's anybody is *apologizing* for a Southampton house these days, is saying something like, it's a half-hour closer to the city, or I want to keep a little distance between me and the other publishers, or some other bullshit. But the smart money is all buying houses in Water Mill, Bridgehampton, Sagaponack, Wainscott, East Hampton—even Amagansett and Montauk, before Southampton. Even the money people. They go to Bobby Van's for dinner. In New York, to Elaine's. They hang around with Jews, too, and all sorts of other undesirables. Something's happened, Freddie, and you have to understand it. Jewish isn't *out* anymore. Southampton isn't *in* anymore. Do you know what's happened, Freddie?"

His mouth was slightly open; he was listening as if it were a suspense story. "No, what's happened?"

"The arts have happened. The media have happened. To be a writer, or a publisher, or a producer, or some kind of TV biggie—that's where it's at. And believe me, it not only doesn't hurt to be Jewish, it helps. That, today, is what being a Wasp banker was fifty years ago: the center of things."

Then came something gratuitous, but she couldn't resist. "Next time somebody accuses you of being Jewish, don't say anything. Just 'thanks.' That's what I do."

Again, he couldn't tell if she were serious. "How many people accuse you?"

"Not enough," she answered. "Not nearly enough."

Freddie had enough of this excursion. He proceeded briskly to business. "All right then, what's the important club to join in the Hamptons?"

"The gliterati."

"Never heard of it." He couldn't quite make this woman out. "There's a club at the beach in East Hampton, but the name is shorter than that."

"Oh, you're thinking of the Dale," Bea said. "That's passé just like the Maidenhead. You really *do* have to love grass courts to join that one."

"What did you say the name of the other one was?"

"The gliterati."

Freddie caught it. "Oh! You mean like literati, with glitter added." He was angry at her, controlled himself. "Why do you enjoy teasing me, Bea?"

"I guess I'm being a little mean. You're so famous for being a powerful man, I figure this is my only shot at having you sit at *my* table, needing something from me. Sorry, Freddie. Anyway, you got it right.

It's not a formal club. It has no admissions committee, and its member-ship is changing, people drifting in and out, moving to the center and back to the fringes, staying for a while and then disappearing. It has no clubhouse, unless you count Bobby Van's in Bridgehampton and Elaine's in New York."

"I've never been to Bobby Van's."

"Have you been to Elaine's?"

"Yes, once, with Johnny Wainwright. I didn't like the food."

"The food is irrelevant. People don't go there for it, they go for the other people. Writers are the core. They start going, they set the tone; it becomes known as a literary hangout. Publishers start going there, then media figures, and theater and film people, actors, directors, pro-ducers and God help us, agents. Then those two undefinable cate-gories, celebrities and personalities.

"Then around those, the money people, the society people, a couple of politicians. And around all *those*, the beautiful women who don't belong to any category but their own, and are brought by men from one of the other groups. And sure, a few beautiful men, brought by women. Even a few beautiful men brought by men."

"How does one join this club?" Freddie looked interested.

Bea smiled. "There are no fixed membership rolls. The club exists in concentric and interlocking circles, and all the edges are blurred, kind of like a Ballantine Beer three-ring sign, out of focus. Book people are the inner circle. They're the 'in' crowd."

"But how can I become a book person?" Freddie wanted to know. "I'm not a writer."

"That doesn't stop anybody else these days," Bea said jokingly. Then added, seriously, "Then become a publisher. Money is one of the prime requisites. Publish a big book, and the club will love you. Well, per-haps not the other publishers, but God knows, the writers will!"

Freddie nodded. "Publish a big book. . . . I am on the board of WTI, which owns Saxon. Perhaps . . . perhaps I could acquire a big book. Perhaps, Bea, you could help me find one. After all, that *is* something I could buy. Writers *do* like money, don't they?"

She flashed her teeth. "They certainly do, Freddie!"

"Then help me, Bea. Who's writing a big book?"

She stopped joking, but kept smiling. "Why . . . *I* am, Freddie!"

He looked at her, unsure if she were serious. "Would you like an-other drink?"

"Freddie, I'd love some champagne."

He ordered a bottle of Dom Perignon. Both of them were elated. When the first glasses were poured, she raised hers, and said, "To a big book."

And he echoed, "To a big book!"

When, some months after their dinner at "21," Bea's two-part "WashingtonShock" piece came out in *Scope* magazine, Freddie's reaction to it was more vehement than most. First, there was fear. The barely fictitious names fooled no one, and although he and the Governor were briefly mentioned, the mention was devastating, and it carried the promise, the threat, of more to come in the full book.

After fear came greed. Freddie realized Bea's flip remark about writing a big book was not a joke. She was writing it to get rich, and in wanting to get rich she was playing Freddie's game. If Freddie bought the book for big money, he might get Bea to tone down the parts about him and the Governor. He might be able to delay publication until after the gubernatorial elections in '78, so the damage to the Governor's career could be minimized. He might also buy himself entrée into the Hamptons, and into the inner circle. He might even make money on the book!

How does one go about buying a book? Freddie didn't know, but he was on the board of directors of WTI, which owned Saxon. And the president of Saxon, John Wainwright, now that Freddie had bought a home in East Hampton, was a neighbor. What are neighbors for? Freddie asked himself. What are corporate directorships for?

The two men had dinner at Bobby Van's one clear December Saturday. Johnny was not overjoyed to be there; still, any friend he could make on the board of WTI couldn't hurt. Freddie was not there to help Johnny's publishing career, he was there to start one of his own, but he did not reveal that at dinner. Wainwright, tough and able but of the old school, was not prepared for Freddie Kohl's deviousness. He assumed Freddie's questions were personal curiosity, with perhaps a touch of interest as a director of WTI.

Unable to imagine that anyone would elicit information as a friend and then use it as a competitor, Johnny was suckered.

"How valuable do you think Bea's book will be?" Freddie asked. "After all, she's never written one before."

"She got $100,000 for her two-part piece on Washington from *Scope*; that's a record, it beat the $75,000 Truman Capote got for "Answered Prayers" in *Esquire*. They know what they're doing over at *Scope*, and from what I hear they got their money's worth. Washington was really shook up.

"From the Washington pieces we can tell that Bea can really write. She's funny, she's got a lot of bite, she's as commercial as Jackie Susann. There's a big paperback in it; there's a movie or a TV series, maybe both. Maybe two series, one on Washington, another on the Hamptons. It's got just what a TV series needs, a large cast, glamorous people, plots and subplots."

Johnny's eyebrows went up. "I began working up a proposal," he said, "and I realized there was big money, seven figures, in the book. And believe me, her agent, Irv Schnell, is the best in the business, he's not going to let any of it get away." He smiled his muscular smile. "And can you imagine the sequels? New York City? Then maybe one on L.A.? London? Paris? Acapulco? Palm Beach? Key West? It's a god-damned gold mine! Money. Sex. Gossip. Glamour. It doesn't matter if you've never been in Bobby Van's or Elaine's or the Beverly Hills Hotel. You're still turned on! If it works, the idea is a gold mine for Bea; she can retire on it."

To Freddie, this was beginning to look better and better, yet worse and worse. The bigger, the juicier, this book, the more competition to get hold of it, and the more harm it could do him and the Governor. That was the bad news.

The good news was, the more danger to the Governor, the more he'd have to rely on Freddie. The more he had to rely on Freddie, the more Freddie could ask of him, perhaps some day a cabinet post in Washington. After all, Kissinger was foreign-born—and had a heavier accent than Freddie did.

There was more than political clout in the book, though, Freddie figured. It could make him a force in the book world, and therefore in the Hamptons. And it could even show a profit! God knows, Freddie didn't need the money, but he'd spent his life keeping an eye on the bottom line, and he could not turn away from it now.

Just suppose, he said to himself, he could offer Bea enough to retire on right now. Might she not be willing to write him and the Governor *out* of the book? Or at least sanitize them?

"What makes you talk about Bea's retiring?" Freddie asked.

"I mean as a writer of gossip," Johnny answered. "Bea doesn't like being thought a disher of dirt, another Jacqueline Susann. But she likes insolvency even less. I think as soon as she feels financially secure she'll never dish another bit of scandal again."

"Well, gee," said Freddie—"gee" was a word he used when he wanted to seem ingenuous—"it takes a fair amount of income to make you secure. How much do you suppose Bea would need?"

"Hell, I don't know," Johnny said. "She doesn't live on a grand scale. She walks around in jeans; her kids are taken care of by their father. But if she has a dozen people for dinner once in a while, she likes to put a good Pouilly Fumé on the table instead of soave in a jug, and she wants to be able to plunk down a hundred bucks for a half-pound of Beluga caviar without counting the pennies in her purse."

"Well, then take a guess. How much a year?"

"I don't know." Johnny shrugged his wide shoulders. "Maybe $100,000 a year."

"After taxes."

"Sure, spendable income. That would take $200,000 before taxes, which is a lot of money."

The computer in Freddie's head began to whirr. Suppose it was in tax-free municipals? Let's say at 6 percent. That would take a principal of $1.66 million—in his mind, he saw the sixes stretching out to infinity. To get that sum, Bea would need to earn double it, or $3.33 million —again his computer mind stretched the threes out to infinity—before taxes.

Three and a third million dollars was not all that much money, he said to himself. If it bought what he wanted.

"Have another drink, Johnny. Let me ask you another question." Freddie's bony hand lifted in a gesture to the waitress. When he rested it on the table again, it was right near Johnny's, which was twice its size. It reminded Freddie of the thick-knuckled hands of the farmboys in his home town—those farmboys who could toss little Freddie Kohl around with such indifferent ease. Now Freddie could toss big-handed men like these around just as easily. He preferred now to then.

"Does Saxon want Bea's novel?"

"You bet we do," Johnny said, "and I think we're in a good position to get it."

"Why do you say that? Have you made an offer?"

"Not yet, but Irv Schnell knows I'm interested. He also knows I'd like a chance to make a pre-emptive offer, because I'd rather not get into an auction."

"Why should Schnell let you make a pre-emptive offer? What's in it for him?"

"He knows me and trusts me," Johnny explained. "He knows Saxon can do a good job on the book, on advertising and promotion, on distribution. He knows we can handle the paperback sale to get a lot out of it. He also knows a pre-emptive offer is money in hand, while an auction is always risky. Of course in this case an auction is not really *too* risky, so the offer is going to have to be a big one."

Freddie smiled. "How many publishers will Schnell go to for pre-emptive offers?"

Johnny stopped his drink halfway from the table to his mouth. "One, of course! If he asks me for one, and I think he will, he'll either take it or turn it down. But he's not going to ask several publishers simultaneously for pre-emptive bids!"

"Why not?" Freddie was genuinely puzzled.

"Because then they wouldn't be pre-emptive, would they? We'd be in a kind of sealed-bid auction."

"So?"

"It would be dishonest. When you ask for a pre-emptive bid, you are in effect saying, I am asking only you, and if you offer enough, you'll get the book. If you do that with a group, and it becomes known— which it always does—your reputation in the industry is destroyed. Nobody trusts you or wants to do business with you."

Freddie wondered at this business, concluded it was ripe for plucking. "How big an offer do you think you'll make?"

"I'm working on a hard-soft package, that is, a deal which combines the hardcover and the paperback rights, and of course means a lot more money. I've been discussing it with Sally Majors, the editor-in-chief of Greyhound. We don't have a firm figure yet, but it will be in seven figures."

"Might it go over three million?" Freddie asked, having in mind the magic figure which would give Bea her retirement income.

Johnny laughed. "God knows she might make that, with subsidiary rights sales, but we're not going to offer it up front. Sally Majors is daring, but she's not crazy!"

Johnny Wainwright would not be hard to beat, Freddie said to himself. Harder with a paperback tie-in than without—this Sally Majors sounded like the bolder of the two—but eminently beatable either way.

Then Freddie had a disturbing thought. Supposing it was like a private club—like the Maidenhead—where they would snub him merely because he was an outsider? Supposing all his money didn't do him any good, as it hadn't at the Maidenhead? No, he told himself, he could expect nothing from these people that he didn't claw and muscle to get. And they could expect nothing from him.

"You haven't even mentioned tying up the movie and TV rights," he said to Johnny. "It would seem to me there would be big money in them. Perhaps the biggest of all."

"As a rule, they are retained by the author. I don't know if they're worth *more* than the paperback, but they're worth a hell of a lot. As I told you, it's a big book, Freddie."

"Then why don't you try to deal for the film and TV rights, too?"

"Because I'm a book publisher. I'm not in the film or TV business, and don't want to be."

Freddie couldn't understand such lack of initiative, but he didn't complain; it made things easier for him. "Is it ever done?" he asked.

"Occasionally. Not often, but it's done. There's a thing called a buy-out, where you acquire every aspect of the book, all its royalties, all its subsidiary rights, everything. It's rare, but done."

Freddie's hand twisted the glass of Perrier in front of him. A buy-out, he said to himself. He liked the term; it sounded good, and it was exactly what he had in mind: to own the book completely. For a moment he was tempted to ask Johnny if a buy-out entitled you to take the manuscript and tear it up and throw it away, not publish it at all. He decided not to.

He changed the subject. "Are you worried about what Bea might say about you in her book?" he asked.

Johnny shrugged. "We've all done things we aren't proud of, things we'd rather have kept quiet. I won't cry before I'm hurt."

"How much of the book do you get to read before making your offer?"

"That's the beauty of the 'WashingtonShock' installments, from Irv Schnell's point of view. He can say, if you want to read part of the book, here's a copy of *Scope*; the Hamptons part will be just like it: juicy, well-written, funny. He may show an outline of the Hamptons segment, but if he does, it won't give away many of the titillating details. He doesn't have to."

Then Johnny turned Freddie's question back on him. "Are you worried about what's going to be in the book?"

Freddie smiled, tried to stay as cool as Johnny had. "I can always sue!" Or I can get control of the book, he said to himself. And knew he'd rather get control of the book. But he'd have to move fast, before Johnny and Sally Majors threw a big number at Irv. He'd have to be there first, with a bigger number. Maybe he'd also try to get to Sally Majors to break up her alliance with Johnny. Freddie had no compunctions whatever. He'd use the information Johnny had just given him to screw Johnny. He'd use Johnny to screw Sally. Anyway it worked would suit him fine, for these people—from the Maidenhead down, or up, whichever it was—were hostile to him. He owed them nothing.

The thought of dirty fighting stimulated Freddie; he felt almost exultant. "Well, Johnny, my boy, it sounds big! Shall we drink to success?" He picked up his glass of Perrier.

Misunderstanding Freddie's enthusiasm, Johnny was pleased by it. It wouldn't hurt to have his plan backed by a member of the WTI board. "Yes," he said, "let's drink to success."

"By the way, Johnny, I'm having some people drop by for lunch tomorrow. Please join us."

Johnny tried to be vague. "I think I've got a lunch date tomorrow, don't know if it's definite or not. Let me find out and call you. If I can make it I sure will. Thanks."

Yes, a lunch date, Freddie said to himself, at the Maidenhead, no doubt. The club Freddie was not good enough to join. This man is one of the enemy, Freddie reminded himself. He always has been. Freddie would use him, and enjoy it. But Johnny Wainwright would remain the enemy and Freddie would never forget that.

The first use Freddie made of him was to secure an introduction to Irv Schnell. The next day, Freddie phoned the agent.

"What can I do for you?" Irv asked, keeping his tone neutral.

"I'd like to take you to dinner, to talk about the book business."

Freddie did not have to have dinner with him to learn the book business, Irv knew that. He thought he knew what Freddie really wanted, and decided he owed it to Bea to listen. But first he wanted to set Freddie straight on the tone of the dinner.

"I have a rule," he said. "I treat all occasions on which I talk about business as business meetings. And I never allow anyone else to pick up the check. Understood?"

"Understood," Freddie replied. "How about Elaine's?"

Irv made a point of getting there early so he could say all his hellos without having to include Freddie. He watched Freddie enter, hungry to be welcomed, getting only a few tepid greetings.

Freddie didn't take too long getting to the point.

"You know what a buy-out is, Irv; well, I want to structure a buy-out of Bea's book."

Irv thought he was ready, but this startled him. "You're talking about big money," he said.

"Yes, I'm talking about big money. And you know I can back up the talk. How much?"

Using the same income figure for Bea Freddie had used—$100,000 a year after taxes—and then tacking on a little fat for bargaining purposes, Irv said $4 million—to himself. To Freddie, he said: "Make us an offer."

Freddie was ready for it. He didn't want an offer to be chewed over or haggled over. He wanted to make it a knockout. He paused for a moment, said softly but clearly:

"Five million dollars."

"That's a big offer," Irv said. "Tell me, Freddie, why do you want to get into the book business?"

"I'm always interested in new ventures. And I believe in going in big. This would be the biggest single book deal in history, wouldn't it?"

Irv shrugged. "I've never heard of a bigger one. But then I'm not the industry historian, I'm only an agent."

Freddie knew the man was unwilling to give him anything, but he was used to that, it wouldn't stop him. "And the agent's commission, Irv, would then be the biggest in history, too. $500,000. It *would* be the biggest, wouldn't it?"

This time Irv let out a small snorting laugh. "Why do you keep talking to me about breaking records? I'm not Bruce Jenner. I told you, I'm just an agent."

Freddie looked puzzled. "Who's Bruce Jenner?"

"He's an Olympic athlete, who . . . never mind, it doesn't matter. Yes, five million is a big number, Freddie. And it comes with a big tax bite."

"There's a lot to bite into. And if you're concerned about taxes, maybe I can structure an arrangement to help you there."

Irv just nodded. "Of course, if I just sell the hard and soft cover, we can get a lot of money for the film and TV on our own . . ."

Freddie laughed aloud. "Are you afraid you'll lose money on the offer?"

"No, it's a big number, I told you. But if you're trying to snow us, I just want you to know it's not out of the ballpark." Irv leaned forward in his chair. "And you mustn't forget it comes from someone with no track record in the publishing business. We'd have to know what your publishing plans are, and your subsidiary rights arrangements, and your timing, and advertising and promotion. We'd have to know who the editor would be, we'd have to know lots of things."

"All negotiable, Irv. If the money package satisfies you, I'm sure the rest can be worked out. Does the money satisfy you?"

Irv's look was noncommittal. "I'll have to talk it over with Bea, of course."

Irv was not pleased. He didn't like Freddie, didn't want to have to take his offer to Bea. Nor could he just turn down $5 million. He didn't have the authority to say no. Only Bea could do that. He wondered if she'd be able to.

Freddie was pleased. The book could do a lot for him. About one thing, though, he didn't fool himself. These people would never love him. Not Bea, not Schnell, not Johnny, not any of them. They all made their disapproval, their contempt, clear. Yes, Freddie wanted to get hold of that book. And as he did, make them all crawl. And then screw them all.

In fact, he decided, their hatred delighted him. Let them hate him! What could they do to him?

Labor Day Weekend, 1977; Sunday (continued)

WISNIEWSKI WATCHED the body being wheeled off to the hearse, then sat on a yellow and white chaise and sipped his mug of coffee. He'd asked Sophie a lot of long questions and she'd responded with a lot of short answers. He wondered about those. Two answers he did believe: that Kohl had no history of heart trouble, and that he couldn't swim. He believed them because it would have been more convenient for Sophie to have answered the opposite.

He'd phoned to ask for an autopsy right away, but he'd bet on drowning as the cause of death. And of course someone who knew Kohl couldn't swim would choose to kill him by drowning him. Someone who knew, and had the strength to push him under and hold him. Someone like Sophie. Sophie looked like she could drown a linebacker, but come to think of it, Kohl was a small man, and it wouldn't take much to drown a non-swimmer his size. Once you got him into the pool, that is, Wisniewski added to himself, but that could have been done by trickery or surprise, as well as by brute force.

Sophie walked up with a pot of coffee. "Yeah, thanks," he said, and then, on an impulse, asked, "Do you use the pool much, Sophie?"

"Every day."

"Bet you're a good swimmer."

"Yes."

No matter what he was working on, Wisniewski always found it useful to go beyond questions and answers, cop-versus-civilian, to easy conversation. He was good at it; it worked. Not with Sophie.

"How good?"

She shrugged. He tried to help, to open her up. "I mean, I can swim enough to make it maybe across the pool and back twice. If you can do better than that, you're a good swimmer to me."

"Then I'm a good swimmer."

"How many laps do you swim?"

"It depends on how much work I have."

"If you have a lot of work?"

"Twenty laps."

"If you have a little?"

"Fifty. Sixty."

"Every *day*?"

"Yes."

"You're a good swimmer."

She didn't even shrug at that.

"Anybody swimming at the party last night? Aside from your boss, that is."

"I wouldn't know. I told you that before."

"Uh, yeah. I thought maybe . . . yeah."

"Will there be anything else?"

"No, I guess not. Thanks for the coffee."

Sophie nodded, turned away. She was wearing a tan summer wrap-around skirt, almost the color of her suntan, and a cream-colored jersey top. As he looked at her big arms and shoulders, he thought again how he wouldn't like to go to the mat with her. Then added, he'd like even less to have to grapple with her in the water, what with his four-lap once-a-year capability and her twenty, fifty, sixty laps a day. She'd taken a dozen steps, when he called to her.

"Sophie, would you do something for me?"

She turned and came back, stood there.

"Is the Governor still asleep?"

"I believe so, but I don't really know."

"Does he know about . . . Mr. Kohl?"

"I haven't told him."

"Have you told anyone?"

"The doctor and the police. No one else."

The Governor was the logical next step for him, but how do you handle it, he wondered. Go in and wake him, and say, I've got a few questions, Governor? He'd always felt a little uncomfortable in the presence of the higher-ups, in the Marine Corps, at the FBI school, even at headquarters. And nobody he'd ever dealt with was as high as the Governor of New York State. Should he just leave him alone, and go off and question someone else—someone like Bea Fletcher, who was a friend of Kohl's? Wisniewski knew for sure that his first step would be Kohl's sleeping guest—if that guest were not the Governor. Which told him it *had* to be the first step now.

"Would you go and wake the Governor, and tell him I would like to speak with him right away? Say it's important."

She merely nodded and started to turn away.

"Oh, and Sophie, don't volunteer anything about Mr. Kohl, but if he asks, tell him."

This time she didn't even nod, just walked off.

Ten minutes later the Governor was there. He was in pajamas and a robe, but the detective could see he'd shaved and combed his hair. And he was alone, which surprised Wisniewski. Not even the press secretary was with him. The Governor walked straight to Wisniewski, stuck out his hand.

"Hi, I'm Mike Hughes. What can I do for you?"

"My name is Detective Stanley Wisniewski of the East Hampton Village Police, Mr. Governor." As he spoke he got to his feet, fumbled for his wallet with the detective's shield in it. He tried to keep the awe out of his voice. He tried not to seem too clumsy getting the shield out. He showed it to Hughes, who looked quickly. "Thank you for coming to talk to me; I'm sorry I had to have you awakened."

"I was not asleep, Detective Wisniewski"—Wisniewski noticed he got it right the first time—"I'm happy to help. What seems to be the matter?"

"Mr. Governor, your host, Friedrich Kohl, is dead. His body was found by his housekeeper this morning, floating, face down, in the pool."

"How terrible! He was a brilliant financier, and of course a trusted friend. How did it happen?" Hughes registered surprise, shock, concern so quickly and amply, Wisniewski thought it a professional job. Then he figured the Governor would probably be good at that sort of thing by now—almost like an actor.

"It's hard to say, sir. At this point we don't know if it was drowning, or a heart attack, or maybe even something else. We don't know how he got into the pool, either. That's what my job is—finding out, if I can. I'd like to ask you some questions . . ." He fought off the impulse to add "if I may." But he let his voice trail off so Hughes could infer the words, if he wanted to.

"Please, go right ahead."

"Are you staying here for the weekend?"

"Yes, I arrived yesterday morning, and intended to stay until Monday. Mrs. Hughes is joining me this afternoon."

"Can you tell me what happened last night, sir?"

"I'm happy to tell you what I know, of course." He said it briskly. "We all came to the house after dinner—I guess it was close to midnight—I had a sip of Perrier, and I guess I was just bushed, so after a couple of minutes I left the others and went off to bed."

"Would you mind telling me who the others were?"

Wisniewski thought the Governor looked guarded for a moment, but he began his answer with perfect ease.

"Well, Freddie, of course, and there was Carlotta Reilly, the television newswoman, and her ex-husband, Buster Reilly. But they weren't together. He was with a young woman, an actress, Betsy . . . uh, Betsy Shore. Then there was Bea Fletcher and her agent, Irv somebody, don't really know him. And two people in the publishing business: Johnny Wainwright, and a young dark-haired woman. I've met her a couple of times, let's see, Sally or Suzie. I'm not sure. And another couple, an attractive young blonde and a writer, a big fellow. I suppose I should be better at names . . . politicians are supposed to be . . . and . . . I can't remember anyone else offhand. . . ."

"I understand your press secretary is out here, Governor. Was he . . ."

"Oh yes, of course! Warren Daniels. I forgot . . . it's like forgetting you have a shadow. He's always with me. And, yes, Warren had a date, a girl with one of those names you can never remember like Smith or Jones or Doe. Warren is the kind of guy who puts in a sixteen-hour day, and a seven-day week. I try to see to it that he has a little social life, and what could be better than a weekend in the Hamptons? That's why I was looking forward to the arrival of my wife. Of course, now . . ."

The detective saw Hughes's face turn properly grave.

"Governor, I notice you travel without a bodyguard . . ."

"Whenever I can. I find his presence depressing, and it creates a barrier between me and the people."

"Is your press secretary licensed to carry a gun? Does he also serve as . . ."

Hughes interrupted with a laugh. "Warren? If anything physical happened, I have a feeling *I'd* have to protect *him.* I used to be a police officer, you know."

"No, I didn't! Where?"

"New York's finest. Eleven years, while I went to college and law school at night."

"You don't by any chance carry a weapon yourself, do you, Governor?"

"No. Of course not. But I can handle myself in a fight. You don't grow up in Hell's Kitchen without learning how to use your fists. Not to mention a knee now and then. Ever since I was on the force, I've tried to keep in shape."

"You ought to let more people know you were a police officer, Governor, if I may say so. There are a lot of us who'd feel good knowing there's an ex-cop in Albany."

"You're right, Detective, absolutely right. Now tell me, is there anything else I can do to help?"

"Let's see. Can you remember anyone else being here last night?"

The Governor's eyes narrowed in a noticeable effort to recall. "No . . . I . . . don't think so."

"Did anyone go swimming, Governor?"

"Not that I saw, but as I said, I wasn't up for very long."

"Was there much drinking?"

"Not while I was there. People had drinks, but if you mean, were they drunk . . . I didn't see . . ."

"Who was serving the drinks, Governor?"

"Why, Freddie's housekeeper, of course. What's her name, the big woman . . . uh, Sophie."

"And Governor, were you awakened by anything, or did you hear anything at any time that was unusual?"

"Nothing. But don't forget my bedroom was on the opposite side of the house from the pool."

"Do you like to swim, Governor?"

Hughes shrugged. "It's not a sport a kid from Hell's Kitchen specializes in."

"How about Mr. Kohl?"

"Did he swim, do you mean?"

"Yes. Did he?"

"I never saw him swim a stroke. I've seen him splash around in the shallow end, but never swim."

"So if he fell into deep water, he'd be in trouble."

"Oh yes."

"Or if he was pushed." The detective made it sound like conjecture, to get a reaction.

"Do you have any reason to think he was?"

"I don't know, sir, I'm just considering the possibilities. I wonder if you could help." Wisniewski thought he saw the Governor become careful again. "Did Mr. Kohl have any enemies that you know of?"

"You don't get where he got without making some enemies."

"Anyone specific?"

Hughes appeared to be thinking. "No, no one I can think of off-hand."

"Any love interest?"

"He went out a fair amount, but there was no woman in particular. He'd been married twice, you know. I guess he was afraid of getting burned."

"Did he discuss it with you?"

"You mean his marriages, his love life? No."

"You were very close friends, though?"

"Uh, I wouldn't say so." Now Wisniewski was sure the Governor was tiptoeing. "He was the finance chairman of my campaigns. I wouldn't say he was a very *close* friend. He was a very *trusted*, a very *useful* one. Is there anything else?" The Governor was edgy, Wisniewski could hear it.

"No, that's all, Governor. Thank you."

Hughes stood. "If I can be of any further help, I'll be here."

"You are planning to stay through tomorrow, Governor?"

"I had been planning to."

"I'd be very grateful if you could stay. It would help to have the people who were close to Mr. Kohl nearby, in case I needed them."

The Governor didn't like that, Wisniewski felt, and was trying not to show it. "Of course." He reached out, shook the detective's hand, turned and left.

Wisniewski watched him go, wondering why he'd been so guarded. Wondering just how close and how useful Kohl had been to the Governor. Of course, he said to himself, a public official has to be very careful, and having his host found dead might seem suspicious no matter how innocent the Governor was. Anyone caught close to a death like this one *would* be careful, might even lie, he reminded himself. Take Sophie, for example. Why did she say she hadn't seen any of the guests—when the Governor said she'd served them drinks? Something about a corpse made everyone nervous, and a politician the most nervous of all.

Watching the Governor walk back into the house, Wisniewski suddenly found himself thinking of Chappaquiddick. He wondered if the Governor was thinking about it, too.

An April Weekend, 1977

Lying in the dark of their West Side bedroom, Mike Hughes rolled over and reached out to pull his wife to him. Rosemary allowed him to move her, just enough to let him know she was ready. In the twenty-six years of their marriage Rosemary had hardly ever said no, and hardly ever enjoyed it, enjoyed it even less than he did, and though he couldn't be sure—she would never talk about it—he didn't think she'd ever had an orgasm. Sex had yielded them six wonderful children, him one orgasm a week and her the satisfaction of doing her duty as a good wife.

"Yes, Mikey, yes," she said, she'd always say, when he was in her and getting close. She'd stroke his broad back and repeat, "Yes, yes," until he came, which never took all that long. Then the stroking would be replaced by a series of short pats which seemed to say, there, now I've done my job again and it's over until next week.

Like Mike, Rosemary was from a traditional working-class Irish background; she'd been a blooming, red-cheeked, blue-eyed girl, with silky, lustrous reddish-blond hair, strikingly pretty until she let her-self get heavier with each successive child and began to look older than Mike, although they were the same age. They'd met at a church dance right there on the West Side, found each other attractive, smart, sympathetic, hard-working, suitably ambitious and a perfect fit by re-ligion and background. A computer couldn't have matched two people better—which is not to say that romance wasn't there, too. While courting, they reached for and clutched at each other with an eager-ness that presaged a richer sex life than they were ever to experience together.

The things written about Victorian marriages in which the mates never saw each other naked, were almost true of Mike and Rosemary. She'd never been naked before him in full light, or he before her, without her being severely embarrassed. At first he'd try to get into the shower with her; she'd laugh and push him away and pretend to scold. If he persisted, she'd push harder, stop laughing and stop *pretending* to scold. He gave up. The sight of each other's body became a rarity, the enjoyment of that sight nonexistent.

As their routine developed, they were never even fully undressed in bed, in the dark, while making love. He'd have his pajama bottoms off, she her nightgown pulled up until the feel of it bulging between her stomach and his became a regular and repugnant part of their sex act, which invariably took place at night, at first because that was when Rosemary thought it proper, later because there were growing num-bers of young children wandering around.

Neither of them knew any better. When they married, Rosemary was a virgin, Mike close to it. But while she didn't seem to want any more from her sex life than her children and the satisfaction of her husband, he knew there was more, and he wanted it.

His Catholic upbringing told him not to want it; he told himself not to. There were more important things: home, children, compatibility, career. Especially career, for he was an intensely ambitious man. The sexual problem, however, would not go away. It confronted him each time he rolled off his wife after a perfunctory session like the one on this April night.

"Good night, dear," she said, and leaned to him and kissed him. She sounded content; she'd done for her husband what he wanted, all the more a gesture of her love because she enjoyed it so little herself. She would fall asleep quickly and serenely.

"Good night, dear," he echoed. He would have trouble falling asleep. In recent years, after each of these routinized orgasms, resentment would sweep through him—against Rosemary, although God knows it wasn't her fault, against himself for what the inadequacy had led him to.

When Mike was first elected to Congress in 1968, he and Rosemary decided that, because the children were in school, the family would not move to Washington, so he became a regular on the shuttle. He was no Tuesday-to-Thursday Congressman, though; during his first session he allowed himself nothing but hard work, winning a reputation as a pragmatic liberal who would work with people, compromise, yet fight for what he wanted.

He spent his evening hours tiptoeing through Washington, careful about parties, careful about drinking, because he knew he was in a town full of willing women, eager women.

In his second year in Washington, he met Freddie; through Freddie, he met trouble. Raising funds for his first Congressional campaign had been a mad scramble. Almost at once he had to think about re-election. The West Side being a maelstrom of factionalism, he expected a primary fight as well as a tough general election. He needed people with money, and so he was introduced to Freddie Kohl. Mike could never say he wasn't warned, and early, by a New York newspaper reporter.

"Beneath Freddie Kohl's superficial shadiness," the reporter told him, "deep down, there is *real* corruption."

"Clever," said Mike. "A good line. Did you make it up?"

"Yes, but it's no line. You see, when Freddie Kohl gives you money, or anything, he wants something back right away—that's the surface shadiness—and you say to yourself, hell, I can deal with that! But while you're dealing with it, Freddie has something deeper, something *really* crooked, planned for you—and that's what you've got to watch out for. Remember! Don't say I didn't warn you!"

Later, too late, Mike would remember, think about the warning, again and again.

Freddie gave money and raised money and asked his immediate *quid pro quo*. Sometimes Mike had no trouble: he could deliver a service he'd legitimately perform for any constituent, on a passport problem, or some import regulation. Sometimes Freddie would push for a bill or an amendment Mike would have supported anyway; and he was political enough to suggest Freddie had some input into his decision. Sometimes Mike just said no.

As he got to know Freddie better, he became aware that the dark-haired, dark-eyed businessman, though he lived in New York, spent a lot of time in Washington. Freddie would call him often, invite him to dinners or parties at the $400,000 Georgetown house Freddie kept open and staffed the year round. Freddie gave first-rate dinners and cocktail parties; the food and wine were superb, the guest list impressive, the women beautiful. Mike sampled the wine in moderation; he knew he could handle alcohol. He did not sample the women.

He got through a tough primary against a wealthy opponent, and won in November by a comfortable margin. Without Freddie's fundraising he might have done neither, and he had to face the fact that he went to Freddie's parties not only to fill his midweek loneliness, but because the financier was important to him.

The deeper corruption in Freddie took him beyond asking Mike Hughes for small favors; it made him plan Mike's seduction. Freddie wasn't sure which of Mike's appetites to work on first: ambition or sex. He decided on the first, because while he didn't know about the sex, the mere fact of Mike's being a politician made the ambition a sure thing.

Freddie asked the second-term Congressman to arrive early for one dinner party, and then sat him down in the library, with a glass of twenty-year-old Scotch.

"Mike, I've been wondering about you. What's going on inside that brain of yours? Where do you see yourself six or seven years down the road?"

Mike was amused by the avuncular tone; he'd just turned forty, Freddie was six years younger. He offered the standard disclaimer. "I don't think that far ahead. I'm happy being a Congressman. I just want to do a good job."

Freddie's eyes slitted as he smiled. "Don't be coy, Mike, this is Freddie you're talking to. I sense something in you that wants to take you further. I wouldn't be this interested in your career if I didn't sense it."

"Like where?"

"Oh . . . Senator."

Mike thought for a moment. "No. It's a powerful job, lots of prestige and all that . . . but it's a policy job, and . . ." He came to a dead stop.

Freddie went after that like a cat after a mouse, and caught it on the first pounce. "And you want to *run* things, don't you?"

Mike didn't play around. "Yes. I think I could run things."

Freddie let himself start thinking aloud. "Mayor? No! The most

famous dead-end job in American politics. *Not* Mayor." He looked at
Mike and liked what he saw; Mike was shaking his head no. He no
more wanted a dead end than Freddie did. The man was ambitious.
Freddie was pleased.

"You know, Mike, you *could* be Governor." Freddie said it as if they
had already agreed that this was *the* possibility. "You could. You're a
Democrat; you're big in the city, but you're Catholic enough and
middle-of-the-road enough to do well upstate. We'd have work to do in
the suburbs, but work is no problem, and money is no problem."

"Oh hell, Freddie, I've just started my second term in the House,
and I love the job. This talk is ridiculous; let's see how I do here. You
know it takes a few terms before you build up enough clout to get
anything done!"

But he didn't say no. That they both knew. And each time Freddie
raised the subject Mike's replies sounded less and less like a no. When
the time came for them to talk about re-election to a third term in the
House, Freddie said, "Mike, we need a solid win, a *big* win, to show
the party you're of gubernatorial caliber."

When Mike looked a little startled, Freddie added quickly: "I'm not
saying you're *going* to run for Governor—that's up to you. But I think
you've got to give yourself the option for '74, should you want it."

Mike couldn't argue with that. He didn't have to say yes, which
would have been a major commitment. But what he wanted even less
at that moment was to have to say no. He got what he wanted.

Freddie got what he wanted, too. Two weeks after they'd agreed a
major victory was needed, one of Mike's big contributors approached
him with the suggestion that a finance chairman be formally named, so
a structure could be set up for the campaign—and campaigns to come.
The natural choice was Freddie. Afterwards, neither could remember
which of them had first suggested his name.

The sexual seduction began later, but was consummated sooner, and
so easily even Freddie, with his infinite belief in human weakness, was
surprised. His campaign began and triumphed with an invitation to
supper and Monday Night Football on TV.

"Just a couple of friends," Freddie said, not saying who the friends
were, or that he didn't give a damn about football, Monday night or
any other time.

When Mike arrived at 7:30, only Freddie was there. "The others will
be late," he said as he led Mike into the quiet opulence of his living
room. "I thought we'd have a couple of drinks here, and then go up

and eat off trays in the TV room for the game. What would you like to drink?"

Mike had a Scotch on the rocks; for himself Freddie splashed a little white wine in a glass with Perrier and ice. The others were quite late, and the two spent an hour or so talking. For reasons Mike couldn't fathom—not then anyway—Freddie forsook his monomaniacal pre-occupation with politics and Mike's career to talk about women—what a wonderful town Washington was for women, how tough it was for men like Mike to be without their wives all week.

"I've had two marriages, Mike. Neither worked out. You don't know how sorry I am for that, how I envy you your long marriage and your wonderful family. How happy that must make you!" Then he paused, as if to give Mike a chance to respond. When nothing came, Freddie went on.

"Yes, I regret not having the blessings of children, a loving wife, a happy home. I suppose it is one of the curses of working as hard as I have. But you know, Michael"—Freddie used the full name rarely, when he wanted to underline his earnestness and sincerity—"I have not let it interfere with another part of my nature. You see, I believe man has two natures. I'm sure you agree . . ." He paused to let Mike agree.

"At least two, Freddie . . ." Mike was feeling mellow.

"There is the Godlike in us, the quality that makes man the highest form of life. Then there's the animal. We *are* animals, too, Mike, and we can't pretend we're not, except perhaps for those rare ones among us who are saints. But I am not a saint, and I suppose I may say you are not either." He looked at Mike for a reply; Mike just laughed and shook his head.

"And if we ignore our animal side, pretend it doesn't exist, or worse, try to suppress it, do you know what happens, Michael?"

Mike didn't know what Freddie was driving at, although he knew it was something, Freddie's brain was never idle or even merely ruminative. The Scotch was so smooth, the sofa so comfortable, he thought he'd just relax and wait and find out. He laughed again. "No, what, Frederick?" He mimicked Freddie's use of his full name, but didn't use Friedrich because he knew the other man detested it.

"If we do not satisfy the animal part of our nature, it does not go away. It stirs in us, it impinges on our higher abilities. If the beast in us is not fed, its hunger upsets all of us, keeps us from working, from thinking. Do you understand what I say?"

"I'll tell you as soon as I refill my glass." Mike got up, poured himself another drink. The twenty-year-old Scotch, a private label, was as smooth as silk. Mike couldn't bring himself to dislike luxury. It made him feel guilty.

When he sat down, he replied, "No, I'm not sure I understand what you say. What do you say, Freddie m'boy?"

"I say, feed the beast, keep him happy and well fed, and he will leave you free to go about your business. I am not ashamed to say I feed the beast in me. Nor am I ashamed to say I sometimes feed him exotic food. Steak and potatoes are fine, Mike, but not at every meal. Don't you agree?" Freddie looked at Mike, but this time didn't wait for a response.

"Have you ever been in bed with two girls, Mike? Two beautiful young girls who are entirely devoted to your pleasure, and extremely adept at gratifying it? If you haven't, let me give you a warning, my dear friend. Beware. Once you have tried it, you may never again want to settle for steak and potatoes!"

Mike was saying nothing, but he was listening, and interested. He tried not to show it, but he was; they both knew it. He was also getting drunk.

Freddie knew when to stop. "Ah well," he said. "What's the sense of talking about that? People think differently on the subject and I have no wish to impose my views on anyone else. I happen to think the pleasures of the flesh are nothing to be ashamed of and not to be denied. That's *my* feeling, Mike. How's your drink?"

"My drink is fine. Thanks."

Freddie smiled; he could see Mike was slightly drunk, which pleased him. "All right then, tell me about tonight's football. I'm sure you know much more about the game than I do. You look like you played the game in college, Mike."

Mike laughed. "I got most of my higher learning at John Jay College, at night. Did you ever hear of the John Jay football team?"

"To be perfectly honest," Freddie replied, "I've never even heard of John Jay College. Where is it?"

"In Manhattan."

"Really?"

"Really. In a former shoe loft on the West Side. Its full name is the John Jay College of Criminal Justice, and it's part of the City University system. Its student body is mostly cops."

"*Really!* What were you doing there?"

"What was I *doing* there? I was a cop for eleven years, you know that, don't you? I worked my way through part of college and all of law school while I was on the force. It's in my campaign literature—the stuff you help pay for. Don't you ever read it, Freddie?"

"I guess I'm too busy raising the money for it, Mr. Congressman. It's for your constituents to read. I'm not even in your district. But now that I know you were a policeman, I'm going to be more careful!"

The phone rang; Freddie picked it up, said, "Good. Please show them up."

"My friends are here now," he told Mike, and got to his feet. When the friends walked in, Mike suddenly realized why Freddie had been softening him up with all the talk about the beast in men. The two friends were young women named Sharon and Mona, and Mike, with the practiced eye of a New York cop, could see at once they were high-class hookers. Very young, no more than twenty-two or twenty-three, very classy, dressed in elegant, quiet clothes that reminded Mike of Freddie's living room. But hookers—although Mike now modified that in his mind to the subspecies he knew as East Side call girls.

Mike shook their hands, exchanged a few polite words with them, until Freddie looked at his watch and said, "Well, the game goes on the air in fifteen minutes, shall we go up to the TV room?"

"I've never seen your TV room, Freddie," Mike said. "I didn't know you ever watched TV."

"I don't much," he replied. "It's kind of an all-purpose play- and recreation room." Mike stepped into the playroom and looked around. All-purpose, indeed, he said to himself. He could guess what its primary purpose was, and it was *not* TV watching. Mirrored ceiling, quilted walls of tan leather, most of the floor covered by the same quilting. No tables or chairs, just some low, built-in settees and overstuffed hassocks.

Freddie removed his jacket, sank to the floor, leaned against a hassock. "Whew! Not a bad way to watch a ballgame." He tried to make it sound weary and innocent.

"But where's the set, Freddie?" Mike was amused and drunk. Sharon and Mona took off their tailored jackets; their figures were not merely good, they were gorgeous, bosomy yet trim, obviously well tended and beautifully suited for their work. The girls sat easily and gracefully on the floor near Freddie.

For an instant, Mike hesitated. Then, decisively he removed his jacket, loosened his tie, dropped onto the floor next to the girls, moved a hassock to prop himself against. "I played a little high school football. Didn't play well; didn't play much. Just enough to hurt my back and to have to lean against things. Freddie, where *is* the set?"

His host reached to a door on the wall at his elbow, opened it, pressed a button, and a panel in a set of cabinets on the wall opposite them slid open. Using the wall controls he switched on the set, found the channel with the game. Then he pushed another button and a second wall panel opened to reveal a small bar. Freddie got to his feet.

"What would you like to drink? Ladies?"

Sharon and Mona asked for Scotch and soda; Freddie poured a Scotch on the rocks for Mike without even asking. He added a bit of Perrier and ice to his own glass.

"Let's enjoy the drink," he said, "then I'll ring for supper whenever you'd like it."

The ladies said nothing. Mike said, "Sounds fine," and sipped at his drink.

Three plays into the first quarter the phone rang. Freddie picked it up, listened, then said, "Oh no, not today! Are you sure?" Pause. "Well, all right. I'll be right down."

He hung up, got to his feet. "Someone is in town from one of my Coast companies, says I promised to give him some time this evening! I don't remember that at all! It will be a while, but just pick up the phone and order supper whenever you're ready. I'm terribly sorry. I don't *believe* it!"

Mike didn't believe it either; it smelled like a setup. What the hell, he said to himself.

Freddie walked to the door, started out, then remembered something. He opened a low cabinet, reached in and clumsily brought out a football, which he tossed awkwardly to Mike.

"Here! An authentic Washington Redskins football, from Coach George Allen, no less. I'll be back as soon as I can, but it will be a while, alas."

Mike almost laughed at the go-ahead signal. The scent of the setup was now overpowering. What the hell, he said to himself again.

On the tube, the Redskins were playing the Dallas Cowboys. Billy Kilmer threw a short pass over the middle; no receiver was near it. "Broken pattern," the commentator said.

"Do you girls understand the game?" Mike asked. Sharon, slightly the blonder, ampler and bustier of the two, replied, "Yes. You tackle the one who has the ball, and try to take it away." She looked at the football cradled in Mike's lap.

"He tries not to let you," Mike countered.

"But if you're very determined, you get what you want," said Mona, who looked like an SAS stewardess.

In answer, Mike just smiled and held the ball up in his square-fingered hand, challenging Mona. She reached for the ball, he pulled it away and she fell onto his lap; he could feel the softness of her breasts on his thighs. Sharon reached over her friend for the ball, and Mike half shoved, half cuffed her over on top of Mona, so that both were on his lap, one on top of the other.

"I hope I'm not making better friends of you than you want to be," he said.

"Oh no," Sharon replied. "We're intimate friends, as close as any two people can be."

"Are you really?"

"Would you like to see?"

"Uh-huh."

The girls stood, kissed each other on the mouth, put their hands to each other's buttocks, pressed each other close. Then they took a half-step back and unbuttoned each other's blouse, took them off, ran their hands over each other's breasts, Sharon's larger, softer, with bigger, darker nipples, Mona's smaller, pointier, the nipples paler. Sharon leaned over, kissed Mona's breasts, then her navel, then removed her pants and underpants. She stood and then Mona, like a mirror image, echoed the process on Sharon. This was no spontaneous act, Mike told himself, it was almost choreographed. And exciting. Damned exciting.

Sharon lay on the upholstered leather floor and Mona began kissing her, starting at the mouth, working her way down until she was kissing between her legs. Then without taking her mouth away, Mona put her legs over Sharon's face.

Mike watched, riveted. He'd gone to a couple of porno movies, found them a turn-on, but nothing like this. Suddenly, the women stopped, both got to their knees, facing Mike, and Mona said, "You see what good friends we are?"

"Yeah, I see." Mike was embarrassed at how hoarse he sounded, tried clearing his throat.

"We don't want to leave you out," Sharon said. "Won't you join us?"

"Freddie . . ." Mike's voice didn't sound any better to him.

"He won't disturb us." Mona sounded sure, and as she spoke, she was undoing his pants. Sharon started unbuttoning his shirt. When he was lying naked, first Sharon, then Mona kissed his penis and took it into her mouth. Once, while Sharon was sucking him Mona looked him straight in the eye.

"Do you like this?"

"Yes!" He said it on one long exhalation of air. "But I'd like some of you."

"You want some of us?" Again, they seemed rehearsed as they responded to him. With Mike still on his back, Sharon got to her knees and straddled him at the hips, Mona moved forward, and carefully, delicately, gracefully straddled his head and neck.

And each offered some of herself to him.

Freddie, watching the two-on-one through a peephole in an adjoining room, was titillated, at the same time regretful he hadn't yet set up facilities for filming scenes like this one. But that would come; there'd be other chances, for he'd now uncovered Mike's sexual as well as his political appetite. Such a man could be worked with. Such a man could be handled. There'd be more election campaigns with this man, more *scènes à trois* to film.

In 1972, at the age of forty-two, Mike Hughes was re-elected to a third term in Congress, by a landslide. His campaign was efficient, sophisticated, colorful and well financed; a newsmagazine called it the newest look in political salesmanship. He was seen as a leading contender for Governor.

Also, by 1972, Mike was hooked on the sexual tidbits Freddie served him. Customarily they included more than one girl at a time; and more and more the girls got younger and younger. To Mike they never seemed younger than eighteen, but he realized he may have chosen not to notice. One turned out to be a lot younger than eighteen, nearly five years younger. But what was even more embarrassing, she turned out to be the daughter of a high Pentagon general. Mike sweated that one out, until Freddie took care of it, with a payoff—cash, he told Mike, plus a unique, four-year, all-expenses-paid college scholarship for the girl . . . when she was ready for college, which would not be for some time. As Mike knew, the offerings were not prepared only for him. He'd been at suppers where other government figures were led off to their own special desserts; Freddie wanted to let him see it was common practice, that they were all in it together. That was the reason that sometimes, when Freddie led Mike to group splashes in his hot tub, Freddie joined in. The girls—what Bea, in "WashingtonShock," called his Rubber Ducks—were always there, of course, and always young, though rarely as young as the general's daughter.

But although Mike was quieted, he was not reassured by the idea that others were in it, too. The unwritten law of silence, the taboo against reporting sexual goings-on in Washington, was helpful, a recognition that it was part of the American way. But splashing around with teenage girls, he feared, might stretch the unwritten law to the snapping point.

Mike rationalized: as long as he did a good job in Congress, his private life was his own business. As long as you did your job, as long as you kept your private life discreet—the Wilbur Mills-Fanne Fox Tidal Basin episode was, of course, disgraceful—no harm was being done. Some of the time Mike even believed his arguments.

The rising young Congressman from Manhattan's West Side did not really know the rising young Washington columnist Bea Fletcher, although they'd been introduced once or twice at parties. He considered her neither friend nor enemy, and did not delude himself about the probability that she knew of Freddie's sexual setups and Mike's participation in them. The Monday night sessions at Freddie's became as celebrated an institution as the football games themselves—celebrated among a select group, to be sure, but even select groups talked, and the people they talked to, talked. But the more Mike played without being caught, the more he told himself he was safe.

Still, when in 1973 he began his run for Governor, a part of him welcomed the chance to break with the Washington sexual connection. In New York he would no longer be *a* Congressman, he'd be *the* Governor, and he'd be watched—and glad of it, he told himself, for it might do for him what he couldn't do for himself.

His 1974 gubernatorial campaign was a triumph, starting with a decisive primary victory over a more liberal opponent, which gave him a moderate image in the state. In the general election he once again grabbed the center, this time with the Republican to the right, and he was elected by a solid margin.

Once again Freddie, now the finance chairman of his campaign, did a masterful fundraising job. He'd put together a smooth apparatus and didn't want to waste it. He now had a Presidential horse to use it on, and didn't want to waste him, either, and so he would have hated to see either Mike's political or sexual appetite sated. He devoted himself to keeping Mike hungry.

In Mike's first term as Governor, Freddie made two housing moves, both suited to his plans for Governor Hughes. In 1975, he sold his Fifth Avenue cooperative apartment and bought a townhouse on Beekman Place. To be able to look out on the East River was inspiring; to be able to enter and leave without going by doormen and elevatormen was comforting. The next year, he bought a Southampton house, which he kept only a few months before moving to East Hampton, after his Maidenhead rejection.

The elaborate play facilities he built in each house were shown to the Governor; the filming facilities were not. The Governor tried to say no to the play, but he couldn't make it stick. He played less often, but he played. Again, he had the rationalizations: he was doing a good job and his private life was irrelevant.

Freddie tried to introduce the Governor to tennis, too, on his all-weather court in East Hampton. Mike laughed at the idea of a kid from Hell's Kitchen playing tennis. "I'll stick to jogging," he told Freddie. He thought of that response later, when the "WashingtonShock" pieces came out, and he said to himself: that's what I should have told Freddie when he offered me the girls.

After a while Freddie started talking to Mike about re-election and after that, the Presidency.

Talk about 1980 came up late one Saturday afternoon, after Freddie and the Governor had just been through a nude splash in Freddie's East Hampton pool with four young women. The girls safely out of the way, the two men sat in terrycloth robes sipping drinks, looking out at the calm summer ocean.

"Suppose, just suppose, the fellow in the White House does badly or doesn't want to run again. The picture would be wide open, Mike."

"A ridiculous supposition, but yes, it would be wide open."

"Well, just for fun, Mike, whom would you favor?"

Mike thought for a moment, then mentioned a few names. Freddie smiled at him. "None of them would be as viable a candidate as you, Mike. You know that."

Mike just laughed.

"Why do you laugh?" Freddie asked. "Don't you believe that?"

"Want me to be charmingly modest, and blush and say, no, I never even thought of myself as a possibility? It's not true. I was laughing at your . . . chutzpah"—Mike was always using Yiddish expressions with Freddie and then regretting it—"that means balls—in talking about the Presidency of the United States right after you and I have been doing what would be guaranteed to get us on page one of the *News* and the *Post*, maybe even the *Times*, if we ever got caught. Jesus, you've got balls, yes indeed, Freddie."

"Don't be foolish, Mike. Shall I remind you of at least one revered President, and at least one honored Governor whose tastes were similar to yours?"

"Yes, and the whole world has been told about them."

"Not while they were in office, not even while they were alive. You're worrying for no reason."

"I'm being realistic. The taboo is breaking down. Memoirs are being written. Things are being said out in the open that nobody would dare say ten years ago, even five years ago. You can always make a mistake —like Chappaquiddick, or the Tidal Basin. Yeah, or even a heart attack in the wrong bed. And your careful planning is all screwed up. That general's daughter could have been my Chappaquiddick! It scares the hell out of me! Doesn't it scare you, Freddie? Here you are, a famous banker, director of God knows how many corporations, museums, cultural organizations, charities—the financial adviser to the Governor—doesn't it make you nervous?"

"Nothing's going to happen, Mike. People understand these days that a man's private life is his own, and nobody's business, as long as he does his job. And you're doing yours brilliantly—*Time* magazine just said so. They also called you Presidential material, you know that. I'm not nervous, nor should you be. It's a waste of your energy. You should be thinking about 1980—more than thinking about it, working on it."

Mike decided to pretend Freddie was right, and sometimes he was almost able to convince himself the pretense was reality. When in the late fall of 1976 he got advance word of a two-part piece Bea Fletcher had written for *Scope* magazine, the pretense suddenly seemed flimsy. He knew of Bea's columns in Washington, knew how cutting she could be. The first thing he did was call Freddie, to ask about the article.

"Don't worry," Freddie said. "There aren't a dozen people outside of Washington who'll recognize that the lines refer to you. And even they won't understand what the hell they mean."

"Lines? What lines? What the hell are you talking about?" Mike was stunned. Freddie knew something, and there was something to know.

"It's nothing, a line or two about a Congressman, that's all. Forget it, Mike!"

As quickly and as quietly as he could, Mike got hold of an advance copy of the piece. In the first part, he was not mentioned or referred to; feeling easier, he began the second, and was virtually finished with it before he found them.

He read the lines to Warren Daniels, his press secretary, who already knew all about his visits to Freddie's various establishments.

"Listen, this is the narrator talking:

" 'And so I left this *pen* of iniquity, thinking how I envied Molière his genius for describing scoundrels. Even more, envying his compassion and humor. How I wish I could be as kindly and funny as he! But when I see them with their snouts in the public trough, their manners as dirty as any pig's, and their morals a lot dirtier, I feel no compassion or humor, just anger and contempt: for their immorality, their hypocrisy, their betrayal of the public trust, their pilferage of the public money.

" 'Most of these so-called public servants I leave behind me with no regret—well, regret only that they remain alive and well and thieving in Washington. As I move on to a livelier pen of more talented scoundrels, I shall encounter a few of my old Washington "friends." There is, for example, and kindly forgive the mixing of livestock, Congressman Marty and his Rubber Ducks. Marty and his super-rich Svengali have gone on to make a bigger splash, and I'm sure I'll encounter them again. I'll be fascinated to find out if in the move to the bigger pond, Marty has left his cute little rubber ducks behind. Alas, I fear what the answer will be, for they say, and I fear I'm turning my tale into a real animal farm, they say you can't teach an old drake new tricks. Just *buy* him new tricks. Or new ducks?' "

Mike stopped reading; he was so angry, his eyes refused to take him further. He did manage to notice, at the conclusion of the piece, a short item in italics about this being part of a novel-in-progress by Ms. Fletcher, the second and major part of which would be about life in the fashionable Hamptons.

"My God!" he shouted to Warren. "And Freddie thinks almost no one will recognize me! He's *kidding!* And what about the rest of the goddamned novel? What in hell is she going to do to me in *that!*" He stomped out of the room, went to a private line and phoned Freddie.

"What the hell are we going to do about it?" he demanded. He'd never been as harsh with Freddie.

"Easy, Mike, easy . . ."

"Hell, *you* can say easy. You're not an elected official!"

"But I have a reputation in my own field, and as you've said, I'm now financial adviser to the Governor, and I don't want to be humiliated any more than you do, for your sake and mine. Nor do I want your chances for the White House to be hurt—for your sake *and* mine, because you may find some role on the national scene for me, some *major* way I can do something for the country that's been so . . ."

"Oh cut the shit, will you, Freddie? I'm worried about a Hamptongate, and you're in there pitching for a cabinet post! Talk about chutzpah!" This time he said it to annoy Freddie. "If that book delivers what the first part promises, forget the White House! Forget re-election! I'll be back at Start. Worse than that: I'll go directly to jail, will not collect two hundred dollars."

"That's ridiculous. They can't send you to jail, there's no . . ."

Mike interrupted again. "I didn't mean it literally. What I meant was I'd be out of office, with less than zero chance of getting back in. Look, if someone won't vote for you because your opponent gets his face in more TV ads, or because the economy is bad, you can always come back. You can raise more dough; the economy can get better. But if you lose because the voter hears you've been . . . fooling around . . . you're remembered that way for life!"

"For Christ's sake, Mike, don't weep until you get hurt . . ." Under tension Freddie's ear for the vernacular deserted him. "Suppose the book is not harmful to you at all? Suppose it comes out *after* the '78 elections? That would give you two years to neutralize it. You don't think we're going to sit back and let her destroy us, do you?"

Trying to assuage the Governor, Freddie outlined the two prongs of his attack: Clean the book up; delay publication until after 1978.

When "WashingtonShock" came out in *Scope* in late '76, Mike barely knew Bea Fletcher, but with Freddie's cultivation of the gliterati, Mike saw her more often. They spoke occasionally, briefly. Both were polite, reserved, at arm's length, the Governor wanting to seem secure enough not to be bothered by "WashingtonShock," Bea wanting to keep open her lines of communication to power.

Then the word began spreading that the book would be hardcover dynamite and Mike decided he wanted to have a long talk with Bea. His press secretary called her, said the Governor was seeking the input of a number of writers before he appointed new members to the State Arts Council, and would Bea have lunch with the Governor?

She refrained from asking why the Governor would want input from a Washington gossip columnist who was barely a New York resident. She said, "I'd be glad to help the Governor in any way I can, but it's hardly necessary for him to take me to lunch, I know how busy he is. I could talk with him over the telephone if he preferred. Or respond to any specific questions in writing."

"Oh no," Daniels replied. "The Governor would much prefer to do it at lunch, the give-and-take would be freer. He considers time with members of the cultural community well spent."

She said, "If that's what the Governor would like, I'll be happy to have lunch."

They met at "21." For a time he discussed the arts council with her. Patiently, he asked her views of certain writers, of the relationship between government and the arts. Patiently, she replied, although she warned him her views on writers were idiosyncratic and she thought the only relationship writers should have with the government was to keep an eye on it. Patiently, he listened, did not go for the bait she dangled before him.

It wasn't until after the main course, chicken hash for him, a salad for her, that he got around to the purpose of the lunch.

"How's the book about the Hamptons coming, Bea?"

"Coming, hard but coming, Governor. You know it's not easy to force yourself to sit down and put time in every day when there's no time clock to punch, no boss to make you work, and no daily deadline. I'm a little behind schedule—but then the schedule was set up so I could fall a little behind."

"Got a publisher?"

"Not yet, Governor, but we've got a lot of interest. We're talking to people."

"Listen, Bea, if I can be of any help, my financial adviser, Freddie Kohl—but of course you know him, don't you?"

"Doesn't everybody?" She couldn't help smiling slightly.

Mike saw it, left it alone; this was not the time. "Well, Freddie is on the board of everything, and that includes publishing interests. If you want . . ."

"Thanks, Governor, but . . ."

"Would you make it Mike? The other sounds so formal."

"All right, Mike. While we don't have a publisher yet, I must say I have the world's best agent, Irv Schnell. If I could write the book as well as he can sell it, I'd have *War and Peace* on my hands, and in my typewriter right now. But thanks, it's kind of you to offer."

She waited; they both knew he'd have to get down to business.

"Would you like another glass of wine?"

"No, thanks. But I would love a cup of coffee."

He signaled to the waiter. Bea sat there, volunteered nothing. He could see she wasn't going to make this easy for him.

"May I ask you a question about your book?"

"Of course."

"Is it going to be like the article in *Scope?*"

"I don't know how to answer that. Yes and no. It's not going to be *The Sound of Music*. But . . . what do you mean? Like it in what way?"

"Is it going to take people apart? Ruin their good names?"

"Mike, I don't agree that 'WashingtonShock' did that, at all. I think it went after a lot of *bad* names, maybe ruined a few, I certainly hope so. A lot more should have been ruined. It didn't—it *couldn't*—ruin anybody's *good* name."

"You're being disingenuous, Bea. You know what I mean."

"No, I'm not. I do know what you mean, though—you mean I damaged some political futures. To that I plead guilty. No, I don't plead it, I proclaim it. They are people who don't deserve to have their public lives left unscathed. They are not worthy of public trust. Among other things, they're liars; leading the public to believe they are something they are not. I, on the other hand, plead guilty to telling the truth. And I defy you to show me where I have lied. Have I been sued? No, I have not."

"You're still being disingenuous, and very clever. First of all, I'm sure you know how difficult it is under current law for a public figure to win a libel suit. Damned near impossible. Then, you've passed the article off as fiction, so in order to sue, first the person must say: The fictional Mr. X is really me. To which of course the public would respond: If you didn't do the nasty things Mr. X did, what makes you think Bea Fletcher is writing about you? So there you are on the defensive again. If you lose the suit, which is easy to do, given these circumstances, then of course you're branded guilty of the things in the article. And if you win? It's still a million dollars' worth of publicity for the article or the book. No, there's too little to gain and too much to lose by suing. So just because no one has, doesn't mean everyone in your article is guilty, as innuendoed."

Bea looked annoyed. "All right then, Mike, forget the legalities. Person to person, across this table, show me one case where I have said something untrue. If I have, I want to know about it."

"I am not interested in specific cases. They're not the point . . ."

"Then what *is* the point?"

"Here's the point: Someone in public office owes the people a job well and honestly done. A Congressman—for example—owes his constituents vigorous representation of their interests, tempered by his own best judgment and political principles. He should keep his promises. He should do his job: show up for sessions and committee meetings. Get on committees which can use his skills and help solve the problems of his district—and of the country, too. He should introduce bills he and his constituents believe in. He should not be reachable by special interests. If he does his job, his private life is *nobody's damned business!*"

The Governor was getting red in the face; he blew out some air, but when Bea tried to say something, he held up a hand. "Please! Let me finish. Let's just say Jack Kennedy used to screw around *all* the time and Nixon never did. Who would you rather have as President?"

"No, no, no," she responded. "I don't agree with that at all. You assume that private morality and public morality can be separated. I say no, they can't. You bring up Kennedy and Nixon as if sexual immorality were the only kind there is. It isn't. I never said it was. So Kennedy was playing around, and Nixon wasn't. That doesn't mean Nixon wasn't cheating in other ways—which he sure as hell was.

"I want a Congressman I can believe, Mike. One who passes himself off as a faithful man, while he is playing around with I don't care what—women, girls, boys, dogs, sheep, it doesn't matter—he's a liar. And he can't turn that off in public life. Even if he wanted to. Often, being in bed with all sorts of creatures in his private life puts him in bed with all sorts of special interests in his public life."

She looked hard at Mike, who didn't react. She went on. "So he's doubly suspect. I mean, who knows when a legislator is voting his conscience or voting on behalf of someone who's doing him favors—or blackmailing him? How can you tell? You have to rely on his honesty, don't you? And if the core of his private life is cheating, how can you rely on it? Is there such a thing as nine-to-five honesty? I doubt it. And even if it starts that way, how long can it stay that way? Anyone who's leading a double life is vulnerable to blackmail, either the straight-out, brutal kind or the subtler, more dangerous kind: pressure, manipulation. Soon the Congressman begins to convince himself he really believes what it's convenient for him to believe."

Mike was shaking his head throughout the last part of her lecture. "Hell, you don't want a human to represent you, Bea, you want a saint.

And I don't know where you're going to find one, because with the possible exception of Jerry Brown, saints do not put themselves up for public office. And there are even some nasty rumors Brown may be human. You must have one hell of a job pulling the levers when you get into that voting booth!"

"You're damned right I do! And it's all the harder when you've lived and worked in Washington for a while. It's hard, so damned hard it's a disgrace, to find a politician who's privately and publicly honest. But does that mean I should settle for less? No! I say, a plague on both your houses! I do more than *say* it, I shout it, scream it, and hope a lot of people hear me."

By now they were both angry. "You hope a lot of people will *hear* you?" he asked. "Don't you mean: will *buy* your book? And see the movie? And make you rich? Isn't that what you mean?"

"Listen, if honesty sells, why shouldn't I sell a lot of it? And if it makes me rich, hell yes! If, on the other hand, I had to be a crook, or a cheat, or a liar to get rich, then I'd have a serious problem—a problem that doesn't seem to concern many politicians."

"Oh, is that what you're selling, honesty? I've got news for you, kid, there's no particular market for honesty, and you know that as well as I do. Try calling it gossip. Try calling it scandal—that's what sells. Gossip is what you're peddling, malicious gossip. You're not interested in fairness, you're interested in making a buck."

"Tell me, Mike, how can honesty be unfair?"

"Oh, that's easy. I'll tell you what, just for the purposes of the argument, I'll go along with calling it honesty. What it is, is *selective* honesty." Mike Hughes knew he'd now be getting down to cases, specifically *his*, but he didn't care.

"Let's take our Congressman, for example. Let's say he has a damned good record: works hard, fights hard, represents his district, is in nobody's pocket—no one can fault him as a representative. Let's also say he has a private life which is . . . let's say it's not the American dream. Let's say he's done things he'd rather keep quiet. Now, this Congressman decides to run for higher office, let's say to be a senator, or mayor . . . or governor.

"Meanwhile, some writer, for whatever purposes, decides to advance himself, or *her*self, by writing a book that airs a lot of dirty linen, and some of it is the Congressman's. So he, or *she*, hurts the Congressman, hurts his chances for higher office. In all fairness shouldn't his opponent's private life be examined, too? Think it would be any better?

But no, the writer doesn't do that, because he, or *she*, is not after truth, or fairness. He, or *she*, is after a best seller, and if it takes distorting, telling only *part* of the story, to do it—that's tough. On the Congressman."

Then Mike dropped any pretense about being hypothetical. "What I'm saying is, I don't know how to stop you from peddling your gossip, Bea, but I'm sure as hell not going to hand you any Pulitzer Prize for it. You ought to *think* about your book. I hear it's supposed to come out just before next year's elections. *Think* of the timing. Think of its effect on the election. Think of who might get elected to run this state. Think what his views might be on issues which may be of some importance to you: abortion, capital punishment, women's rights, energy —all major issues that mean a hell of a lot to the people of this state— which includes you. Do you want that man in Albany? Are you going to give *his* private life equal time? Or are you going to let him go simply because he spends his leisure time in the Adirondacks instead of the Hamptons, and you're not interested in the Adirondacks?

"That may be *your* idea of honesty and truth. It's *my* idea of dishonesty, distortion, unfairness, perversion of truth. And as I'm sure you know, *that's* what I really came here to say."

Bea nodded. "You've got a problem," she told him. "The standard problem of anyone who gets caught: Why me? Why me, when others park illegally and get away with it? Why me, when the other kids stick their fingers into the cookie jars? Why me, when they all cheat on their income tax? Why me, when every politician fools around?

"Tell me, Governor, what would you like? Would you like no one to be caught until everyone is? And would you like that to apply to muggers, rapists and murderers, too? Because then, of course, no one would *ever* be punished. Because then it wouldn't be enough to blow the whistle on your November opponent, would it? Because after that, you could say, what about opponents in the primaries? Mind you, not that I don't think we'd find stuff on every last one of them, if we had the time and the staff—I've lived in Washington long enough to know that—it's just that no one would ever get around to blowing the whistle on anyone. New politicians and new crooks spring up all the time. It'd be like not giving out a ticket for illegal parking or running a red light, until you caught every violator. Never happen, would it?

"If half the Congress is on the take, one way or another, I'd rather put 'em in jail one at a time than let 'em all loose until we can collar 'em all. No, Governor, the cry, Why me? is not the answer. The answer should be: *I'm clean*. If you're a public man, you should be an honest man. If you're an honest man, you can look people in the eye and answer for your life. If you can't answer for it, *don't blame me for asking*."

Both cups of coffee sat on the table, untouched, growing cold. Mike's hands were on the table, clenched into fists.

"You're a tough woman, Bea; you can't seem to understand that politicians are humans, with all the frailties that go with the species. So let me tell you something: I'm tough, too. You don't get brought up in Hell's Kitchen, you don't ride in a squad car all day and then go to college and law school at night—slugging through books at three in the morning when your head hurts and your neck and shoulders are so tight your wife has to stand there and rub them while you study— you don't get elected from Zabar Country as an Irish Catholic, you don't get all of that done without being tough.

"And yeah, I'm ambitious, too. But I tell you, as a cop, as an assemblyman, as a Congressman, as Governor, I have never been on the take, not to the tune of one penny. And I have given the public value for every penny of my salary—and believe me there haven't been too many pennies, and I haven't saved a damned one of 'em. I could step out any time, go into a law firm for $150,000 a year, $200,000 a year, more. But I don't. Because I want to get things done for people. I've been poor and an underdog in Hell's Kitchen. And so I know what it's like to be poor and an underdog in the South Bronx and Harlem and Bed-Stuy. I don't expect you, with your facile good-guy–bad-guy cartoons, to understand or believe this—but I have made a difference to those people! And that means something to me.

"But yeah, I'm ambitious, and so the ambitious politician butts heads with the ambitious gossip columnist. Well, kid, don't mistake the nature of this collision. You're up against someone with a hard head, who is not known for backing off. You may come out of it with a bad headache. Don't say I didn't warn you."

His eyes held hers, and she didn't try to look away until she'd said: "My goodness, Governor, there's no point in even asking, is that a threat? Nothing could be clearer. I can only say I'll have to rely on the truth as my shield and armor. And thanks for lunch."

Later, Mike Hughes thought long and hard about that lunch and wondered if it had been a mistake. Bea had offered him nothing; nor had she assuaged his fears. She'd just held her ground, and of course he *had* threatened her. Now he had to figure out how to back up the threat, what, if anything, he could do about her book. Once again, the answer he came up with was named Freddie Kohl.

As he got to like the man less and less, he was pulled closer and closer to him. As he more and more wanted to break away, he more and more needed him. The man is detestable, Mike said to himself. He's made me cunt-crazy. How in hell did I get along without it all those years? I don't know, but I did. He's a slimy pimp, Mike thought. And then asked himself: What are you—a child molester? Damned near.

I should walk out on him and his goddamned orgies, Mike told himself. He's pulled me down into the same snake pit he's in. Well, then climb out! Mike answered himself: It's too late now, he said. You're already damned for it.

Bullshit, that's just rationalization.

Yes, it is, he admitted. But he didn't want to stop.

As long as you don't stop, he reminded himself, you can't dump Freddie. Then he had to admit, it was not a question of not wanting to dump Freddie. He *couldn't*.

True, Freddie had gotten him into this mess. But Freddie had also helped get him into Congress. And into the Governor's mansion. And maybe into the White House. And Freddie was the man to blunt Bea Fletcher's hatchet. If anyone could.

No, he couldn't dump Freddie. Not yet.

Labor Day Weekend, 1977;
Sunday (continued)

THE DEATH of Kohl, if it was suspicious, could be dangerous to the Governor's career—Wisniewski could see that. He could also see that the two men had been closer than Hughes was willing to let on. Yet he felt it unthinkable that the Governor of the state would kill anyone, and he had to force himself to ignore that feeling. Hughes had made a point of his toughness and he'd been close to Kohl, and Wisniewski had learned that in a murder—if it *was* a murder, he had to keep reminding himself of that, too—first look to those closest to the victim.

But the Governor? Well, maybe not Hughes himself, but it would be easy for him to get someone else to do it. He mustn't rule anyone out. After all there'd been, counting the two he'd already talked to—he tallied them mentally—thirteen people besides Kohl at this house last night. Maybe more. Maybe a casual intruder in the early hours of the morning—someone who'd arrived to rob the house, or steal one of the cars, who'd encountered Kohl and killed him. That was possible too. A fourteenth person. But first he'd have to deal with those he knew.

The Governor. Sophie. The press secretary, Warren Daniels, and his date. Bea Fletcher. Bea's agent, Irv somebody. John Wainwright. A writer and his date, a young blonde. A young woman in publishing, Sally or Suzie. Carlotta Reilly, the TV anchorwoman, and her ex-husband—the Governor had called him Buster. His date, an actress named Betsy Shore.

Wisniewski fished a small pad out of his jacket pocket, found a ballpoint pen, listed the thirteen, sat there staring at them. Then he put checks next to Sophie and the Governor. Two down, eleven to go. He got up, headed for the house to find a phone book. He only had a few last names. First, Bea Fletcher. He found her number, jotted it down on the pad. Then Wainwright. John Wainwright lived only a few hundred yards away from Kohl. That might be his first stop. He picked up the phone, heard someone's voice speaking on another extension.

"... set the thing down right here on the lawn and get the Governor the hell ..." The voice stopped; the speaker had heard someone lift the other phone. "Who is this, please?" he asked sharply.

"This is Detective Wisniewski of the East Hampton police. Who is this?"

"This is the Governor's press secretary."

"Mr. Daniels?"

"Yes."

"Mr. Daniels, the Governor has agreed to stay here for a while. I think you know what's happened. It's important that I speak to you downstairs right away."

"Please hang up this phone!"

"Mr. Daniels, I'm sorry, I picked it up by accident. The Governor is not going anywhere for the time being. Please don't make any plans to have him leave. And please come downstairs so that I can talk to you."

"I'll be right down. Now hang up the phone!"

"Yes. I apologize for interrupting."

Daniels was down in a couple of minutes, tall and thin, in Ivy League uniform, Lacoste shirt, chino pants, topsiders with no socks. He strode angrily into the library, where the detective was still sitting next to the phone.

"You had no business listening ..."

"I said I was sorry, it was an accident."

"You can't order the Governor to stay here."

"I didn't order him to. I asked him to. And he agreed to."

"Well, he's changed his mind."

"I'd like to talk to him about that."

"You heard it from me, and that's good enough."

"I'm afraid it isn't."

"You have no right to keep the Governor . . ."

"Yes, I do."

"I'd like to see you try!"

"If he tries to leave I'll arrest him as a material witness."

"The courts will never let you, you'll be sued, you'll be destroyed."

"I'll just have to take my chances."

"We'll get you . . ."

"*We?* Who's the 'we'? The Governor? You? Get me for doing my job?" Now Wisniewski was angry and a little reckless. "I'll tell it all to the papers and the TV: How I was trying to do my job. How I had to arrest the Governor as a material witness in a homicide case. How you threatened to *get* me."

The look on Daniels' face changed. "The Governor has important business. He would always be available when you needed him."

"May I ask what the business might be on Sunday of Labor Day weekend?"

"Do you think that's any of your business?"

"Yes, I do, because just a few minutes ago, the Governor told me he'd been planning to spend the day here. That his wife would be joining him this afternoon."

"She won't be."

"Why is that?"

"Because we just called her and told her not to come. Do we need your permission for that, too?" Daniels voice was heavy with sarcasm, but his attack had been stopped and they both knew it.

"Of course not. *She* wasn't at the scene of a death which is under investigation. But the Governor was, and I'm grateful that he has agreed to stay." He waited for Daniels to disagree; the press secretary said nothing, so Wisniewski went on.

"And I hope you will stay, because you're a possible material witness, too." Now the detective could make the threat he hadn't wanted to make directly against the Governor. "There are two police officers in front of the house. I hope you won't make any plans to leave, or to bring in a 'copter."

Daniels just glared at Wisniewski. He was accustomed to having detectives open car doors for him and his boss, not order them around.

"I'd also appreciate your staying here for a couple of minutes right now to answer some questions about last night."

The press secretary seemed to be thinking about it. Then he said, "All right."

"Thank you, Mr. Daniels. Tell me what time you got back and who was here."

Daniels' account jibed with the Governor's, but he added names to the descriptions Wisniewski had. Irv Schnell, Harry Majors, Nellie Brandon, Sally Majors, Lolly Jones. Wisniewski now had a name for everyone.

"Can you tell me as much as you remember about what happened after you got here?"

"The Governor and I both went right to sleep, so I can't tell you about anything after that."

"Did you and the Governor sleep in the same room?"

"Of course not!"

"Adjoining rooms?"

"No."

"Would you tell me where his room is and where yours is? And where Mr. Kohl's is?"

"The Governor was given a bedroom at the west end of the house, mine was at the opposite end, overlooking the pool. Mr. Kohl's bedroom is next to mine. They're all upstairs."

"And you went right to sleep? Actually fell asleep right away?"

"Yes."

"So you can't really tell when the Governor fell asleep, or even if he stayed in his room, can you? I'm not trying to give you a hard time, Mr. Daniels. I just want to know what I can count on, and what I can't."

"The Governor *told* me what he did, and that's good enough for me!"

"He told me, too, Mr. Daniels. I'm not doubting his word, I'm just trying to find out what you actually saw and heard."

"You sound like a prosecutor."

"No, just a detective who knows enough law to do his job."

"A little knowledge is a dangerous thing."

"That's true, I suppose, Mr. Daniels. I do the best I can. Would you tell me about your date? Uh . . ." He looked down at his pad. "Miss Lolly Jones. Where was her room?"

He'd caught Daniels, he could see it on his face. The question had been perfunctory, innocent, but he'd tripped him up. His face flushed as he replied, "She stayed in my room, with me."

"Mr. Daniels, I don't mean to be rude. You say you fell asleep right away."

"I was very tired."

Wisniewski would have been less suspicious if he'd changed his story and admitted to having stayed awake for a while. Now he felt the press secretary was covering something. What? That he'd made love to his date? Not very embarrassing. That she hadn't been in the room with him at all? If not, where had she been? In her own room? Daniels would hardly hesitate to admit that. In someone else's room? Possible. But whose? Kohl's? Daniels wouldn't worry about protecting him. The Governor's room? Wisniewski would have to wait for answers. At least he was working up some good questions.

"Of course, Mr. Daniels. Was she in your bed? If I may ask?"

"Uh, yes."

He believed Daniels less with each answer. "Are you a light sleeper?"

"Moderate."

"Would Miss Jones have been able to get up and leave the room without awakening you?"

"I doubt it."

"Is she still asleep?"

"Oh no," Daniels said, quickly. "She had to catch the early train to the city, the eight-something, so I drove her to the station."

The station wagon that had been used this morning! Wisniewski had his explanation. And some new questions. "You drove her to the station at about eight?"

"A little before eight."

"And saw nothing? Didn't see Mr. Kohl's body in the pool?"

"Of course not! If I had I would have done something about it."

"Does your window look out on the pool?"

Daniels seemed to stop short. "Yes, but I didn't look out. I think the shade was drawn, and I was groggy. I just got her into the car to make the train." He paused a moment, added: "And you can't see the pool from the door I used. Or from the place where the station wagon was parked."

He was defending himself, Wisniewski could hear it. "And you drove right back and got into bed?"

"Right back into bed."

"What time was that?"

"Probably wasn't even eight-thirty."

"Did you wait for the train?"

"No."

"Did Miss Jones mind?"

"Is that any of your business?"

"No, I guess not."

"No, she didn't mind. She asked me not to stay."

"Did you fall asleep again?"

"I told you I was tired."

"When did you wake up?"

"The Governor awakened me to tell me about Mr. Kohl."

The detective paused. Sure, the whole story could be true. What could also be true was that the girl was *not* with Daniels, and his first move in the morning was to get her the hell out of there. Because he knew Kohl was dead? Because he knew who'd played a part in the death? Because *he'd* played a part in it? Or she had? Or the Governor? All possibilities. And nothing more—for the moment.

"Thank you, Mr. Daniels, for your cooperation. And for agreeing to stay around. If I have any more questions I'll look for you. Thanks."

Daniels said nothing, just nodded, turned and walked away.

Wisniewski picked up the phone, dialed John Wainwright's number.

"This is Detective Wisniewski of the East Hampton police. I'm conducting an investigation you may be able to help me with. May I come over and ask you some questions?"

In ten minutes, at Wainwright's beachfront house, he told him about Kohl's death, and found out that Wainwright, too, had seen and heard nothing. Had had one drink, talked to a few people, then gotten into his car and gone home. Didn't remember the time, probably about one or one-thirty. Wisniewski had the feeling this was the way it was going to be with all of them. Wainwright was hanging tough; he looked tough. Wisniewski took in the muscled body, figured he'd have little trouble disposing of Kohl in any way he wanted to. Then something happened that softened Wainwright. The day was growing hot, and the detective removed his jacket, sat there in his short-sleeved shirt. Wainwright spotted on his forearm the tattooed letters usmc.

"You were in the Corps?" he asked with a burst of interest.

"Yes, four years."

"I was, too, during World War Two. Pacific theater. First Division."

"*I* was in the First Division," Wisniewski replied. "I was in Vietnam."

Wainwright grinned at him, and was easier after that.

"Did Kohl have any enemies you know of?"

Wainwright laughed. "Everyone who knew him."

"Everyone?"

"Let's put it this way. I didn't know anyone who liked him. He was a tough, rude—yeah, ruthless—businessman. He was invading areas which were accustomed to gentleness, and he was ruining them. In my opinion, anyway."

"What areas?"

"The publishing business, for one. East Hampton, for another. Both happen to be sacred to me."

"Would it be fair to say you were an enemy?"

Wainwright shrugged. "Let's put it this way. There were times I could cheerfully have killed him myself." He smiled. "Of course I wouldn't say that if I *had!*"

Memorial Day Weekend, 1977

BETWEEN GEORGICA and Hook ponds the white beach stretched nearly two miles, and each morning he was in East Hampton Johnny Wainwright walked the few yards through the dunes from his house and then ran, first west to Georgica Pond and back, then east to Hook Pond and back. He'd start easily, at a jog, for the first mile or so, then begin punctuating the workout with a series of intervals, each a little harder and longer than the last, a training habit he'd gotten into as a quarter-miler at Exeter before World War II and then Yale after it.

He'd been using this stretch of beach that far back, too. At eight in the morning it seemed no different these days—just Johnny and a few gulls and sandpipers to share the sand and the ocean. Sure, if you kept your eyes on the dunes you saw some new houses—not many. Johnny and all the other owners of the big houses off Lily Pond Lane and West End Road kept this hunk of beach pretty well protected; thank God—and lots of dough—for that, Johnny said to himself.

But this beach, at this time of morning, was about all that had stayed the same around East Hampton.

In a few hours on this sunny Saturday in late May, Main Beach would look a little like Coney Island, and Main Beach was only a half-mile from his house. What he felt, Johnny would assure himself and anyone else, was an esthetic resentment, not an ethnic one.

He was thankful that the Main Beach masses were too lazy to make their way the half-mile down the beach to his house to destroy his privacy, but he had little else to thank them for. From Memorial Day to Labor Day—on weekends, but increasingly during the week, too— the village was a nightmare, the sidewalks jammed, the roads even worse, like a parking lot, cars crawling bumper-to-bumper through the village.

What everyone wanted in the village, Johnny couldn't imagine. To shop at the A&P? Have an ice cream cone? Browse in the bookstore? In July and August, when Johnny had to go into town on a weekend, he used a bicycle. To pick up his Sunday *Times*, he'd drive in before 8:30, and even then it was crowded. To get groceries, he'd telephone for a delivery, or have his housekeeper do the buying during the week.

Johnny was thankful for the beach at eight in the morning. He moved from his warmup jog into a brisk trot for fifty or sixty yards and then, breathing hard, slowed a bit. Except at the start, Johnny didn't believe in the dawdle most of the *arriviste* joggers used as an excuse for running. What a sight they were! On days he wasn't playing tennis, Johnny would stretch out on the beach, his own four miles well behind him, and watch all those unsuitable types make believe they were runners—hairy men with pot bellies and fleshy breasts wobbling, mincing along at a ten-minute-a-mile pace. Fat-bottomed, flabby-thighed women quivering like bowls of Jell-O as they plodded forward, hardly moving—Johnny could walk faster than they were jogging.

Johnny disliked *arrivistes*, in running, in East Hampton, in publishing. He recognized his bias, insisted it was only a question of style. Newcomers were always pushing to get in; they never knew how to act once they got in; they could never stop talking about having gotten in. They always seemed frantic, and to Johnny, the essence of style was ease.

At Yale he'd been a 50-second quarter-miler and in the late '40s that was damned fast. Even now, at fifty-two, he was lean and fit, could still run away from the men ten, fifteen, twenty years younger who bored the hell out of people with talk of their mileage and their injuries, and their shoes and the marathons they either ran or wanted to run.

His breathing slowed again, he began another interval, accelerating to about 80 percent of full speed, holding it for 100 yards, easing up. Johnny was in great shape for his age, and delighted in it; he loved the feel of his body responding to the demands he put on it. At Yale he weighed under 170 for track, a few pounds more when he won the school's light heavyweight boxing championship. These days he stayed under 180, none of it fat.

On the tennis courts of the Maidenhead—another place things hadn't changed, thank God—Buster Reilly was the only man over forty who could beat him, although not lately. Buster had gotten paunchy and boozy, and didn't play much, partly because he was in such bad shape, partly because he owed the club a lot of money and was embarrassed about it.

Watching Buster fall apart frightened Johnny. For one thing, he liked the man. For another, which hit closer to home, they were contemporaries, both athletes, both veterans of the war, both men who were used to doing business in a certain way, a way that seemed to be going out of style.

Thinking of Buster made him drive himself harder along the beach, pleased with the response of his feet, calves, thighs. He slapped himself on the gut to remind himself how lean and tough he was.

But a paunch was not his problem, and obsolescence was not a danger to be held off by situps and windsprints. The danger was, Johnny admitted, in his attitude. He hated to contemplate changing to suit the times. He wanted things to stay the way they were when he was twenty-five. Of course they hadn't; they were eroding. He fought like hell before giving up a single inch—this was his Verdun—but they were going.

He wanted the beach to stay the same, clean and unending and empty. He wanted the village to stay the same, serene, uncluttered by too many cars and too many people carrying too much Gucci. He wanted the Maidenhead to stay the same: convivial people, courteous bartenders who knew how to make dry martinis the way he liked them, perfect grass courts, with never a wait to play, manicured golf course, with never a wait to tee off, quiet dining room, with never a wait for a table.

He'd wanted his marriage to stay the same, but five years ago, Crackers—her real name was Mary; Crackers came from her maiden name, Graham—had taken the three boys and moved out. He'd been devastated. He'd liked the old way, and for the twenty-two years of their marriage, thought she had, too.

What had ended so badly in '72 had started in '50, in a golden glow. They'd married in June, right after he was graduated from Yale and she from Smith. They were a beautiful couple, both tall, both blond, both aristocratic, both from families with money and social cachet. In a year they had a son, John van Rensselaer Wainwright V, two years after that a second son, Graham, and two years after that the third, William Brewster, after his godfather.

Crackers was forty-four when she stood at the door, ready to walk out of their Park Avenue co-op. She looked him straight in the eye and said coldly, "In the twenty-two years of our marriage you have not given me one single orgasm."

Johnny was stunned. He hadn't known that; worse, he realized he hadn't ever thought to find out. Their lovemaking had never been voluptuous to him, and in recent years had been less and less frequent. More and more, Johnny slept with other women, although he never regarded them as a threat to his marriage.

As she turned to walk away, Johnny stopped her, saying: "You have not had *one* orgasm, in twenty-two years?"

She shook her head. "I didn't say I hadn't *had* one. I said . . ." and she pointed a finger at him, ". . . *you* never gave me one." Then she walked off.

In the years afterward, he brooded about that often, wondering if the orgasms she *had* had were achieved by her own hand or with the help of others, and if so, who those others were. He even had moments of conjecturing about there being other women, and to his surprise discovered he didn't care whether they were men or women, that he felt not a scintilla of jealousy.

What he resented, true conservative that he was, was the change in the status quo. If Crackers hadn't liked things as they were, why hadn't she said so before? Why, after twenty-two years, had she decided she resented his not giving her orgasms? Why, after twenty-two years, had she decided she resented his sleeping with other women? What changed things? What changed her? Damn, how he hated change!

Most of all, Johnny wanted publishing to stay the same, and that had changed on him, and hurt him, most of all.

His father, Big John Wainwright—no one ever called *him* Johnny—

was twenty-eight when, singlehandedly, he founded Saxon, and forty-one when after three unsuccessful tries at having a son—which was Big John's indelicate way of saying they'd had three daughters—his namesake was born. Big John would be ninety-three if he were alive today. Thank God, said Johnny, he wasn't; he was spared knowing what was happening to his business and his publishing house.

The Wainwrights and van Rensselaers were two old families with old money—lots of it—and so Big John had a running start when he set out to become a publisher. His goal was to publish good writing, and make money at it, which meant he'd take losses for a while to bring a talented author along, and might even take losses indefinitely on a few authors he believed in—provided the profitability of the rest of his list could absorb them. Those few prestigious writers he'd regard as loss leaders who attracted favorable attention to Saxon and made agents and writers want to do business with the house.

But those were the days of small, genteel publishing companies and small, genteel advances. Back then, *Publishers Weekly* and the *Times Book Review* rarely mentioned money at all, let alone the incredible six- and seven-figure deals one now read about every week.

Big John died in 1965 at the age of eighty-one, spared the vulgarization of the business he'd loved. He'd made a lot of money for Saxon and its authors, while insisting on publishing quality—Johnny reminded people of that.

Nine years later, in 1974, Johnny fought to remind his three older sisters of it. But they preferred listening to their investment advisers, who told them to grab the offer made for Saxon by a huge conglomerate, WTI.

WTI—Western Tire, Inc., a goddamned tire company! Even now, years later, the thought of it gave him angry energy, made him pound hard with those thigh muscles, lift the knees, drive across the hard sand, arms pumping, elbows high on the back thrust.

A goddamned tire company!

They'd gotten a splendid deal from WTI; Johnny had no money worries, but then he hadn't from the day he was born. And for the moment he had no prestige worries, for he'd stayed on as president of Saxon. But from 1975 on, when the WTI deal took effect, Saxon was no longer Johnny's company. He had to report to an executive vice president, account for the numbers on his balance sheet, just as if he were running a division turning out truck parts, auto seat covers, sporting goods, kitchen hardware, tires, or any of the other diverse enterprises in what their TV commercials called "the WTI family of companies."

How did you tell a VP who'd climbed to the top as a super mer-chandiser of tires that such-and-such a novel, on which Saxon had lost so-and-so many dollars, had been nominated for a National Book Award, which made it all worthwhile? Or that you turned down a Hollywood gossip novel because it was trash—even though it did get a half-million dollar film sale?

He began to see that WTI looked at books and tires in exactly the same way. It saw two colors, black, which was good, and red, which was bad. Red ink meant something had to change, and the first change WTI made was to put a watchdog-in-residence at Saxon, a thirty-two-year-old MBA named Rod Lannon, whose title was corporate liaison officer and whose job was to keep an eye on costs and on Johnny.

Lannon called Johnny "Jack," which he hated. He began to undercut Johnny's authority, which he hated even more. Lannon would question the advances being paid, question why Saxon hadn't got such-and-such a best seller, question the sales figures of Saxon novels. He began to talk directly with Molly Eckhardt, Johnny's editor-in-chief.

Johnny found it out when the editor walked into his office and told him. "The damned fink!" she said. "He wanted to know what books I'd liked that had been turned down, and how I thought we could get more *big* books into the house, and said if I spotted anything really *big* I should feel free to bring it directly to him!"

"What did you say?" Johnny asked, trying not to show his fury.

"I told him that right now I was bringing books directly to the best executive in publishing, John Wainwright, and I had no intention of changing that."

"Thanks, Molly. But I guess they have every intention of changing it. I've got a title and an office, but I'm only a paid employee. Since the Wainwrights don't own Saxon anymore, I run it only as long as it pleases them. It's becoming clear that what pleases me doesn't please them, so it looks like one of us is going to have to go—and they own the place."

"Don't go, Johnny."

"Why not? If I'm going to turn out the kind of drivel they want, I accomplish nothing by staying. By leaving I can avoid being an ac-complice in the crimes they're committing."

Molly Eckhardt was a bright woman in her mid-forties who'd worked with Johnny for a long time and was not afraid to disagree. "That's one way to do it, Johnny. The neat, clean, romantic, chivalrous, nineteenth-century way. Avoid complicity. Also avoid responsibility."

"Christ! Even my friends think I'm outmoded! I'm beginning to feel like a dinosaur, just waiting to topple over and sink into a bog. I thought the name of this game was to find the next James Joyce. Or at least the next Scott Fitzgerald. Hell, I'd settle for the next Joe Heller! Now what are you asking me to do? Join the hunt for the next Jacqueline Susann?"

"Maybe I am. Because maybe that's the only way you can also stay in position to find the next Joyce, or whomever. Maybe I'm just being selfish. I know you can walk away with your head held high, and your flags flying and your principal, with an 'a-l,' intact, which will yield you enough income to let you keep your principles, spelled with an 'l-e,' intact, too.

"I also know there are a lot of good people, and modesty does not prevent me from saying I'm one of them, who can't afford to walk away with you, who'll have to keep on working here, or somewhere in this business, and who will gladly join the hunt for the next Jackie Susann, in return for a shot at the next Joyce. Or maybe not the next Joyce, but someone like Bellow or Heller or Vonnegut who, *mirabile dictu,* is both talented *and* profitable. Each time another White Knight in this business gallops off in a cloud of righteous indignation, we working slobs lose one more chance to continue our furtive search for quality."

Johnny got up and kissed her on the cheek. "You stop me short, Molly, as usual. Why are you always so damned sensible? The problem is, my being here will make no difference. WTI and its errand boy Lannon will do the same thing with me as without me." He was waiting for her to prove him wrong; she did a good job of it.

"I've done a little reading about WTI—you know me, Johnny, always the researcher—and they're interested only in the bottom line. If a division shows a profit, they leave it alone. If it runs in the red, they send in an 'errand boy,' you call him. I call him a hatchet man. Saxon has been in the red for a couple of years now. Get it in the black and they'll call Lannon off. Get it in the black and they won't give a damn if you publish nothing but obscure poetry and leatherbound Proust. I would cheerfully devote some of my time to the schlock hunt if it kept you around and gave us some time and money to look for quality. If you go, Johnny, schlock hunting is *all* we'll do. Think about it, will you? Give us a break."

The more he thought about it, the more he came to respect Molly's view. But a new fear developed; Johnny began to question his taste in junk. What could be more embarrassing than to go for a piece of trash—only to have it flop! He'd have to slink off with neither publishing house nor dignity.

Then he read "WashingtonShock" in *Scope*.

Several things about it impressed him: Bea was a skillful writer, no one to be embarrassed about. In writing about the foibles, sexual and other, of the gliterati, Bea had an immensely salable commodity. Johnny knew Bea. He also knew her agent, Irv Schnell; they'd worked together on several projects and respected each other.

Soon he found out "WashingtonShock" was the beginning of a book, the main part of which would be not the scandals of the Washington world, but of his own Hamptons. He hated gossip and scandalmongering, but he kept replaying Molly's words about saving Saxon.

Finally Johnny made an appointment with Robert Warfield, the senior vice president, something he'd never done before. Usually he had to be dragged up from his offices at Park and 33rd to the WTI headquarters at Park and 50th; this time he volunteered, was shown into the VP's corner office. From the start Warfield had known enough to call him Johnny, not Jack, and asked to be called Rob, not Bob.

"How's it going, Johnny?" Warfield asked. He was about forty, very tall, trim, hair just a bit too short to be mod, a bit too long to be square, cleverly designed to fit in at Le Club and the Yale Club, without being typical at either place.

"We've got some exciting prospects, Rob . . ." Johnny knew publishers always began that way, but he said it nonetheless. "We've also got some problems."

"I know." Warfield said it to fit either the prospects or the problems —in the middle, like his haircut.

"Our biggest problem is morale," Johnny continued. "A lot of our people are worried that Saxon is no longer running its own ship, that our house, which after all is one of the most, perhaps *the* most, prestigious in the business, is not being given a chance to . . ."

Shaking his head, Warfield snapped an interruption. "Your biggest problem—*our* biggest problem—is not morale. It is your profit-and-loss picture, which for the past three years shows no profit, and more and more loss, and looks like it's headed that way again for '77. That is the problem from which all your problems—*our* problems—stem.

That's why Lannon is there. You see, Johnny . . ." Warfield looked at his watch, walked to a bar in the corner of the office. "It's four-thirty; I'll allow myself a glass of sherry. What would you like?"

None of your executive martinis or Scotches, very civilized, Johnny thought. He decided he didn't want to be all that civilized or even particularly civil. "Nothing, thanks," he said.

Warfield gave a small shrug, poured his sherry and walked back to his desk.

"You see, Johnny," he began again, "WTI bought Saxon with the intention of turning it around, making it profitable. That's my job. The president of this corporation is watching. So is the chairman. So are the directors and the stockholders. If, at the end of this year, Saxon shows another loss, as it will, Johnny, as it will, they'll ask me why. They'll ask me what I'm doing to change it, and when it will change. And I must have answers. I *will* have answers. And your 1957 annual report will not do as an answer. Nor will the number of National Book Awards Saxon has . . ."

"Rob, a book is not an automobile tire!"

Warfield smiled, almost patronizingly. "I knew you'd get around to that. It might interest you to know I majored in English lit at Brown, gave serious thought to going for my doctorate, and teaching, on the *college* level. I like to think, John, I am aware of the difference between a book and an automobile tire."

Johnny hated the dripping sincerity; hated the way Warfield was leaning forward, gesturing with his horn-rimmed glasses like a doctor in a patent medicine commercial. He wanted to tell him to shove it, then get up and walk out; the feeling came close enough to make his thigh muscles tense, to begin lifting him out of the velvety-soft black leather chair he was in. Then he thought of Molly and all the other editors who had to work for a living and couldn't follow him out. He'd be walking out on them; he'd also be walking out on Saxon, a damned fine name. He cursed himself for not making some provision for holding on to the name of Saxon—but he realized it was the name WTI was buying. The name was, in fact, all they wanted. If he left, he'd be leaving the name to the exploitation of people like Warfield and Lannon.

He untensed his legs, sat where he was. "Brown, eh? I remember they had a fine English department, Rob. I happened to major in the same thing at Yale, and I wasn't suggesting you didn't know the difference. I was just . . ."

Warfield had seen the rebellion, and seen Johnny come back into the corral. "What I was about to say, John, was that while I know the difference, I also know the similarity. In running each division, in merchandising each product, from tires to books and everything in between, our objective is profitability. That is what we're responsible to our shareholders for. Now I've done a little homework in your industry; there are houses making money. Our job is to find out why Saxon isn't one of them, and then *make* it one of them. And from now on you people on the front lines at Saxon are going to have a lot of expert backup, from me, from Rod Lannon, from the whole WTI organization, in merchandising, sales, market research, advertising and promotion, accounting, everything, and you should think of us as a support team, helping to make Saxon a winner."

Johnny almost felt he should jump and yell, "Yea, team!" but Warfield wasn't finished. His prim, handsome face turned stern. He gesticulated again with the horn-rims. "And make no mistake, Johnny, we've *got* to make Saxon a winner. We *will* turn it around. Other houses have done it."

"By publishing junk."

"That is negative thinking! Perhaps you don't understand me. We are not in business to satisfy the *New York Review of Books*. Or the American Academy of Arts and Letters. Saxon is not the conscience of the industry, it is a *part* of it, and we intend it to be a profitable part of it. We have nothing against encouraging a few worthwhile young writers, but that is secondary. Profitability is first. Saxon is no longer one man's, or one family's plaything; it is accountable to corporate ownership. If you find that unpalatable, Johnny, for both our sakes you should say so, so you and we can make our separate plans, go our separate ways. I'm not going to threaten you by telling you we're going to turn Saxon around *with* you or *without* you. We prefer it to be with you; you're a respected man with a respected name. But you must understand the direction in which things are moving. Think it over. We don't want to pressure you . . ."

Without saying the "but," he left no doubt it was there. Then he rose from his chair, walked around his desk and held out his hand. Johnny had no choice but to stand and take it. The meeting was over.

"I hope we understand each other," Warfield said as he walked Johnny to the door.

"Yes, I think we do." Johnny *did* understand Warfield, and decided Molly Eckhardt was right.

"One thing more," Warfield said. "We're going to have to see some dramatic development this year. The wolves are already howling." Johnny was amused at the way Warfield referred to the wolves as if he were not one of them—and the chief howler, at that.

"Well, I hope we understand each other," Warfield repeated, and Johnny repeated, "Yes, I think we do."

"And just let me know what I can do to help," Warfield added as he closed his office door.

Johnny walked away less and less inclined to quit. Molly had said WTI was essentially interested in the bottom line, and so they were. There'd been many years when Saxon's bottom line had been a healthy profit, while they were turning out fine books. That could happen again. Johnny deplored the changes in the business, but he knew his choice now was to try it the new way or quit. More and more the new way in publishing resembled the tinsel and the schlock of the movie business, yet Johnny saw something redeeming in that. If one blockbuster could turn a studio around, maybe it could also save a publishing house.

Maybe Bea Fletcher could save Saxon for Johnny.

And she wasn't a bad writer. Not bad at all. That made the medicine a lot less bitter. Of course he was disturbed by what he heard about the hatchet job she was doing on the Hamptons. He didn't like gossip in general; he didn't like the idea of her fouling her own nest, especially when it happened to be his nest, too. He didn't like the possibility he might be a lead character. And he liked least of all that, after all his protestations, Johnny Wainwright, of the fine old house of Saxon, might be publishing the book. He pictured the derision in the publishing world, if John van Rensselaer Wainwright IV should not only publish gossip, but Hamptons gossip at that!

Yes, there was a lot for Johnny to worry about. More worries piled in; he picked up his pace along the beach as if to get away from them. Supposing he went after Bea's book, and couldn't land it? Then he'd have traded in his good name for nothing. Supposing he got the book, published it, and it bombed? Then he'd be leaving Saxon, but not with his head high and his flags flying.

Moving at a good clip now, Johnny reached Hook Pond, turned and headed into the home stretch. He had perhaps a half-mile to go, and he began picking up, lengthening his stride. It'd been a couple of months since he'd decided to go for Bea's book; it'd be a couple more before he knew the outcome. He'd been in a lot of book negotiations, and thought he was pretty cool about them, but this one had him in suspense.

He still had trouble taking in the size of the hard-soft offer he'd let Sally talk him into. Their original talk of a $1.5 million figure had been wild enough. But their final offer, $2.3 million, was almost beyond his comprehension. And for a book of Hamptons gossip!

Of that amount, $500,000 would come from Saxon and $1.8 million from Greyhound, a prodigious sum for a first novel, but one that they'd get back in sales—especially paperbacks, when the movie or the TV series came out—Sally assured him of that. Johnny could see clearly that Bea would make a lot of money, a $2.3 million advance, plus film or TV rights. What he couldn't see so clearly, what worried him, was what Saxon and Greyhound would make. They'd have to sell a hell of a lot of books to make that advance back.

Something else worried him even more. He'd made the half-million-dollar commitment without first clearing it with Lannon, Warfield or anyone at WTI. It had been a risky move, which he made for several reasons. First, he was afraid he might get a no from the corporate brass or get tied up in red tape while they tried to make a decision. Then there was ego: Johnny felt he'd be diminished, in his own eyes, in the eyes of the industry, if he had to get permission to commit Saxon to the offer.

If WTI found out, they could disown the offer, they could fire Johnny for it, or at the very least, humiliate him publicly. As of now the offer was secret, nobody but Johnny, Sally, Irv and Bea knew—at least Johnny hoped it was only the four of them. Should WTI refuse to go along, Johnny had another idea: get some backing and publish it under his own imprint. But there was a hitch there, too. Johnny had made the offer as an officer of Saxon. WTI could choose to honor it—and still fire Johnny for having made it. They could get Bea's book, and unload Johnny at the same time, which would leave him without Saxon and without the book.

He couldn't trust WTI. He *knew* he couldn't trust Freddie. And he wondered if he could trust Sally. She was devoted to winning, and if that meant deserting him, would she refuse to? If that were in her mind, shouldn't Johnny beat her to the punch, and join Freddie first? No, Johnny didn't do things like that. Not the old Johnny, anyway. But he was trying to be the *new* Johnny, and what the new Johnny would do, should do, not even the old Johnny knew.

A hundred yards from home, Johnny leaned forward a little and drove ahead as hard as he could. Running didn't solve the problems but it did dull the pain they caused; it made him feel young and strong and vital, not like a fifty-two-year-old dinosaur. Perhaps, come to think of it, he'd rather *be* a dinosaur, and not survive to see the day when snots like Lannon and philistines like Warfield ruined a great publishing house, when wheeler-dealers like Kohl contaminated the business with outlandish offers, when a snip like Sally could lead a Johnny Wainwright by the hand into the realm of big money—when the object of all this greed was a destructive bit of gossip about a place which was once the realm of elegance.

In a burst of speed, he broke an imaginary tape, slowed to a trot, then a walk, breathing hard, covered with sweat, feeling good. Yeah, he told himself as he headed to the house, maybe it was better to go the way of the dinosaur than adapt to *that* kind of change. Thank God for the quiet of the beach, the easy swooping of the gulls, the eternity of the ocean waves. Those things at least would stay the same. God, how he hated change! How he'd love to destroy those dark angels of change who were destroying the world he loved.

Labor Day Weekend, 1977;
Sunday (continued)

"MAY I use your phone, please?" the detective asked Johnny.

"Want privacy?"

"Yeah, please." Wisniewski said it with a smile. "Got to explain to the little woman why I'm gonna be late for dinner. She won't like it."

"Of course. People do die at the most inconvenient times." Wainwright smiled back, led him to a small study, pointed to the phone.

"Yeah, no consideration. Thanks." He sat down next to the phone, watched the publisher leave and close the door. Then he looked at the list he'd put together, for which Wainwright had supplied addresses and phone numbers. His eye ran to the next man's name on the list. Had he been accused of being a male chauvinist, he'd have been surprised. To him it was only natural that when you dealt with a possible crime of violence you checked out the men first. And there was no doubt, the more he thought about it, that if there was any crime here, it was a violent one. Kohl *could* have hit his head as he'd fallen into the pool and been knocked unconscious, but that wasn't likely. What was more likely was that if he'd fallen in accidentally, or been pushed in, he'd have shouted for help, and someone would have heard. On the other hand, if he'd been pushed in and his head had been held under . . .

The next man on the list was Buster Reilly and his number began with 537, which meant it was in Bridgehampton. He dialed it; a sleepy voice answered.

"Mr. Reilly?"

"Yes."

"Pardon me for disturbing you, sir, this is Detective Wisniewski of the East Hampton police. It's important that I ask you a few questions about an investigation I'm conducting. May I drop by to see you?"

"When?"

"In ten minutes. This is important."

"Well, then, OK."

"Thank you; I'll be right there."

"It's the second house on the left on Ocean Road, after Bridge Lane."

"Fine, thank you."

It wasn't until he hung up and checked the remaining man's name, Harry Majors, that he noticed it was in East Hampton. Maybe he should go there first. No, he'd already told Reilly he'd be over. He dialed Majors' number, identified himself, asked him not to leave until he got there.

"How long?" Majors asked.

"Less than an hour."

"OK, it'll take me that long to unstick my eyes."

Wisniewski hung up, wondering about these people. He looked around the study, at the richness of the leather-bound books on the shelves, the oil paintings, the paneled walls. He figured the stuff in this room alone cost more than his whole house. He'd been in the Wainwright mansion—that's what they all called it—once before, perhaps twenty-five years ago, when he was a kid, helping his uncle, who was a plumber. He'd been overwhelmed by it, and he realized it still awed him. Of course Kohl's house was pretty impressive, too, although everything seemed newer. Perhaps Kohl's stuff cost even more. And right now Kohl was lying cold and stiff, maybe already being cut apart by the medical examiner. His big house and furniture and money hadn't helped him. The opposite, Wisniewski figured, it probably hurt him, maybe killed him. On the way to the top he'd made enemies. Who'd said that? Wisniewski thought for a moment: they'd *all* said it, Sophie, the Governor, Wainwright.

So his money wasn't doing Kohl any good now. And the number of enemies he'd made wasn't helping Wisniewski much. He let out a sigh; he guessed he should call home and warn Lee not to plan an early dinner.

When he finally walked out and found Wainwright, he could truthfully say, "Thanks. My wife thinks I'm actually getting thoughtful in my old age."

"Oh, you're welcome. Anytime."

"And Mr. Wainwright, I'd appreciate it if you kept our little talk to yourself."

"Of course."

"One more thing. Were you planning on going back to the city today?"

"No, I was not, and am not."

"Good. It's important."

"I *am* staying, Detective Wis . . ."

"Wisniewski."

"Sorry, I didn't quite get it the first time."

"Almost nobody does."

Wainwright smiled, stuck out his hand. The detective took it, felt the strength of his grip. Oh yeah, Wisniewski thought, that hand could do the job. Hell, he might even give Sophie a tussle. The detective walked to his beat-up Toyota, which was parked next to Wainwright's 450SL. The car, he figured, was worth around $25,000, the house, three-quarters of a million, maybe a million. His total life's earnings would add up to the cost of Wainwright's weekend house. Another world. How could he ever hope to find out what was going on? He shrugged, turned on the ignition, drove off to the highway, left at Ocean, to Reilly's driveway.

He looked up at Reilly's house; this one might cost him only twenty years' pay, he figured, which didn't make him feel a lot better. His first look at Reilly did nothing to improve his mood—here was someone else who could have tossed Kohl around with ease, have held his head under water or done anything else he'd damn well felt like. Reilly was going to flab—the bags under his eyes alone looked like they weighed more than all of Freddie Kohl—but there was power in the neck and the arms and shoulders.

Reilly's response to the news of Kohl's death was surprising. "If you're waiting for me to say how sorry I am, I hope you brought an overnight bag, because you've got a wait."

"Did you know him well?"

"Well enough to know he was a bastard. But then if you've talked to anyone else I'm sure that's not news to you."

"You didn't think of him as a close friend?"

"Are you kidding? Did anyone?"

"I was going to ask you that."

"No one I know of."

He went on to the same questions he'd asked the others, and got the same answers. Reilly had got there about midnight, had been drinking a fair amount, stayed awhile, talking to everyone and no one in particular, then left.

What time?

"God knows, I don't think I could tell time when I drove home."

"That's kind of dangerous, Mr. Reilly."

"I know it. Is all this really a coverup for a drunken-driving investigation? No, forget that. I don't mean to be flip about it; you're right. Maybe I'm trying to kill myself."

"I'm thinking of the other people you might kill. Other drivers. Other people in your car. Was there anyone in the car with you?"

"No." He paused, looked confused. "My God, then where's Betsy?"

"Miss Shore?"

"Yes, she was my weekend guest. She had dinner with me and we went over to Freddie's. I left without her. I guess she must have fallen asleep there and spent the night."

"May I use your phone for a moment?" Almost without waiting for an answer, the detective phoned Kohl's house. Sophie answered.

"Would you put the Governor's press secretary on, please, Sophie?"

He waited. Finally a man's voice said, "Yes?"

"Mr. Daniels?"

"Yes."

"This is Detective Wisniewski again."

"Yes, I know."

"Mr. Daniels, a young woman named Betsy Shore spent the night at the Kohl house. May I speak with her, please?"

There was a pause. "She's not here."

"Where is she?"

"She went back to New York."

"When? How?"

Another pause. Then the voice, reluctantly: "I drove her to the station with Miss Jones."

"Why didn't you tell me that, Mr. Daniels?"

Now the voice was tight, defensive. "You didn't ask. You asked about Miss Jones."

"Did you drive anyone else to the station?"

"No."

"Is there anyone at the house besides you, the Governor, Sophie and the two police officers?"

"Yes, two Suffolk County detectives arrived to dust for fingerprints."

So the county guys were in on it; he guessed he'd have to expect that, after the body was taken to the morgue, but he wished they weren't.

"Anyone *else?*"

"No, no one else."

"Mr. Daniels, would you call one of the East Hampton officers to the phone, please?"

"Just a minute."

Another voice came on. "Wiz? It's Billy."

"Hey, Billy, do two things for me. Check all the rooms to see if anyone else is there besides the Governor and his assistant and the housekeeper. Don't let any of them leave. OK?"

"Sure."

"Thanks. And Billy, don't tell the county boys anything you don't have to. Don't tell 'em I called. OK?"

"OK. Where are you, by the way?"

"Just talking to some people. On my way from one place to another. I'll call you later."

He walked back to Reilly. "Thanks. Your guest supposedly took the morning train back to the city. Do you know where she lives?"

"Sure."

"Do me a favor, will you, Mr. Reilly? Give her about another hour to get home, and then call her and ask her to come back out here. By train, by jitney, Rent-a-Car, any way she wants. We'll pay for it. But she must be back here. We'll send a police car for her if we have to."

"That important?"

"Mr. Reilly, we found a dead man this morning floating in his own pool. It could have been a heart attack, but more likely it was drowning. We don't know if it was accidental or not, but we know it happened sometime last night. We also know there were a lot of people at the house last night, yet no one I've talked to so far heard anything or saw anything. This is not just a coverup for a drunken-driving investigation. Or for illegal parking. It's serious. OK?"

He saw the temper flare and then fade in Reilly's blue eyes. "Yeah, OK. Anything else I can help you with?"

"Would you describe Miss Shore?"

"You've probably seen her, or her type, on television. Mid to late thirties—don't ever tell her I said that—platinum blonde, medium height, about maybe 115, 118 pounds, very sexy, big bosom for a little girl."

"Is she athletic? Play tennis? Swim? Jog?"

"Not that I've ever noticed. I have heard her talk about exercise classes, though."

"Would you say she was a strong woman, Mr. Reilly?"

He smiled at the detective. "Strong enough to drown Freddie? She's a dainty thing, wrists like a bird. Of course I don't think Freddie could swim, I've never seen him do anything but splash, so maybe it wouldn't take much. Still, he was a wiry little guy; he could get surprising velocity behind a tennis ball, if he hit it right—which he did once every couple of sets."

Reilly stopped smiling. "But Freddie had a way of humiliating people that would give his eighty-year-old arthritic grandmother enough strength to kill him. That's if he *had* an eighty-year-old arthritic grandmother. I'll tell you something else: if he had one, and if she got in the way of a deal of his, he'd try to humiliate *her*, too. So you better question her."

"Did he ever humiliate you, Mr. Reilly?"

Reilly looked at the detective and paused. "What makes you ask? Checking me out as a suspect? Listen, I wouldn't have to bother with drowning him. I'd get a kick out of snapping his neck." Reilly gestured with his big hands, and Wisniewski didn't doubt he could do it.

"Well, his neck was not at a funny angle, Mr. Reilly," he said. "So I guess that lets you out."

"Unless I also snapped it back into place."

Wisniewski smiled at him. "Then I better keep an eye on you. You are going to stick around town, aren't you?"

"If you'd like—I was planning to anyway."

"And please call Miss Shore. It's important that she get right back here. I *will* send a police car for her if I have to."

Both men stood. Reilly was an even bigger man than Wisniewski had thought, four or five inches taller and perhaps forty pounds heavier than he. When they shook hands, Reilly gave an extra squeeze that made the detective wince. He knew the big man had done it as a joke, so he nodded. "Yes, you *could* snap his neck."

Reilly laughed. "But I didn't. After all, what the hell did I have to be angry at him for?"

A June Weekend, 1977

BUSTER AWOKE suddenly, dazed, not knowing where he was, what day, what time of day. That happened often lately, when he was out drinking the night before. Then he remembered it was Saturday, he could relax. The air was cool, the sun coming through the window promised a lovely day. He squinted at his watch: 10:50. He got the feeling he should be somewhere, sat up quickly.

The real estate office, at eleven! A second time he looked at his watch: 10:51, he'd never make it. As he looked down, he noticed the rolls of flab around his middle. Disgusting, but what he deserved. Fat, out of shape, broke, divorced, a boozer, at a dead-end.

Oh Christ, he told himself, don't be so cheerful!

I've got nothing to be cheerful about, he reminded himself. Nearly fifty-four and in bad shape in every way. So bad, he was going to sell this house he loved. God, how he hated that!

He got to his feet slowly, to ease the throbbing of the hangover that awoke with him every morning these days, walked to the phone and called Bruce Boys' real estate office. One of Bruce's boys answered; Buster hated the inflection of so many gay men's voices, and no one but gays worked for Bruce. People called them Boys' girls, but Bruce had one of the best real estate offices in the Hamptons, and Buster didn't have to take a shower with them, he just wanted them to sell his house.

"Tell Bruce that Buster Reilly will be a little late. Thanks."

The prospect of selling this house, which he loved, was appalling, but Buster was broke. To a lot of his old friends from the South Bronx, who'd become cops, firemen, construction workers, especially priests, it'd be tough to explain how you could be broke and in debt on $100,000 a year. To people in the Hamptons, for whom $100,000 was merely the fringe of solvency, it would be easy.

Start with a huge tax bite, add one child at boarding school and two at private day schools ($13,000 a year), one apartment ($12,000 a year), taxes, upkeep, mortgage payments on the Bridgehampton house ($800 a month), plus child support, restaurant and bar tabs, clothing, and the rest of the inflated life style he'd taken on, and the answer was easy. The addition was dismaying. The wonder was that he could make it at all; in fact, he no longer could. And when his contract at UBC expired at the end of the year, the chances were he'd not be rehired. Buster was no longer in step at the network. He suspected that his last contract was a sop to Carlotta, star anchorperson.

Moving as fast as he could, Buster reached the real estate office just before 11:30. He was led by one of the slim young men into Bruce Boys' office.

"Honestly, Buster," Bruce said, "there's so little money in a winter rental, I personally don't think it's worth the wear and tear on the house."

"I wasn't . . . actually . . . thinking of a winter rental." Buster could hardly take the pain.

Bruce's eyebrows lifted. "The summer? Of course. We'll get a wonderful price for it; I just thought you were *mad* for your summers out here."

"Oh . . . I've been thinking about a change of scene. You know, nine years is a lot of summers in one place. In fact, I've been considering the possibility, that if you got a good offer . . . the possibility of . . . selling the place." He found it tough to make the words come out.

This time Bruce's carefully tanned, carefully tended face showed real surprise. "Do you want me to list it?"

Buster tried to keep the talk academic. "What do you suppose it would sell for these days?"

"Let's see." Bruce touched his face under the left eye, looked toward the ceiling. "How many bedrooms?"

"Five. Three baths."

"About a mile from the beach?"

"Less. Almost two acres. Concrete twenty-by-forty swimming pool—heated. It's in top condition, well insulated, new oil burner, hot water heating. Low heating bills, low taxes."

"It's a *marvelous* house. Is there room for a tennis court?"

"Absolutely. I've been thinking about putting one in. I . . . just never got around to it." He didn't want Bruce to smell need, although he figured it was too late, the aroma was all over the place.

"What do you think it could sell for?"

Bruce pursed his lips, hesitated. "I'd say two hundred fifty thousand. Maybe two seventy-five."

Buster nodded. Nine years ago, he'd bought the house for $55,000, put in a pool for $9,500, put another $25,000 into it. Not a bad profit. But how he loved that house! How he didn't want to sell. He winced at the prospect; Bruce misinterpreted the wince.

"I think with some luck, with the right buyer, we might even get three. Shall I list it?"

Buster took a deep breath, tried to seem casual. "Yes." He shrugged. "Yes, list it." He spoke the words very quietly, and at once turned to walk out.

"Uh, Buster, would you mind filling out this card?" Bruce handed him a 5-by-7 card and an old-fashioned fountain pen.

Depressed, humiliated, Buster tried to concentrate as he filled it out, barely looked at Bruce as he handed him the card. "Let me know, will you?" And without waiting for an answer, Buster stood, half-waved, turned and walked out.

"Shit!" He shouted it as he walked toward his car. Then he said something he thought of often these days. "Bring back the war!" He'd never say that to anyone, even thought it childish when he said it to himself. But he meant it. World War II had been glorious for him. Exciting. A triumph. He'd left it with the gold leaf of a major, a bemedaled paratrooper—a war hero.

He'd also come to say something else about the war: that the glory, the excitement, the triumph of it had probably fucked up his whole life, because after it, everything seemed dull, an anticlimax. Every time some asshole pygmy vice president spent three hours weighing the "boldness" of buying one carbon-copy comedy series or another, Buster would think about the danger, the thrill of the war.

In his network job there was no thrill. Especially after the "new breed" of scientific programmers took over, he approached the work with cynicism, aloofness, a feeling of What am I doing here? With the help of the GI Bill, he'd gotten there via Dartmouth, an unusual route for a construction worker's son from the South Bronx.

As a scholar, Buster made Phi Beta Kappa; as a single-wing tailback, he made all-Ivy, all-East and a couple of All-America honorable mentions. He turned down a pro-football offer to get an MBA at the Amos Tuck School. Pro football, he decided, was not classy.

When he got out of school in 1950, he was not quite twenty-seven, a war hero, a football hero with an excellent academic record, and a handsome, eligible bachelor. In the next years he ran through three executive training programs and one marriage. The marriage was a total failure—one good year, two terrible years, then a divorce. The training programs led him to a bank and two major corporations, and were only a partial failure, for by the time he was thirty-five he'd reached the middle executive level, despite the flightiness of his career.

When he was thirty-five, an Amos Tuck classmate suggested he consider a broadcasting career, and set up an interview with a UBC executive to discuss the expanding realm of television. Buster was charming and impressive; and he was interested. He was hired as a middle-level administrative executive. Once again, he skated easily on the surface, until he saw an area in which he wanted to dig in: programming. By forty, he was a vice president, second in command of network programming.

He'd thrived on "artistic" decisions, on dealing with creative people —only to find, within a few years, as he was pushing his way into programming, the artistic and creative criteria were being pushed out by marketing criteria. Numbers and demographics were the code words.

But if a career malaise was beginning to set in, the crisis was still years away. At forty, his life was exciting enough to make him forget his incipient dissatisfaction. Successful, glamorous, he was one of the most eligible men in town. Floods of invitations arrived at his East Sixty-sixth Street apartment; beautiful women arrived with fair frequency, too.

He was in a perfect spot to make an advantageous marriage; he dated women with money, family, connections, who could insure his career. But just before his fortieth birthday, he met Carlotta Barnes.

She was twenty-six, had just come down from Boston to do a local half-hour talk show on UBC's New York station. She was regarded as bright and capable, the best of the dozens who had auditioned, yet hardly destined for the popularity and power she was to achieve.

In that match, Buster was the "catch" and Carlotta, the young unknown, the lucky one. They met one morning in the UBC cafeteria. He noticed her on the coffee line; her good looks, the fearless pride in her eyes, the set of her head.

When he saw her go off with her coffee to sit alone, he said to the two men he was with, "Fellas, you're going to have to excuse me."

One of them, who'd seen him staring at Carlotta, asked with mock severity, "For how long?"

Buster grinned. "For as long as it takes."

Cup in hand, he walked over to where she was sitting, sipping her coffee and looking through a newsmagazine.

"Excuse me," he said. She looked up, those bold eyes asking why he was interrupting. But Buster was secure with women.

"I noticed you sitting alone, and I happened to be alone . . ."

"No you weren't," she said, but her smile said it was all right.

"No, I wasn't," he admitted. "But I was afraid if you were a fast coffee-breaker you might be gone before I could think of anything better. You are such a fine-looking woman, what I really want is to meet you. May I?" He nodded toward the chair.

"Yes, please."

"My name is Buster Reilly."

"Buster?" She was amused, also unaware of who he was.

He was pleased that she didn't know. "Buster's just a nickname but it's the only thing I've been called for a long time. The name actually is Brandon, named for Mount Brandon on the Dingle Peninsula, County Kerry, Ireland. Brandon is a variation of Brendan, as in Saint Brendan the Navigator, who *really* discovered America, centuries before the Vikings or Columbus—at least that's our Irish party line. My grandparents came from the town of Brandon, which is in the shadow of the mountain. I guess I got the Buster because I was such a strapping lad. I'm so used to it, I don't hear how silly it must sound."

"Not silly. Different. Actually, quite cute, if a little short on dignity.

But who needs dignity?" He could see she was young, apparently new, yet bold, almost sassy, in her responses.

"What's your name?"

"Carlotta Barnes."

"Are you new at the network?"

"I'm not at the network. I've just been signed to do a local half-hour talk show for women. We're rehearsing, and tearing out our hair, because we tape our first one next week and no one's ready."

He laughed. "No one ever *is* ready. But life and UBC go on. Where are you from?"

"Originally from Connecticut, but I've been working for the UBC affiliate in Boston. Now you tell me who you are."

"Professionally, I'm in network programming. Personally, the answer is complicated and indefinite."

"Uh-oh, I probably should know who you are."

"No reason to. But I am glad we've met. Where are you rehearsing?"

"Studio 49. All day."

"If I were to stop by and watch for a bit, later, would that disturb you?"

"Of course not!" They made conversation for a few more moments about her show, then she saw his erstwhile companions getting to their feet. "The men you didn't come with are about to leave," she said.

"Then I'd better *not* go with them," he answered, smiling. But he stood. "I'm glad I met you, Carlotta Barnes. I may stop by later."

He took her hand; it was firm, long-fingered, the nails simple with colorless polish. "Glad to have met you, Mr. Reilly."

To herself she said, he's a damned attractive man, and doesn't he know it! She finished her coffee, went back to the task of putting together a five-day-a-week half-hour talk show without enough time, staff or budget.

About three, when they were ready to start taping an interview with the author of a book on mother-hating, Joe Kovach, the stage manager, beckoned her off the set, took his headset off and whispered, "Look good, kid. Reilly's wandering around the control room."

"Who *is* he?" she asked.

"Oh, you *are* new," Kovach replied. "Buster Reilly, second in command of network programming, the heir apparent. He could make you a *star*."

"Suppose I don't want to be a star? Suppose I just want to be a journalist?"

"In this business, kid, they *all* want to be stars, the journalists worst of all. Then they divide into two groups: the many who *don't* make it, who walk around telling themselves how much they *want* to. And the few who *do* make it, who walk around telling others how much they *don't* want to."

Carlotta pointed to herself, shook her head no.

Kovach just smiled at her. "See me five years from today. The loser buys the winner a drink. I drink Chivas Regal."

Three years later, when Carlotta was made local co-anchor, the stage manager sent her a note: "I guess I get to collect early." She sent him a bottle of Chivas Regal.

He put his headset back on. "OK, look good for Buster. They want you back on the set."

Aloud, she would have denied it, but she was aware of a new tension, and couldn't tell whether it was because she was being looked at as a woman or a potential star.

When the taping was over Buster walked from the control room into the studio, bantered with the crew, but kept moving straight toward Carlotta.

"You're really very good," he said.

"Thank you. A couple of hours ago I would have taken that as an ordinary compliment. But I've been alerted. Now I know who Buster Reilly is. Do you have any suggestions?"

"Yes. I suggest you have dinner with me tonight, during which we can spend five minutes talking shop and the rest of the evening *not* talking shop. I realize it's kind of short notice . . ."

She laughed. "You see before you a totally unattached woman, in New York less than a week, with no friends and a social calendar full of blank spaces. I'd like to have dinner with you."

Eight months later, some time after his fortieth birthday, they were married. He was the man to watch at UBC, possibly even a network president someday. She was the unknown, young and good-looking, but not glamorous, rich or famous.

The morning of the day he was going to propose, he called her and asked, casually, "Where would you like to have dinner tonight?" Then he worked her around to Elaine's, which was what he'd planned. He'd also planned with Elaine that they get a table in a rear corner.

At dinner he pretended to be solemn and distracted, until finally she asked, "What's the matter?"

"A major decision affecting me is going to be made soon, and I'm worried, really worried."

"When will you know?"

"Soon enough," he said. "But I don't want to spoil the meal. Let's try to forget it."

"Forget it? Darling, how can I? Won't you tell me any more about it?"

Buster stalled through a second glass of wine and then, as he had planned, the waiter walked up. "A telegram for you, Miss Barnes." He handed it to her. Nervously, she seized it, started to tear it open. "For me? I don't understand! Who knew I was going to be here?"

Shakily, she worked at opening it. "I hate telegrams! They're never good news, always bad!"

"I hope this one won't be bad," he said.

Finally, she got it out of the envelope. It said: "DEAREST WOMAN I LOVE YOU WILL YOU DO ME THE HONOR GIVE ME THE JOY OF BECOMING MY WIFE SIGNED THE MAN ACROSS THE TABLE."

She looked over at him, her eyes teary. "Oh Buster! Oh! Buster!"

"Now you know the decision I'm worried about."

"Oh darling! How could you be worried about it? Yes. Of course I will!" She reached over, took his hand. He squeezed hers so hard, she winced.

"I thought it might be a little too soon, too sudden."

She laughed at that. "I was beginning to think you'd never ask."

He waved at the waiter, who was ready with a bottle of champagne in an ice bucket. "What would you have done with the champagne if I'd said no?" she asked. "Not that it was possible, mind you, not remotely possible. But what if?"

"Actually he had an alternative ready," Buster explained. "Iced hemlock, for one."

"No hemlock," she said. "From now on, it's all champagne for us, darling."

It began as all champagne, and for a while seemed it always would be. They had children at the end of the first, third and fifth years of their marriage, with Carlotta never missing more than six weeks' work for each. Her career moved steadily upward. On the birth of the first, Brandon Sean Reilly Jr., who was called Junior, she was still hosting the women's half-hour, and doing well at it. When Michael Barnes Reilly was born, she was co-anchor of the local news, and when the third, Mary Carlotta, was born, she was working for the network, covering stories and occasionally anchoring weekend news. Carlotta was doing splendidly.

Buster wasn't. The aging first-generation romantics, who'd made programming decisions on instinct, had moved up to the boardrooms and decided the business was too big to be run by romantics any longer, and so ordered in the new breed of programmers and executives, the experts in marketing and merchandising.

Just when Buster should have been succeeding to command, he found himself obsolescent, and couldn't, or wouldn't change.

It was not that he wasn't warned. At lunch one day, Danny Michaels, the grand old man of programming, who was over sixty and a few years from retirement, sounded the alarm.

"Buster, I'm watching these new young guys, with their computers and their demographics, and I find it amazing. They're trying to take the art of programming and make it a science."

Buster scoffed at that. "You think they're getting any better results than we are? Look at those ratings the guys across the street are getting, with all their scientific method. Did you notice how many new shows they dumped after thirteen weeks? By God if that's science then give me seat-of-the-pants anytime!"

"Look, don't make any mistake," Danny said. "Personally I agree with you, but the chairman is impressed by numbers, and by the scientific mumbo jumbo. You may think it's bullshit, and I may agree with you, but unless you learn how to play the game, speak the language, you're going to be in trouble when I retire. You're going to personify the Old Guard, and this is a business where the new is always better. You're smart enough to change, but don't take too long. And, for God's sake, Buster, don't think you can win this one with charm or glamour or heroics. The day of the white knight on his charger is over. Your choice is to get off the horse and go armored, or find yourself flattened under a tank, like the Belgian cavalry against a Panzer division. Which side do you want to be on, Buster?"

"Well, hell, Danny, what a funny thing to say! I don't want to be on the side of the Panzer division! They're the guys you and I fought during the Big War. Remember?"

"Don't nitpick on the analogy, please, Buster. You're too smart and too capable to be flattened. You *deserve* my job. Just adapt, play the game, and you've still got a damned good shot at getting it. Get stiff-necked, and you can be sure you won't."

Of course Buster did get stiff-necked: he'd show these kids and their computers and their statistics and their pseudo-science that they couldn't make any better programming decisions than he. The fact was, they didn't. But they explained them better, and they made Buster fall out of step, which in the network bureaucracy, as in any other, was worse than being wrong.

About a year later, when Buster was called into Danny's office, he'd expected the worst. It hurt like hell anyway.

"I warned you," Danny began. "I kept warning you. Why wouldn't you listen?"

Suddenly, Buster felt old. "All right, Danny. Do me a favor and cut the preliminaries. Just tell me."

"They're kicking me out. Forcing early retirement on me, with a consultancy. Burt's getting my job."

"Burt? That fourteen-year-old wimp?"

"He's thirty-two, and he's a marketing specialist. He's got charts, numbers. He impressed them. Why wouldn't you listen?" Now it was Danny who sounded old and tired, as if he didn't really want an answer to his question.

Buster didn't give him one. "Thirty-two," he said. "Three years younger than I was when I started at UBC ten years ago—without charts. You mean I put in ten years so I can now work for Burt the wimp?"

"No."

"No?"

"They recognize it might be a problem, your being directly under Burt, since he used to work for you. So they're shifting you."

"Without even talking to me?"

"That's what I'm doing now, Buster. I'm talking to you."

"No you're not; you're presenting me with a *fait accompli*. Suppose I say no?"

"No to what, for Chrissake? You don't even know what it is!"

"That's not the point, is it?"

"Let me tell you what the point is!" Danny really liked Buster and admired him; he felt rotten about what was happening and welcomed the chance to get angry, to blame someone. "The point is your dumb stiff-necked pride. Maybe you see yourself as the last of the Lancelots, but I see you as neither the first nor the last in a long line of Don Quixotes. What's the point, Buster, what do you want? You want to get a professorship at a school of communications, so you can tell some kids how TV has gone to hell? And then watch them all run to New York with their tongues hanging out, trying to break into it?"

Buster stood up. "No, I want to go out and have a drink. Or two. Or four." And without even asking which job he'd been transferred to, he stalked out.

The next day he walked into Danny's office and said, "I'm sorry. It's not your fault. I love you, Danny, I really do. What the hell kind of job are they giving me?"

"Believe it or not, Buster, and I know you won't, it's a great opportunity. They want you to head up acquisition of properties for feature films made for TV."

"Features for TV?" Buster was indignant. "The network just bought up the entire film libraries of two major studios, why the hell do they have to make features for TV? What the hell am I going to head up? A secretary and a broom closet?"

"Listen to me! You're dead wrong!" Danny shouted back. "We're not much into it now, but we're going to be. And so are the other networks. You can build yourself a goddamned kingdom! They'll give you a five-year contract at $100,000 a year. That's not so bad, and if the thing builds you can always renegotiate it. This is a great chance for you, Buster!"

"Beaten out!" Buster could shout better than Danny could. "Beaten out, pushed out, by a bunch of pasty-faced sweaty-palmed little wimps with charts! Oh, shit! I'd like to take the bunch of them and shove their charts . . . I could do it with one hand!"

"For Chrissake, will you try to forget the football field and the 82nd Airborne! Not only is this a great chance for you, you're damned lucky to get it! With all the hate you show toward those wimps, you could've wound up on your ass! I've gotta tell you, they don't like you much better than you like them, and they're just waiting for you to look bad so they can move in for the kill. Don't give them the chance!"

Quickly, as quietly as he could, Buster proceeded to look around the industry for another job. When he found that numbers and demographics were winning everywhere, he took the new UBC job and contract, disgruntled and determined to fight it all the way. And drinking all the way. A couple of times he walked into afternoon meetings half drunk. He gave the wimps their chance, handed it to them, deliberately, defiantly.

When he signed his new contract, Buster was forty-five and Carlotta thirty-two. She was by then a network reporter and occasional weekend anchor. More and more she was being noticed; more and more Buster was drinking, rebelling, making less and less of a job which— Danny was right—was to grow into a big part of the network.

Burt *was* a wimp, and his programming did not seem to show significantly better ratings than the old unscientific kind, but he was brilliant and impressive, and had grown contemptuous of Buster. Burt was also something of a bitchy little wit, and as he watched the careers of Buster and Carlotta, he once remarked, "A Star Is Born, right here in our shop!"

Another man might have gotten a feeling of security knowing his wife's strength and income were there as a backstop. Not Buster. Once he'd been the eagle and she the fledgling. Now she was soaring and he was losing strength and altitude, fast. Her money was no help; it hurt all the more.

Carlotta knew the real crisis would come when Buster turned fifty, because he would be hit simultaneously by his age and the end of his five-year contract. Meanwhile, she was gaining more and more network power, as regular weekend anchor, then as co-host of the morning network newsmagazine. At thirty-four, she signed a new two-year contract which for the first time made her income higher than his.

At first she tried to conceal the size of her salary; then reluctantly, because she knew she'd have to, she told him. Buster tried to be happy for her; he broke out a bottle of champagne, which turned out to be less for celebration than sedation.

Two years later, when that contract was up, Carlotta was co-anchoring the network evening news. Her agent told her, "We'll get you big money this time. And a few documentaries. You've got 'em where you want 'em."

But he didn't know quite where she wanted them, and she didn't tell him. She told the president of the network, during a private, confidential lunch, *sans* agent.

"I'm considering switching to your friends across the street, John, because they've offered me a very good deal, and they're interested in Buster for an important job." That was subterfuge and they both knew it; the president also knew he had to play it out. "And I'd hate to think I was competing with my own husband," she added.

"We want you to stay here," the president told her. "And Buster too, of course."

"In one year, Buster's contract is up," she said. "What happens then?"

"We'll give him a new contract."

"How long?"

The president was a good negotiator. "Why, as long as yours, of course."

"He's got to have a raise."

"If you ask it, he'll get it. But between us, he expects to be dropped. If he's offered a raise instead, he'll know you got it for him. Do you want that?"

They settled on a four-year contract for Buster, which would begin in a year, when his contract expired, the pay to stay at $100,000 per year, and a five-year contract to begin at once for Carlotta, starting at $350,000, with healthy annual increments and escalators for doing documentaries. The smart money in TV wondered why she didn't get more; nobody but Carlotta, the network president and a few executives knew the real reason.

Once again, Carlotta dreaded going home with the news. Once again, Buster tried to be congratulatory; he ended up hostile. "You should have gotten more," he said, thinking he sounded jolly, but sounding only drunk. "We might need it for groceries."

Fights started often these days, and she became expert at spotting their beginnings, though she was less expert at heading them off.

"It'll take me up over $500,000. That's not bad; I don't want to be greedy. Besides, you've done a wonderful job of providing the groceries, and everything else, for the past ten years, and I'm not the least bit worried about it."

"Maybe you should start."

"Start what?"

"Worrying."

"Stop it, Buster. You have a lot of friends at the network, who expect major contributions from you in the years ahead . . . even though they think you're holding back at the moment."

"Name three."

"Buster!"

"Let me tell you something, superstar."

"Please don't call me that, darling!"

"Let me tell you something. The only thing they expect in the years ahead is to kick me out."

"You're just wrong about that."

"What makes you so sure?" Suddenly he was suspicious. "Is the superstar protecting her naughty old man? *Old* old man! I'll bet that's it! You are, aren't you?"

"You're being ridiculous, darling!" Hating to lie, she lied vehemently. "You're in a down phase at the moment, but they value you, I know that. You don't need me to help, you never have, you never will. I'm the one who's always leaned on you. Now, at last, I'm able to stand up by myself. For God's sake, sweetheart, applaud me, be proud of me!"

He clapped his hands twice, dispiritedly. "Proud? I'm more than that. I'm grateful."

"Stop it! You've earned everything you've gotten, and more. And if you feel you want to walk away from UBC and go somewhere else, do it! We have the cushion now! I tell you, they'll regret it; they don't want you to go! But whatever you do, let's be happy, darling!"

Shortly before his fiftieth birthday, Buster was called in to see Burt the wimp about the expiration of his contract, expecting to be told they were dropping him. To his surprise, to his suspicion, he was offered a four-year contract at $100,000 a year. "That's the best offer we can make." Burt didn't sound happy about it; he sounded more as if he were daring Buster to turn it down.

"I've got some thinking to do," Buster replied. Then he went out and celebrated the offer by getting drunk for the hundredth or so time and cheating on Carlotta for the first time, with an actress he met at a bar across the street from his office.

Within a week, there was another woman, and another.

Carlotta noticed it as a remoteness, a loss of sexual interest, and for a while took it as anger and hostility over the fading of his career and the burgeoning of hers. She also chose to take the late arrivals, the dinners missed, as time spent drinking. She tried to talk to him about it.

"You're never here anymore," she said one evening.

"I told you," he responded angrily. "I'm out wooing the young hotshots, trying to revive the old career. How many times do I have to tell you?"

She didn't know what he was doing, but she knew that was a lie. She chose not to contest it. "That's not what I mean, darling. What I mean is, even when you're *here*, you're not here."

It was nearly eight. Buster had been home only forty-five minutes, with an obvious two-drink head start, but already he was well into a pitcher of martinis that were 99 percent vodka. "In that case, if I'm *not* here when I'm here, I may as well leave. There's no point in my staying." He got to his feet.

She stood, too, walked to him, put an arm on his shoulder. "Buster, please! You're destroying yourself. You're destroying us. Stop. Sit down. Let's have dinner, let's talk. Let's do something before it's too late."

"You don't understand." He said it with mock pedantry. "Since I'm *not* here when I'm here, maybe I'll *be* here when I'm not here. Why don't we give it a try?" He moved toward the door, a bit unsteadily.

"Oh honey, I'm talking about saving us, and you're playing word games. What happened? Have I done anything? Is it wrong for me to be successful? Do you hate me for it? Is that why you're never home anymore? Why aren't you happy for me, Buster?"

"Are you happy for me, Carlotta?"

"I'm not happy for the way your career's going. You're too talented for it to go the way it has. But you can change it. I'm not happy for the way our marriage is going. We love each other too much for that. But we can change that, too. We should, we must. I'm not happy for the way you're drinking and staying away from me and the children and your home. What you're doing I don't know and I don't ask. But *that* can change! I know I'm taking a terrific chance by saying these things, but I'm beginning to think I've got nothing to lose, and a lot to gain. I suppose I should say *re*gain: us, our love, our home, our marriage, our family."

He chose to pick on one part of what she said. "What do you mean, you don't know what I'm doing and you don't ask? I've told you. If you don't believe me, say so. If you think I'm seeing other women, say so! Go on!"

"I can't talk to you! I don't want a confrontation, I don't want to win a conviction. I'm not a DA, I'm your wife, remember? I want to save us!"

"You want to be a bitch, and a saint, too! I won't let you! You think I'm sleeping with other women, say so! I dare you! Go on, be a bitch, bitch!"

If he was trying to get Carlotta to come out fighting, it was working. "Do I think you're sleeping with other women? Yes, I do. That is, I think you're *making love* to them. You're *sleeping* with me. You sure as hell aren't making love to me, that much I know. There, now I've said it. Does it make me a bitch? Have I walked out? No. Have I told you to get out? No. Have I even brought it up? No. You've pushed me to it, pushed and pushed, and you've finally succeeded. Now all I can say is, I want to go right by it. All I want to do is fix us up, make us work again."

"You mean, make *me* work again!"

He stood ready to leave, she stood near him, imploring him to stay. Now she took a step back. "All you want to do is pick a fight. This is one I can't win, so I'm going to bed."

He would not even let her make that move uncontested. "Ah-ha! Saint Superstar wants to steal the exit away from naughty old husband, does she? No, this one thing she won't do. I go first." And he turned and stomped out the door.

That night, for the first time, he didn't come home at all. In the weeks ahead there were many reconciliations and confrontations, each confrontation angrier than the last, each reconciliation weaker. Four months later he moved out, to a two-bedroom apartment on East Sixty-sixth Street, just a few doors from his old bachelor apartment.

Two months after that, his lawyer called hers about a legal separation. That evening she kept phoning him until finally he was home, drunk, and answered the phone.

"All I want to tell you is this shouldn't be happening."

"Yeah, I know, I know," he said. "You want me back. You're not the one who wants the separation. My lawyer told me I'd be hearing that. For the record. To protect Carlotta's millions. Only it's supposed to be in writing. It's not good over the phone, you're wasting your breath— and my time. Just have your lawyer send the letter, and leave me alone." He hung up.

She called again. "I don't want to be separated. I want to stop the destruction of the marriage. I want to stop your destruction of yourself!" She began to cry, tried to stop sobbing so she could speak. "For God's sake, there are a wife and three children here who love you! Stop!"

Buster hung up, took the phone off the hook.

He was fifty-one, she thirty-eight when they got the legal separation. Her annual income was then about $400,000 and she wanted no money, but he insisted on paying child support and tuition totaling $20,000 a year. His lawyer told him that was quixotic, that it was way out of line with his income, that Carlotta could afford it much better than he.

"At least let me make some of it alimony, so it's deductible!" his lawyer pleaded. And Carlotta was willing to have most of it called alimony, so she'd pay the taxes on it. Buster refused. He began to use his savings, to sell some of his UBC stock; he took a second mortgage on the Bridgehampton house, which gave him a new debt.

His assets ran out along with his four-year contract, which despite his misgivings, he had signed. He'd made some desultory stabs at other jobs, but programming techniques were changing everywhere, and moreover, Buster hated being in the position of supplicant, so he didn't try very hard.

Nor did he try very hard to build his position in the acquisition of TV film properties. He stayed stiff-necked, wouldn't mesh. When one of his friends at the network argued with him—"For Chrissake, Buster, what the hell would you like to buy? Bergman? Rohmer? Fassbinder? *You* don't go to see their movies either! You're working for a mass medium, you've got to buy a popular product. You're not running an art cinema! The only question is: Whose popular taste do you want to satisfy, yours or the network's?"—he had no rational answer, for he made no claim to being a highbrow, he just didn't want to be part of a formula. His position was silly, he would have admitted, were he admitting anything then.

Along with his assets and his contract, his marriage was ending. Twelve years after their wedding, one year after their legal separation, Brandon Sean Reilly, fifty-two, and Carlotta Barnes Reilly, thirty-nine, parents of Brandon Jr., eleven, Michael, nine, and Mary Carlotta, seven, got a New York State no-fault divorce.

In the next year and a half Carlotta kept watch over Buster. It would have been hard for her to say whether she continued to love him the same way, or if she was just worried about him. She knew she'd stopped expecting a reconciliation; too many variables were awry. And she knew he was still the same rebellious boy he'd been, although she'd hear that once in a while, when his heart was in it, he would negotiate deals for some excellent properties.

More often though, he was turned down by his network superiors on books, stories or ideas he wanted to buy. And when his choices were approved, more often than not, they failed to pull ratings. Buster blamed the failures on lack of support—stingy budget, bad scheduling, puny advertising and promotion. He was, to an extent, right, for the fact was, Burt the wimp didn't *want* him to do well. Burt wanted to unload him when his contract was up, and a success or two might muddy the waters, give the network president an excuse to keep

Buster. With the contract down to one year to go, Burt wanted to be able to point to Buster's thorough failure. Burt wanted to be able to say to the network president: if you want to keep him, that's your business, but move him somewhere else, his job has become too important for him! And Danny Michaels had been right, the job was growing immeasurably; movies for TV were becoming a huge operation, one Burt didn't want in hostile hands.

Since the breakup of her marriage, Carlotta had become more and more friendly with the president of the network, John Silverstone, and his wife Liz. They invited her to dinner often, usually as a single woman for whom they provided a dinner partner. Partners were easy to find; men she was interested in, almost impossible. She had no shortage of men to go to dinner or the theater with; a romantic liaison was another matter.

Once when she'd lamented this to Bea, her friend had replied: "They say that even Marilyn Monroe used to sit home Saturday nights because men were afraid to call her."

"Yes, but she wasn't as sexy as I am," Carlotta replied. "Anyway, you're sweet to say it."

"A good line," Bea replied. "I may use it some time, without credit, of course." They were having lunch at a new seafood restaurant on the Sag Harbor waterfront, one of those long, easy Saturday lunches where one glass of white wine stretches to three and two o'clock stretches to four.

"You've got a great life ahead of you, Carly—exciting, productive, satisfying. Don't wear Buster like a millstone. You need a man who can match your strength, not a millstone. What we're going to find you is a great big sober successful hunk of strength and security—you've had enough of the other kind."

Talk like that made Carlotta fiercely protective. "Don't put him down, Bea! That man has been in my mind and heart for damned near fifteen years now. He's the father of my three children, and every time, every day, I look at them I see a little of Buster. You're talking about the one man in my life!"

"Yes, I am," Bea answered. "I had one like that, too, remember? And we had kids, and every time I look at them, I see a little of Staunton in them. Staunton! My God, do you know how long it's been since I spoke that name aloud? Yes, I know what that is. I also know that you forget. No, you don't forget you *once* loved that man. You don't forget that once, when you picked up the phone to dial his number, you started smiling, in anticipation of the sound of his voice. That when you answered the phone and you heard him, your heart gave a bounce that scared you. You don't forget that once all your dreams and your energies were tied up with having that man with you, for life. *Once* you felt all those things—you don't forget that. You're just unable to summon up that uncontrollable smile, that bounce of the heart, just as you're unable to come up with the words to a song you've forgotten. You're sure you knew them, *once*. But that's not the same as knowing them *now*. It will happen, and you'll be the better for it. God, will you be the better for it!"

Carlotta could no more feel Bea's detachment than Bea could remember her involvement. "You make Buster sound like a human Edsel," she said. "A kind of model that doesn't work and has to be thrown on the junk heap. And you're so wrong! But that's because you've known Buster only this last year or so, which has been his worst time. He has done some wonderful things. He has *been* some wonderful things."

"I don't want to sound flip, but as the old saying goes: What has he done for you lately? Or in this case, what has he done *to* you lately? The answer is, a lot—all of it bad, and getting worse."

"This is not show business, Bea. There's more to it than just 'lately.' This is marriage, commitment. You don't have three children and a home based on what you've done for each other lately. To me, children and a home are what they say in the ad about diamonds. They're forever. Or is all that passé? Is commitment out of style? Well, it isn't for me. Besides, Buster is far from a millstone. He is a very smart, very capable man who's going through some rough times—part of which I'm responsible for. . . ."

"Oh no, Carly, no! You're not buying that guilt, are you? Talk about millstones!"

"I'm not buying anything. I didn't say I was to *blame*. I said I was partly responsible. Can you see the difference? If I weren't making so much money, if I were not such a celebrity, if he felt pressure to be the breadwinner, instead of pressure from the upward motion of my career and income, things might be different. No, I don't feel *guilty* about my success or Buster's problems. I put in for my success, and I suppose he put in for his problems. But things just aren't that simple."

"The word for him is *failure*," Bea told her friend. "I know you don't like to use it, but that's the word."

"You're wrong." Carlotta's voice was strong and decisive. "Dead wrong. Buster's dropped into a trough the past couple of years, granted. But he's had a lot of successes too, and he'll have more. The final verdict is not in yet. You know, Bea—" Carlotta took a deep breath and plunged in, "Buster really is a first-class producer. Even lately, on the few chances he's been given, he's put all the elements together, and done a damned good job of it, considering. He's got taste, he's persuasive, he's organized, he's a good negotiator, and when he wants to, he can charm the hell out of anyone. All he needs is a real chance."

Carlotta didn't look at her friend as she spoke the last sentence; she tried to make it sound casual, undirected. They both knew what she meant.

"There's nothing you wouldn't do for that man, is there?" Bea didn't know what else to say.

"I guess not. I'd even risk alienating my best friend."

"No way, Carly honey. You're stuck with me as a best friend for as long as . . ." She hesitated. "But . . . oh, my . . . I don't see how Buster . . . well, you know . . . Irv handles all that . . . oh, *shit*, Carly!"

Carlotta squeezed her friend's hand. "Please, no. I'm sorry to put you through this. Forget it. I'm so sorry, this is my problem, and I shouldn't make it yours."

"That's wrong, honey," Bea answered. "I want to share your problems with you. But this is *not* your problem. It is precisely the problem you've *divorced* yourself from. Your problem is continuing to take on a problem that's not yours. That's what I want to help you with."

"You don't understand," Carlotta said, sorrowfully.

"Yes, I do. It's a kind of illness, and I want to help you get well."

Back in the fall of 1976, when Buster heard about Bea's book, he too saw a chance to score a dramatic coup. His first try should be to get the rights for UBC. To do that, he'd have to go to Burt the wimp. He detested the prospect.

Then he examined his other prospects. The Maidenhead was posting him for arrears; he'd blown his savings, cashed in his stock; he'd run up huge tabs on his credit cards and at a couple of saloons. He was about to fall behind on his child support, and that, above all, he didn't want to happen.

He swallowed hard, and phoned the wimp for an appointment. After the humiliation of a two-day wait, he got in to see him.

"Yes, Buster, what can I do for you?" Burt was not cordial.

"I've got a line on a property that would make a superb mini-series."

Burt took on a look of noncommittal professional interest. "Tell me about it."

Buster explained that it was a book about the Hamptons, still being written, by Bea Fletcher, and a continuation of the "Washington-Shock" pieces about to appear in *Scope* magazine.

"Well, of course, I'd like to read it when it's ready."

"It will be long sold by then."

Burt shrugged. "What makes you say so?"

"Because it's a hot property; a lot of people are interested right now. There's going to be fierce competition." Buster hated himself for having to plead his case this way, for not being able to tell the wimp to fuck off.

"Have you read it?"

"No, but . . ."

"I don't understand then; what is it you're asking?"

"Well, if I can finish my sentence . . . I'm *suggesting* that based on my experience and judgment as a programming executive, I be authorized to negotiate for this property, something I am uniquely qualified to do because I am a close friend of Bea Fletcher and her agent."

"What kind of bucks are we talking?"

"At this point, perhaps median six figures. If we wait, more like seven figures."

"You're kidding!" Burt said it cuttingly. "Do you seriously expect us to authorize you to throw around that kind of money?"

"Well, as a matter of fact, yes I do. For a property like this one—you bet I do! OK. Don't say you weren't asked. Don't try bullshitting anyone about how you wished we had a shot at it when it's too late, when someone else makes a goddamned fortune on it. Thanks for the audience." Without waiting for Burt to say anything he stood and headed out of the office.

"Buster!" The younger man tried to sound peremptory, then waited for Buster to stop and look back. "If you really hoped we'd give you that kind of money to spend, all by yourself, you are not living in the real world. Try coming back into our world."

"Your world?" Buster could feel the anger creeping up. He knew he should control it, couldn't bring himself to try too hard. "I can't come *back* into your world because I was never in it to begin with! God save me from *ever* being in it!"

Burt smiled patiently, like a grownup trying to calm an unruly child. "Get a grip on yourself, Buster."

Buster's face reddened. He clenched and unclenched his big fists. "I wouldn't worry about that, you little asshole. If I were you, what I'd worry about is my getting a grip on *you*." He leaned over the desk.

Burt stood, looking a little scared, trying to maintain his superiority. "Easy, Buster, you're no youngster . . ."

That did it for Buster. He took two strides around the desk, grabbed Burt under the arms, lifted him high off the ground.

"Stop it!" the young man shrieked.

"How's this for no youngster?" He walked him over to the big leather sofa along the side wall and slammed him down onto it, stormed out of the office, out of the building, into the nearest bar, where he ordered a double martini.

He took a deep drink and said softly, "Fuck UBC." He bet Bea's book would be dynamite. He'd get the film and TV rights for himself. But how? Using what for money? Hell, he reminded himself, he knew all the right people, Bea, Irv, Carlotta, publishers. But that wouldn't get him the money to buy the rights.

Money. Money. His *friend* Freddie Kohl had the money, all the money in the world. His *friend*, who always wanted to be taken to the Maidenhead to play tennis. His *friend*, whom he always allowed to beat him, or come close, at tennis. His *friend* Freddie would do something for him.

Yeah, fuck Burt the wimp. His friend would help him. There was only one catch. Even drunk and angry he knew that by comparison Freddie made Burt seem like a veritable Albert Schweitzer.

Labor Day Weekend, 1977; Sunday (continued)

WELL, HERE at last, Wisniewski said to himself as he sat down with Harry Majors on the terrace of Majors' house, is someone who doesn't look like he could or would tear Kohl apart.

"Sure I can't get you a cup of coffee?" Harry asked as he sat himself in a director's chair. "Or a bloody mary, or something?"

"No, thanks. If you just let me ask you some questions, that'll be fine." As Wisniewski said it, he got out his pen and pad.

"Could have been a heart attack, of course," Harry said. "But it sure doesn't sound like it."

"I hope we'll know in a few hours; meanwhile I've got to go ahead on the basis that it wasn't. That he was drowned, maybe pushed in, maybe held under. If that's wrong, OK, nothing lost. Anyway, would you start by telling me who was there?"

Harry repeated the names Wisniewski already knew; when he finished, the detective asked, "This Nellie Brandon, where is she now?"

"Asleep upstairs. Want to talk to her?"

"Don't disturb her now; maybe I'll talk to her later. Describe her."

"Oh, maybe five-six, skinny, a hundred ten, a hundred twelve pounds, reddish-blond hair, freckles."

"Athletic?"

"God, no. I have to help her lift a wineglass to her mouth."

"Really?"

Harry laughed. "No. But she's no strapping lass. She couldn't give Sophie much of a tussle. But then who could?"

Wisniewski had to smile at that. "Does—did—Miss Brandon know Mr. Kohl well?"

"Not at all, really. I introduced her when we went over last night after dinner. I don't think they spoke two words to each other after that."

"No business or romantic contact between them?"

"God, no, she's a clothing designer, he's a financier. I'm sure he would have liked to have romantic contact, but as I say, they never met."

"Was Kohl much of a ladies' man?"

Harry thought for a moment. "He tried hard, had a lot of good-looking women around. But he never seemed to be enjoying them; and the women didn't seem to be enjoying him. Of course, I don't know what went on privately, but I never heard any woman talk about Freddie Kohl with any real feeling. Yes, I did. Hatred. But never real affection."

The detective pounced on that. "Who?"

"Oh, no one in particular. Just what I know about women's attitudes toward him."

He could see Majors was being careful; there was no point pushing him. "Tell me what you remember of the evening, from the time you arrived."

"I guess I'd had a fair amount to drink." He looked at Wisniewski's expression, smiled. "Everyone tell you that? There's nothing like a possible murder to make people get vague, is there? The fact is, though, most people out here on a Saturday night *do* tend to drink too much. And I know they were doing a lot of it at Bobby Van's, and then at Freddie's. Anyway, I don't think it was much before midnight that we left Bobby's, and that meant we'd have gotten to Freddie's house ten or fifteen minutes later—around midnight. Nellie went for a swim in Freddie's pool with no clothes on, which always attracts attention. I had a drink. We went into the library and talked for a while. I had a drink. Talked some more. Had a drink. It was after the third that we left, probably around one, perhaps one-thirty."

"Who was in the library, talking?"

"Oh, at one time or another, they were all in there. Someone would come in and sit and talk, then go out, wander around, come back in."

"Did you do that?"

"No. Once we walked in we stayed until we left the party for good, but don't forget we didn't go in until after Nellie's swim, so we didn't stay all that long."

"Did anyone leave ahead of you, or were you the first?"

"I don't really know. As I said, people were all over the place."

"How about cars in the parking area when you left?"

"There were a lot, so I'd say we were one of the first to leave, if not the first. But I can't tell you they were *all* there, or whose car was missing."

Wisniewski had a feeling that for the first time he was talking to someone who was not holding back. "What did you think of Kohl?" he asked.

"I suppose I found him detestable, but I can't get too excited about it; I feel like he's a creature from another planet—the work he does, the things he wants, the way he deals with people. Every little conversation with him is an adventure—I keep saying *is*, when I should say *was*, you'll have to excuse me."

"What do you mean about the conversation?"

"He was never relaxed, he never seemed to just talk. He was always wheeling and dealing, always seemed to be *after* something."

"What was he after with you?"

"At first he'd keep probing, trying to find out what I had that might be useful to him. Then he found out: nothing. I'm just a comedy writer. He didn't covet my body, my business, my book, my house, my anything. The only thing I had was a few bad one-liners, and he doesn't even laugh at *good* one-liners. So he just stopped talking to me, which was fine with me."

"How about the others?"

"Most of them are involved in publishing, Wainwright and Sally, my ex-wife; Irv Schnell. Bea Fletcher, who's writing a book. Reilly is a producer, his ex-wife is a TV celebrity. All of them are part of Freddie's plan to gain status in the Hamptons. So he wants something from all of them. *Wanted*—I keep forgetting. The poor guy has gone beyond wanting."

"How could he gain status from them?" Wisniewski asked.

"Lots of ways. Just by being seen with them. You see, the media crowd is the 'in' crowd in the Hamptons. More than that, though. Do you know Bea Fletcher?"

Wisniewski smiled. "Remember the storm last December? The detective who stopped by and looked at the furnace?"

"Oh, yes! You?"

"Me. I know Bea Fletcher. Besides, I've seen her on Johnny Carson."

"Yes, haven't we all. Well, anyway, she's writing a book, a gossipy novel about the Hamptons. And everybody figures two things about it: that it's going to make a lot of money, and that it's going to embarrass a lot of people."

"Why should it embarrass them?"

"Because all the characters are going to be based on real people, and very close to real people."

"Recognizable?"

"By those who know the real people, you bet! And just in case there's any doubt, she's using the same initials as the real people's, although the names will be different."

"An FK for Friedrich Kohl?" the detective asked.

Majors smiled at him. "How about a cup of coffee? I'm going to get myself another."

Wisniewski smiled back. "How about an answer?"

"I don't know. I haven't read the book."

"How do you know so much about it, then?"

"Bea Fletcher and I are . . . good friends."

"Girlfriend and boyfriend?"

"Formerly. Now just friends, sometimes not even that, you know how it is."

"Yeah, I suppose." Wisniewski's shrug said he didn't know how it was, and it didn't matter.

Harry was on his feet all this time, heading for more coffee. Finally, the detective said, "I will have a cup, thanks, cream and two spoons of sugar."

"Coming up."

While he was gone, Wisniewski looked out across the double dunes, shining green and white as the sun lit up the dune grass and sand. This was a modest house, but he knew it would be damned expensive because of its location. He suddenly thought it funny, that though he lived little more than a mile away, it was halfway round the earth. His house was on a suburban half-acre and he almost never made the one-mile trip to the ocean, which was what these people paid all that money for. He liked the ocean, liked the beach, the dunes, wondered why he never came out here, decided it was because he never had the free time in a big enough block. Then had to correct himself—the ride took five minutes, less, a free hour would do. Before he could come up with an answer, Majors was back with the coffee, in a mug, with a spoon sticking out of it.

"Thanks." Wisniewski stirred the coffee, started to take the spoon out, didn't know where to put it, decided to leave it in. He took a sip. "Good. My wife brews a good cup of coffee, but this is terrific."

"Glad you like it. It's a special blend from Zabar's."

"Where?"

"Zabar's."

"Never heard of it."

"In the city."

Wisniewski smiled. "You mean *New York* City? We never go there."

"Oh, well, Zabar's is a store on Broadway that has things like coffee and cheese, kind of a fancy delicatessen."

"Anyway, the coffee's very good. Now can I ask you about the book? Do you know *any* real people who are in it? Are you? Are any of the people who were at Kohl's last night?"

"Look, I'm just not sure; you're going to talk to Bea Fletcher, aren't you? Why don't you ask her? I don't want to speak for her book. *Are* you going to question her?"

"It's my next stop." At any rate it is now, Wisniewski said to himself. "But there are a couple more things I want to ask you."

"Go ahead."

"Do you know if Kohl had any particular enemies?"

"My guess is, anybody who dealt with him, but that's just a guess, and I bet you've heard it before. He was a hard man to deal with. Which takes me back to the point I was making before: Bea Fletcher's book. Freddie wants—wanted—to buy control of it so he could make money from it, so he could try to cut out of it nasty stuff about himself —don't ask me if there is any, ask Bea—or about the Governor, whom he was very close to."

"Very close to?"

"*Very* close. If Hughes ever gets to be President, Kohl thinks—thought—he could be Secretary of State."

The information was coming too fast, Wisniewski tried to keep it sorted. "Are you saying there *is* stuff about the Governor in Mrs. Fletcher's book?"

"No. I'm not saying that. I'm saying that Freddie was trying to get hold of the book because that's what *he* thought."

"Yeah, but was he right?"

Majors smiled again, threw his hands in the air. "As I said before, ask Bea Fletcher."

A July Weekend, 1977

BY BECOMING the object of their thoroughly divergent desires, Bea came as close to reuniting Harry and Sally Majors as anyone ever had. Which was not very close. Nothing could have brought them together for long; their reunion was a brief meeting for convenience, which momentarily flared then cooled at once.

Harry loved Bea and within the limits of his flexibility and idiosyncrasy would have done what he could to get her back. To which Bea would have replied: his flexibility is so limited and his idiosyncrasy so unlimited, there's no way.

Sally loved Bea's book, desired it, sight unseen, and would have done what she could to get the paperback rights, within no limits whatever. To which Bea would have replied: make me an offer. If Sally had been told that Harry could help, she'd have made *him* an offer.

Harry, on the other hand, even if he knew that dealing with Sally could get Bea back, would have said: no way. He had a nose for success; anytime he whiffed it, he ran the other way. The smell made him nervous.

Harry and Sally were a thoroughly Hamptons romance; they'd met there and split there. He was a writer, she an editor. Their names offered a certain Hamptons cleverness, for her maiden name was Myner and the meeting of Majors and Myner was not only amusing, but an ironic twist on what people took to be their stature. People said she became the major figure, which was fitting, while he, no matter what his name, had been a minor one all along.

They met in the summer of '67 on the beach at Amagansett. She was twenty-two, fresh out of Ohio State and the proud possessor of a job as an editorial assistant at Saxon. He was thirty, already once divorced, already a moderately successful comedy writer for television.

Then, as later, Sally's body was trim and economical, hardly voluptuous, but with beautifully formed limbs. Then, as later, her dark brown hair was silky, her nose small and fine. But the shiny brown eyes of the twenty-two-year-old were to lose their softness, their ingenuousness. Later, they would look that way only when she found it useful, but during that first summer in New York, they shone with genuine openness and an eager embrace of her new life. In a world of taller women, sexier women, prettier women, more glamorous women, Sally had those eyes. And a lot of brains. The toughness was still to come; it came fast.

On the beach in 1967, Harry overwhelmed her. Sally had never known a man so clever, so sophisticated, so compellingly blasé; Sally had never known a man who was thirty. Harry was almost as unaccustomed to a woman so enthusiastic, so forthright in her admiration for him, so straightforward. It was disarming.

They were married at City Hall in the spring of '68. That summer, in a little rented A-frame near the beach in Amagansett, was an idyll. By the summer of '69, when they rented the same A-frame, they were coming apart—largely due to her discontent and ambition, he said; largely due to his passiveness and lethargy, she said.

When Harry worked, he made two or three thousand dollars a week, but he never worked more than half the year, which kept his annual income below $75,000. Sally wanted to know why he didn't work more; he explained that increasingly the work was in California. She wanted to know why he didn't spend more time there; he explained that he didn't like California. She wanted to know why he didn't try writing screenplays or Broadway plays or novels in his spare time; he began to get annoyed at her relentless pushing, but instead of fighting back, responded in his characteristic passive-aggressive pattern.

"I get nervous at the prospect of a six-figure income. I might have to turn in my hair shirt."

They actually split on an August Sunday in '69; they'd walked to the beach, Sally weighed down by a manuscript, part of the extra work-load she assumed in her drive to move up from the very junior editor-ship she'd reached by then. Harry carried *The New York Times*, a ballpoint pen and the blanket, and as soon as they sat down, he began his fast, flawless excursion through the crossword puzzle.

Watching him, Sally suddenly turned furious. "Harry, is that what you want to do all your life, live in a tacky, rented one-bedroom bungalow and do the *Times* crossword in ink?"

What Harry wanted to say was, I am not an ambitious, high-pressure overachiever. I write good comedy material, which satisfies me. I make a decent living, which also satisfies me. And if it doesn't, the surest way to get me to deny it is to push me. I thought you knew the kind of man you were marrying. Why try to make me into some other kind of man? But Harry could never bring himself to say those things. He preferred offhand sarcasm.

He looked up from the puzzle. "Well, I could switch to pencil, if you think it would help the marriage. Or would you prefer that I do it in blood? And if so, whose?"

"Frankly, that's an improvement," she replied. "I didn't think you were willing to do anything to help it." She stuck her face close to his, as if by proximity to force straight talk upon him. In her face, little love remained, she was by this time angry and contemptuous. "Don't you want to carve out a little hunk of this world for yourself, Harry?"

"Oh? I thought you were carving out a piece big enough for two—at least."

"I thought the man was supposed to do that. The big, strong pro-vider."

"Actually, I thought I'd leave the old world alone and enjoy it just the way it is, uncarved. Don't want to spoil my 100 percent rating from Friends of the Earth."

"You're thirty-two years old and you're flitting around like Peter Pan. When are you going to grow up?"

"I'm living out the childhood you never had, Sally. Were you ever *not* grown up?"

"I find you lazy, cowardly and contemptible. You repulse me, you nauseate me." Her eyes were blazing.

In his own way, Harry was angry. His way was not to show it. "Then, as the old joke goes, I suppose a fuck is out of the question. You don't know that joke, do you, Sal? But then you don't know any jokes, do you? Except me, that is! Ha ha. Anyway, this disgusting, filthy, smelly bum is sitting on a park bench, eating a vile sandwich, picked, bit by bit, from a trash basket. Along comes a very prim and elegant society girl who, because of the crowded park, is forced to sit on the same bench as the bum. He offers her a bite of his sandwich. She looks at him and says . . . well, she says exactly what you just said to me, right to the 'you nauseate me' ending. And *he* says, 'Then I suppose a fuck . . .' "

Harry didn't bother to finish, for as he was getting near the punch line, she was getting up, grabbing her manuscript and heading back toward the house. It was just like Harry to sit there and finish the puzzle, in ink. By the time he got back to the house, Sally had left in their rented car. And it was just like Harry that he didn't try to call her, or go back to the city, just stayed out in Amagansett through the week and into the next weekend, when a letter from Sally arrived. It was a long harangue, ending with, "You just don't care, do you?"

And it was just like Harry that his answering night letter contained just one word: "Right."

Something in Harry said, This is no way to walk away from a marriage. Words deserve to be spoken, your position defended, justified; hers attacked, disproven. That something was voted down. Instead he resolved not to tie himself so completely to one person again, not to let any woman get fingerprints all over his ethos as she tried to reshape it in her image.

They went their separate ways, Sally marching to the top of the publishing world, Harry marching through the ranks of the attractive women of New York and the Hamptons like Sherman through Georgia.

A good many men, with a good deal of envy, would speculate on the secret of Harry's success with women. Certainly he was not rich and could not enthrall a woman with charm bought at Cartier's, Gucci and "21." He was no jock; though big and broad-shouldered, he was soft, out of shape and decidedly unathletic.

Nor was he noticeably handsome; he *was* good-looking, gray-eyed, strong-jawed, although his face was getting soft and his black hair, gray. Women said he had bedroom eyes, but no one thought he "came on" with the drive or determination that many Hamptons men did. He was neither famous nor social; he was not a celebrated stud.

But Harry paid attention. When he was with a woman, he focused on her; he listened, he responded. He was gentle, funny; he never tried to impress a woman, or oppress her by pushing her around physically or emotionally. He neither wanted to dominate nor to be dominated; his ideal was to find a woman whose hopes and needs matched his, so they could both be happy without either prevailing over the other.

And he was easy. In the New York–Hamptons world of high-powered, high-pressure men, women bloomed in his relaxed warmth. Their petals opened. Because he was attentive, responsive, easy, he was good in bed. He was skilled, too, but that was mere sexual craftsmanship; caring made him an artist.

More than any of these things, what made him a great ladies' man was his reputation for being one. In his world there was so much hype and illusion that if people *thought* you were something, that was good enough to make you it. Harry was a lover.

He was not a tennis player, a golfer or a jogger. He did not ride, play croquet, softball or touch football. He did not do push-ups, sit-ups or any other calisthenics; he did not go to a gym. Walking the beach was to him a romantic or social activity, never an exercise. Nor did he swim, although on the hottest of days he would briefly immerse himself in a pool if one were handy, or failing that, in the ocean, if it were warm enough and calm enough, conditions which did not usually prevail until August.

Drinking, reading, making love, going to movies—lots of movies—watching TV, having long talks at dinner when he felt like talking and was with people he felt like talking to, writing comedy material—those were the ways Harry spent his time.

And, though he kept it quiet, surfcasting. It was the closest thing to a sport he could claim, but far from claiming it, Harry concealed it whenever he could. He kept his ten-foot fiberglass rod and spinning reel hidden in the house, and if cornered, would make a joke of it. "Yes, I'm a desultory surfcaster," he'd admit. "But it's almost impossible to find any desultory surf these days."

Yet he'd take that rod down to the beach more often than he'd admit, and spend an hour or two or three casting and reeling in, more often than not coming away with no fish, but always coming away more serene than he'd arrived.

He came by the fishing through a kind of friendship with a Bonacker, and sometimes when he thought about it, Harry realized it was the only instance he knew of where a gliteratus spoke to a Bonacker for a purpose other than asking him to work on his car, his roof, his furnace, his toilet, his lawn or his pool.

Bonac was the shortened version of Accabonac Creek, in East Hampton, and Bonacker the local term for a native. Bill Edwards was a Bonacker, born in East Hampton, as many generations of his family had been before him. Bill worked in his family's fish store, worked for his brother-in-law, who was a building contractor, and on summer weekends filled in as a part-time bartender at Sam's Pizza, where virtually every Friday night Harry went for pizza and red wine.

For several years Harry had been following the same Friday night routine, either bringing in a date or meeting friends. If the latter, he'd arrive a bit early, sit at the bar and sip a vodka and tonic while waiting for the others. Almost the first time he'd done it, he'd noticed the difference between Bill Edwards' hands and his, as the bartender put the drink down and he reached out to take it. Edwards' were so thick-fingered and callused, so rough, so leathery, Harry was amazed he was able to bend them around the glasses and the tools of the bartender's trade—although Edwards seemed to do it easily enough.

Harry asked him what else he did for a living. Edwards answered openly and pleasantly. After some initial reserve, he accepted Harry as a fellow human rather than as an exotic writer from the city who was paid too much, drank too much and worked too little—which explained the soft hands.

One September Friday, Edwards said he had to be up early the next morning to go fishing.

"Where?" Harry asked.

"Oh, I try a few spots near Main Beach, see if I can find out where they're runnin'."

Almost to his surprise, Harry heard himself ask, "Can I go with you sometime?"

He was even more surprised when Edwards replied, "How about tomorrow?"

"I don't have a rod."

"I've got a couple."

"What time?"

"I'll pick you up at six-thirty."

"Six-thirty? Do the fish always get up that early?"

Bill Edwards chuckled. "High tide is about six-thirty, and the best fishin' is a little while before it, and after it. What do you say?"

Again, to his surprise, Harry said yes. "What should I wear?" He sounded to himself a little like a girl on her first big date.

Bill shrugged. It had never occurred to him that you had to wear anything special. "Shirt and a jacket, in case it's windy. Old pair of pants you can roll up. Or shorts, bathing suit. Pair of sneakers."

"I don't know how to cast," Harry said, half afraid he'd be turned down, half hoping he would.

The bartender grinned. "Take you about a minute to learn."

"Six-thirty?" Harry hoped he'd relent, try to catch the next tide.

"Yup, six-thirty."

Harry nodded.

He set his alarm for six, and when it rang he hauled himself out of his stupor, cursing himself for his dumb idea. Why hadn't he waited until high tide hit at 10:30 instead of 6:30? Ten was a good time to be getting up on Saturday—on any day. Ten, then have a cup of coffee and read the papers. Do the crossword puzzle. He didn't even like nine o'clock rehearsals or production meetings, and those he *had* to go to.

Lurching around, he managed to boil some water, make a cup of instant coffee. He lit a cigarette. He was trying to break the habit, and rarely let himself begin that early, but he decided anyone guilty of such premature awakening deserved premature emphysema. He found a pair of old chinos, a torn cotton button-down shirt, sneakers, a nylon windbreaker he had ready for times he couldn't talk a date out of walking along the beach.

At 6:30, sharp, Edwards was there, in a dune buggy.

They drove along Further Lane toward the west, onto Beach Lane, then onto the beach, continuing west until they got near the narrow strip which separated the Atlantic on the south from Georgica Pond on the north. He stopped the dune buggy just above the high-water mark. At 6:40 the sun was already bright, the day still hazy but cloudless, already warm, presaging high sun, high temperatures in a few hours.

From the roof of the vehicle, Bill took down two rods, one about eleven feet long, the other slightly shorter, and handed the shorter one to Harry. Then he plunged two holders into the sand, put a rod into each.

"What are we trying to catch?" Harry asked.

"Supposed to be some stripers, but nobody's havin' much luck."

"Then why are we here?"

As he clipped lures to the lines, Bill grinned. "Nice time of day."

Again, to his surprise, Harry found himself agreeing. The beach was quiet, clean, bare. Now that he'd gotten by his grogginess, Harry was beginning to enjoy it, and he realized that without a purpose like surfcasting, people tended not to get up this early.

"What do we use for bait?"

"We don't. We use lures. These things." Bill pointed to the two silvery bits of metal at the end of each line. Each was perhaps three inches long, each had a couple of nasty hooks on it.

"You mean the fish fall for that?"

"Sometimes." Bill smiled again. "The stripers swim along lookin' for baitfish. They see the lure movin' through the water, bein' reeled in by you. They think it's a fish, go for it. Sometimes."

Bill leaned against the dune buggy, removed his boots and socks, rolled up his trousers a few turns, walked to the shorter of the two rods and picked it up.

"You hold your right hand here. Your left down here. You open the bail, so the line'll pay out when you cast. You leave about three feet of line past the tip of the rod. You hook the line with your right index finger, like this, so it won't go out till you're ready, and you don't let go till the pole is almost straight up in the air. Let go too soon, the line'll go straight up in the air, and come down too close to you. Let go too late, it'll go straight down toward the water. Either way is no good, especially on a calm day, when you want a good distance on your cast."

Effortlessly, Bill brought the rod up and over; the line sailed out, the lure hitting the water nearly a hundred yards out. "Then you close the bail, like this, and start reeling in, easy."

Several times, Bill repeated the cast, talking his way through it. Then Harry tried, got the line out perhaps thirty yards.

It felt uncoordinated, yet pleasant. He tried it again, reeled in again. Then had a thought. Harry turned to Bill, who was by then also reeling his line in.

"What happens if something bites?"

"Be there in a minute." Bill put his rod in its holder, and walked over, pointed to the knob in the reel. "That adjusts the drag. When you feel a bite, first pull on your rod to seat the hook; then you've got to play the fish. He'll pull on the line, and take it out with him. How easy he does it depends on the amount of drag on the line. You don't want to make it too easy, but you don't want him to snap the line, either.

You let him drag; when he rests, you reel in. As he gets tired, you tighten up on the drag, until you can bring him in."

"But how do I know how much to tighten up on the drag, how do I know when the fish'll snap the line? How will I know if I get a fish on the line, to begin with?"

Bill smiled at him. "When one bites, you'll know it. Some of 'em damned near take the rod out of your hand. When you feel one, you just seat the hook and call me. From the look of things today, that's not gonna be a problem."

And it wasn't. For an hour the two men stood there, twenty or thirty yards from each other, casting, reeling their lines in, neither getting so much as a nibble. Yet Harry felt a great sense of serenity come over him. Soon he was able to stop thinking about the steps in a cast, and could perform them mindlessly, letting the repetition of the task, the warmth of the sun, the lapping of the ocean at his feet, tranquilize him. When Bill said, "Let's stop for a beer, we won't be missin' much in the way of fish," Harry almost hated to interrupt the routine. He felt he could go on with it forever, even though a growing fatigue in his arms and shoulders told him he couldn't.

"Do this often?" he asked as he and Bill seated themselves on the sand, each with a can of beer in hand.

"Yeah, especially in the fall; it's the best time."

"Catch a lot?"

"Nope." Bill took a long swig of the beer.

"Why do you do it?" But even as Harry asked the question he knew the answer.

"Peace and quiet. A man can be alone. No kids yellin'. No wife naggin'. No TV. Nobody givin' you orders. Nobody rushin' you— you're doin' things *how* you want to do them, *when* you want to do them."

"Got you." Harry grinned at Bill, and said to himself: this man knows what his problems are, knows how to solve them, as few of my friends do. Harry realized the morning was having the same kind of effect on him. No thinking about funny lines, none of the habitual anxiety about the next project, which special, whose comedy material he was going to work on.

Bill said nothing, just sat staring out at the ocean, and Harry, to his immense satisfaction, understood there was no need to keep a conversation going—of any kind, let alone the brittle exchanges of gossip and

wit he was accustomed to. Harry sat back and bathed in the ease of
it.

He watched Bill bringing the can of beer to his mouth. In his powerful, callused hand, the can looked the way it did in the beer commercial when the football player tore the top off: small, fragile, tearable,
although in Harry's hand it felt rather sturdy.

Then he looked at Bill's face, leathery, a little beefy, padded to go
with the beer belly that topped his belt. The man's look suited his life,
a life so different from Harry's. This man worked in a fish store in
season, worked for a contractor in season, tended bar in season and he
would do that for the rest of his life. Could he be happy at it?

Then Harry thought, hell, Bill would probably wonder how Harry
could do what *he* was doing for the rest of *his* life—if Bill wondered
about things like that. Probably not, and probably he was the better
for it. In most ways, Harry figured, Bill was in better shape than he.
Bill had a wife and kids, a settled family life.

Harry had none of that, and he realized it was so far from his mind
that he never raised the question. He and Bill had done a fair amount
of talking, yet he had no idea how many kids Bill had, what their
names were, what their sexes were. At dinner parties, Harry turned
away from parental talk of kids and their problems, their achievements, their schools. The most interesting people, he found, could turn
into the biggest bores when talk of children started.

Sitting there, sipping beer, Harry realized that the concrete possibility of having a family had never occurred, in either marriage. He and
Sally hadn't even talked about kids. If they had, Sally would have
expected *him* to raise them, Harry figured. Hell, she'd have expected
him to *bear* them—she wouldn't have the time.

With admiration, Harry watched the way Bill was content to sit
there, sipping the beer, saying nothing, until, after a while, he finished
it, crushed the can in one hand, murmured, "Ah, good!" and stood and
got two more from the cooler in the back of the dune buggy.

As he handed one to Harry, he said, "Surf fishing kind of tame,
huh?"

"That's what I like about it," Harry replied. "It's also the most exercise I've had in a while. I can feel it up here," and he ran his hand
across his chest and shoulder. "If it weren't for that, I could stand
there forever. Anyway, what kind of exciting things do you think I do
with my time?"

Bill just shrugged, as if preparing an answer, but in no hurry to begin it. As Harry waited, he realized he'd been thinking about Bill as an older man, but looking at him closely, Harry saw they might both be the same age, late thirties.

"Oh, tennis, golf, croquet, jogging, swimming, softball. Lots of parties—all the things you people set up for yourselves."

Harry had to give a loud laugh at that. "First of all, I don't set anything up for myself. This morning, surfcasting, is the closest I've come to that in a long time. As for the list, the only thing on it I participate in are the parties." It was strange, he thought, that Bill should refer to Harry and the outsiders in a lump as "you people"; he thought of Bill and the Bonackers in the same way.

"Bill, you and I must be about the same age. How old are you?"

"Thirty-six."

He was two years younger than Harry, and not aging well. "You're a bit younger, but close. Yet each of us thinks of the other as being some kind of foreigner. I guess we are, in a way—to each other. But we also think of each other as some kind of group lump, not as an individual. Look at all those things you think I do, when actually I do almost none of them. And, the fact is, since I don't build courts, or pools, or houses, or patios, or saunas for 'you people,' I don't even know how to describe the lump I put 'you people' in. I don't even know if this makes sense, but . . . oh hell. Bill, tell me who you think 'us people' are."

"Rich," said the other man, promptly. "From New York City. Drive Mercedeses. Spend a lot of money on clothes." He smiled.

"Why'd you smile?" Harry asked.

" 'Cause when you people come into Sam's, you're always wearin' work clothes, country clothes, I don't know what you want to call them, but they look funny on you. People who talk about books and TV and movies and money all the time, and they're wearin' jeans and denim work shirts and boots, pretendin' to be farmers, or somethin'. Why should you want to look like workin' men, when you can afford not to? When all the workin' people want to do is get out of their work clothes and dress up on a Saturday night?"

"I suppose everybody wants to change out of what he considers the uniform he *must* wear, and put on something different, something that represents fun time to him, instead of work time."

"Yeah, I guess so," Bill agreed. "But you people look so funny in jeans and that other stuff, like they're too new, or too expensive, too fancy. Like the bodies are just wrong for them. I don't know, maybe *we* look just as funny in jackets and ties, like we're wrong for them."

"What else about us people? Do you natives look at us as intruders?"

Bill popped another beer, took a swig, thought for a moment. "Can't blame you for comin' out here. Sure is a beautiful place, ain't it?"

"It sure is. Do you resent us for being here? Do you think we're trying to take it away from you?"

Bill laughed. "Hell, you ain't *tryin'*, you're *takin'* it!"

"You don't have to sell. *You* people are making a lot of money on our taking it."

"Well, yeah, some people are makin' a lot of money. I guess we're all doin' all right. That's why none of us really want you to leave, 'cause we're makin' a livin' off you. I don't know if we could make a livin' at all if you weren't here. But, yeah, a lot of us resent you, 'cause you're rich and kind of noisy, and you throw your money around, do a lot of showin' off.

"My wife sees it. She works the parties at the big estates. She doesn't like the way you people treat her. She thinks you look down on her. And a lot of the local people feel the same way, that you think you're better than we are. That's why some of 'em don't mind overchargin' you, or givin' you a hard time; some of 'em are in favor of screwin' you any chance they get. You think we're dumb, so we like to show you. Besides, we figure you got the money, so it don't make any difference what the price is."

"But how can you accuse us of looking down on you? Don't you understand that most of us are in terror of your power? We *need* you desperately. Nothing can run without you. I've heard *us* people begging *you* people—the contractors, plumbers, electricians—to come. Begging! Promising anything! We're at your mercy!"

Bill just looked at him goodnaturedly for a while before answering.

"Yeah, but would you invite us to one of your parties?"

Harry smiled and held up his beer in salute.

"Touché."

Soon after, Harry bought himself surfcasting equipment—rod, reel, line, lures, tackle box, the whole thing—and often walked over the dunes to cast for an hour or so. Sometimes he'd go with Bill. And he'd see him regularly on Friday evenings. But he never did meet Bill at a party.

By the time she was twenty-five, a year after she and Harry had split, Sally had the title of senior editor, but she knew that the big time

in publishing lay in the buying, selling and merchandising of manuscripts, not editing, so when the job of manager of subsidiary rights
opened at Saxon, she pitched for it and got it. She became expert at
selling the paperback, foreign and serial rights to books, even more
expert at spotting their commercial possibilities. In business dealings
she was unsentimental to the point of ruthlessness; "quality" was a word
she seldom used. "Is it commercial?" became her favorite question.

When an aggressive young paperback house, Greyhound, offered
her the job of editor-in-chief, at a substantial raise, she went to her
boss at Saxon, Johnny Wainwright, and told him about it, waited for
him to match or top it. But that was not Johnny's style, and so they
parted, staying casual friends. Their next business dealing was over
Bea's book, and this time it was clear that Sally, not Johnny, was the
leader. She set the opening figure, $1.5 million for their hard-soft offer;
she decided they'd better be ready to go up as high as $2.3 million.
Unsure, disbelieving, Johnny followed.

Sally could feel herself taking charge, and Johnny moving her way,
which she liked. He was useful—but not indispensable. There were
other houses, and there was always Freddie Kohl. He was going to
make, perhaps had already made, an offer. There was money to be
made on the book; there were skins to be saved: Freddie's and the
Governor's. She didn't trust Freddie, knew he'd push her to the wall if
she were weak; but she also knew she could take care of herself. Yes,
she'd deal with Freddie if she had to. As a last resort.

Ahead of Freddie, there'd have to be someone who had access to
Bea. There was Johnny. There was Carlotta, Bea's closest friend, but
Carlotta would be in there pitching for Buster. Besides, Sally was not
a close friend of Carlotta's, nor could she offer her anything.

Then there was Harry.

In the years since their split, Sally sometimes thought about him and
the causes of their breakup. Crossword puzzles? Wisecracks?
Lethargy? Lack of ambition? Cynicism? Yes. And no. In Sally's mind
none of those reasons would have been serious, had not the magic
ingredient been missing—and that was money. Had Harry been rich,
none of the other things would have been important. Sally happened
to believe that money mattered, and if you didn't have it, you
shouldn't be sitting on your ass doing crossword puzzles. If, on the
other hand, you *were* rich . . .

Although she didn't know Bea well, Sally assumed Bea felt the same
way about money. After all she wasn't writing to win a National Book

Award; she didn't spend time in the Hamptons to hide her light under a bushel or play humble. She wanted money, and the fact that Harry didn't have any, and wasn't trying to get any, may have played a part in *their* breakup, too.

For Sally to have said that to Harry during their marriage would have been to wave a red flag at a bull. But maybe now, after his split with Bea, he'd see the pattern. Maybe now he'd be willing to try something. . . . She doubted it, but figured there was no harm trying.

She needed an excuse to see him, and she thought showing him her new house might offer it.

What she first had to do was engineer a casual meeting. She had to be careful. She couldn't call him; Harry was always suspicious of her wheels within wheels, always suspicious about which axe she was grinding.

She decided the place should be Sam's Pizza, in East Hampton, on a Friday night. The first Friday she drew a blank; the second, she found him at the bar.

"Can I buy you a drink until your date, or whoever, arrives?"

"Whoever. Why not? I'll have a beer."

"Cheap date."

"And worth every penny of it."

"How are you doing?"

"Doing OK, Sally. I don't have to ask how you're doing. *Publishers Weekly* is full of it. You deserve to be their woman of the year. Or would the gender disappoint you?"

"Still funny funny funny, huh, Harry? Still read every magazine?"

"Yup, and do every crossword puzzle. In ink."

"Nothing's changed, eh?"

"Nope. And I like it because the more things don't change, the more they stay the same. How about you? Changing all the time, I'll bet."

"I hope so, Harry. That's what life is all about: change. Just finished redoing my new house, and I'm proud as hell of it. You really ought to see it . . ." She paused as if the thought had just occurred to her. "Why don't you? Stop by sometime this weekend, let me give you a drink and a tour. It's very feminine."

"Showing off, eh!"

"Unashamedly. I think I've done a hell of a lot with a little money. Why don't you stop by? I've got some passable soave—you still drink it, don't you?—and a super little house. Let me show off."

For a moment, Harry just looked at her. She was attractive, yet he couldn't remember loving her. He thought it would be OK to have a look at her house.

"Maybe Sunday, if I'm not too busy jogging, swimming, croqueting, golfing, tennising and crossword puzzling."

She smiled, because he was funny, and because she was pleased at getting what she wanted. "Make it around noon, to give you a break between morning and afternoon sports."

On Sunday, when he hadn't arrived by 12:30, she phoned him, trying not to seem too eager.

"Oh, damn!" he said. "I've been so busy with the push-ups, the sit-ups and the weights, I lost track of the time. You still want me there in a half hour? Or have I already thrown you off schedule for the week? You know once you fall an hour behind, you *never* quite make it up . . ."

"Shut up, and come over! What else have you got to do? It's too crummy a day for surfing."

"You've talked me out of the surf and into a cold glass of soave. See you in half an hour."

It was chilly for May, and rain had begun to fall. Sally had bemoaned the absence of fireplaces in her new house, so in her den she had put a handsome, open-faced, cast-iron stove. Except for her bedroom, which she'd painted orchid and just adored, the den was Sally's favorite room, done simply in brown and white, walls of rough pine painted white, sofa, chairs, drapes all the same bold brown-and-white print. She lit a fire in the stove, curled up on the sofa with a manuscript.

In thirty-five minutes she heard his car drive up; she stood, looked out. It was a compact and, she could see by the Z in the license plate, rented.

"Same old Harry," she said after she kissed his cheek. "Rented house, rented car, always ready to pick up and move. No mortgages."

"That's right. I can never afford the payments. Now shut up and let's have a drink and a tour."

"Bloody mary? Red wine? White wine?"

He looked around the living room, dominated by whites, creams, pale pastels. "Better make it the soave, a spilled bloody mary around here would ruin everything."

She poured him the wine, then showed him the living room, all its old sofas and chairs re-covered in off-white with stripes and piping, a plethora of throw pillows brightening the room. She was especially proud of the two theatrical posters, one a Mucha—"more than I could

afford, but a real prize. I could sell it now for double what I paid"—
the other a Cheret—"not nearly as expensive, but lively, don't you
think, and the colors are perfect for the room."

She walked him into the dining room, with its big oak table, its
reupholstered chairs bought for almost nothing at a garage sale, its
second Cheret poster, its bone china standing proudly in a glass cabinet. Then her favorite, the brown-and-white den, and upstairs, the
orchid bedroom, with its canopied double bed, and finally a quick
glance at the second and third bedrooms.

"I haven't had the time or the money to do those yet," she explained.
"So don't look. Just take my word they're going to be terrific."

He found the tone of apology amusing and charming; she seemed
more feminine than he'd remembered her in a long time.

When they finished, she took him into the den, where the fire was
burning.

Again, he was amused. "Living room too fragile for just anyone,
right? I don't blame you. Ordinary people would get those creams and
whites dirty in no time!" He smiled as he said it.

She almost blushed. "Oh shut up! What do you think of it?"

"You've done a hell of a job, Sal, really. It's in such good taste—but
then you always did have good taste, except in husbands. And it's so
feminine."

"Thanks, I was hoping you'd like it. Does it surprise you that it's
feminine? I *am* feminine, you know—even though I'm ambitious. Can't
a woman want to be rich and successful and still be feminine?"

"Forget it, Sal. I didn't mean to suggest anything. God knows, one of
the many blessings of our not being married is that we don't have to
fight over things like that. We've agreed to disagree, which is just fine.
You can be *very* feminine; you're more attractive than you ever were."
He raised his glass. "Here's to a good-looking house, and the good-
looking woman who owns it." He took a sip of the wine.

For a moment the two of them just sat there, silently. Then Harry
said, "In the eight years we've been split, this is the first time we've sat
down together with no purpose other than to ask: How've you been? So
how've you been? Can you sum up the eight years in a word?"

"Do I have to?"

"No."

She thought for a couple of moments, then said, "Busy."

"I would have said, Driven."

"Nobody asked you. If you want to supply one word, do it for your own eight years."

"All right, let's see." He hesitated. "Easy."

"I would have said, The same," she offered.

"Nobody asked *you*. Besides, that's two words."

"Will you allow it?"

"Sure. I don't mind."

"Wow, Harry, you should mind. It's not much to say about your life, do you realize that?"

"No, I don't. Not at all. Depends on whether you like what you're doing. If you do, the same can be terrific."

"I disagree. Different is always valuable. New things. Changes. That's always an interesting way to go."

"Not if you're happy where you are."

"Are you, Harry? Or just too lazy to change?"

"The answer to that is a definite yes—and no. Some of each, I suppose. But I do know a lot of what people call change is really staying the same. Just substituting new trivia for the old."

"Sure, some of it is the same. I still read a lot of manuscripts, I still buy books. Some of it's different, though. I don't have to wade through the real shit anymore, someone filters that out for me. I don't have to let someone else make the ultimate decisions anymore, most of those I get to do myself. Life is not an excursion, I'm not a tourist. If you've got a goal you believe in, you go after it, and if that means doing some drudge work, some work you don't like, you do it anyway. Your advantage there, Harry, only it's your problem, too, is you don't have a goal."

"Yes I do. My goal is not to have to do anything I don't like."

"And does it work for you?"

"I told you: yes and no. And does yours work for you?"

"Yes."

"I'm waiting for the 'and no.'"

"There is none. Just yes."

"Sure of yourself, huh?"

"Sure I'm after what I want. And on the way to getting it."

"Never wanted to marry again?"

"I could ask you the same, Harry."

"I did marry again. You. It didn't work."

"Lots of people thought you were going to marry Bea Fletcher."

"I wasn't one of them."

"That's not what I heard."

"I don't give a damn what you heard, and that's the name of that tune. You haven't answered me. Didn't you, don't you, want to marry, have kids? After all, you're thirty-two—you don't have all that much time for kids."

"I guess I do want kids, but I'm hot on the trail of a career right now, and I don't want the scent to get cold. Each time I meet a man who has even the remotest of possibilities as a husband and I think about children, I wonder how much it will set me back; I start thinking of it as a diversion, a red herring."

She sat back, sipped her wine, looked at the fire. "I'm always on the move, but one thing I don't want to change is this room and that fire and being able to sit here this way. For the rest of my life, I'll be content to light the fire and sit and stare at it."

Harry smiled at her. "Here's to your doing that—as long as you want to." He raised his glass.

"What do you mean, as long as I want to?"

"What I mean is, in a couple of years, maybe sooner, you'll want a fireplace, not a stove, and a house south of the highway, not north. And a couple of years after that you'll want a marble fireplace, not just a fireplace, and a house on the beach, not just south of the highway."

She didn't deny it. "You're quibbling," she answered. "The principle is the same."

"Far from it. The principle is quite the opposite. You're talking about your being contented. I'm talking about your being discontented. My guess is that half the time you spend in front of any stove, or any fireplace, you'll spend thinking, planning how to get a better one. I don't call that contentment."

"Oh, how I disagree! Thinking ahead, planning ahead, makes me happy. I can spend blissful hours sitting here thinking how I'm going to improve this house, how I'm going to buy a bigger one some day. That doesn't mean I'm not content in front of *this* fire."

"If you want to say you're contented being discontented, I'm just not going to argue that one. But tell me, what happens if things *don't* get better all the time? How do you handle setbacks? Or has every single thing improved for you in the past eight years?"

"You have a funny idea of the way the world works, Harry. Setbacks disappoint me, the way they disappoint anyone else. They also make me determined—to make things work better the next time. That's the way a lot of people handle them. There are people who decide the way to avoid disappointment is not to try for anything. I'm *not* one of those. Has everything gone the way I've wanted in the last eight years? Of course not. Although I'm *trying* to make it work that way. Shouldn't everyone?"

"Name one thing that hasn't."

She stopped staring into the fire, and looked at him, hesitated, started to speak, stopped.

"Go on," he prompted. "We're letting our hair down. Say it."

"Sex."

She caught him; it was one of those rare times when he didn't know what to say. "I'm sorry," he finally managed, and then had to add, "I mean it, I'm not being flippant. You and I made love beautifully; it got to be the best thing we had, in fact it got to be the only good thing we had. If the others had worked as well . . ."

He looked straight at her. In her eyes he suddenly saw the hope and vulnerability of the twenty-two-year-old he'd met ten years before.

"Sometimes I tell myself I'm in too much of a hurry, too mono-maniacal." It sounded almost like an apology. "You know, I never said I had all the answers. I never said one doesn't have to pay a price for choosing one direction over another. You said those things for me."

Impulsively, he leaned from his end of the sofa to hers, took her hand and squeezed it. "I know it. It suited me to pretend you said them."

"As long as we're letting our hair down," she said, "I've got a confession to make. There were times, not in the first year after the split, when I was still angry, but after that, times I was lonely—successful and lonely—times when I heard or read you were between gorgeous women, just polishing off one conquest, with the next not yet announced, when I was tempted to pick up the phone in the evening and call you and ask if I could come over and slip into bed for the night. No talk, nothing serious, just a night of making love, lying there with your arms around me, with your big, overweight body pressed against me. My hand was actually on the phone a couple of times. Other times I thought of just taking a chance and walking over and surprising you, ringing your bell and walking in."

"Why didn't you?" Suddenly, in a flood, he could remember loving her, making love to her, missing her, wanting to touch her, thinking about living happily ever after with her.

"Partly, I guess I didn't want to give in. Partly I didn't want to get a no from you. I didn't want to walk over only to find you there with

another woman. And I didn't want to give you the impression I wanted
us back together, because I didn't. Bed time was never our problem. It
was the *rest* of the time we couldn't make it." She shrugged, smiled,
made a gesture with her hands, then let them drop into her lap.

"You would have surprised the hell out of me. I'd never dream of
that kind of impulsive, spontaneous thing coming from you. I would
have given you a lot of points for it." He laughed. "As if points from
me are any big deal."

"But would you have said, Come over?"

He thought for a moment, nodded his head. "Yes. Yes, I would
have."

They stared at each other, as if it had just occurred to them they
were alone, in front of a fire, on a rainy Sunday with nothing to do.
Nothing better than making love.

He leaned over and kissed her. Her mouth was soft, her lips parted.
He reached into her blouse, touched her nipple. Even as they kissed,
he could feel her jump as he touched her.

For a long time they kissed, then he drew his face away. "Is this why
you wanted me to come over?"

"I'm glad this is happening. But I didn't expect it. Or plan it."

"Was it to see the house?"

"Yes."

He knew her well. "But there was more," he said.

"Let's talk about it later."

"Now."

"Something that could mean a lot to both of us; please, we can talk
about it later."

"Bea's book, isn't it?" He sat up, pulled back from her.

"Harry, just listen for a . . ."

"I've just remembered a previous engagement I'm about to make."
He stood. "Nice place you've got here. You'll be able to make a bundle
on it when you buy the big one down on Lily Pond. You must remember to invite me over to see that one, too. Bea's *next* book should be
ready about then. See you around. And next time you're thinking of
picking up the phone, or stopping by—don't."

He turned, walked out of the house.

She took a sip of her wine, listened to the car pulling out of her
driveway. Harry had saved her from herself, and she was glad of that.
But now she might have to deal with Freddie Kohl. He'd try to slaugh-
ter her—she'd be ready for him.

Labor Day Weekend, 1977; Sunday (continued)

BEA FLETCHER seemed to have the answers to all questions, Wisniew-ski told himself as he drove to her Sagaponack house. It was not the house she'd lived in when he met her the year before; that one had been rented, this was hers, an old farmhouse that would be a bitch of a maintenance problem. He never did understand why these people were so anxious to pour money into the purchase and upkeep of what was old, when they could afford something new and headache-free.

He'd called first, so when he knocked at her kitchen door, she opened it at once.

"I'm Detective Wisniewski."

"How do you do? Come in." She paused, stared at him. "You're . . . the man who came to help during last year's storm!"

He smiled. "You've got a good memory."

She walked him to the living room, gestured toward a sofa.

"That's my business. I always meant to call your headquarters to thank you, but never did. Thank you. Better late . . ."

"Oh, you're welcome, it was my job."

"By the way, do you remember that Freddie Kohl was one of the people here?"

"Yes, I do. Who were the others? Mr. Wainwright, right?"

"Right."

"And Mr. Majors?"

"Right again."

"Any others?"

"No."

"You all seemed to be having such a good time. I'm surprised to learn how people disliked Mr. Kohl."

"Yes, I suppose they did."

"Did you?"

"Yes. Does that make me a suspect?"

"If disliking him made someone a suspect, there'd be nothing but suspects. It takes more than dislike. It takes a real motive. The person's whereabouts at the time of the act. His or her capability to perform the particular act. For example, if the act took great size and strength, that would eliminate a smaller, weaker person."

"But would it take great strength to drown Freddie? Could he even swim?"

"Don't you know?"

"I have no idea. Come to think of it, I've never *seen* him swim."

"From what I've heard, he couldn't. Not a stroke."

"That means a lot of people could drown him. Perhaps even I could."

"Are you a good swimmer, Mrs. Fletcher?"

"Not bad."

"Then maybe you could have."

"So could most anyone at Freddie's house last night. That gives you a lot of suspects. Including me."

"There's the matter of motive. Disliking isn't enough."

"What kind of motive would be enough?"

"I was going to ask you that, Mrs. Fletcher. I hear all the answers are in your book."

"I wonder who was kind enough to say that? And you can tell Harry to mind his own business."

"He's not the only one. Isn't your book what they're all after?"

"Some of them are, but I hardly think anyone wants it badly enough to kill."

"I just don't know that, ma'am. I don't even know that he was killed by anyone, not on purpose. It could have been a heart attack, or an accident, or maybe even suicide. I'm trying to find out a lot of things. I hope you'll help me."

"Aren't you glad you showed me how to turn on the furnace? Now I owe you one."

"I'm investigating a death, maybe a murder, Mrs. Fletcher. I hope you'll tell me what you know in order to help, not because you owe me anything."

"Sorry," she replied. "It was a bad joke. I'll try to help."

"Tell me who was there last night."

Once again, he heard the same names.

"Who did you talk to?"

"Oh, a little to everyone. No one special." Then she added, "I did have a long talk with Buster Reilly in the library."

"Oh. What about?"

"About his ex-wife, Carlotta, who's my best friend. About his career." She paused.

"About the book?"

"Yes, about the book."

"What did you say about it?"

"Buster wants to produce the movie version. We talked about that."

"Will he produce it?"

She hesitated. "That's not up to me."

"Who is it up to?"

"My agent, Irv Schnell. The kind of deal he makes."

"If it were up to you, would you let Buster Reilly produce the movie?"

"I don't know. But it's *not* up to me."

"Would you have let Friedrich Kohl produce the movie—if it were up to you?"

"He made an offer to buy *all* the rights to the book, hardcover, paperback, film and TV, everything."

"A good offer?"

"A *lot* of money."

"Would you have taken it?"

"I would have left it up to my agent."

"Would he?"

"It was a big offer. But he didn't like Freddie."

"Add another name to the list. Did the offer make you like Mr. Kohl any more?"

She seemed to think for a moment, then: "I continued to detest him. I would have preferred that he not get any part of the book."

"Now he won't. That must please you."

"I'm not pleased that he's dead."

Sitting in an easy chair across from him, she shifted her weight, recrossed her legs. She was in shorts, and despite his efforts not to look, Wisniewski noticed how slim and beautiful her legs were. He looked away uneasily, embarrassed at having stared. He wondered if Freddie had ever looked at her legs.

"Did Mr. Kohl and you . . . was there ever . . . any romantic interest between you?"

"Not on my part, and as far as I could tell, not on his either."

"Mrs. Fletcher, I understand that some people out here were afraid of what your book might say about them. Was Mr. Kohl afraid, do you suppose?"

"I'm writing a novel, it's not about real people."

"Oh, Mrs. Fletcher, I hear it's very *close* to real people. Please level with me, I'm a detective, I'm not a book critic, or a professor. Is there a character in it that's close to Mr. Kohl?"

"Yes, I guess there is."

"Would Mr. Kohl have any reason to fear the things said about this character?"

"I guess so."

"Would other people be afraid of what's in it about them?"

"Yes, some might."

"Which ones?"

"You'll just have to read the book!"

"I'd like to."

"It will be available in hardcover in the spring."

"I'm afraid I can't wait that long. How close are you to having it finished?"

"Very close. I'm right up to the ending, which I've got to work on. Freddie's death is going to change some of my plans."

"Do you bring the events right up to date, Mrs. Fletcher?"

"I spent this morning writing about last night at Freddie's. That's how up to date it is."

"It's about the South Fork?"

"Most of it is."

"Do you like it out here, Mrs. Fletcher?"

"Yes. Everything but . . . I suppose I shouldn't be flippant, but what the hell. The place is gorgeous. I like everything about it but the people."

An August Weekend, 1977

A GRASS court!

Bea scuffed her way back to the service line, trying somehow to caress the thick green carpet of lawn through the soles of her tennis shoes. Johnny Wainwright, her doubles partner, strode over to her.

"Are you all right? You're walking strangely."

"No, I'm not all right," she replied. "I may have an orgasm. I do believe the feel of this grass is the single most sensual experience of my life. Including sex." She flashed her grin at him.

"Never mind the big smile," he said. "Concentrate on the big serve. Hit it deep. You're doing just great." He had to smile back.

The sun was brilliant, the day exhilarating; the few puffy white clouds served to make the sky a deeper blue by contrast. The white of the impeccably drawn lines of the doubles court accentuated the green of the grass. If there was any breeze it was not felt in this hollow behind the dunes where the Fentons had cleverly built their court, the only private grass court in East Hampton, as they proudly pointed out.

As they also proudly pointed out, it cost about $10,000 a year to keep up, which at an average use of twenty-five times per summer, meant $400 per use. They were even prouder of the beachfront mansion, on eight acres, which cost $75,000 a year to run and was worth over a million dollars.

Bea loved playing on grass, hadn't done it since she was a girl in Nashville. She toed the service line of the forehand court, set herself, brought her racket back as if to scratch her back, as she'd been taught by the pro at the country club back home, threw the ball high and straight, hit it deep to Gerri Fenton, who managed a weak return to the center of the court. Johnny took it with a forehand volley, obviously easing up on the return. Gerri hit a soft cross-court shot toward the alley on Bea's side of the court, and moving toward the net, Bea was in perfect position to hit it right down the alley, passing Bob Fenton, who made a futile backhand lunge for it at the net.

"Good shot!" Fenton said.

Bea and Johnny walked across their side of the court. "Nice going, Bea!" he said. "I should have teamed up with you long ago!"

"Oh, I haven't played in ages!" she responded happily. She'd been a fifth choice, phoned in desperation when his regular partner cancelled. It had been years since her last tennis game, as she'd told them all before she started the match. What she hadn't mentioned were the six lessons she'd taken in the past couple of months. She'd always loved tennis; besides, it was an important part of the life out here, and she didn't want to be left out of it.

She looked across the net, saw Bob Fenton standing ready. Serve it deep, she told herself. Don't let him move in on your serve. She brought the racket back, tossed the ball high, remembering to keep her eye on it. She hit it deep, trying to get it to Fenton's backhand, but he ran around it, took it on the forehand, returned it to her forehand. Bea hit it hard to Gerri Fenton, hoping she'd go for it with her backhand, rather than letting it go through to her husband's forehand. Gerri obliged, barely getting her racket on it, sending it squiggling over the net at a speed and angle which made it impossible for Johnny to reach.

"Ah, you devil!" Johnny said to Gerri, shaking his head and grinning as he crossed the court.

"Good shot! Wonderful!" Bea shouted. She wanted to keep the game cheerful. She prepared to serve, announced, "Forty-fifteen!" She took a deep breath, looked around. How sumptuous, how gorgeous all this was, and how she loved it! She forced her attention back to the game. She got her first serve in, and deep. Three first serves in a row, she said to herself, not bad for a teenage mediocrity, many years removed.

Bob Fenton, tall, dark, thin, was not quite as fanatical about tennis as he was about making money. Nor was he as good at it. But fanatical enough and good enough to spend the money on the court and to want to win. His wife was a terrible player, but to her the court meant a distinction she could achieve in no other way. She would sooner talk about the court than play on it.

Fenton hit Bea's serve straight back at her, hard and deep to her backhand. He wanted to keep the ball away from Johnny, to break Bea's service and win the game, which would bring the Fentons to 4-5 in games and keep them alive in the set.

Bea hit a good backhand return but did not get by Fenton, and he slammed it to her backhand again. Challenged, Bea got off another good backhand and this time went to the net behind it. Fenton tried to lob it over her head, but the shot was short and weak, and she smashed it right at him, handcuffing him. The ball got by his racket and hit him squarely in the groin.

Bea ran around the net, but by the time she reached him he was straightening up.

"Oh Bob," she said, "I'm so sorry! Are you all right?"

He was walking around now. "Yes, of course. You play a hell of a game."

Meanwhile, Johnny had hurdled the net. "You all right?"

Fenton said, "Oh, sure. Where did you find her, Johnny?" The four of them headed off the court. He added, "Bea, you've got an instinct for the jugular."

"Only I hit a little low," she answered, and they all started to laugh. "I was mighty relieved," she continued, "when you didn't answer me in a high voice. For a moment there I was afraid it was game, set and macho."

"What do you think of playing on grass?" Gerri asked.

"May I tell you," Bea responded earnestly, "you have one of the most beautiful hunks of turf in the western world? The feel of it underfoot, the bright green look of it in the sun; the sky, the house, the sparkly white of the tennis outfits—how delightful it is to see us all in white; anything else would have been defiling . . . I'm glad there are some purists left—all of it is just so delicious, I wish I could eat it up."

Gerri Fenton loved appreciation. "You'll have to come back again!" she said. Her husband added with a smile, "Provided you don't get too good for us." He was only half kidding, Bea knew that. She picked up a towel, daubed at her face, let a look of utter weariness come over it as she did.

"Beginner's luck," she replied. "You began by assuming I couldn't play at all, and now, in reaction, you're overestimating me. When you're on your guard, you will, I assure you, be able to thrash and humiliate me thoroughly."

Bob Fenton laughed. "I'll drink to that," he said. "What would you like?" He walked them over to the pavilion where the Portuguese couple who worked for the Fentons were tending the bar and buffet.

"A glass of white wine would be lovely." Bea took the delicate goblet in her hand, relishing the luxury of it, accepted a plate of lobster salad, walked over and sat next to Irv Schnell, who'd been watching the match.

"I guess you surprised everyone, Bea."

"I guess I did pretty well."

"Maybe a little too well?"

She leaned toward Irv, lowered her voice. "Remember this, sexy. I never kiss ass unless it is an absolute high-level business necessity. Let 'em call me a bitch. Let 'em call me a gossip. Let 'em call me a castrating female. But let 'em never say I threw a tennis game just to get another shot at the grass court, the Mâcon and the lobster salad."

"That's a wonderful line, Bea. I hope you'll remember it for the book."

It was a year and a half earlier that Irv, serendipitously, heard his first wonderful Bea Fletcher line. He was in Washington to have lunch with a former Secretary of State who wanted Irv to handle his memoirs, and dinner with the Vice President, who wanted Irv to sell his book on crises in American society. To the Secretary he'd probably say yes, to the VP, possibly no. While he realized the VP might someday be President, he was not impressed. Ten years earlier, Irv would have taken him on with calculation of future benefits. But at Irv's age, with his income, he didn't have to take on anyone who didn't interest him, not for money, not for prestige, not for future benefits. He had to like a writer. He could afford to indulge himself.

One of his indulgences was that he wouldn't try to catch the late plane back to New York the same night, but would book a suite at the

Watergate and take his time about flying up to New York the next morning.

He checked in after lunch to grab a nap before dinner. Before he opened his overnight bag to hang out his blue suit, with the habit of a media addict he flipped on the TV set. He heard a man's voice, then a woman's, then a second woman's with a Southern accent. The Southern accent seemed to be doing most of the talking; the others the laughing. Irv paid little attention; he undid his tie, unbuttoned his shirt, took off his shoes, sighed with relief.

He began to listen; in response to a question from the host, the Southern woman said: "Our Congressmen the intellectual elite of our nation? Tom, either you are tryin' to be provocative, or you're a press agent for the majority leader. With the possible exception of a snake's belly, the only thing lower than a Congressman's moral standard is his IQ!"

Irv wanted to see what this viper looked like. He saw a handsome, animated woman who appeared to be in her mid-thirties, with delicate, regular features and a toothpaste-ad smile. The other two apparently regarded her as an expert on Washington mores.

"Wouldn't you say, Bea, that Washington morality has been elevated post-Watergate?" the woman asked.

"It would be hard for it *not* to. As they say, when you're at the South Pole, the only direction you can go is north!"

She's damned clever, and personable, Irv thought. But Bea who? And what else did she do besides tear Washington apart on a local talk show? He leaned forward for more.

"How do you reconcile your low view of our government with the fact that we're the leader of the free world, Bea?" the man asked.

"Leader of the free world?" she repeated, mockingly. "Have you noticed lately just where it is we're *leadin'* 'em? Have you turned around to see if anyone is *followin'*? Anyone, that is, who doesn't have his hand out?"

The woman had a knockout punch, Irv told himself, and knew just how to use that cute Southern accent. Nor was she above a bit of distortion for effect.

Irv liked her; he was interested in her. But who in hell was she? Then the words "Bea Fletcher, Washington Columnist" were superimposed on her picture. Irv spotted the call letters of the station and phoned it.

"My name is Irv Schnell, and it's important that I speak with the Bea Fletcher who was just on your talk show."

He couldn't get through to her, so he put in a call to the Vice President, whose press secretary supplied her home number.

A maid answered. Mrs. Fletcher had gone to her son's dancing class; the maid didn't know where that was. Irv got the VP's press secretary again. There were two proper dance classes in Washington. Irv got both names and numbers. He called the first, Miss Farmington's Classes. Yes, Mrs. Fletcher's son, Staunton, was in the class, in fact Mrs. Fletcher was supposed to help out today—parents took turns doing that—and she was expected momentarily.

The class was in a small ballroom in an old downtown hotel; Irv wrote down the address, dressed, ran out of the room and found a cab.

In ten minutes he was slowly opening the door to a rococo ballroom. Quietly he stepped in, looked around. He saw a pianist and two teachers, both in white gloves, primly dressed, looking like Irv's idea of finishing-school headmistresses. There were perhaps twenty children, all about twelve or thirteen years old. Irv could see no Bea Fletcher.

The older of the two teachers was speaking. "You *must* listen to the beat of the music as it tells you step, step-together-step. And remember that since the man leads, he must always see where he is going so he can guide his partner and avoid colliding with other couples."

Irv stood at the door, not knowing how to approach, not wanting to interrupt the class, yet unwilling to leave without asking about Bea Fletcher. The pianist began playing; unaccountably, it was the 1940s tune, "It's Been a Long, Long Time." He looked at the pianist; the man was his age. Irv smiled.

Then the younger of the two white-gloved women detached herself from the group and started toward him with an upper-class self-confidence befitting a dance-class teacher.

"May I help you?" she asked as she got closer.

Irv began his answer just as the music stopped and his voice rang out in the room, which disconcerted him. "Well, actually, I . . . I'm looking . . ."

She grinned. "I'm sorry, the classes for the *older* boys meet on Thursdays."

"You're Bea Fletcher."

"Yes, I am." Her smile began to fade.

"Actually, I'm here looking for you. Do you have a couple of minutes? My name is Irv Schnell, and . . ."

The smile disappeared. "I'm afraid I don't know you, and in any event I'm busy with this class."

Irv was not about to let her get away. "I am a friend of the Vice President."

"Of the hotel or of the country?"

"Of the country." He smiled at her. "I'm a literary agent. A very well known one, even though you've never heard of me. I'm down from New York to talk to the Vice President about a book he is thinking of writing, and I happened to see you on TV, and . . ."

She looked at him, hard. The dancing-class teacher was gone. "May I buy you a drink?" she asked.

"I was about to ask you the same question."

"I'd be delighted, either to buy, or be bought for," she said. "This hotel has a lovely old bar which has gone just seedy enough to make it picturesque. Why don't you go down there and wait till the class is over, after which I'll see if I can get my son a ride home with one of the other junior Fred Astaires, and meet you in about twenty minutes."

"Fine, Mrs. Fletcher."

"Please call me Bea. And repeat your name to me."

"Schnell. Irv Schnell."

"All right then, Mr. Snell, I'll see you in twenty minutes."

"Irv." He beamed at her.

Irv was amused by the inability of many gentiles, especially southerners, to pronounce the "sh" of his last name. He was also elated by this woman, by the alacrity with which she responded to his occupation. She was no shrinking violet; she was ambitious, quick to go after an opportunity. Of course she looked a little too refined to be the kind of clawing cat he'd seen on the tube. And while he didn't know what kind of book he had in mind, he knew he didn't want it from a genteel lady with white gloves and a gripe. Only a real bitch would do, and at dancing class Bea Fletcher didn't look the part.

He found the bar, ordered a glass of club soda and waited.

Twenty-five minutes later, Bea strode in. Too elegant by half, he told himself as he watched her approach in ladylike silk blouse and tweed suit. She slid into the banquette alongside him.

"My, this is exciting! Did you really just see me on television?"

"Yes, an hour or so ago, for the first time. I thought I might talk with you, ask a few questions, to see if the ideas I have cooking have anything to them. What would you like to drink?"

"Just a club soda or Perrier for me, too, please. The problem is, I don't have much time now. My maid can only stay till five, so I've got to start for home in"—she looked at her watch—"in a half hour. I'm sorry. I'd invite you to take potluck with us, but I know you're having dinner with the Vice President . . ." He looked at her, and she flashed her gleaming, flawless teeth at him. "Yes, I checked you out, too. If you were after my body, I wanted to know it so I could shower first."

"So you're assuming I'm not? Should I be hurt?"

A cautious look came into her eyes, which surprised him. "I'm not assuming anything. Nor am I letting down my guard. It's been my experience, Mr. Snell . . . Irv . . . that most men are after most women's bodies. That view may be distorted, jaundiced, invalid, but it is a lesson I have learned from the experiences of my distorted, jaundiced and invalid life."

This was not merely a society matron, Irv said to himself. Not even merely a cat. This was also a wounded woman. There might be a hell of a book in her. Assuming, of course, she could write.

"The last name is Schnell, Bea. With an 'sh' sound in it. But I like it even better when you call me Irv. Whatever you want to call me, I am *not* after your body. I *may* be after your mind and talent, though, both of which are unknown quantities to me at the moment. So let me ask you some questions. Have you ever thought of writing a book? How much writing have you done? What kind of book would you like to write, if any?"

He put his hand up to forestall any answers. "But, first, so you take my questions seriously, and answer them seriously, I want to tell you some things about myself. *Time* magazine has been kind enough to call me the best literary agent in the country. Believe it or not, I'm also a modest man, I just tell you this so you'll understand I'm not fooling, or trying to pull the wool over your eyes. My authors have won a Nobel Prize, four Pulitzers, three National Book Awards. I've also had seven books number-one on the *Times* best-seller list. I told you I was here to talk to the Vice President about a book, and you know that's true, because you checked up on me, which I think is cute. I also had lunch with a former Secretary of State today about his book. Both of them will be my authors, *if* I want them to be. But I'm fussy. I'm over sixty, I have more money than I need and I can afford to be fussy. I won't take on anybody who doesn't interest me, no matter how many books he or she can sell or has sold. I could give you some names, but why should I cast aspersions?

"When I saw you and heard you on TV, I said to myself, there might possibly be an interesting book in this person. So before you answer my questions, you must decide if the subject is worth pursuing. Otherwise, let's not either of us waste our time."

She answered, "Now I know who you are, from the Vice President's office and from you. And I'm impressed. I *have* done some writing, four columns a week for the *News*, a regular column for a magazine called *Month in Washington*. And yes, I have thought of writing a book. I'm not sure what kind, although I do know it would turn out to be cynical. *Mean*. Don't expect any happy endings, I don't believe in them. No, I'm not wasting my time talking to you, and I hope you're not wasting yours talking to me."

She looked down at her watch. "Pardon me, but I don't have any more time to talk now. I'm sorry, damned sorry. Perhaps another time . . ." She looked at him, shrugged, waited for him to offer something.

"How can I see what you've written?"

She thought for a moment. "If you tell me which hotel you're at, I'll drop off my book of clippings. Take them with you, read them at your leisure, and mail them back to me, I'll put the return address on the envelope. Then, if you're interested, and you're ever down here again, or I'm up in New York . . . but hell, you probably *won't* be interested. After all, National Book Awards and best-seller lists, I mean . . . hell! Whatever you do, please don't lose the clippings, they're all I have!"

"Don't worry," he replied. "I'll have someone pick up the scrapbook in a couple of hours, and return it tomorrow. I'll call you from the airport in the morning and we'll talk about it."

Bea was frightened. She was going to be judged, by high standards. By *New York* standards. "Can you form an opinion by tomorrow morning?" she asked.

"By tomorrow I could form an opinion of *War and Peace* or *Remembrance of Things Past*."

She laughed. "And what would it be?"

"Tolstoi, I'd handle. Proust, I wouldn't. No movie in it." He shrugged, smiled. "By tomorrow morning I'll have an opinion."

At 6:30 that evening a messenger rang the bell of her Georgetown house. Bea kissed her clippings book before she handed it over. She couldn't sleep all night; she was glad she didn't know the hotel he was at, for the temptation to call him might have overwhelmed her. It's all right, she kept telling herself, you're not really ready yet. Besides, it's not fair that you be judged by those columns. It's just as well for you to be turned down, so you'll have a chance to write something "serious" to be judged by, not gossip columns.

At 7:30 in the morning she began waiting for the phone to ring. She told herself she was being ridiculous, that he'd said he'd call from the airport, and there was no reason to think he'd be at the airport so early. Nine, ten, eleven, would be more like it. She kept telling herself that, and kept waiting for the ring, lying in bed, at first trying not to look at the phone or think of it, then giving in and just staring at it.

Nine, ten, eleven, she kept saying to herself. That's when it'll ring. It rang at 8:20. She reached to the night table for it; her hand trembled as she put the receiver to her ear.

"Hello?"

"Good morning, Bea, this is Irv Schnell. I hope I didn't wake you. I was afraid you might leave for work, or something."

"No, no, I've been up for some time." Like all night, she wanted to add, but didn't. "It is kind of early for you to be at the airport, though, isn't it?"

"I'm not at the airport, Bea. I'm still at the hotel. I figured as long as I was in town, I might stay a little longer, and take you to lunch. If you're free, that is . . ." Her heart gave such a fierce leap, she wasn't sure what he said next, something, she thought, about returning the clippings.

"I *am* free for lunch," she managed to say.

"I think you have a lot of talent. I think we might work something out. I also think you have a lot of anger in you. Cynicism. Bitterness. However, since I'm an agent, not a psychiatrist, I'm primarily concerned with the talent. Where would you like to have lunch?"

"It doesn't really matter. The Sans Souci, I guess. Do you want me to make the reservation?"

"I'll take care of it. How about 12:30? We can have a long, leisurely lunch."

"Sounds fine. Wonderful!"

She fidgeted away the morning, unable to concentrate on anything.

At lunch, the first thing Irv said was, "These columns are really strong stuff. You know how to write. The columns are vivid, with a lot of very good imagery. Believe me, it's a long way from a book, and whether you can go the distance remains to be seen. Anyway, so far, so good. But as I said over the phone, you're an angry, bitter woman. You don't seem to *like* anyone you write about. Which is all right for a columnist, but lousy for a person. And dangerous for a novelist."

Bea was wearing a well-tailored tan pants suit, with a black blouse. To Irv she looked sleek and a little tough. "You said you weren't going to be a psychiatrist," she warned. "And there you go again. I feel as though I've been charged with something, with a lot of things, and I don't know which to defend myself against first. All right, then, to start, there *are* people I like, but I don't write about them in my columns. Yes, I'm angry at a lot of people in Washington. Mostly men, because they're the ones in power in this town. Mostly men, because I'm a woman and men have fucked us over for a long time."

Her face softened, but only for a moment. "Please excuse my language," she said. "Now, as for my personality being unsuitable for a novelist, first of all I think you're wrong. But if it is, then I won't *be* a novelist. If we're here to talk about a new direction for my writing, wonderful. If we're here to talk about a new direction for my personality, forget it. If you want to play superagent to my superhopeful, I bless you. If you're here to play Henry Higgins to my Liza Doolittle, thanks for lunch."

Irv didn't get upset easily. "OK, OK, no psychoanalysis. I've got enough trouble just being an agent. I admit I did wonder why such a talented, beautiful woman should be so bitter, but I'll never ask again. Have you got a book in you? That's all I want to know."

Bea spoke indignantly. "What does being beautiful have to do with being bitter? Would you ever say to a man, you're so handsome, what have you got to be bitter about? Of course not! Why do you say it to a woman?" Then she stopped herself short. "Sorry, Irv. How to lose friends. Forget it. You were born into the system, just as I was. Let's talk about finding out if someone has a book in him—or her. How do you go about it?"

"Usually I ask the person to tell me the story of his life. Or her life. To you it'll seem like the analyst's couch."

"Tell you what," Bea said. "You keep me off the analyst's couch, I'll keep me off the soapbox. And I'll tell you the story of my life."

Over a long lunch, she did. She told him how the proper upper-middle-class girl from Nashville had married the handsomest man in town, Staunton Fletcher. How Staunton, then a thirty-four-year-old lawyer, had been appointed to the Securities and Exchange Commission, how they'd moved to Washington. How that had opened the eyes of the thirty-one-year-old Southern matron. How she'd been appalled by the venality and the immorality—especially the sexual immorality, with the man cast as predator and the woman as victim. How she'd been sure her marriage—"steel, anchored in bedrock," she'd called it—was impervious to Washington ways.

She told him of the horrid evening on which she discovered the steel and the bedrock shattered. She'd come back from a Nashville visit one day early, so she could surprise Staunton on the eve of his birthday. And what a surprise it had been! A bottle of champagne in her hand, she'd quietly entered the house, tiptoed upstairs—and found Staunton in bed with another woman. He swore it had never happened before, promised it would never happen again.

But it did happen again, soon, and this time he did not promise anything. He'd become hardened, become a "Washington husband"—which, she supposed, made her a Washington wife: suspicious, defensive. Mocked. Out of her sadness, her isolation, she had an abortive affair, brief and unsatisfying, but long enough to enable Staunton to find out, and impose a punitive divorce settlement which left her eating peanut butter sandwiches three nights a week until she could hack out a career for herself. She began as a receptionist in a public relations office, was graduated to writing press releases, then column items. Then came the monthly column, the daily column and the TV appearances.

Irv listened. "So sum up for me," he said, "what the experiences of the seven years in Washington have taught you. Let's see, seven years, that makes you thirty-eight. You certainly don't look it. That's another chauvinist remark, I suppose."

Bea nodded. "Yes it is." But she smiled, and went on. "OK, let's see. What I have learned in seven years in Washington. It is dominated by men. It is corrupt. It is run by second-raters who are neither intelligent nor principled, but rather cunning in a bestial way.

"I have learned that no matter how pure your intentions at the outset, you cannot rise in Washington, or even *survive*, without selling out along the way.

"I have learned that like any power structure, it tends to corrupt people and bring out the worst in them. That women are among its chief victims, since they have very little chance of rising to real power and are therefore forced to become petty cheats, as opposed to major ones, like their husbands and lovers.

"That Washington is a company town, monolithic and boring.

"That I want to live somewhere where there is a hierarchy of talent rather than cunning, where women aren't forced into second-rate citizenship by the very fact of their sex.

"That on the level of personal relationships, I'm on guard against all men, because they have a tendency to want to fuck me—both sexually and metaphorically—merely because I'm a woman. And, conversely, I feel close to women, as sisters and allies, merely because of our shared status as victims."

Irv started to object as Bea paused to sip her coffee, but she held up her hand.

"I know, I know, there are some wonderful guys in this world and some rotten gals. Granted. I'm talking about the roles imposed on us by the society, and in Washington they generally fit. I also know, before you say it, that this is a lousy attitude to go through life with. *But I didn't choose it.* I didn't take it out of a library, the way you do a book. Or go into a gallery, and point, and say that's my picture of life right there. Life handed me the book, the picture. Life *forced* it upon me. It took me a while to learn it. A while and some pain. But at last I did. I'd have to be pretty dumb not to."

Irv shook his head. "There's almost nothing I can say that won't sound like a couch session. We'd better stick to what kind of a book you want to see come out of these experiences."

That was not a tough question for Bea; she'd thought about it, a lot. "Somehow I'd like the world to know what kind of place Washington really is. Especially I'd like the American voter and taxpayer to know. To know just how rotten those shining examples of virtue, their elected representatives, are. Kind of an exposé. And, though I don't know if the two things mesh, also I'd like to write a novel. It would be fun."

"How about a memoir? Your own life. Your own experience."

"Oh God, I don't think I could stand the pain."

Irv shook a stubby finger at her. "A minute ago you used the word 'fun.' Now you use the word 'pain.' What makes you think writing a book is supposed to be fun? What makes you think there's not supposed to be pain? You want fun, go to a disco. You want a hobby, collect stamps. What I'm talking to you about is being a pro! Because that's all I deal with, pros. Sure, some of it will be fun, more fun than you've ever had. And some of it will be pain, more pain than you've ever felt, because you'll have to poke into spots that have never healed and hurt like hell. Believe me, unless you're different from most of the other writers I know, the time will come when you'll be sitting and wetting your typewriter with your tears.

"But the thing you'll find most of all sure as hell won't be the fun, and it won't even be the pain. It'll be the plain hard work, work when you don't feel like it, work when you're tired, work when you want to be playing tennis, or whatever it is you play, work when you think you've got nothing to say. Work like going to the office every morning, and putting in a full day, whether you feel like it or not, or are hungover or just plain lazy.

"That's the difference between a pro and an amateur. An amateur does something for the love of it, which means when he doesn't love it, he doesn't do it. A pro, if he's any good, has got to love it too, but that's not enough. A pro is also doing it as a commitment, for the money, maybe, but as a commitment. He's got to be counted on. When I was a kid, people used to say there had to be a truck driver somewhere who could knock out Joe Louis with one punch. Just the way you hear today all the people who say they could write a better novel than the pro's. That's a lot of . . . crap . . . if you'll pardon my French. The difference is, a pro *does* it. An amateur beating a pro is just a lot of talk, because an amateur *plays* at what he does, and a pro works at it. And believe me, this is no couch talk, this is *business* talk."

He reached a hand across the table and squeezed Bea's. "It's also too much talk and too soon. Let's first see if we've got a book at all. I've been thinking that the things we both want might be combined in one book. An exposé. A novel. A memoir. A first novel is always some kind of memoir anyway, it comes from the writer's own life. And if you write a *roman à clef*, based on your own experiences in Washington, with the characters based on the real corrupt people you know, it'll be an exposé. If you do that, you can have at least one good guy, which is important because if your book has nothing in it but the rats you seem to say inhabit Washington, people might not want to read it. You've got to have at least one good guy."

"And whom did you have in mind for that role?" Bea asked.

"The good guy? Why, you, of course, Bea! As heroine and as victim."

She laughed. "Oh God, are you wrong, Irv! Don't you see, I'm just as bad as the others! I've survived and prospered by learning to make a buck off corruption, too. By writing nasty little cracks about it. If a miracle should happen, and everything should turn pure, I'd be out of work. Victim, or rather *former* victim, yes. But a heroine? God, no!"

"You'll need a hero—or heroine—someone to root for," he said. "But the lovely thing about a novel, Bea, is that you are not bound by the facts of any particular lives. You can find your own kind of truth for your own characters. Maybe it'll be different from the truth about the real people your characters are based on. But so what, it'll be true anyway. Maybe you'll find yourself writing about a woman who *does* have heroic parts to her character, and that woman will be based on Bea Fletcher—even though you insist there's nothing heroic about the real you."

She started to shake her head, but Irv stopped her.

"Look, what's the point in my insisting there must be a hero and your insisting there can't be, when we don't have word one of a book yet? It's wasted breath. Let's first see if you're interested. Then let's see if we can come up with an idea that will work. *Then* let's see what actually happens when you start writing the book. Maybe we'll both be surprised. Will you listen to some advice that comes from age, if not from wisdom? As much as your book needs a hero or heroine, your *life* needs one even more. And as much as it may be good for your book the way you hate people—all right, hate *men*—that's how bad it is for your life. You see, a book you start, you work on it and you finish. Good or bad, it's over and you start something new. You don't finish one life and start another.

"As an agent, I see this woman with possibly a good book in her, and I'm happy. As a human being, I hope as a friend-to-be, I see this intelligent, beautiful, charming woman with a miserable life in front of her—of sneering and hating, of being sneered at and hated, and I'm unhappy."

"I told you before, Irv, I didn't choose this. Life assigned it to me. At first I *was* the sweet, docile, affirmative, loving creature you're looking for in me, and do you know what it got me? Divorce, disgrace and peanut butter sandwiches. So I picked myself up and came back fighting, and, yes, mean, cynical, sneering, calculating. And do you know what it got me? Strength, independence, security. Even some success and power."

In the next few months they talked many times more, some of them at Irv's house in East Hampton. At first Bea took her kids along, picking them up at school on Friday, flying to MacArthur Airport in East Islip, where Irv picked them up on his way out from the city. Then when it became apparent that Irv had no sexual designs on her—or on any woman, as far as Bea could see—she'd sometimes leave the children with her housekeeper and make the trip herself. Through the winter months she loved the bleak beauty of the Long Island shore, the empty wind-scrubbed beaches, gray and white with the winter shades of the ocean, the whipped foam, the striated sand, and the gulls—who did not leave after Labor Day.

Dressed in long underwear, three sweaters, windbreaker, jeans, boots, gloves, stocking cap, Bea walked the beach until she was stiff with the cold. She suffered happily, she told Irv—who did not usually go with her on her walks—for the joy of the wind "blowing through my head, cleansing Washington and its dirty little people out of it."

She also loved East Hampton's easy sociability. If you wanted company, there were people around, even on winter weekends. But you could choose to be alone without being offensive. She liked the choice, and at first she liked the people. They were competitive, bitchy, aggressive, possibly no less venal than those in Washington. But there were two big differences. The Hamptons people fought over books, film deals, TV, theater, which seemed to her far better issues than porkbarrel and primaries. And in the Hamptons women were equal combatants, not merely victims or trophies.

As she worked on her Washington *roman à clef*, she realized it was coming to a dead end, just as her life there was. She began making plans for a getaway. But what plans could she make about her book? She put the question to Irv, who watched over her and her work like a mother hen.

"What do I do now?" she asked.

"May I read what you've written so far?"

"Uh, oh, yes, I guess so. I'm so scared to let you do it. For God's sake, remember, it's only a rough draft, *very* rough!"

Irv took it, called her the next day. "It has a lot of marvelous stuff in it, Bea, but I can see you're running out of interest in Washington."

"What shall I do?"

"Why not take the book with you to the Hamptons as your protagonist moves there? Notice I'm not calling her a heroine?"

"Can I do that?"

"Why not? The thread is this one woman, her life, her problems, her view of the world. What you have up to now will make a wonderful first part of a book. And a marvelous magazine piece! A sensational piece! It would not only make you some money, but would build a real demand for the novel. In the right magazine, it could make a national figure out of you instead of just a Washington figure."

The idea worked splendidly, because the piece was so juicy, the style so bright; because Irv had such clout. *Scope* magazine bought it, 30,000 words to be run in two installments, at a price of $100,000,

$25,000 more than *Esquire* had paid Capote for "Answered Prayers."
Bea was on her way to becoming a national name. When the pieces
came out she'd be booked by Carson, Griffin, Douglas, Donahue. She'd
be good, Irv knew it. She'd be asked back. Ability to promote a book
on talk shows was a prime requirement for a best seller these days.
This would drive the price up.

For Bea it was an answered prayer. Ahead she could see security, a
way out of Washington. Best of all she could see a stretch of Hamptons beach to walk, not as Irv's guest, or anyone else's, but as someone
who *belonged* in this rare, nervous, flashy, competitive community,
where a woman was allowed full membership.

The move would not be easy. She must get to know the place well
enough not only to sustain her social life but, much tougher, to sustain
her writing. It was mid-1976 when she began to run out of steam on
Washington and spoke of moving, both her life and her book. The two
Washington pieces for *Scope*, to be entitled "WashingtonShock,"
would appear in late '76, and Irv wanted her to finish the Hamptons
book by Labor Day of '77, so it could be published in the spring of '78.
So she'd have a little more than a year to learn enough about the place
to write about it, a hell of a lot less than the time she'd put in in
Washington.

But in the Hamptons she had several advantages. Here she'd be a
member, not the wife of a member. Here, her journalistic technique
would be honed from the start; she'd done her learning and prac-
ticing in Washington. And the people here were so much more talented and interesting, one dinner party might offer more than a month
in the capital.

She rented a house in East Hampton while she looked around for
one to buy. She decided the potato fields of Sagaponack had the openness and the serenity she treasured, and it was there she would buy
her house.

Irv watched her with a bursting avuncular pride. He liked her despite her cynicism, he liked her for her honesty. He didn't need the
money that would come from another Jacqueline Susann; at sixty, he
did want and need the fun, the excitement of sculpting a star, of playing Pygmalion to her Galatea. But unlike Pygmalion, he would not fall
in love with his creation—although he did wish *she* would fall in love
with somebody. He watched with anxiety the absence of any romantic
interest in her life. She was thirty-eight when he met her, and had
been an unattached woman for six years, in which time she had

never once been in love. She'd had lots of dates and invitations, but no beau.

Her criteria for judging men were a strange assortment of cynicism and principle. She liked important places and men who took her to them; she'd learn a lot for her columns and her book, she'd advance her career. Yet she resented the smugness that usually went with "important" men. She liked men who offered wit and responded to it, resented men who were unwilling to let her compete conversationally.

She wasn't surprised that Washington hadn't yielded her a serious love affair. Men in politics and government tended to be sexist, and the more independent and successful the woman, the more she put them off. They wanted a woman to add up to the sum of their expectations, no less, no more.

Bea's first encounter with the Hamptons told her it was a better place than Washington to meet the right kind of man, which in its turn would bring a new kind of problem, a threat to her independence, to what she called "Control of Me." She waited for a love to come along to pose the problem. None came.

Then one day that summer at a big party on the lawn of a network vice president, she saw Harry Majors. A drink in each hand, he was making his way across the grass in that pigeon-toed walk of his, big, square-faced, broad-shouldered, gray hair flopping as he walked. He wore what she would come to know he always wore, chino pants and button-down oxford. She was on the fringe of a cluster of people, but momentarily turned away from them; he was crossing an empty patch of lawn. For a moment it was as if they were the only ones there.

Harry saw her staring at him, and he stopped dead in his tracks as if he were a child to whom someone had yelled, "Freeze!" Ten yards from her he took the horn-rimmed glasses pushed up onto his hair, slid them down over his eyes and stared back at her. He feinted a step to his left, as if going to deliver the second drink, then, grinning, headed straight toward her.

"Hello," he said when he got close. "I thought I knew every beautiful woman round these parts."

She smiled back at him. "*These* round parts," she replied, "are usually found in Washington."

He nodded appreciatively. "Not bad. Not bad at all, stranger. But I've got to warn you, I'm known as the fastest quip east of the Shinnecock . . ." He paused for a moment. "Or is it the Shinne*quip?*"

"Now you're just showing off," she said. He was tall, perhaps six foot two, he had pale skin, gray eyes, and he was not in the best of shape. She didn't know why he looked so irresistibly attractive, but he did.

"Harry. Majors."

"Majors? As in baseball?"

"As in baseball. Is it a league you'd like to play in?"

"Don't know. What's your game?"

"I'm a comedy writer, at least I thought I was until I met you. Now I may have to turn in my card. A joker, of course."

"So say something funny."

"All right, how about: thirty-eight."

"I don't get it."

"Perhaps you didn't like the way I told it."

She looked puzzled. "I still don't get it."

Harry laughed. "No reason you should, if you don't know the joke. Gagwriter invites friend to gagwriters' dinner. Explains that they all know every joke so well, they assign a number to each and instead of telling it, just get up and say the number. And the others laugh or not, depending on how well they like the joke. The friend, wanting to be one of the guys, asks gagwriter for the number of a really socko joke. Gagwriter tells him thirty-eight. Friend waits to be recognized, stands, and says, 'thirty-eight.' No one laughs. Mortified, the friend turns to gagwriter and says, 'I thought you said thirty-eight was really great. How come they didn't laugh?' Gagwriter replies, 'I guess they didn't like the way you told it.'"

"Oh," she said, "I don't do set pieces. I improvise."

"Yes, I noticed. And so well *I* had to fall back on a set piece."

"Hope you didn't get hurt."

"Nope, just help me up." He switched both drinks into his left hand, reached out his right hand. She put her long slim fingers into it. He squeezed. "Good to meet you," he said. "Good to have a new face around, especially one as beautiful as yours."

She was beginning to say something sweet in return, when a voice from off to her right bellowed, "Hey, Harry, do I get my drink, or what?" Bea looked in the direction of the voice, saw a huge, red-bearded man.

"That's Pete Stein," Harry said. "He's not usually without a drink this long, and if he leaned on me, it would hurt a lot worse than falling back on a set piece. I'd better move out smartly. I'll see you again. Soon." He gave her hand another squeeze, looked into her eyes, hard.

"Hope so," she replied, and watched him walk off.

"Not another one!" The voice made her jump; she turned and saw it was Johnny Wainwright, who'd seen the last moments of her talk with Harry.

"Not another what?"

"What do you all see in him?"

"The others will have to answer for themselves. I think he's very attractive, and funny. Who's got her hooks in him?"

Johnny laughed. "What a romantic way to put it! He's been going out with the widder Braxton, but I hear they're about at the end of the road."

"The widder Braxton? I don't see no old ladies standing around with their hair in a bun, Johnny."

"The dark-haired one next to Harry."

Bea saw a tall, athletic-looking woman, with strong cheekbones, perhaps thirty-five years old, no older. "You mean the young tennis type, the Amazon?" she asked. "She don't look like no widder nobody!"

"Sorry about that!" Johnny smiled at her.

"Is she his weekend date?"

Johnny shook his head. "She's got one of the loveliest houses you've ever seen, in Wainscott. She's not anybody's weekend date."

"What are you doing for dinner tomorrow night, Johnny?"

"No plans. We could drive into Southampton and . . ."

"How'd you like to have some people over? I'll do the cooking."

"Well, well, well," he said, teasing. "Whomever could you have in mind?"

"You got it!" Bea answered emphatically. "And another couple. And a single woman, not too attractive, please. Definitely not the widder whoever!"

Johnny agreed, set it up. The next morning he asked Bea, "What's on the menu? Besides Harry."

"Oh come on, Johnny! All I want to do is get to know the man." To herself she said, he's right. And what a forward creature I have become! How far from the demure Nashville girl, who would never have dared the conversation with Harry at the party, let alone the boldness of setting up the dinner.

Bea threw together a bouillabaisse, which she did well, a salad with three kinds of lettuce from the Amagansett Farmers Market, and for dessert French bread, ripe Brie, fruit and coffee.

Johnny sat at the head of his old oak dining table, Bea at the foot. On Bea's left sat big, bearded Pete Stein, on her right, Harry. Between

bread warming in the oven! I'll be right back." She fled to
, face crimson, asking herself if they were all laughing at
already sliced and buttered the bread, so all she had to do
ut of the oven and into a basket. She managed to drop three
he floor. Come on now, she warned, control yourself. Com-
elf.

de back into the dining room, asking, "Who wants more
give herself an entrance line, although there already were
ottles of Pouilly-Fumé on the table. Covered by a chorus of
hank you's, she managed to sit and get a spoonful of the
se to her lips. By now it was cold, but she couldn't say

d, not bad at all," she murmured, then leaned toward Harry.
tly cool, haughty, collected, was I? Neither Dina Merrill
Kelly will ever play *me* in the movies. Nor, for that matter,
play *them*. Although they might play each other!"

too bad," Harry replied. "Because when Paul Newman plays
ot going to settle for anyone less playing you." He said it
ion, leaning toward her as he did.

m do you see as me?" She had to laugh to herself, as she said
ip Jewish-inflected "so" with which she began the sentence
npeccable Sweet Briar "whom" following it. She'd come a

see anyone as you but you. Comparing you to any actress is
ng you, doing you an injustice. I'd rather cast you as your
rean namesake, Beatrice. Bright, funny, sassy, strong-willed,
nt, yet wanting to find a man who'll love her—who'll accept
ote, unfeminine, unquote, characteristics—and still love her.
cept them, *embrace* them."

ts Dina and Grace, any day. Thanks! But let me tell you
, fella. Any man who can accept all those things, even love a
espite them, let alone *embrace* them and love a woman *for*
s much a rarity today as he was in Good Queen Bess's day. A
m pretend, which takes the form of patting you on the head
you're a cuddly little novice. But the minute you begin to
them in even the smallest way, letting out the merest hint
t be an equal, you become a castrating bitch. Either you
balls or you've already got three of your own—all brass."
nany do you have?" he asked.
nany are you missing?" she snapped back.

Harry and Johnny sat Pete's wife Joan.
woman writer, Estelle somebody, Bea
name. Johnny had his orders: tie up Joan

Bea spent most of the time before din
she sat down, she and Harry barely spo
table and sat, took a deep breath, eyes ca
her blue eyes—made all the bluer by
careful to wear—stared straight into his

They were about the same age, thirty
his hair gray, his eyes tired, his faced
eyes. He did all the things you weren't su
ing. He didn't do the things you were s
ging, swimming. His face showed it all; sh
Their conversation began with the intin
each other a long time.

After a few moments of deep, silent
tired."

"I am. Of waiting for you. Where hav
been doing?"

"Since six-thirty yesterday evening, sch
I made it."

"*We* made it," he answered. "No way
evitable. And it's so new, so breathless. S
it."

She knew he was right. It was so heady
it, began regretting the end of this ever
mean, tomorrow no gasps?"

He shook his head no. "Tomorrow son
row and every day for a lot of days. But
problems."

Her eyes kept coming back to his; she c
at her food, couldn't concentrate on eating
After all, with only six at the table, how
embarrassed. She didn't give a damn. She
her meal.

"Oh Bea! It's scrumptious!" Startled, sh
asm of Estelle What's-her-name.

"Glad you like it," she responded, and
waiting for mine to cool down." Then she
tendre and to cover her blushing, leaped t

forgot th
the kitch
her. She'
was get i
pieces or
pose you.

She st
wine?" t
two open
no's and
bouillab
that.

"Not b
"Not exa
nor Grac
will I eve

"That'
me, he's
with affe

"So wl
it, at the
and the
long way

"I don
type-cas
Shakesp
indepen
all the,
No, not

"It be
somethii
woman
them, is
lot of th
as long
challeng
you mig
want the

"How
"How

Harry and Johnny sat Pete's wife Joan. Between Pete and Johnny sat a woman writer, Estelle somebody, Bea could never remember her last name. Johnny had his orders: tie up Joan Stein, leave Harry to Bea.

Bea spent most of the time before dinner in the kitchen, and so until she sat down, she and Harry barely spoke. She put the plates on the table and sat, took a deep breath, eyes cast down. When she looked up, her blue eyes—made all the bluer by the azure T-shirt she'd been careful to wear—stared straight into his gray ones.

They were about the same age, thirty-nine, but Harry looked older, his hair gray, his eyes tired, his faced lined, a little puffy under the eyes. He did all the things you weren't supposed to do: smoking, drinking. He didn't do the things you were supposed to do: sleeping, jogging, swimming. His face showed it all; she thought it fatally charming. Their conversation began with the intimacy of people who'd known each other a long time.

After a few moments of deep, silent staring, she said, "You look tired."

"I am. Of waiting for you. Where have you been? What have you been doing?"

"Since six-thirty yesterday evening, scheming to sit next to you. And I made it."

"*We* made it," he answered. "No way we couldn't have. It was inevitable. And it's so new, so breathless. So special. We ought to bottle it."

She knew he was right. It was so heady she didn't want to talk about it, began regretting the end of this evening even as it began. "You mean, tomorrow no gasps?"

He shook his head no. "Tomorrow something new, special, tomorrow and every day for a lot of days. But today is for the respiratory problems."

Her eyes kept coming back to his; she couldn't take the time to look at her food, couldn't concentrate on eating, feared the others noticed. After all, with only six at the table, how could they not? She was embarrassed. She didn't give a damn. She had to try to eat; this *was* her meal.

"Oh Bea! It's scrumptious!" Startled, she looked up to the enthusiasm of Estelle What's-her-name.

"Glad you like it," she responded, and added, lamely, "I've been waiting for mine to cool down." Then she heard her own double entendre and to cover her blushing, leaped to her feet. "My goodness! I forgot the bread warming in the oven! I'll be right back." She fled to the kitchen, face crimson, asking herself if they were all laughing at her. She'd already sliced and buttered the bread, so all she had to do was get it out of the oven and into a basket. She managed to drop three pieces on the floor. Come on now, she warned, control yourself. Compose yourself.

She strode back into the dining room, asking, "Who wants more wine?" to give herself an entrance line, although there already were two open bottles of Pouilly-Fumé on the table. Covered by a chorus of no's and thank you's, she managed to sit and get a spoonful of the bouillabaisse to her lips. By now it was cold, but she couldn't say that.

"Not bad, not bad at all," she murmured, then leaned toward Harry. "Not exactly cool, haughty, collected, was I? Neither Dina Merrill nor Grace Kelly will ever play *me* in the movies. Nor, for that matter, will I ever play *them*. Although they might play each other!"

"That's too bad," Harry replied. "Because when Paul Newman plays me, he's not going to settle for anyone less playing you." He said it with affection, leaning toward her as he did.

"So whom do you see as me?" She had to laugh to herself, as she said it, at the hip Jewish-inflected "so" with which she began the sentence and the impeccable Sweet Briar "whom" following it. She'd come a long way.

"I don't see anyone as you but you. Comparing you to any actress is type-casting you, doing you an injustice. I'd rather cast you as your Shakespearean namesake, Beatrice. Bright, funny, sassy, strong-willed, independent, yet wanting to find a man who'll love her—who'll accept all the, quote, unfeminine, unquote, characteristics—and still love her. No, not accept them, *embrace* them."

"It beats Dina and Grace, any day. Thanks! But let me tell you something, fella. Any man who can accept all those things, even love a woman *despite* them, let alone *embrace* them and love a woman *for* them, is as much a rarity today as he was in Good Queen Bess's day. A lot of them pretend, which takes the form of patting you on the head as long as you're a cuddly little novice. But the minute you begin to challenge them in even the smallest way, letting out the merest hint you might be an equal, you become a castrating bitch. Either you want their balls or you've already got three of your own—all brass."

"How many do you have?" he asked.

"How many are you missing?" she snapped back.

"I've got the regular number, I suppose. Haven't even counted lately. That's how secure *I* am." She saw, or thought she saw, or *hoped* she saw, in his eyes an acceptance, more, an embracing, of all of her—warts, wisecracks, all. "If I take your hand under the table," he said softly, "it has nothing to do with this conversation, but is merely for the purpose of giving it a squeeze and telling you I think you're terrific. *And* feminine. OK?"

"I'm reaching," she replied, just as softly. He found her right hand with his left, grasped it gently, tightened, tightened, until the pressure grew pleasurable almost to the point of pain. Then he relaxed the grip slowly, gave another short, sudden squeeze, kept pressure on as he let go, allowed his hand to slide down hers, pressing as it went, down the palm, the fingertips, to the last, reluctant tip of her middle finger.

"That was the best hand squeeze I have had in my entire life," she said.

"A modest talent," he replied, leaning to her. "You on the other hand are a marvelous cook. *And* funny. *And* sexy. And beautiful. But you must hear that all the time."

"You *must* be joking! One by one, rarely. All at once, the way you did—and right after squeezing my hand so that I almost fainted into my own bouillabaisse, never! Makes me damned glad I set this dinner up. Set *you* up, that is, retiring creature that I am."

"I'm delighted you did," he said. "Flattered. I would have called you."

"When?"

"Soon."

"Not soon enough for me."

"Will you spend the night with me?"

"I thought you'd never ask."

Somehow Bea got through the meal, began waiting for the others to leave, silently urging them to go.

They stayed forever—until 11:30, and then Harry took Bea out into the starry summer night. Saturday, July 15. Bea would always remember that night.

He put his arm around her shoulders, she put hers around his waist. He was half a foot taller than she; it was a perfect fit. "You have children?" he asked.

"Yes, Staunton is fifteen and Amanda is thirteen, and they're both away at school, so we can spend the night anywhere you say and please don't tell me you've changed your mind."

He stopped, turned to her, put both arms around her. The bulk of him was comforting. He kissed her very gently, his mouth closed, his lips soft. Then again, their mouths relaxing. Then a third time, their mouths open.

"Changed my mind?" he repeated. "Oh no! Have you?"

"God, no! Why do you think I set up the dinner?" She stretched up and kissed him again.

"My house is right on the dunes," he said. "It would be fun to walk out on the beach and look at the stars."

"Sounds wonderful."

"Follow me."

They got into their cars, drove out to the highway, to Dunemere Road, to Further Lane, down the long private road to his rented saltbox. Driving behind him, Bea found it hard to believe she'd engineered this night; she was so far from the proper Nashville girl she'd once been, she was amused. Yesterday she'd seen Harry for the first time, at a cocktail party, and barely spoken with him. Today she was going to spend the night with him. And she'd arranged the whole thing.

Okay, she was pushy enough to join the group. Was she talented enough? Would she ever be wealthy enough? The jury was still out, but she knew this, for sure, as she'd never known anything: she loved writing, and the idea of being a writer. She thought she was good at it, and if it worked it would give her money, give her Control of Me. What a dreamy combination: gaining security and independence by doing something you loved. She *had* to make it work, she simply had to. No one, nothing, must get in her way.

As she got out of the car and walked toward Harry, she fluffed up her hair; she wore it short and wavy these days, its natural silky straightness didn't seem fashionable to her. Bea looked toward his house as she walked; it was a tiny saltbox, probably moved from the town, with a small brick patio between it and the dunes. She wanted a house of her own, her mouth watered for it, and she'd have one, not right at the beach—the ocean was a little bleak and scary in winter, and the houses were too expensive; even a modest one like this would cost around $250,000—but she'd have one, and soon, a citadel of repose out here, where she wanted to be. Perhaps the people here didn't know much about repose, but that didn't matter; one of the charms of the place was that you could take the social life or leave it alone, and mix it with as much ease and solitude as you wanted. Nobody dropped in. Nobody strolled by your house. Nothing was forced upon you, but it was there for the phoning.

Harry took her hand as they walked to the beach, held it tight. His hand was warm and dry, the pressure of it made her woozy, as it had at the table. She had trouble walking the narrow path through the dunes; luckily a three-quarter moon lit their way.

"May I tell you how good your hand feels?" he said. "And how good it is to be out on the beach, with the moon up there, and you down here?"

"You may. And it feels just as good where I'm standing, although . . ." She hesitated, didn't know if she should go on. "I hear you say that to all the girls. And they all love it."

"Not true. I don't come to the beach with many women. I say what I said to you to very few. And some of those don't like it." He touched her face with his fingertips. "And I want you to know I enjoy having to explain myself to you."

She touched the hand on her face. "Good. But for how long?"

He shrugged. "Try me."

"I really shouldn't poke into your life, but you have the reputation of being a great ladies' man."

"Well, you're a great lady, so it . . ."

"Give me a straight answer."

"OK. A straight answer. More than half the men my age are married. Half the rest live with a woman. Half the rest live with a man. Half the rest live with their mothers. Half the rest are gigolos; half the rest, walking wounded; half the rest are unbearable male chauvinists; half the rest fuck and run. That leaves me and a guy with a harelip and a limp. And *that's* how I got the reputation for being a great ladies' man. That is exaggerated, but only slightly."

"In any event," she replied, "I'm holding on real tight." She pressed his hand to her cheek.

Harry wrapped his big arms around her, tightened gently as he kissed her. She put her arms around his neck, held on; they kissed three long, open-mouthed kisses before he said, "You call that holding on real tight?"

She tightened her arms.

"Better," he said. "Much better. And you'd *better* hold on tight. You don't have much choice."

"I don't want much choice."

He stood there looking down at her for a few moments, then said: "Harry Majors, speechless!"

"Is that so bad?"

"It's just that there's so much I want to say. About how special this moment is, about what I'm feeling for you . . . but . . . I guess I don't have the equipment. . . ." He laughed. "Whoops! *That's* not exactly what I meant. I mean the equipment to write fourteen-line love sonnets instead of one-liners. I mean the moment is beyond my words. Not Shakespeare's or Elizabeth Barrett Browning's. But beyond mine. I feel like a young boy. I feel so happy!"

He let go of her. "Let's walk." They began strolling down the beach, near the water.

"I know what they mean," he said, "when they put those lines in songs about not wanting the night to end."

"Maybe we can hold on to what's here after the night does end?"

He squeezed with the arm around her shoulders. "We can sure as hell try."

She squeezed back. "Let's *not* let it get away. After all, it only just got here."

"OK, let's hold on for a while."

"For a *long* while," she added, and then thought, it's just like a woman to make that correction.

He smiled down at her, and echoed, "For a *long* while." After a few more steps he said, "This is making me drunk."

"You sure it wasn't the brandy after dinner?"

"That was only 80 proof—near beer, compared with being here with you."

"How many proof are we?"

He thought for a moment. "I once met a guy who was with General Mark Clark when his army hooked up with the Russians at the end of World War Two. They broke out 190-proof vodka to celebrate. That's us."

"I didn't know there was any proof that high."

"Barely. Proof is twice percentage, so 190 proof is 95 percent alcohol, and that's about as high as you can get."

"I suppose we're jinxing ourselves?"

"I suppose. Let's change the subject."

"OK. So you don't have a harelip and a limp, eh?"

"Not since the operations."

"And you don't fuck and run."

"I can barely jog."

"Let's see . . ." She thought for a moment. "Gigolo?"

"Ran out of pomade."

"Chauvinist?"

"Wear an ERA button pinned to my chest always—which can really smart when I'm not wearing a shirt. Proudly carry the *Ms.* Seal of Approval."

"I won't ask where. Married?"

"Tried it on twice. It was a lousy fit."

"Let's see, what else? Living with a woman?"

"There's no living with a woman. And they say the same about me."

"With a man?"

"I'd probably do it, except I'm afraid he'd always be trying on my things."

"With your mother?"

"She's already living with a man—my father."

As they walked on, Bea chewed over his flippant views on marriage and on living with a woman. Her first reaction to them was disappointment, then she realized how irrational that was. She *knew* that right now she was not in the market for a live-in relationship or marriage. So why was she bothered? She wanted this man to be in the market for them. This man whom she had met all of thirty hours ago. Ridiculous!

"I've got a good idea," he said. "Let's go back to the house, get into bed, put our arms around each other."

"Sounds wonderful," she said.

For a while they lay on his bed fully clothed, embracing, pressing their bodies together, before he whispered, "Let me undress you."

"Yes," she sighed, although he hadn't waited for an answer. She felt warm, relaxed. The dreamy excitement she felt on the beach was still there, but the tension, the anticipation of making love to this man for the first time, was no longer making her anxious. Everything was beginning to feel loose, easy.

He unbuttoned her blouse. She wore no bra; her breasts were small enough and firm enough for her not to need one—and she was proud of it. Gently, with his left hand he cupped her right breast, stroked it, touched the nipple. Gently. Then he put his mouth to it, kissed, sucked it. As he did, his hand went between her legs, stroked the insides of her thighs, then her crotch, his middle finger pressing her clitoris—with amazing accuracy, she thought, considering she still had on jeans and underpants.

"You're so good at this," she whispered.

"You're so inspiring," he replied. He brought his head up, kissed her mouth.

"Sit up," he said. She did; he slipped her blouse off. She lay down again, her bare breasts pressed against the cotton of his shirt. Then his hand deftly lowered the zipper of her jeans, slid under her bikini pants, between her legs. Gently, his fingers found the lips of her vagina, his middle finger slipped between them. She was moist, more than moist, wet. For a moment the Southern lady in her wondered if he would think her wanton to be so aroused so quickly. But only for a moment, then she didn't care, all of her was moving, slowly, irresistibly, like a wave, building. Normally, she wrote the first time off; she was that sure she wouldn't have an orgasm. This time she wasn't so sure.

Then his hand was out of her; with both hands he took hold of the sides of her jeans at the waist, said, "Raise your hips," and with one continuous motion, slid jeans and underpants off her hips, legs, feet. Still fully clothed, at the foot of the bed, Harry kissed her toes, then her feet. He licked between her toes, took two of them in his mouth.

"Oh, no!" she cried. "Unclean, unclean!"

"Not anymore!" he replied. She felt embarrassed, and ashamed to feel so; she raised her head, looked down at him. "They really aren't clean, I never . . ."

"Oh, shut up," he said. "It's your middle-class propriety that's upset, not your hygienic standards."

She was lying entirely nude on the bed, propped up on her elbows, looking down at him. He was on his knees at the foot of the bed, fully clothed, looking up at her, as he kissed her feet. She found it deliciously erotic. All at once, he stood, stretched himself out full length alongside her. Deliberately, tenderly, he kissed each of her closed eyes, each side of her nose, each side of her neck just beneath the jawline. Then her mouth. Then her left ear, into which he whispered: "I'm going to start with your toes again, and work my way up with great thoroughness, not letting a single square inch of you go untouched. If I miss any place, I hope you'll tell me."

He didn't wait for an answer, just moved to the foot of the bed again. She lay there, expectantly, breathlessly.

He took each toe into his mouth, one at a time. He kissed the soles of her feet.

He kissed each arch, each instep.

He kissed a circle around each ankle. Up the shinbone and calf of each leg to the knee, first the left leg, then the right.

He continued up the right, kissing a straight line up the center of the thigh, veered to the outside until he reached the hip, then worked down, this time along the inside of the thigh.

Then he went back down to the left knee and worked his way up the same way, down the same way.

She just lay back, breathing hard, not sure if she wanted him to continue these preliminaries forever, or hurry to the main event.

He kissed his way up the left thigh again, this time ending with a kiss on her pubic hairs. He went down again to the right knee, kissed up the thigh, working his way to the inside of the thigh. Only this time he never made it as far north as her pubic mound.

She opened her legs to make it easier for him, put a hand to his long gray hair, so she could stroke him, touch him as he licked her.

Her body began to undulate—all on its own, without asking her permission, or even telling her it was going to. She put both hands on his head.

"Oh, God, Harry, please come into me!"

He ignored her.

"Please! Harry! Before it's too late!"

He ignored her.

"Harry! It's so close! Too close!" She shoved his head away, gently but decisively. He let himself be shoved, raised his head, kissed his way in a straight line up her body, pausing briefly at the navel, making side trips to each nipple, then lifted his head for a moment to say, "Here. This is what you taste like down there." And he kissed her mouth.

The taste was only slightly different from that of saliva, but saltier, more pungent. The idea of it was exciting! Scandalous! And how it aroused her! She was getting so close to an orgasm, she was almost disappointed when he stood to take his clothes off. She didn't want to come down off her peak.

"I hope you taste as delicious to you as you do to me," he said as he undressed. Before she could answer, he had climbed on top of her. She continued to be surprised by his grace and delicacy; he was a big man, over two hundred pounds, yet there was nothing heavy about him. He kept most of his weight on his hands, arms, legs, feet, most of the time he was on her. When he let his weight press on her, it was always in control, never a throwing of all his bulk on her.

He kissed her. Between her legs, she could feel his penis, hot and hard, not yet in her.

"You slide me in you," he whispered.

It was easy; he was so rigid, she so wet, with his saliva and her own juice. She'd come down only a short way from the peak of a few moments ago, and as he slid in and out, giving his body an easy, upward drive at the end of each stroke to make contact with her clitoris, she got back to the height, then beyond, up, up, up, flying, exploding in a shower of fireworks.

Harry felt her orgasm, and then he let himself come, too, in an eruption of pleasure.

She floated in a long, blissful glide, losing altitude slowly, slowly, slowly, finally arching to a landing so light she hardly knew when she'd touched the ground. They lay there, he still in her, her arms around his back, both of them oiled, cooled, from head to toe by a film of perspiration.

Naturally, easily, she said, "You're a wonderful lovemaker, how wonderful you are!"

"How could any man not be, with you?"

"They've managed."

"Oh, the poor fools. I guess I should thank them, though, for letting you get away."

"You not only make me feel so good, you make me feel so wanted, Harry. No wonder women can't keep their hands off you. Well, I don't care, I . . ."

"Oh, stop it!" He almost sounded angry. "Women in great numbers manage to keep their hands off me, which is not surprising considering I'm an aging, graying, sagging, journeyman comedy writer. You're the prize, and I'm lucky to be here with you."

She shook her head. "That may have been the most wonderful orgasm I've ever had."

He whispered, "You mean, the most wonderful *so far*." He turned toward her, kissed her long and deep, and they were ready to try again.

The months that followed were the happiest, most exciting of her life, and when they were over, when their love affair began fraying, Bea would remind herself of Harry's words "so far." They were merely the happiest times of her life *so far*. There'd be better times, she'd tell herself. But she'd have a tough time believing it.

Better lovemaking? How could it be any better? More fun? A man she cared for more? Where? How? Who? It would be lovely to think the best was yet to come, but for fun, for lovemaking, for *love*, she just couldn't imagine it.

They were wonderful months, and when she and Harry parted she told him so. He'd introduced her to a whole new bunch of people in the Hamptons and New York, and told her so much about the people and the places, she sometimes felt he deserved co-authorship credit on her book. She couldn't have done it without him, she told him, which was ironic, because he came to disapprove of the book so strongly.

Often he just gave her bits of information and let her interrogative skill and tenacity get the rest. Bits about Freddie Kohl and his buddy the Governor. About Carlotta and Buster Reilly; about his ex-wife, Sally, about the structure of the literary crowd. And he introduced her to everyone, writers, film people, journalists, playwrights, bankers.

She discovered that for better or worse, all of the groups made a good show of talking each other's language, so it became hard to tell the good guys from the bad guys, the idealistic artists from the evil capitalists, without a program. Except for Freddie; he seemed so blatantly crude and aggressive, she could not at first believe he was serious. Then, when at last she did believe him, she almost pitied him. She might have left him out of her book entirely, had she not run into him in Washington. And had he not gone after the book.

His desire to buy her book created in Bea's mind a certain artistic necessity, rightness, for including him in it. It also created a conflict. She didn't want to deal with him. She did want his money. Memories of mending four-year-old dresses, of unpaid bills, weekends spent vacuuming, scrubbing, laundering; memories of waiting for super-market sales, skipping steak, stocking up on the cheapest chopped meat to go along with the endless spaghetti. Memories of the peanut butter. These days when Bea went to the supermarket, she over-bought, she wallowed in the luxury of stuffing her shopping cart with anything she wanted—the expensive stuff!—steaks to cram her freezer, Häagen Dazs ice cream at a buck and a half a pint, instead of the A&P house brand, seedless grapes when they first hit the market—she'd once seen them at $3 a pound, and after an instinctive first reaction of self-denial, she laughed to herself, and bought two pounds just to show herself she could do it. And she didn't even like them very much!

She made a lot of money in 1976—$70,000 from the daily and monthly columns, the TV show, occasional lectures and short magazine pieces, plus some child support from Staunton. Plus the $90,000, after commission, from the "WashingtonShock" piece. She enjoyed it, without feeling secure in it. A magazine piece, a book, was one-shot income; the next one might make you rich, or it might, after months of work, make you nothing. A newspaper columnist was always dependent on the whim of a new editor, or owner, and the TV and lecturing depended on her clout as a writer.

Besides, her accountant reminded her, the tax bite was horrendous; she could plan on keeping about half of what she earned. And the money just didn't go very far, what with frequent trips to New York and the Hamptons, the houses in Washington and East Hampton.

Bea wanted to do more than just rent a house out on the Island; she wanted to *own* one, wanted it to be *hers*. She did not have title to the Washington house, and didn't want to. It represented her days of bondage. To her it was Egypt and the Hamptons The Promised Land. Like Freddie, she wanted full citizenship, and as social acceptance was the key for Freddie, so money was the key for her. To get it by writing a book about the Hamptons seemed deliciously fitting to her. To get it from Freddie, one of the villains of the piece, seemed downright poetic. It also bothered her.

The conflict within Bea caused by Freddie and the book was nothing compared to the conflict it caused between Bea and Harry.

"Why do you want to take his dirty money?" Harry asked. They were standing on Freddie Kohl's lawn, at an elaborate Sunday brunch where vintage Moët et Chandon was being poured the way soave was poured from jugs at other parties.

"It's no dirtier than anybody else's," she replied.

"All right then, why are you so frantic about *anybody's* dirty money?"

"Because I was raised in a comfortable upper-middle-class home, raised expecting to be taken care of, and suddenly found myself putting peanut butter and jelly on my table for dinner, wondering how I was going to pay the phone bill so the company wouldn't disconnect it. I found myself abandoned, with no one taking care of me, with no skills, no way of earning a living. And I got scared! And I'm still scared, that I won't be able to take care of myself. I *have* to be able to! Who's going to support me, Harry, if I can't myself? Tell me! Who? Are *you* going to support me, Harry?" Merely talking about it made her apprehensive, and her voice grew harsher as she asked the questions.

Harry looked at her with distaste. "No. I'm not. Any more than you're going to support me. A lot of people have the same worry; I'm one of them. But you don't see me in the mad scramble to get rich, do you? You don't see me willing to do anything, deal with anyone—any damned slob—to pick up a buck. Do you?"

That made her furious. "I'm a writer, Harry, and you make me sound like a hooker. I think that's a strange attitude for a *TV comedy writer* to have, don't you?"

Harry loved good champagne; he'd been having a fair amount of Freddie's, and his eyes showed it. "Uh-uh, kid. You're dragging the old red herring across the trail to try to get me off in the wrong direction, but I won't go for it. Being a writer is not what I'm talking about. Making a deal with the devil is what I'm talking about."

"No! You won't make a deal with the devil!" She was shouting in a whisper. "But you'll go to the devil's parties! You'll drink the devil's champagne! What in hell are you doing here, Harry, prostituting your high ideals—you who've used that fine mind of yours for fifteen years to write *TV comedy?* What is the purist doing slumming this way? Why aren't you sitting in an apartment on West End Avenue reading *Partisan Review?* Stop corrupting yourself on *his* lawn with *his* champagne! You won't even go over and talk to your host, will you? How can you contaminate your purity with his filthy Moët et Chandon? No, you mustn't! I'm doing this for your own good!" With that she reached out and swiped the glass from his hand, knocking it to the grass. He bent over and picked it up, gave her a cold smile.

"I did it for you," he said. "I thought you wanted to come, and you wanted me to come with you. Did I want to? Not particularly. Do you think that as long as I'm here I should drink cheap wine? I will. Show it to me. I haven't seen any."

"You did it for *me?*" she shouted, softly, but not as softly as before. "Well, I don't want you here! I'm going over to talk to the devil. I may not be as pure as you, but I do have my own code of honor: if I drink the devil's champagne, I say hello to him! And I don't want you around looking down from your peak of self-righteousness at us ordinary lice crawling around on the ground. Get out of here!"

She stalked off across the lawn, straight to Freddie, and afterwards went out to dinner with him. Harry drove back to his house and drank himself to sleep on white wine—from a jug.

The next day he phoned her and they went for a pizza at Sam's. Both said they were sorry; they spent the night together. Neither was sorry enough. Both had things they couldn't honestly say they were sorry for; both felt they had an irreducible truth to their positions and they couldn't rearrange that or apologize for it. The blood stopped flowing, but the scabs were there to be picked at and they never healed. It was never the same again.

Bea's impetus to buy a house rather than keep renting came from the critical and public enthusiasm for the "WashingtonShock" pieces in *Scope*. One reviewer called it "a scathing *roman à clef* in which Washington's high and mighty are stripped naked, allowed only the filmiest veil of fiction between them and the public gaze. Three things are sure: Ms. Fletcher is going to be read, reviled—and rich."

Walking with Bea on a cold, crystal-clear late November day, Irv agreed about all three attributes. They walked from his shingled Victorian mansion down Lily Pond Lane toward Georgica beach, their feet crackling the leaves which had fallen from the big oaks, elms and maples. Irv didn't like the cold, he was bundled up, overbundled, against it, but he'd agreed to go as far as the beach.

"I guess I can't go home again, huh?" she asked.

"No, but you can come back to my house before we both freeze our whatevers off!"

She looked at him, a smile cracking her cold, reddened face. "I tell the jokes, fella. You tell it like it is. Can I go home?"

"Why do you want to? All the things you didn't like about Washington are said so beautifully in your writing, they convince me you don't *want* to go home. Don't they convince *you*? What's nice for you now, or anyway will be soon, is that you'll have enough money not to go home if you don't want to. Enough money to do what you want. A wonderful thing to be able to say!"

"Wonderful to be able to hear! So wonderful, I can't believe it. I'm afraid I'm going to be jinxed just by listening, or talking about it. I got more than Capote did for that magazine piece! I can't believe that, either. How did it happen?"

Irv, his face stiff and blotchy with the cold, his eyeglasses misted over, a sheepskin hood revealing nothing in the way of ears, chin, forehead, managed to get a smile through. "Maybe you've got a better agent than Capote. Maybe you've got a better story."

"No doubt about the agent, my dear. But I'm not well known, and how many people outside of Washington have any inkling of the real people behind my characters? And they'll know even fewer of the Hamptons people!" She pushed her hands deep into the pockets of her tan down parka, and shuddered, not from the cold. "I can't believe that this won't end. That I won't wake up, fall off the cloud and find myself flat on my ass, every bone broken, surrounded by peanut butter sandwiches."

"Bea, this is my business, let me tell you a few things. You think most readers knew or cared about the real-life identities of Capote's society ladies having lunch at the Cote Basque? Or the real people behind Jackie Susann's characters? Not for a minute. They may care about the *fact* of real people behind the characters, to give them an immediacy. But they care more about the style, about being let into the lives of people who can afford the art, the furniture, the yachts, the food, the wine, the fashions, the mansions, the whole glamour scene the readers themselves cannot afford. And especially they want to read about scandal—sex, intrigue, treachery, infidelity—in the lives of the beautiful people. That way, the readers can have their cake and eat it, too. They can enjoy the fooling around vicariously, knowing they can never be caught at it, and at the same time they can have the glow of feeling superior. They can tell themselves, see, the rich are not as honest as I am, not even as *happy* as I am."

"And you think my book will give them that?"

"You bet! And so do the publishers. I've already gotten phone calls."

"Irv! No kidding?"

"No kidding, Bea. Don't buy any more peanut butter."

"What kind of money, Irv?" She was almost afraid to ask.

"Big."

"What *is* big?"

"What'll make the 'WashingtonShock' money seem small."

Irv was a couple of inches shorter than she, and it was easy for her to throw an arm around his shoulders. "Let's walk back," she said. "I'm cold. And there's something I want to do."

"What?"

"Buy a house."

Two months later, on a bleak winter Saturday, she took possession of a late eighteenth-century white clapboard farmhouse on Sagg-Main Street in Sagaponack. It was about a mile and a half from the ocean, and a steal at $115,000, the real estate agent told her. She knew it, for her two months of intensive house hunting had been preceded by months of more casual looking; in fact ever since she'd started spending time in the Hamptons, she'd never *not* looked for a house.

She'd seen many at $150,000 that weren't as nice as this one. Run down, but livable; she could move in at once, and re-do it bit by bit as the money came in.

Staunton was now a rich Washington lawyer and had agreed to send the children to boarding school, so Bea felt freer to move between Sagaponack and Washington, as she began phasing the first in and the second out. This white farmhouse which she stood admiring was the key to the change.

"My house," she said aloud, just standing there, although the wind was so frigid it froze her face and made the words feel strange coming out. Irv kept edging toward the door to get in out of the cold, but Bea wouldn't move.

"My house, Irv! Mine. I own it. Nobody is giving me the right to live here, and nobody can take it away—not as long as you do your work, dear agent."

"Congratulations, Bea, it's really wonderful. Why don't we go in?"

"In a minute. I'm experiencing my house." She didn't move; finally she turned away. Irv waited for a moment, shivering, and when she remained motionless, he walked around so he could see her face. She was just standing there, staring at *her* house, tears rolling down her cheeks. When she saw him staring she managed a smile. "OK," she said, "the silly girl is ready when you are. Do you have the screwdriver?"

He put his arms around her and squeezed, then said, "Yes, I have the screwdriver."

At last she stepped forward, put the key in the kitchen door, turned it. They walked in. Although there was a more formal entrance around the left side of the house, the kitchen door was just off the driveway, and everyone used it.

They stepped into a large country kitchen that held a huge old working fireplace as well as a battery of modern appliances: oversized refrigerator, dishwasher, clothes washer and dryer. At the right rear of the kitchen were the back stairs, at the left a door and a small hallway through to the dining room.

"Do you have the screwdriver, Irv?"

"Yes, again. Why do you keep asking?"

She pointed to the door leading to the dining room. "Because I want you to remove that door. Unscrew the hinges. Can you do it?"

"Bea, you want some things done, I'll have a contractor come in, and . . ."

"Irv, please, this is not 'some things done,' this is a ceremony." She reached into the canvas sack she was carrying, pulled out a split of cold champagne. "First the door, then the champagne. Go to it, sweetheart."

Irv had to do some huffing and puffing for the screws were many times painted over, but he was surprisingly handy and in a little while door and hinges were leaning against a nearby wall. Bea pulled two wineglasses from the sack. "You're so good at unscrewing, sweetheart, how are you at cork popping?"

He opened the bottle, filled both glasses, handed one to her. "May we drink to this house?" she said. "This wonderful, special house. My house! And to the happy times my friends—and you're one of the dearest, Irv, you know that—and I are going to have in it."

"To the house!" Irv said, and they both drank. Then he added, "And to the lovely lady who owns it. *L'chaim!*"

"Yes," she said, excitedly. "Like in *Fiddler on the Roof.* To life, to life, *l'chaim.* . . ." She pronounced the "ch" as if it were a "k." Irv grinned at her, and raised his glass again.

"And to the joy that will move into this house with you, and stay with you, for all your life!"

She ran over and kissed him on the head. "Yes! Joy in this house! But no peanut butter! Not a single jar anywhere in the place!"

Irv remembered, and looked over to the kitchen door. "And doors?" he asked.

"Oh yes." She stared at him for a moment. "Irv, when you stand in the kitchen and look through that hallway, where the door used to be, what do you see?"

He looked through, searching for a catch, then said, "Why, the dining room!"

"All right, now come with me," Bea said. Both clutching their champagne glasses, they walked into the dining room. "Now look through the hallway from this direction, and tell me what you see."

Again, he thought for a moment to see if he could spot a trick. "What are you driving at, Bea?"

"Just tell me what you see, sweetheart!"

"The kitchen, what else? But why?"

"Because . . . in my house in Nashville, and in my house in Washington, or I should say the houses I *called* mine which were not mine, the doors between the kitchen and the dining room had *always* to be closed, by order of my husband. Staunton said it was unsightly, but really it was his way of closing me off, of keeping me in my place, of separating the man's part of the house, the elegant part, from the woman's, the drudgery part. Almost as if when I was being the servant, I had to be treated like a servant.

"So in this house, which is *really* my house, there will be no closed door—and no possibility of a closed door—shutting off the kitchen from the 'important' part of the house, because I happen to believe the kitchen is as important, as noble and as beautiful as any other part. And I tell you, it will be more beautiful yet, when I'm finished having it done over. And I tell you something else, any man who comes into the house is going to have to move freely from the 'important' parts of the house into the kitchen—and to damned well know how to help once he gets in there."

"Give me a dish towel, sweetheart," Irv said exuberantly. "And let me be the first to audition!"

"Oh no you don't," she replied. "Your first tryout will *not* be in the kitchen, sexy. But for now, show me how good you are at pouring the rest of that champagne."

It was several months after she bought the house that Bea came to realize Harry would not be the man in her kitchen. The blow-up at Freddie's champagne brunch was still months away, but already it was growing clear. From their meeting she began to think about the possibility of walking hand in hand into the sunset with him; just as early, she began to believe he never thought about the possibilities at all. He never said he was for marriage, or against it. He didn't bring it up at all; when it came up, he dismissed it humorously, but with the back of his hand.

Nor did he raise the possibility of living together, although for several months they reached an approximation of that. She spent many nights at his East Seventy-sixth Street apartment in New York, he spent some nights at her house in Washington. Little Staunnie was at boarding school; Amanda was going away in a matter of months. The time was ripe, but the idea never seemed to occur to Harry. It occurred to Bea often. She was afraid of it; she didn't know if it could work. She'd be willing to talk about it, though, even willing to try it. But not suggest it.

"I love you as I have loved no other woman in my life," he would tell her; sometimes she could see tears welling up in his eyes as he said it.

Then he'd go off to Hollywood to work on a TV script, and not call her for a week, at which point she'd pick up the phone, call him at the Beverly Hills Hotel. But he'd never take the call; he'd return it three days later, sounding as if he were not in California but on Mars.

Less than a week later, he'd be back in New York, wanting to spend time with her, telling her how he loved her.

"Where were you the last couple of weeks?" she asked.

He looked puzzled. "In California. At the Beverly Hills Hotel."

"I know that. I mean, *where were you* while you were at the Beverly Hills Hotel?"

"You know I get tense when I'm working. I go far away. I can't help it, I don't like it, but it happens. And when it does I'm not fit company for any living creature."

"God knows, I like you better when you're not working. Why don't you stay in the East, and let me support you? You can be the live-in lover of Sagaponack."

She said that mainly as a joke, but she did want to see what kind of response it would get. He laughed at it.

"In three weeks you'd be phoning California, trying to find work for me. I'd be losing a lover and gaining an agent."

She got the response, and didn't like it, and saw something else she liked even less. Remote as the prospect of her supporting him was, the prospect of his supporting her was even remoter. He never made more than $75,000 a year, some years less, which was OK for a single man, but not for anything more. She made more than he did; and if a book or two clicked, she could go a lot higher. As long as he kept his current schedule and aspirations, his income would not.

Once she asked him, "What do you want to be when you grow up?"

"A boy," he answered. "Just like I am now, young and foolish and carefree."

It was a rebuff, and he tried to soften it. "I'm a good comedy writer, Bea. I make a living at it. I have no pretensions."

The softening didn't help. She was put off by it, but she kept quiet. What she wanted to say was, to hell with pretensions, how about ambitions? None of those, either? What do you see in the future? For you. For us. Or don't you see an "us" in the future at all? She could not bring herself to ask the questions, and he never seemed interested in answering them.

❊ ❊ ❊

She started dating other men, a Senator in Washington, a publisher. She slept with the publisher. He offered to take her and her children down to Olaffson's in Haiti for a week. She accepted the ride on his company jet, insisted that she pay her and her kids' hotel bills.

Meanwhile, she'd heard that Harry had resumed his grand march through the attractive women of New York. For several nights after her week in Haiti, he didn't bring it up. One night, at dinner at Elaine's, he did, so abruptly it startled her.

"Why, Bea?"

"Why what?"

"You know."

"We're not headed anywhere, Harry."

"How about where we're at?"

"Where *are* we at?"

"We're in love with each other. Where else is there? *What* else is there?"

"Other places, other things."

"You mean like Haiti, with a rich man?"

"I'm going to answer that. It's going to get us in a lot of trouble, but what the hell, we're already in a lot of trouble. So I'm going to answer. That man knows I have kids. He invited them, too. Do you know I have kids, Harry? Have you ever invited them anywhere?"

"I thought you wanted a lover; I didn't think you wanted a nanny. I'm not a nanny; nor am I Santa Claus; nor am I rich. Sorry about all that."

That made her furious. "You see, I knew if we started talking about this, I'd be cast in the role of the bourgeois villain. Well, hell, a good part of me *is* bourgeois, Harry, and I don't think it's villainous. A good part of me wants a man who'll offer to take care of me. I'm not all dry wit and wet clitoris!"

"If you said dry wit and wet clit, you'd have a snappier line."

"Is that all you have to say!" she shouted. "Go fuck yourself, Harry!" She said it too loudly; the people at the next table turned to stare. Angrily, she stared back, and snapped, "What are you looking at? You come here to see the famous in unguarded moments, right? So here we are! Just throw money! Or mind your own business!"

The people turned away; she turned back to Harry, eyes flashing anger.

He reached for her hand. "Anyone ever tell you you're beautiful when you're angry?"

She was not to be assuaged. "No. Because until now I never hung around with creative literary sensibilities like you. Did anyone ever tell you to go fuck yourself, Harry? Well, now you're being told again, only this time not loud enough to disturb the neighbors." She leaned forward intently. "Go fuck yourself, Harry!" She reached into her purse, grabbed two twenty-dollar bills and threw them on the table. Then she stood up and walked away, waving to her friends as she left.

Lying awake that night, and many nights after, she would tell herself, I'm glad it's over. I was going soft and mushy, forgetting who I was and what I was doing. Forgetting what I was after. Forgetting Control of Me. I had no room for Harry, no need for him. My book doesn't need a hero, I told Irv that right away. My book won't *have* a hero—just villains, and plenty of them. Yeah, they're teaching me villainy, and I'm going to execute it better than they dreamed. Execute, that's the word. I'm gonna kill 'em.

Labor Day Weekend, 1977; Sunday (continued)

"You say your book goes right up to last night at Mr. Kohl's house, Mrs. Fletcher?"

"Yes, it does."

"Does it *include* last night?" Wisniewski was setting her up and trying to sound casual about it.

"Uh-huh." He could hear her wariness, see it. She would not be easy to set up.

"Then I admire you for knowing what happened. I guess you're a better detective than I am. No one I've talked to can remember anything."

She answered with a half smile, as if to tell him she knew what he was up to, and didn't mind. "I'm not any kind of detective, Mr. Wisniewski. I happen to be a novelist."

"Are you saying that the people in your book, and the events that occur, are not real, are made up?"

A look of mock horror came over her face. "Oh, you don't *ask* a novelist a question like that!"

"Why not?"

"Because characters are usually taken from life—partly—and then by an act of imagination they are made into something new, the author's creatures."

He shook his head, let himself look puzzled, a little more puzzled than he was. "I guess I don't understand. I told you, Mrs. Fletcher, I'm not a book reviewer, I'm a detective. It would be . . . interesting . . . to me to know that the people I might read about in your book, the things they do, are based on real people and real things, that if I read an episode in your book, I could say to myself, it actually happened. Could I say that?"

She looked at him without speaking, got up, walked over to get herself some wine. As she put the ice in the goblet, she asked, "Would you like something?"

"Just an answer, Mrs. Fletcher. It's important to me."

She poured her own wine, carried the glass back, sat, looked at him, sipped.

"*Please*, Mrs. Fletcher!"

"By and large, yes. Essentially, they happened."

He shook his head. "I wonder why people would open up to you that way?"

"Because I'm their friend. Because I can't arrest them."

"But they're afraid of your book?"

"Oh yes, but they're all media creatures. Publicity is mother's milk to them. People out here—most people everywhere—can't keep their mouths shut, about others or about themselves. If they know something damaging about someone else, they're impelled to tell it, partly just to gossip, partly because they think if they feed me raw red meat to chew on, I won't chew on them. I used to be a gossip columnist, and I've seen it work—every time. But the least explainable part is why they're so willing to gossip about themselves. Yet they are. After a while, the trick is not to turn them *on*, it's to turn them *off*."

He stared at her, feeling puzzled. He'd never met people who lived and died by words as completely as these did. "With all this talking about people," he said, "all this . . . dirt"—he didn't know if that was the proper slang for it these days—"you'd think nobody would be on speaking terms with anybody else. You would think they would all hate each other."

"Well, of course, they *do*, in a way. But that doesn't mean they aren't going to *talk* to each other. They have to, they can't help themselves. They simply must stick together. They *have* no one else!"

"Don't you think Mr. Kohl's death may change that?"

She just shook her head. "Surely you are joking! If you think anything or anybody will change, even pause for a moment, I suggest you peek in at Ernst Heinemann's party tonight. Do you think a single soul will be missing—except for Freddie, God rest his soul? Do you think you'd see even a single black armband?"

"Will you be there?"

"Of course!" She shrugged. "I have a journalistic obligation. That's my excuse; everyone has one reason or another for being there. But they'll be there!" Then as if she were a bit appalled by her own callousness, Bea added: "I may cancel my annual pre-Heinemann drink, though."

"What's that?"

"Oh, an old Hamptons tradition I began last year. I invite a group of friends over for a drink, and we all go on to the Heinemann party together. In that way, we get our stories straight. . . ." The sudden leap to attention in his eyes made her stop, then say: "I'm only joking!"

"Who will be at your pre-Heinemann drink?" He leaned forward in his chair, realized he was acting too eager, slumped back again trying to make all the movement look meaningless. But her answer told him she understood.

"Guess," she said.

"The same ones who were at Mr. Kohl's last night?"

"Same old crowd."

This time he sat forward, made it purposeful. "Look, Mrs. Fletcher, I need your help. Would you, for me, *not* cancel your pre-party drink? And would you invite only the people who were at Mr. Kohl's house last night?" He stared at her, waited.

When she didn't answer, he added: "It's important; it would mean a lot."

All at once she felt she was being forced into the role of an accomplice, of a spy against her friends, and she didn't like it. "Why?" she asked. "What do you hope will happen?"

"If I'm lucky, I can find out more about the killing. Maybe get a lead to the killer—if there is a killer."

"Oh," she said. "Do you intend to be here?"

"That's the other thing I wanted to ask." He smiled. "Would you invite me, too?"

He could see she was feeling trapped. "Don't ask too much of me, Detective Wisniewski. Yes, I'll do this one thing, but don't ask too much."

"I appreciate it, I really do."

She shook her head. "I don't see what you hope to accomplish by it. If one of them is the killer, do you think he will show up? He . . . or *she!*"

"He . . . or she . . . would probably feel *compelled* to."

"Don't forget," Bea said, "I'll be here. Hope that won't give you any wrong ideas."

"Oh, they'll all be here," he said. "Thanks to you and your book. No one would *dare* miss it." He paused; he wanted to slide into something new, and make it unnoticeable, seamless. "How I envy you your power to get them to talk—it's a detective's dream. Do you suppose there's anything they wouldn't tell you?"

"Well, I can't know *that*, can I? The nature of the thing they won't tell me is precisely what I *can't* know." He could tell from her voice and face the seams had been noticed, but he decided to charge ahead, anyway.

"Do you suppose, Mrs. Fletcher, anybody'd tell you who killed Friedrich Kohl? If anybody knew, that is. Or would anybody confess?"

"Why in the world would anyone do that?" she asked.

"The reasons you mentioned a few minutes ago," he said. "You know, Mrs. Fletcher, policemen see the same thing in people you were talking about—the irresistible urge to confess, to talk, to get something off their chests, even if it's harmful. Even though they know we can arrest them, testify against them. And the urge is even stronger when they've done something wrong, something criminal; it's called a guilty conscience. You lay awake with it enough nights, and nothing is worse, not even criminal prosecution."

"Yes, I suppose you're right." She didn't seem to want to pursue the point.

But he did. "Well, did anyone?"

"Did anyone what?" She was stalling. They both knew that.

"Tell you who killed Friedrich Kohl! Or confess!"

She laughed at him. "You *must* be joking!"

"What does that mean?" he asked. "That no one told you? Or that you wouldn't tell me if someone had?"

"No one told me," she answered firmly.

"If someone had, would you tell me?"

She sat there as if thinking about it. "I might. I'm inclined to think I would. Yet . . . it depends . . . if it were someone close . . . someone who pledged me to secrecy . . ."

He decided to try in another direction. "You could be subpoenaed, you know, made to testify under oath." Her eyes grew frightened, her face closed up. "Please understand," he went on, quickly, "I'm not saying I'm going to do that, Mrs. Fletcher. I'm just asking for your help. Your friend is dead . . ."

"I wouldn't exactly call him a friend."

"Okay, I withdraw that. Friedrich Kohl, who offered you a lot of money for your book, died last night. Maybe was killed. Maybe it had something to do with the book. This morning you were writing an ending to that book. Maybe writing about how a man died . . ."

"I am a novelist. I am writing a novel . . . fiction!" Her voice sounded tense.

But he was going to press now. "Yes, but maybe something you are writing could give us a lead . . . something you are not even aware of. You know a lot that no one else knows. I'm asking your help. Is that unreasonable?"

"I'll try to answer any questions I can."

"Thank you. Are you close to finishing your book?"

"You are tenacious, aren't you? I'll tell you again. I'm working on the ending. I do not know who killed Freddie Kohl."

"You work on the manuscript out here?"

"Oh yes, here's my workplace, here's my material. I wouldn't consider anyplace else."

He made his face as open and disarming as possible. "You know, I suppose it's none of my business, but I have no idea how a writer works. Do you write on a pad in longhand, sitting in an easy chair? Do you type at a desk? People must bother you with questions like that all the time."

"Not detectives." He thought she seemed relieved by the innocuousness of his questions, which is what he wanted. "I type all the time, it makes my work look more professional. I use an electric at my desk"— she looked toward a small den off the living room—"or if it's an irresistibly beautiful day, I'll sit on a chaise outdoors with a small manual portable on my lap."

He nodded. "Thanks. Writing is kind of a mysterious thing to most of us. I don't read much, mostly war books, but I wonder sometimes how you go about writing a book. I wouldn't know where to begin."

She smiled. "At the beginning. At least that's the way I did it, but then it's my first, and I don't know all that much. You do one page at a time, then one chapter, and it mounts up, and you begin to feel proud of the pages and love the pile of them just sitting there." Again, her eyes went to the little den.

"I'll bet you *must* be proud of it." He smiled again. Now he knew where the manuscript was. "The question is," he went on, "how can I learn what's in your book that would be important to me in investigating Mr. Kohl's death?"

"I said I'd answer any questions I could."

"Yes, but you see, Mrs. Fletcher, I don't even know enough about the people who were there last night to ask the right questions."

Again, she was wary. "I don't see what I can do about that."

"What you can do, what I'd like, is to be able to read the manuscript."

"Mr. Wisniewski, no one has read that manuscript; not even my agent has read all of it. No one is going to. I'm going to have to look it all over, because of Freddie's death. I don't want anyone saying anything that might be taken the wrong way."

"You mean something incriminating?"

"No, I don't mean that at all!" He could see her anger flare. "I mean something ungracious, or embarrassing, something that need not be said now that he's dead. Surely you can understand that!"

"Yes, I can, Mrs. Fletcher, and I don't mean to upset you. Surely *you* can understand I am trying to find out the truth about a man's drowning. I'm not going to gossip. Isn't the truth worth a little embarrassment?"

"Mr. Wisniewski, I do not believe I am going to let you read my manuscript."

He sighed. "We can subpoena it, Mrs. Fletcher."

She looked at him, leaned over to the end table, picked up the phone, punched out a number, waited. "Irv," she said, "Freddie is dead, did you know that? Yes, found this morning in his swimming pool . . . wait, wait . . . there's an East Hampton detective here now, asking me questions about it. He wants to read my manuscript. . . . I *did* say no. He says he can subpoena it." She listened for a while, then, "All right, yes, I will. I will. No, no, you don't have to, I'll ask him to leave. I'll see you at the game, anyway." She hung up.

Now Wisniewski was angry. "He told you to get me out of here, didn't he? Said he'd come over if you were afraid, didn't he?" The detective pulled his shield from his pocket. "Mrs. Fletcher, I *am* on the side of law and order, you know. I'm not anyone to be afraid of. I want to find out about Mr. Kohl's death. I'd think you'd want to, too. I entered on your invitation, and I'll leave if you ask me to."

"I'm sorry, I don't want to offend you, but Mr. Schnell is my agent, and my friend, and he's a lawyer. He told me a detective can't subpoena anybody or anything, a court can, or a grand jury. If you want to arrest me, you should, but I am not to say anything more, or show you anything, and I'm to ask you to leave." She got to her feet, smoothed down the front of her shorts. "Please leave."

He stood, too, tried not to let his anger show. "Mrs. Fletcher, did you kill Freddie?"

She hesitated, then said fiercely, "Of course not!"

"Then why won't you help me?"

"And just what do you think I have been doing?"

He tried to control himself, for he still needed her. "I think you have been answering what is convenient for you, in a convenient way"— his voice was calmer—"but a death like this isn't convenient . . . not for any of us. It would be convenient for me to be home with my family on Labor Day weekend."

"Then I suggest you . . ." she began, but he interrupted. "The reason I'm *not*, is that I'm trying to find out about the death of an important . . ."

"It's your *job*," she said. "It's not mine."

"It's your job as a citizen to . . ."

"I dislike civics lectures, on Labor Day or any other. My agent said if you would not leave, to call him and he'd . . ."

"I didn't say I wouldn't leave, Mrs. Fletcher. Believe it or not, I know what your rights are—as well as your agent does. I wasn't intending to violate them. I was just asking for your cooperation." He was heading for the door as he spoke.

"I'm sorry," she said.

"I'll be here for your pre-party drink—with your permission, of course. And if you'll tell me the time."

"Seven," she said. "A little after."

"Thank you, Mrs. Fletcher," he said.

"You're welcome, Detective Wisniewski," she replied.

He turned and walked out.

As he climbed into his car, he looked at his watch. A few minutes before one. He didn't have to be back here until seven, which would give him a few hours with Lee and the kids on Sunday of Labor Day weekend, after all. Maybe even dinner, if they ate early enough.

On the way home, he stopped at headquarters.

"Hey, Larry," he said to the man at the desk.

"Hi, Wiz, how you doin'?"

He shrugged. "Heard anything from the hospital on Kohl?"

"Yeah, just a few minutes ago. Drowning. Water in the lungs. A few small discolorations on the back of the neck. From fingers, that's the best bet."

He was not surprised. "Any problem with his heart?"

"Nope," the desk man said. "At least they didn't find any."

Again, Wisniewski was not surprised. Kohl was drowned, his head probably held under. How he would love to get a look at Bea Fletcher's book!

Labor Day Weekend, 1977; Sunday (continued)

As soon as the detective left, Bea did what Irv had told her to: locked the manuscript in her desk. Then she brushed her hair, thought about touching up her eyes, decided against it. She stared at herself in the mirror, asked her reflection: Am I obstructing justice? Should I let the detective read the manuscript?

Why not? She had to admit to being just a little irrational about that, since in less than a year a lot of people—an awful lot, she hoped —would be reading it. But she didn't want to undress herself or anyone else in public any sooner than she had to. And it was still a work in progress; there was material in it she'd change or cut, material *no one* must see in its present form.

She gave the desk drawer a final tug to make sure it was locked, found her purse, went out the kitchen door, pulled it shut and headed for her car. Then she paused, went back, reached into her purse for her keys and did something she never did out here—she double-locked the door.

Bea was amazed that the annual softball game hadn't been canceled. After all, Freddie *had* subsidized it, but even if he hadn't, they'd all known him, been to his parties.

Of course, she said to herself, *I'm* here, *I* haven't stayed home. She walked around the field wondering who knew, wondering who of all those who'd been at Freddie's last night would show up for the game. She saw Harry.

She didn't know what to say. The first thing she thought of was: "What a horrible thing to happen!"

"Yeah." She waited for more; nothing came.

"How could . . . what do you suppose . . . ?"

"I was going to ask you," was all he answered.

She looked up at him with exasperation. "When you want to, you can say less than any human I know. Can't you just make believe you're telling jokes?"

"What's funny? What would you like me to say?" She could see the tightening of his lips. Some men battled; Harry tightened his lips.

"I don't know! What do *you* think happened last night? Did you see anything? Things like that."

"Are you picking up where Polack Holmes left off?"

"Polack Holmes?"

"Yeah, the guy from the police . . . Wisnewitz, whatever his name is . . . can't you just see him sitting and cogitating, smoking a cigar instead of a pipe and playing Polish polkas on the accordion instead of Paganini on the violin? There. More like the old Harry?"

"Yes . . . alas. The name is Wisniewski, and he seems like rather a nice guy. He grilled you, too?"

"Yeah, once over lightly. Before he went to see you. I told him all the answers were in your book."

"Thanks. No wonder he wanted to read the manuscript. I said he'd have to wait and get it through the Book-of-the-Month Club, or see the movie, or the TV series . . ."

"I tried to phone to warn you, but your line was busy, as usual."

"Intelligence network operating, as usual. I guess you wanted to foist him off on me so you could get back to corrupting the morals of a minor." When he didn't answer, she went on. "Well, did you turn Nellie to jelly last night? Not to mention this morning?"

"Yeah, she was too weak to come to the game."

Bea was trying to keep it light, but not liking this exchange she had started. "For God's sake, will you allow me the dignity of my jealousy without your five-and-dime flippancy? Aren't you ashamed, at your age, of having to do with someone her age? How old is she? Fifteen? And you must be damned near fifty by now!"

He laughed. "I happen to have just turned forty. As you well know. We happen to be the same age."

"You and Nellie? Never! I don't believe she's forty, any more than you are. I'll give her . . . all right, seventeen, not a day more."

"No, kid, you and I. Remember you and me?"

"Vaguely. It happened sometime before you let your insane lust for nineteen-year-olds take hold of you."

"She's twenty-eight, and aging fast, breathing the deadly air of the Hamptons."

"You say twenty-eight as if it were just right for a man your age. It happens to be all wrong."

"You mustn't let what used to be my insane lust for older women distort reality. For a young man my age, a young woman her age happens to *be* just right. There's a formula, made up by the sagacious French, I believe, for determining the proper age ratio. The woman's should be half the man's, plus eight. Which means a man of forty *should* be with a woman of twenty-eight. And—I hate to break this to you—a *woman* of forty should be with a man of sixty-four."

"The sagacious French, eh? I'll bet a sagacious French *man* made up that formula."

"You know women are no good at math."

"Did you come here this afternoon for the great American pastime, or to taunt a woman?"

"I thought that *was* the great American pastime."

"And it's past time it stopped."

"You ought to try writing comedy."

"You said that, or something like it, the first time we met."

"I meant it. Still do. It's a compliment, you know. Although now that you're a big-time novelist, I suppose you don't think . . ."

"Stop it, Harry."

"OK. How is the book coming?"

"Coming."

"And the rest of your life?"

"Assuming you don't intend any crude sexual double entendre, the book *is* the rest of my life—at any rate, the most important thing in it at the moment."

"That's too bad."

"Why, what should be?"

A tumult of cheering and applause sounded from the crowd. Neither of them turned to see what was happening in the game, but the noise obscured his answer.

"I didn't hear you!" she shouted.

"I said *I* should be!" he shouted back, but by then the crowd noise had ceased, and his answer sounded loud in the stillness. "I said *I* should be," he repeated quietly.

For an instant she felt her eyes mist; she fought it. "We tried that, remember? It closed out of town. You were billed above the title: Harry Majors in 'The Life of Bea Fletcher.' We lost a bundle on it, remember?"

"You'd rather have had it 'Queen Bea of the Hamptons.' "

"No, I'd rather have had it 'The Bea Fletcher Story,' with Harry Majors in a supportive role. . . ."

"Sure you don't mean with Harry Majors in a walk-on? And walk-off? As needed?"

"It suits you not to understand. I just want to be the star of my own life, with your support. And vice versa. You wanted to be the star of my life, with no support."

"Bullshit. Pure distortion."

It made her angry. "Why did you come over to talk to me?"

"I thought you came over to talk to me."

"It doesn't matter," she said, dully, and started to turn away. His voice stopped her.

"I don't know why you came over to talk to me, if you did, but I know why I came over to talk to you, if *I* did."

"Why?"

"Because I miss you. Because I'd rather wake up with you than anyone, of any age."

"Why can't you just say that without the splints underneath the fingernails first?"

"I don't start that, Bea. I'm just the counterpuncher."

"Counterpuncher? I'm not sure what that means, but aren't you mixing up my metaphor?"

"While you're mixing up my life."

"How? How do I mix up your life? Other than by my mere existence? If that's it, then I plead guilty—to existing."

He shook his head. "Here we go again. We've picked up too much emotional baggage along the way, haven't we? It's gotten too heavy. Hostility has such high specific gravity, doesn't it?"

"Oh hell, Harry, you always mix things up, on purpose, I think. Hostility's not the cause, it's the result. You just refused to do anything about the cause, and it . . . oh, forget it, what's the use. I'm glad you miss me. I miss you. And it's all so damned pointless. And sad."

"Can we talk about something else?"

"Oh, please!" she answered. "Anything."

"Poor Freddie. Nobody seems to care. Nobody stops, or even slows down, for a second. I remember as a kid in school reading a poem by Wordsworth about someone dying, and one line in it is something about . . . 'But she is in her grave, and oh, the difference to me.' Freddie doesn't seem to make any difference to anybody."

"Maybe to the person who killed him," she said. "Maybe it's making a difference to that person."

"That's not what I meant, but I suppose you're right. Who do you think it is? Someone we know?"

"A lot of people would *want* to kill Freddie—but only as a figure of speech, if you know what I mean. I can't imagine anyone we know *really* killing anybody."

He nodded. "Nobody thinks he knows any killers. Every time they catch an axe murderer, or some fiendish rapist, the press always gets a neighbor to say, 'he wasn't the type, he was such a *good* boy, such a *quiet* boy.' "

"I don't envy that detective," she said. "To come in from the outside that way, and try to find out who did it. I don't see how it can be done."

"Well, if anyone can't do it, Polack Holmes can't."

"That's nasty, Harry, and snobbish. It's not like you."

"Okay, okay, so I turn in my brotherhood award, and am sentenced to three doubles matches at the Maidenhead. Am I properly chastised?"

"We can't go very long without snarling at each other, can we?"

"Yeah. Hell. Change the subject again. What's happening in the softball game?"

"Do you care?" she asked.

"I don't give a damn."

"Neither do I."

"Then let's go have a drink."

"Oh Harry, and get into a fight every three sentences? No."

"You're right. You're sensible. As always."

"You even turn that into an accusation."

"I'm hopeless. You going to be at Ernst's party tonight? Do you think there'll even be one?"

"Why not?"

"Freddie."

"You must be joking. Who cares? Anyway, it's too late to call it off—even if anyone wanted to. The fact is, not a tear will be shed."

He nodded. "You know, when Hamlet is dying, he says to . . . someone . . . I don't remember, 'absent thee from felicity a while.' I guess that's what we all hope, that people will stop for a couple of minutes, be *upset, not* want business as usual, sure as hell not parties as usual, because our being dead makes a difference to them."

"God, you're being literary . . . and morbid. I almost think I'd rather have you argumentative."

"No pleasing you, is there?" He smiled sadly as he said it. "But then I suppose I'm not all that pleasing. I wish . . . oh hell, see you at the party tonight."

For an instant, she hesitated, almost embarrassed to say it. Then: "I'm having people over for a drink first. Hope you'll be there."

"Not canceling?"

She was tempted to say she was doing it for the detective, but then decided that would be the coward's way. "No. Not canceling. We'll make it in memory of Freddie."

He shook his head. "The dance of death goes on. And oddly enough, the only way out of it *is* death. So Freddie sits this one out, but we keep on boogyin'. How touching."

"Does that mean you won't be there?" she asked.

"Don't be silly. Of course I'll be there." And he turned and walked off.

Labor Day Weekend, 1977;
Sunday (continued)

Wisniewski did get to spend some hours with his family, and to have an early Sunday dinner with them. They generally ate at an unfashionable hour, six. People who had dinner at nine astounded him. The kids got hungry early, and so did he. He'd have perhaps one gulp of beer before dinner and then finish the bottle while he ate; cocktail time was no problem.

On this day, they had only to push dinner up twenty minutes or so for him to be with them. Yet he was *not* with them, he could feel it and he was sure they could too. He was merely killing time before going back to Mrs. Fletcher's house to get to work. In fact, at 6:45, which was sooner than necessary, he got into his car and headed back to Sagaponack and her house.

Traffic was tied up on the highway, and he began cutting first to the north, then, when he hit Wainscott, to the south, which was the longer but clearer route. Still he got to Bea Fletcher's house at a few minutes after seven, which, from the absence of any car but hers, seemed to make him the first one there. He drove past her house, made a U-turn and parked on the road, facing north so he could watch the cars approaching along Sagg-Main.

From the glove compartment he took a pad and pencil and made a list.

Bea Fletcher
Gov. Michael Hughes
Warren Daniels, press secretary
John Wainwright, publisher
Sally Majors, editor
Harry Majors, writer
Nellie Brandon, ?
Carlotta Reilly, TV
Buster Reilly, TV
Betsy Shore, actress
Irving Schnell, agent

Lolly Jones would not be there, but then she had no motive he knew of. If he had to, he could have her picked up later. He didn't think he'd have to.

He watched as the cars drove up, ticked the arrivals off on his list as they walked to the house. He was surprised at how long it took them to arrive. Among his friends, when you were invited somewhere at seven, you got there by seven; by 7:15 you were late. Here it was almost eight before the last arrived.

Wisniewski got out of his car, paused for a moment to think about whether he should take with him the service revolver in his glove compartment. He decided against it. If it were seen on his belt, it would give the meeting a tone he didn't want it to have. To be sure the gun was safe, he locked it in the trunk, then walked to the kitchen door and knocked.

In a couple of moments, Bea Fletcher was there. "I told them you were coming," she whispered as she walked him in. "No one seemed particularly pleased. On the other hand, no one left."

He looked at her, trying to see what attitude she'd taken on since he'd been here, then decided it didn't matter; he couldn't *let* it. He said merely, "Thanks," and then they were in the living room.

She introduced him; again he was pleased with the way she got his name right, pronounced with none of the condescending elaborateness people with names like Fletcher and Wainwright sometimes used.

"I appreciate the chance to talk with you," he began; then reached into his pocket, took out his shield, showed it. "Anyone who would like to examine this," he said, "is welcome to do so."

"I would." Wisniewski looked at the speaker. He was the oldest, smallest man in the room, the only man the detective hadn't met. He had to be the agent.

"My name is Irving Schnell. I am Mrs. Fletcher's agent. I am also an attorney and a member of the New York bar."

"Of course, Mr. Schnell." He handed him his shield in its small leather wallet. Schnell took out a gold pen and a small leather memo book and wrote down the shield number. Meanwhile, Wisniewski looked around the room, realized he hadn't met any of the women but Bea Fletcher, and proceeded to introduce himself and to put the names he already knew with the people he was meeting. Carlotta Reilly was easy—he knew her from television news. Sally Majors was small and dark; Betsy Shore, blond and voluptuous; Nellie Brandon, blond, skinny and freckled.

Schnell handed back his shield, said, "Thank you." The detective nodded and smiled in answer, then began speaking.

"I don't have to tell you that Mr. Kohl is dead. I don't have to tell *most* of you that I have been assigned to investigate his death."

He looked around. Everyone seemed guarded. No one volunteered a word. He realized this meeting could fall flat; it could be embarrassing. But he'd have to go ahead.

"I asked Mrs. Fletcher to invite you, rather I asked her *not* to change her plans to invite you. I also asked her permission to be here. She wasn't happy to do it, but she agreed. And I appreciate it . . ." He looked toward her with a smile and a nod. "Just like I appreciate your help."

Wisniewski leaned forward in the straight-backed chair he was perched on. "Look, I can't force anyone to stay here. And I can't force anyone to speak. You have every right to remain silent and you have every right to get up and go. Those are your constitutional rights, just in case there's anyone here who doesn't know them. And, look, *nobody is being accused of anything.* I'm trying to find out how Mr. Kohl died, and I'm asking your help. If you don't have anything to hide, I don't see why you would refuse to help me, but . . ."

Irv Schnell raised his hand to interrupt. Wisniewski stopped him with a gesture. "*But* there is no presumption, whatsoever, of guilt, or anything, if you leave, or refuse to speak. Did I say that OK, Mr. Schnell?"

"Yes," Schnell said.

"Thanks. Now let me sum up what I know. Friedrich Kohl died of drowning, sometime early this morning, let's say between one and three A.M. It was probably not an accidental drowning. He did not hit his head and knock himself out—which is one way you can drown. There wasn't enough alcohol in his bloodstream to inebriate a flea—so it wasn't drunkenness. Without one of those two conditions, it would be hard to drown under those circumstances even if you couldn't swim —which I understand Mr. Kohl couldn't—because almost anyone who's conscious and sober can thrash his way to the side of the pool. After all, if you fall in, how far from the edge can you be? What we did find was a couple of bruises on the back of Mr. Kohl's neck. They could have been made by a hand—holding his head underwater."

Wisniewski looked around, hoping to find something in the faces of his listeners. What he saw everywhere was guarded attentiveness— nothing else. Well, it was too early, he was expecting too much. He might get nothing from this session, but if he did, it wouldn't be this easy. He took a sip of the ice water Bea had given him, stalling a little, looking around some more before going on. "Now, I've been thinking about whose hand that could have been. Could it have been a bur- glar's? I don't think so. A burglar looks for an empty house, so he can get in and get out—fast. With all the people around last night, it was definitely not an empty house. *Noticeably*, not an empty house. But suppose a burglar *did* go in, late at night, when everyone seemed asleep . . . and then was surprised by Mr. Kohl. If he wanted to kill him, which he probably wouldn't, it seems to me, drowning is one of the last ways he'd do it. First you've got to get the man *to* the pool, then get him *in*, then hold him under. And for all the burglar would know, his victim might be a better swimmer than he was! And maybe drown *him!* No, I say it was someone who *knew* Mr. Kohl couldn't swim. Which is another way of saying someone who knew Mr. Kohl. Last night, a lot of people who knew him were at his house—at around the time he was killed. That includes everyone in this room."

He scanned the faces again; something was different, he wasn't sure what, but maybe it was a kind of early warning fright which had been added to the attentiveness.

"In fact"—he braced himself as he continued, for this would draw a reaction—"at least two of you were at the house *when* he was killed. I say that without any doubt, because Governor Hughes and his press secretary, Mr. Daniels, spent the night at the house."

"Now, wait a minute!" Daniels was on his feet, looking pale. "If you are implying that the Governor of this state . . ."

"It's all right, Warren," Hughes snapped. "Let the detective go on."

"Thank you, Governor. I wasn't implying anything, Mr. Daniels." Wisniewski took another drink of water, sucked in a deep breath and exhaled almost in a snort. "I don't want to waste you folks' time with the ABCs of my business, but there is something I want to explain, something the Governor already knows, having been a police officer himself."

Several of the faces turned to the Governor. Hughes just nodded at the detective. Sure, it was ass-kissing, just a little, Wisniewski knew, but he had the feeling he should grab an ally whenever he could, because there weren't many in this room.

"If it's a homicide, we start by saying: theoretically, anyone could have done it, *anyone* in the world; and then we begin eliminating. Most people were not around to do it, physically were just not close enough, so they're out. And we're down to a comparative handful."

"That's an enormous amount of work to do in one evening, to eliminate millions, *billions*, of crafty Orientals, savage Africans, hot-tempered Latins, brooding Scandinavians. We can't keep up this pace," Harry interrupted. "I think we should all take a well-deserved rest. Or at least another drink." He stood and walked to the bar.

"Shut up, Harry," Bea said, as if admonishing a naughty child.

"I understand," Wisniewski told Harry. "I am sounding too much like a kindergarten teacher. I just want to explain how we narrow down . . ."

"You just want to explain how it is that we're the likely suspects," Harry shot back. "How *we* were there, and how *we* all disliked, maybe hated, Freddie, and knew he couldn't swim, and how easy it would be to . . . you don't have to go back to the creation of the world for that. At least not for me. For my part it would do if you came in just a few steps short of where you snap the cuffs on the killer. Can we have a vote on that? A show of hands?"

Wisniewski didn't quite know how to handle that. After all, this was not anything official, he had no authority to . . . do . . . anything. He got some help from Bea.

"Are you sure you could put your drink down long enough to do *anything* else with your hands, Harry? If you can, why don't you try putting one hand over your mouth and just sitting and listening?"

"OK, sorry." Harry clapped his right hand to his mouth, then moved it slightly away to speak. "Would it be all right if I sipped the drink between my fingers?" Bea gave him an exasperated look. He turned to Wisniewski and said, "I am sorry. I, I think all of us do understand we were in a position to kill Freddie . . . but"—Harry was a little drunk and seemed to have trouble stopping himself—"we're not killers by nature, really, we're good people, quite . . ."

"Oh, Harry, why don't you shut up?" This time it was Johnny who spoke, with a kind of mild impatience.

"No, if you'll pardon me for saying so, it's all right." Wisniewski stepped in. "Mr. Majors brings up a good point. Most killings are by people who are not killers by nature. In fact, from what we know, there are very few killers by nature. Two out of three killings are done by people who know their victims and who kill only once."

"What you are trying to say, sir . . ." Harry interrupted, "and I'll say just one more thing and thereafter no one will be able to *drag* a word out of me . . . what you are trying to say is that . . ." and he paused dramatically, "the killer could be *in this room*."

Although everyone was annoyed with Harry, and although everyone already understood the reason for the detective's being there, the way he put it had an impact. And Wisniewski hit it harder with his answer.

"That certainly is possible, yes."

"Should we be scared?" Bea asked. "I'm not joking."

"I don't think so," he replied. "For one thing, the killer, if he or she is in this room, is not a professional, probably will never kill again. Probably has never killed before—except maybe in the service. I bet that every man in the room was in the armed forces. Am I right?"

After a pause, Warren Daniels responded, "No. I wasn't."

"OK, then all the others were. I know I was. And I was in combat. I killed people. How about you, Mr. Majors? Were you in combat?"

"No," Harry replied, "I was in Special Services. Put on soldier shows. We had some terrific fights over scripts, but all the violence was verbal."

"How about you, Governor Hughes?"

"I was an MP. In Korea. But no combat. Never even had to use my club."

"I know you were in the Marines, Mr. Wainwright, because we discussed it. Combat?"

"Oh yes," Johnny said. "South Pacific. I was blooded."

"You, Mr. Reilly?"

"Yes. I killed up close, face to face."

"So you see," Wisniewski summed up, "we have three of us in the room who have had some experience killing people."

"Ah, Detective," Irv Schnell interrupted. "How is it you haven't seen fit to put that question to me? Do I look too small? Too old?"

"No. I'm sorry, Mr. Schnell, I didn't . . ."

"I happen to have been a combat infantryman in World War Two."

"I am sorry. There are *four* of us." Wisniewski wondered why Schnell should make such a point of that. To assert his manhood? To blur the investigation?

"Suppose we stumble on the killer's identity while we're talking," Bea said. "Couldn't he be dangerous?"

"He *or she*," Wisniewski replied. He couldn't tell if she was serious or teasing. "I don't think we have anything to be afraid of."

"We have an armed officer of the law with us," Harry offered.

Wisniewski didn't know if he was serious, either, but gave him a straight answer. "Not armed. My service revolver is in the glove compartment of my car. If you report that to headquarters, I could get in trouble."

"Maybe you'd better get it before the investigation goes ahead," Harry said.

"Harry, you're turning into a real pain in the ass." Bea stood, went for another glass of wine as she said it.

"Maybe I'm just trying to obstruct justice," he replied.

"Mr. Majors, you don't have to stay," the detective said.

"Yeah, shut up or leave," Bea added.

"None of us has to stay," said Irv Schnell.

"But none of us wants to leave, because we're afraid it'll be taken as a sign of guilt," Harry said. "Besides, no one wants to miss anything. So I'll shut up. It's a promise."

"Let's get back on the track!" Buster exclaimed, almost fiercely. "I am the only one in this room who has ever killed with his hands; let's deal with me first. Freddie was about to get something that could have helped me: the film rights to Bea's book. Therefore I wouldn't kill him."

"Unless of course you knew he wasn't going to give them to you," Wisniewski said. "*Was* he going to?" He looked at Buster, then at Bea, then at Irv. There was a strained silence.

Finally Bea looked at her agent, as if commanding him to say something. "Freddie had nothing to give," Irv said. "None of the rights had been sold to anyone. None of that had been decided on."

"Look," Wisniewski said, "let me blunder in here and ask some direct questions, even though they may sound dumb. What were Mr. Reilly's chances of getting what he wanted?"

Again no one spoke. This time Buster looked around, his jaw muscles clenching and unclenching. And again it was Irv who broke the silence.

"I'd have to say they were not very good. I know in a competitive situation I don't see how I could have awarded him the film rights. Nor had he ever made me an offer. Nor did Bea ever instruct me to give or sell him film rights."

"I never said no," Bea added, desperately. "It was a possibility to be explored." This was for Carlotta, and both women knew it, although neither looked at the other.

"Thanks, Bea," Carlotta replied. "This is a time to tell the truth. You weren't going to let Buster have them, and I . . . ."

Buster broke in. "Look, goddammit! Are you trying to make a case for my killing Freddie? If this is your proof, you'd have to put Bea on my list of targets ahead of Freddie, right? And Irv. And a few executives at UBC. If I were going to kill out of frustration, to *get* people who didn't give me what I wanted, I'd have a pile of bodies stacked up by now."

Wisniewski shrugged. "Sometimes the victim can stand for all the others the killer hated. Things build up, and one may get it for all. That can happen."

"That *can* happen," Buster said softly.

"Sometimes the hatred, the opportunity and the victim all come together." Wisniewski was trying to goad him.

"Absolutely," Buster agreed.

"And you have the strength."

"Yup."

"You knew he couldn't swim."

"I sure as hell did."

"Do you remember what time you left?"

"No. You've already asked me that. I don't. I was loaded, I don't have any idea of what happened the last part of the evening at all."

"No idea?"

"Nope."

"Could you . . ."

Buster interrupted the detective. "Yeah, sure, I could have grabbed the little creep and pushed his head under and listened to him gurgle. And not even remember it."

"That would *do* it," Carlotta broke in angrily. "That would finish the destruction of Buster Reilly that he has been working on so hard these past few years!" She turned from Buster to Wisniewski. "He is as gentle as a lamb. And as grown-up as . . . as . . . an infant! Don't pay any attention to him!"

Wisniewski looked at her. "I don't mean anything by this, Mrs. Reilly, but, as Mr. Majors said before, whenever somebody commits a murder there's always someone near and dear who says, 'He was good and gentle and wouldn't hurt a fly.' "

"You're not suggesting Buster is a suspect?" Carlotta shot back.

"He's not suggestin' anything, ma'am. Just askin' a few questions." Harry made it sound like an all-purpose hero, John Wayne, Gary Cooper and Jack Webb rolled into one.

"Shut up," Bea shouted.

"He's right, Mrs. Fletcher," the detective said. "I'm looking for help."

"OK, you want help," Irv said, "I'll give you help!" The others looked startled; they had never heard such volume from the little agent.

"I'd appreciate it, Mr. Schnell," Wisniewski said quietly.

"Here it is." Irv got to his feet. "Buster? Sure! Wants the book, desperately, sees he's not going to get it. In a drunken rage, kills the man in his way. Johnny: macho war hero, sees his beloved publishing business being ruined, blames Freddie. Needs book, sees he won't get it, blames Freddie. In a drunken rage, kills. Carlotta: will do anything for Buster. Sees Freddie in the way. Plus, the man's probably made an indecent proposal . . . he does that . . . *did* that . . . with everyone. She sees him in or near pool, realizes he's easy target. Holds his head underwater. Next, Betsy: humiliated by Freddie. *She* holds his head underwater . . . killing him and all the men who've debased her."

Irv looked around. "No one will be spared. Not you either, Harry!" He looked back at Wisniewski. "Harry Majors sees the woman he loves being swept into a grand new world, corrupted by Freddie's money. In effect, deserting him for Freddie. Sees his chance: a hand on the back of Freddie's neck. Next, the Governor." Irv stared at Hughes long and hard. "Let's just ask, do you suppose the Governor is happy Freddie's out of the way? You bet. Let's not say any more. Do we have to, Governor?"

Hughes just shook his head.

"As for Mr. Daniels, what the Governor wants, *he* wants. Or maybe we should say, what the Governor wants, he *does*. Let's see now . . ." He surveyed the room. "Sally: Easy. Young woman who wants to get to the top. Nothing can stop her. Until Freddie. Then he suddenly beats her out for a big property—or so she fears. She is furious—and suddenly she sees her chance to eliminate this jarring new force in her industry. And she takes it." He paused, looked around some more. "The beautiful Miss Brandon. Don't know enough about her. Hasn't been around long enough to develop a motive. Of course with Freddie you never can tell. It doesn't . . . didn't . . . take long to develop a motive."

He paused again. Wisniewski started to speak, but Irv put his hand up. "I'm almost finished, not quite. There's one more. There's me. Freddie was ruining *my* industry, too. He was trying to buy Bea away from me. His tactic was to destroy. Destroy an industry, destroy people, destroy relationships. Who wouldn't want to destroy him? He *deserved* to be destroyed.

"So there you are, Mr. Detective. You've got a roomful of motives. And a roomful of suspects. And therefore you have no *one* suspect. And unless you're hiding something, no evidence. You'd be much better off with one suspect than a lot of them. But I'll tell you something else—all you'll find in this room is suspects. And motives. No killer! This is a community of talkers. Of complainers, of threateners. Boasters, backbiters, gossipers. Lots of sharp knives—but they're all verbal. These people all chose their weapons when they chose this business. God knows they can't keep their mouths shut! Someone, for example, tipped Freddie to a highly secret offer made for Bea's book." Irv paused to stare at Bea, Sally, Johnny. He figured he'd make a passing try at finding who'd given away the $2.3 million bid. But he saw nothing in any face. Well, Freddie was dead now and his five-million-dollar buy-out was dead with him, so it didn't matter. Irv went on. "Yeah, the tongues are never still, and the tongues are deadly. Out here the good folks will lay open your reputation. But they'll leave your person alone!"

"I understand," the detective said, almost gently. "They're not the type. The problem with that is, like I said before, two out of every three times the killer is not the type. Until he *becomes* the type. He . . .

or she." Then he held up his hand. "Look, I came here for your help, to find what you know, not tell you what I know."

He paused, waited. No one spoke. He thought for a moment about what he knew now that he hadn't known before. Not much. As Schnell had just said, he had lots of motives, lots of suspects. In fact, too many. He looked around. Still, no one said anything.

After several of what seemed like the longest seconds Wisniewski had ever experienced, Bea looked at her watch. "One thing I know," she said, "is that we better get to Ernst's party; it's nearly nine."

Wisniewski seemed to feel a vast collective sigh of relief fill the room. Briskly—he'd never seen these people move so purposefully— they got up, abandoned their glasses and started to leave.

"Thank you," he said hurriedly. "I know where you're all reachable. I hope I can reach you if I need you."

Some nodded, some just looked at him, some walked out. Wisniewski stood, walked to Bea. "Thank you for your help, and for letting me be here, Mrs. Fletcher," he said.

He almost asked again, Can I read your book? He didn't; he knew what her answer would be. And he knew he could no longer accept that answer. He shook her hand, walked to his car. He was the next-to-last to drive away; her car was behind his as he drove north to the highway. At the blinker light, where he knew she would turn right onto the highway to go to East Hampton, he went straight ahead through the intersection, headed north. But in fifty yards, as soon as he could, he made a U-turn, headed south again, back toward where he'd just been, toward Bea Fletcher's house.

Wisniewski didn't know how long she'd stay at the party, didn't know how much time he'd have.

In the dark September night, the torches planted around Ernst Heinemann's huge lawn, which sloped from his baronial brick mansion to Georgica Pond, made the water shimmer gold and black and bronzed the tanned faces of the gliterati. In the hour and a half the party had been going on when Bea arrived, the sky, the pond, the faces had grown darker, the cacophony of conversation louder, the crowd denser and more nervous. Soon dancing would begin on the wooden floor built for the party; soon enough alcohol would have been drunk so that the irregularities of the lawn would become an obstacle course.

Ernst Heinemann was a tall, jolly man in his late fifties who had achieved what most writers dream about: critical esteem and wealth.

A newsmagazine once wrote that Heinemann should either be called America's only good *popular* novelist or its only popular *good* novelist. His books were assigned reading in high schools all over the country; they sold by the hundreds of thousands annually in paperback. He was also available in deluxe hardcover reprints. From his backlist alone he earned $200,000 a year, and a one-page outline for a novel was enough to get him a half-million-dollar advance.

Like almost everyone at his party, Heinemann was divorced. For the past ten years he'd been living with a magazine writer twenty years younger than he.

Each year he invited three hundred people and four hundred showed up. Almost nobody refused his invitation; many brought uninvited friends. Some people simply crashed.

Heinemann was an eclectic man; he enjoyed talking with a banker, businessman, doctor, or TV producer as much as with another literary light, and that eclecticism was reflected in his invitation list. It also showed in his dance music. He was a traditional jazz fan, and each year hired a Dixieland group. But between live sets, a DJ put on records for rock, fox trot, samba, tango, Viennese waltz and polka—all Heinemann favorites.

Seen from the height of the stone patio, the party hardly seemed affected by the death of one of its most famous invitees. It was a choppy sea of human motion, everybody trying either to meet or to avoid someone, its surface becoming denser and rougher with the darkness, the arrivals, the drinking.

Looking to her right from the patio when she entered, Bea saw the band, the dance floor, the DJ and a bar. A second bar stood straight ahead of her, and a third to her left. Each had a white-clothed table and two white-jacketed bartenders. Each seemed a rock, around which a sea of guests swirled, eddied, paused.

And the stars were out. Straight ahead of her a former Secretary of the Treasury was chatting with an Oscar-winning screenwriter. Next to them a lion-headed old novelist had a young woman book critic by the arm and was talking fast, gesticulating with his other hand, which held a drink. Behind them a Broadway star was laughing at something being said by the chairman of the board of a major brokerage house. On the dance floor a famous architect was leading an interior designer in a step that bore no relation to the music. This evening would be a three-day supply for the gossip columnists.

All the outfits, Bea noticed, were casual-expensive, the women not merely in jeans, but designer jeans, the men not merely in V-neck sweaters, but in cashmere. She had on white jeans, which she could see at once was a mistake, for white jeans were in this year and every second woman on the lawn wore a pair—they became the whitecaps on a turbulent sea of guests.

Looking around, she decided everyone was enjoying himself as if nothing had happened last night. No, she corrected herself, *more.* Now they have something new to talk about, the ghouls. Well, she thought, then what am I doing here? She wasn't sure; she strained to reach for the truth. Did she need the look of the place for the book? Was she trying to show the others she was unperturbed by the detective's investigation, that she was innocent of the killing? Did she just not want to miss a party? She couldn't separate them, decided they were all reasons for her being here.

She walked into the crowd, headed for one of the bars, which was not quickly or easily reached. It took her twenty minutes, six kisses, four handshakes, three brief conversations, and a substantial one, with a magazine writer about the demands of historical truth in a *roman à clef.*

When she got her wine, she decided on one leisurely tour of the lawn, and then out. Those who had been at her house she didn't want to see; even she was surprised at the strength of that feeling. It hit her when she spotted Johnny, who looked at her as if he wanted to talk. There were three or four people between them; Bea threw him a forlorn shrug and then managed to break eye contact. She kept going.

After a half hour, again dotted with embraces, effusive cries, brief, warm chats, she encountered Heinemann.

He gave her a hug and an austere kiss. "I'm glad to see you," he said, and she grinned at him. He was at the moment perhaps the one person in the Hamptons whose greeting she both welcomed and believed. And when she said, "You heard about Freddie," she knew he'd be the only person whose answer she could believe.

"Yeah, I heard." His big brown eyes looked at her, he puffed at his unfiltered cigarette. His look dared her to offer platitudes—what he called "mouth music"—or expect any from him.

She didn't dare. She just said, "What do you think?"

"I don't like to see anyone killed," he began. "That's where my tender feelings end. Kohl was a sonofabitch. Contributed nothing, just milked, milked, milked. I loathed him. Felt sorry for him almost as much. He was pitiable. Also a gate crasher. I never invited him, but he showed up anyway, always with some public figure to make sure I wouldn't kick him out." His brown eyes stared at her through the thick glasses as he took another drag of his cigarette.

"Someone came up to me and said something like, it's too bad, it does put a damper on the party, doesn't it? I told him: Horseshit! Nobody gave a damn for him, which is what he deserved. Then this guy said how sad he thought it was, so I finally said: Then why don't you go home and mourn? What in hell are you doing here?"

He looked at her, this time took a sip of his gin and tonic. "I mean, Bea, it's all such crap! One hasn't time to wade through the crap *and* get anything done, and sooner or later one has to go for one or the other. As you may know, I made my choice." He gave one of his guffawing laughs and hugged her again. "I'm awful glad to see you. Have a good time." Then he gave her a kiss and walked off.

She continued in her circle. Of course, Ernst was right about the horseshit part. If Freddie's death affected her, it wasn't at all because she'd lost a friend, it was because of the effect on her book. Well, it has surely gotten in the way of my enjoying this party, she told herself, then was forced to add: But you never really liked this party before, either, remember? Yes, she admitted, I remember.

Bea looked at her watch. It was 10:15, which meant she'd been there more than an hour. That was enough. She looked around, took in the bronze flicker of the torchlight on the lake, watched a swan glide with serene grace into a band of light and then out of it, and then turned and headed for her car.

Even as Wisniewski was parking fifty yards down the road from Bea Fletcher's house, he was clicking off his headlights. He unlocked the glove compartment, groped for his little flashlight and his big ring of keys and headed around the back of the house.

He didn't know how much time he'd have before Bea returned from the party, but figured it might not be a lot. She might have only one drink and then come home, and he had to be prepared for that. At least he knew where in the house to look for the manuscript: the desk. And where in the manuscript to look for the killer: the ending.

The farmhouse backed on potato fields, so there was not much chance neighbors would spot his light, but he tried to use it as sparingly as possible. Somewhere back here he'd find a weak link in the house's protection—there was always at least one. He had nothing to fear from a burglar alarm—there was none, he'd checked that during his visit.

First he tried two windows; both were locked. Then he spotted a screen door and with his light looked for a hook. There it was. He tried the door; there was some give in it, and behind it a sliding glass door had been left open. This part would be easy. He found his wallet, fished from it a laminated membership card—long expired—in some fraternal organization. He carried it because it was invaluable as a "loid," which would open spring locks—and, he hoped, hooks like this one. He forced the card through and lifted. The hook was off more easily than he'd hoped.

Using his light as little as he could, he made his way into the den, looked at the lock on the desk. This would be easy, too, he could see, but it would take a kitchen knife. Light in hand, he found the kitchen, found the knife. The desk was old and wooden and had enough give so there'd be little, if any, damage to it.

It was only when he located the manuscript that Wisniewski began to sweat. He didn't like doing this—he *hated* it. It was against what he'd been taught, what he believed in. It was what bad cops did, and a big piece of his life was supported by his picture of himself as a good cop. It made up for the money he didn't earn, and the social and family strains caused by his having married a Vietnamese.

This was illegal, and he was amazed at the decisiveness with which he opted to break in. There'd been no agonizing, not even any debate. When Bea had refused to let him read the book, when the meeting with all those people had yielded him nothing new—except the certainty that the book had the answer—he knew at once he'd go after the book.

He had the rationalizations all set. These people would draw a green curtain around themselves, lawyers, power, connections—all bought by money, and he had to act fast. Besides, eventually the damned book was going to be read by the public anyway; it was not as if he were looking at secret documents. Another thing was, he didn't get many cases like this, maybe would never get another, and he was damned if the county boys were going to take it over, or the FBI, or anyone. Sure, he could threaten to subpoena her book, but his chances would be slim in the long run and nil in the short run. He had to read it *now*.

Later, he could confess it to her, tell her why, invite her to make a complaint. As long as he got to read it first. What would be truly inconvenient, embarrassing, was getting caught in the act. That mustn't happen.

His hands were damp with sweat as he lifted the manuscript from the upper right-hand drawer. It was hefty—he looked at the number on the final page: 547. Then he scanned the page itself—it was a writer summing up, no names, no killing. Suppose the killing were not near the end? He asked himself the question suddenly in a panic. Suppose, the way authors do, she put the ending near the beginning! Then he was stuck, because he sure as hell couldn't sit there and read 547 pages with a flashlight! Not unless she were away on a two-week cruise instead of at a party a few miles away!

He'd just have to take a chance. He grabbed about thirty pages from the bottom, and started looking for names. The first he spotted was Fritz Kane. Someone had told him the initials would be the same— who'd told him? Majors, Bea Fletcher herself? It didn't matter. Then he saw Senator Marty Hogan . . . MH . . . Mike Hughes. He continued scanning, saw . . . swimming pool . . . portable bar . . . Hogan glaring at Kane . . .

He went on. His eyes picked up words . . . blackmail . . . film . . . porno . . . taunting . . . a push . . . a splash . . . the Senator in the pool with Kane . . . a cry for help . . . and the Senator's hand . . . on Kane's neck . . .

My God! Wisniewski said to himself. She's given it to me! The killer, the reason—porno films of the Governor! Even the place to look for the film—Kohl's house.

On a dark night, on a quiet country road, the beams of a headlight can be seen a long way, and just as he was going on with the manuscript, he was startled by lights which seemed to climb right into the room. He snapped off his light and waited. The headlights came closer and closer, but did not go by. Instead they turned into the driveway.

Wisniewski began to move, getting the manuscript together, shoving it into the drawer, prying the lock closed with the knife. He moved for the door as quickly and quietly as he could without the help of the light. As he was making his way around the far side of the house, he saw the beams of the car again, realized he'd been thrown into a panic by someone merely using the driveway for a U-turn. He laughed at his own panic; as he walked, the night breeze cooled the sweat on his face, and suddenly he felt a lot better.

There was no hurry now; maybe he even had time to go back in. But he wouldn't. She might indeed be returning. In any event he no longer had to. He climbed into his car, sat there relaxing for a moment, playing back in his mind his break-in, his discovery, moment by moment. And realizing something. When he put the manuscript back, he'd placed the last thirty pages, the ones he'd been reading, on top. She'd spot that instantly! Should he go back?

No. He might get caught. She might not go to the drawer for a day or so, might not even see the rearrangement. Besides, he intended to tell her. No, he would not go back. He would go to Freddie's house.

He now had a suspect. The thought of it made him sweat again. His suspect was the goddamn Governor of the state!

Labor Day Weekend, 1977; Sunday (continued)

In his car, on his way over to the Kohl house, Wisniewski had little doubt what he was after: the porno home movies of Governor Hughes with female companions promised by Bea Fletcher in the ending to her novel. He had lots of doubt, though, as to what he'd do with them if he found them.

He'd have to decide how much he wanted to arrest the killer in this case—arrest him, start the machinery moving toward indictment and trial—if the killer was the Governor.

How much did he want that arrest? And how much did he want to keep his job? There was little doubt in his mind that the moment he mentioned the Governor as a suspect or as a star of home movies, he'd been stepping into a meat grinder. Unconsciously Wisniewski tightened his square, stubby hands on the wheel of his car until, almost surprised, he felt the ache of the pressure, saw his thick fingers white at the knuckles.

My God, he told himself, the clout that would be brought to bear! The mere mention of the Governor as a suspect would be deadly in an election year. The mere existence of those porno films—although they alone would hardly make a murder case—could be fatal to the Governor's re-election chances next year, not to mention his hopes for the White House in three years.

This time he'd taken the highway from Sagaponack back to East Hampton, and was slowed in traffic. For a moment he wished he'd never get there, and in fact that was an option: to make believe he'd never read the manuscript, to forget about looking for any film. To play it safe, keep out of trouble.

Yet when he reached Georgica Road, where he had to turn to reach Kohl's place, he never even thought of playing it safe. As if the car, his hands, were leading him, he drove to the mansion on the dunes, pulled in and parked. He spotted the station wagon, not the Rolls—but that could be in a garage. Nor did he see any other car. It looked as though the Governor and Daniels were still at the Heinemann party. Wisniewski glanced at his wristwatch; it was not quite 9:30. The chances were they would not be back from the party for a while.

As he walked toward the door, Wisniewski was happy he'd told the desk to remove the patrolman who'd been guarding the house, happy not to have to explain to another cop what he was doing there, what he'd come to look for.

He rang the bell, waited for Sophie to let him in. When no one responded, he walked around to the french doors off the pool patio, tried them, found the second open. God, these people made it easy for burglars, he said to himself. He stepped inside, closed the door behind him.

"Sophie. Sophie!"

He waited. No answer. He flicked on his little flashlight, walked through the big living room, into the center hall, found the stairs.

Twice more he called Sophie's name. Again, there was no answer, so he walked upstairs. The big bedroom on the southwest corner, he remembered from the manuscript, was the one at which the camera was aimed. The detective paused for a moment to get his bearings, then headed west, down the hall. At the end he saw three doors. He opened the door on his left—this would be the southwest bedroom. He flashed his light around. The two exterior walls were all glass, with drapes partially drawn. He could get a glimpse of the sea; though the night was partially clouded, with little moonlight, he could still see the luminescence of the surf. He swung his light to the room's north wall. It was all mirrored. Here would be the one-way mirror through which the filming was done, and the filming room would be on the far side of that wall.

Quietly, Wisniewski closed the bedroom door and tried the one next to it. Locked. He turned his light on the knob and lock; it was one of those old-fashioned ones that a skeleton key would open, and he happened to have just the thing on his key ring. In three seconds, the door was open. He flashed his light around, saw this small room—large closet would be more like it—had no window, so he flipped on the light switch. There was the camera, on a tripod, behind it a stool for the person doing the filming, and to his left, the glass through which the filming was done. For a moment he switched off the light, and looked through to the big bedroom and the sea beyond. The only furniture in the tiny room was a table, with a single drawer. On the table stood two empty mugs, both with rings of dried coffee in them.

He tried the drawer; it, too, was locked. Wisniewski took from his pants pocket his key ring, found a key, opened it. He was always amused at what people thought constituted lock-and-key safety. In the drawer were a half-dozen unused rolls of super-8 film, still in their unopened boxes, and four rolls of what seemed to be exposed film in canisters. He picked up the four, slipped them in his jacket pocket.

Now he had the film. If it showed what he thought it did, it meant he had one leg in the meat grinder. Wisniewski walked from the room, switched off the light, closed the door behind him, locked it. For a couple of moments he stood there in the dark and tried to think. Now he couldn't retreat. He might as well search the rest of the house. He opened the third door on the west end of the house, revealing a north-west bedroom, large but not as large as the one the Governor was in. The beam of his flashlight revealed ruffles, pastels. This room was decorated for a woman, probably the woman—or girl—chosen for the weekend by Kohl.

In the center of the house, on the north and south, were two small bedrooms, the southern one barely furnished, a spare guest room, the northern one tiny, furnished like a nun's cell. This, he'd bet, was Sophie's room. He'd come back to it. The bedroom on the northeast corner was medium-sized, and from the look of the clothing and papers in it was being used by the Governor's press secretary. Finally, he opened Freddie's room, on the southeast corner. It seemed to be about the same size as its western counterpart, huge, almost square, with its two outside walls also glass; Freddie must have awakened to the sunrise every morning. But where the counterpart room had a mirrored north wall, Freddie's wall was one long closet. Wisniewski walked over to it, slid a door open, ran his light along the contents. There was one long row of sportcoats, trousers, suits, at least fifty hangers of clothing. He reached out to touch a jacket. Cashmere, maybe five hundred dollars a jacket, he figured. In this closet there was clothing worth maybe two years of his salary. He probed with the light, spotted two racks holding about thirty pairs of shoes. And this was Kohl's weekend house! Life on this scale was unimaginable to Wisniewski.

Along the room's west wall he saw a long, low bureau, walked to it, started opening drawers. There were pairs of socks beyond counting, stacks of underwear, handkerchiefs, perhaps three dozen shirts, many of them silk. He found no papers whatever, no letters, notes, nothing. Then, almost as he was walking away from the dresser, he let his light play along its top. Something was strange. At first he didn't know what, then it came to him. There was on that bureau, in the entire room, for that matter in the entire house as far as he'd seen, not a single photo of a human being, man, woman or child. Back home, in Wisniewski's bedroom, family pictures were everywhere of kids together, of him and Lee together, kids separately, him and Lee separately, pictures of brothers, sisters, aunts, uncles, cousins, nephews, nieces, even relatives who didn't talk to them anymore. To the detective, the absence of pictures was even more foreign than the silk shirts, the alligator shoes, the cashmere jackets. What else he was looking for he was not sure, probably he'd know if he saw it—but nothing offered itself. He left and went back to Sophie's room.

From what he could see, Kohl had only one personal connection— the stolid, massive woman who worked for him, who lived in this austere little room. He opened the door, looked for a light switch, found none. Then with his light he picked out a lamp on the small table near her bed. He switched it on and looked around.

In a house where the big bedrooms were more than 20 feet square, this room could be no more than 9 by 12. On its walls, on its one cheap dresser there was not a single picture or decoration. On its iron single bed was a nondescript spread of a faded tan. Reluctantly, he opened the top drawer of the shabby, chipped white dresser, to see plain cotton underpants and bras. Embarrassed, he almost shut it, but instead forced himself to reach in, beneath and behind the piles of underthings. At once, he was glad he had, for his hand came upon a small leather diary, closed by a little clasp. He stared at it for a moment, then decided to slip it into his pocket. In the other drawers he found shirts, shorts, chino pants, all of them drab, all inexpensive, nothing feminine.

Then he walked over to the closet, opened the door. In it were several skirts and dresses, all so plain they seemed to be cut from the same cloth as the drab bedspread. On the floor were a pair of brown oxfords, three pairs of sneakers, a pair of clogs. No dress shoes, no high heels. Nowhere a touch of silk, no pantyhose, no bright colors.

He closed the closet, noticed the only other bit of furniture, a straight-backed wooden chair, once painted green, now more chips and scrapes than color. On that tiny bit of floor left uncovered by bed, dresser and chair, lay a two- by four-foot brown and cream throw rug so worn its geometric pattern was barely visible.

Sophie represented to him as exotic a mode of living as Kohl did. Alone. No family, no noise, none of the happy cacophony of people talking, shouting, laughing, quarreling. In a house not hers. In her tiny room the big woman trod so lightly she left almost no footprint. He wondered what kept her there. Had she no better place to go? Or did she care for Friedrich Kohl? If she did, she was the only one—at least as far as he'd been able to find. Certainly luxury was not her reward for staying. If she was Kohl's only connection, he was hers.

He wondered if Kohl had deliberately kept her in such shabbiness. Wisniewski decided she preferred it, wore it like a badge. Suddenly, he felt saddened, ashamed, a voyeur, and decided he was going beyond the realm of duty into that of personal curiosity. That he wouldn't allow himself; he switched off the lamp, turned on his flashlight, walked out into the hall and down the stairs.

Then he realized he'd been lingering in Sophie's room because he wasn't sure what to do when he left. In his pocket he had what might be the hottest piece of film since *Deep Throat*, and not because it was explicitly pornographic—although it might be that, too—but because the leading man was the Governor instead of Harry Reems.

He walked out of the house onto the patio, the pool darkly shimmering beyond it. He looked at his watch—not much after ten. Fifteen hours ago his life had bumped into Friedrich Kohl's death. A day that was to have reached its crescendo with a drive to a bay beach had turned into a homicide investigation, the victim one of the richest men in America, the suspects a list right out of a newspaper gossip column, and the killer—if Mrs. Fletcher's book was right—the Governor of the state.

Wisniewski saw himself in an impossible situation. If he had no leads, chances were tomorrow county detectives would take over the investigation. He wouldn't like that. As it was, he had what he wanted, a major lead, some real evidence—and a lot of trouble.

He reached into his pocket for the film, instead felt the diary, which he took out and stared at. Sophie surely knew a lot about Kohl's activities and might have put some of what she knew into the book. She might also have put in private details of the sad life he saw contained in that room. He half dreaded the prospect of reading it. He slipped it back into his pocket, reached into the other pocket for the four cans of film, hefted them. God, how he'd like to walk to the ocean, hurl the film and the diary as far out as they'd go. That was out of the question. He could wish he'd never found the stuff, but having found it, he simply could not destroy it.

Goddamn Kohl! What business had anyone taking pictures of other people in bed! With all his money, luxury, you'd think he'd have something better to do than stare through peepholes, or have a camera do it for him!

Look at this place! Even as he said it, as if a dead Kohl had cued them, the clouds rolled away from the half-moon, which cast a pale light on patio and pool. Wisniewski walked through the neatly aligned outdoor furniture. He knew workmanship; he knew each of these chairs was worth a couple of hundred bucks, each of the chaises at least double that. God knows what the flagstone must have cost! Not to mention the pool. He walked toward it; it was kidney-shaped, larger than any pool like it he'd ever seen. How his kids would love it!

Why couldn't Kohl have been content to sit around this gorgeous place and enjoy it? Because Kohl had no kids to enjoy his pool, no friends to sit on his expensive pool furniture. He couldn't even swim! The pool he'd bought and one of the people he'd bought had combined to kill him. Wisniewski walked closer to the pool. There was such a calmness to water. Where, he wondered, had Kohl gone into the pool? Probably right where he was standing; it was the deepest part, yet closest to the house, as if Kohl's pool had been designed to make it convenient for someone to drown him. Then the detective could see why: a small bathhouse was at the far end, and the shallow part of the pool next to it.

He looked down at the water; in the brighter light of the moon now it was a paler blue, and Wisniewski thought he could see the bottom. He wondered if Kohl's eyes had been open as he was held under, if

Kohl had seen the bottom. He wondered how long Kohl had thrashed and struggled. Kohl was neither big nor strong, whereas the Governor seemed fit and burly, almost six feet tall. It wouldn't have been much of a match, but then, Wisniewski figured, if you're thrown into water over your head, and can't swim, you're in a bad spot even if you *are* strong. And the minute you weaken, let the other person get your head under while he can keep his above the water, you're gone.

At that moment something about the pool seemed so serene, so welcoming; little as he liked to swim, he was tempted; he wished he were rich, with the time and the opportunity to get into that water and let his troubles wash away—as they said in the songs. He wished he could dip his toe in to see how warm it was, and he laughed to himself as he actually reached a shoe to the surface and flicked it with the sole, half expecting the feel of the water to pass through to his skin.

What it was he saw or heard then he didn't quite know—a shadow, the scuff of a foot—but it made him start to turn, which he later realized saved his life, because if that big arm had been able to snake under his chin and make contact with his windpipe, it would have been the end of him, Marine Corps training or not. But responding to the sound, the shadow, whatever it was, he turned his head to the right, and the thick bicep smashed into his chin as the arm circled his head, tightened.

Almost at once he knew it was Sophie. The arm, strong and massive though it was, had a layer of softness which was not a man's. And he could feel the pressure of her big breasts on his back.

There was no way he could keep her from driving him into the water; given his position and her size, he couldn't have prevented that even if he'd been ready and braced for it. Almost instinctively he reached out with his right arm as they hit the water, groping for the side of the pool. His forearm hit it with a cracking pain, but his hand touched the gutter and he held on. It was all so fast, but despite the surprise, the shock, the pain, he knew that if he lost contact with the side of the pool, let himself be carried free into that ten-foot water, he'd have no chance. He knew, too, that while he had only one hand free and she had two, he'd never be able to fight himself free.

With his left hand, he reached up to her encircling arm, groping for a finger—if he got one he'd snap it right off her hand. But there was none; her hands were off to the left somewhere, one clutching the other in the vicinity of his left collarbone, and when he finally slid his hand along her arm to her hand, his own awkward clutch allowed him no leverage. Her response to his grasp was to tighten her stranglehold, try to tilt his head back, force him down, underwater, to break his hold on the side of the pool.

He lowered his chin, drove his head down and forward as hard as he could, pulled as hard as he could with his right hand to keep himself close to the side of the pool. He knew she was damned close to over-powering him; if she could snap his head back, or make him lose his handhold, he was gone.

Just for an instant he consolidated his strength and felt her doing the same, getting ready for a new effort.

Now she was increasing the pressure on his neck. With his left hand, he reached to her hip; he could feel the edge of her bathing suit, below it her skin. He grabbed flesh between his thumb and forefinger; he had to inflict some pain, change the balance of this struggle. Yet . . . he found himself unable to hurt a woman that way.

Do it! he shouted at himself, silently. He pinched as hard as he could. For a big woman, she had damned little soft flesh on her thigh; he wasn't doing much damage, he knew as he squeezed. She just twisted her hip and squeezed harder.

No. That wouldn't do. The pain was damned near unbearable, and the moment he couldn't bear it, relaxed his neck muscles to stop fight-ing it, his head would go under and that would be the end. He had to do better—and fast. His left hand moved around to the inside of her thigh, he snatched at the soft flesh in her crotch, could feel bits of the fringe of her pubic hair. This time he squeezed a handful of flesh. It hurt her; he could feel her react. She brought her left knee up and across her body and, using it as a fulcrum, levered his head back with her arm.

This was new pressure, more painful than ever. Reflexively, his left hand released her flesh and reached for the gutter. He pulled himself as high and as close to it as he could.

Now he had his back fully turned to her, his chin tucked as far into his chest as he could, while she had both hands free to destroy him. He felt her big soft breasts in his back, then her legs opening, one being placed around each side of him.

Fighting the agonizing pain, tensing his arms to keep himself high in the water, close to the pool's edge, he readied himself for her move. She braced her feet against the side of the pool and pulled at his head more powerfully than ever. All he could do was hold on, how long, he didn't know, but not very long.

He remembered all those bridges he'd done in the high school gym to build up his neck, for football, for wrestling. It had grown to a size 17, a big neck for a little guy. He'd been proud of it. God knows he needed those neck muscles now. There was nothing else he could do but hold on. Braced as she was, if he let go with either hand, she'd have him. But if he could hold on long enough she'd have to do something. *If* he could outlast her.

Once, twice, three times, she tightened. Three times, fighting through the pain, he tensed, held. Finally, she made a move and he was ready. She released his neck with her left hand and reached out for his left hand, which was clutching the pool gutter. Now he had to take a chance. He sucked in a breath of air, brought his left hand sharply away from the pool, and grabbed her right, which was clutching his neck and shoulder. With his right hand, he reached for her right elbow, jerking it upward with as much force as he could manage, at the same time ducking his head under to free it from the grip of her right arm. It was the classic break of the back stranglehold, taught in every Red Cross life-saving course, a course he'd had to take as a refresher only last year.

It freed his head, but when he tried the follow-up, twisting her right arm behind her back to get her in a hammerlock, his grip on her wrist slipped, and she wrenched her arm away. Trying to keep her from turning her body so she could face him, he grabbed the top of her two-piece bathing suit; as she twisted it broke open. She managed to turn halfway, the straps of her top coming off her shoulders. Being a rotten swimmer he had to concentrate on treading water, which by itself was a major undertaking. He held on to her bathing-suit top, hoping the straps would bind her arms, but she whipped her right arm clear and threw it around his head.

He could hear her suck in air, feel her start to take him under, and he knew he was in worse shape than before, because now he was exhausted and no longer had a grip on the pool. First one arm tightened on his neck, then the other; he found his hands on her bare breasts, and a ridiculous feeling of embarrassment seized him, an instinctive desire to remove his hands. Instead, he forced himself to grab the nipples, to pinch them as hard as he could.

The pain was too much for her; she made a sound that was half grunt, half scream. Her arms loosened. He pushed her away, with his right hand grabbed the gutter. He brought his left up under her chin, and with an open hand, half shoved, half punched her head back, driving it up and back against the side of the pool. He could feel she was tired, too. Fury, adrenalin, gave him new strength and stamina. He increased the pressure of his hand on her chin, kept her head tilted back, tight against the rim of the pool, brought his body in close to hers, put a leg between hers so she couldn't move.

"Stay still. Don't move a muscle or I'll snap your fuckin' neck!" The strangled sound of his voice, the hatred in it, surprised him. *"Don't move!"*

Her response was to jerk her body around, try to get her right hand onto his left, to yank it away from her chin. He tightened the grip of his right hand on the pool, drove his left knee up into her crotch, jammed his hand up and back against her chin, lifted her another six inches out of the water, propped her at an intolerable angle over the side of the pool.

She let her body go limp and he moved as fast as he could. He slid his left hand over her face and grabbed her hair. She yelled in pain as he pressed down on both hands and without releasing his grip on her hair, heaved his exhausted body out of the water.

Clutching her hair, he brought himself to a kneeling position just above her. Only then did he become aware of the drag of his soaked clothing, the weight of the book and film cans in his dripping jacket. He wondered what kind of shape his evidence was in now.

Then he spoke to Sophie. "You're going to turn and climb out. I'm going to have this grip on your hair, and if you do anything funny, I'll snap your neck. I'm not kidding." He tightened his grip as a demonstration, and then began to twist the hand in the direction he wanted her to turn. She turned and when he began to pull, she put her hands on the side of the pool and lifted herself out.

"Just stay there on your stomach," he ordered. "Put your hands behind your back." He undid his leather belt, pulled it free, used it to tie her hands.

"Okay, now get up." She did, with difficulty, having to struggle to her knees before she could stand. He made no move to help her, just stood there, trying not to look at her bare breasts.

"Sit on that chaise, and don't try anything, or I'll knock your teeth out."

She obeyed. His eyes always on her, he pulled a canvas director's chair up close to her, sat, suddenly overcome by tiredness. It was a good thing he'd won when he had, he told himself, because very soon he would have lost. She was breathing heavily, her chest heaving as she sucked in air. But as before there was nothing in her eyes.

He knew he should get her into the car and over to headquarters, but he wanted to talk to her before she could compose herself, although he had to admit she looked pretty composed right then. Anyway, he needed a couple of minutes' rest.

"Why did you do it? Tell me about it." He tried to sound detached, professional, as if she hadn't just tried to strangle him.

She shrugged her big shoulders. He kept looking straight at her eyes, yet was aware of her breasts bobbing as her shoulders moved. "Because I was the only one who loved him. And I had the right to decide when he should die."

"What?"

"I was the only one who cared whether he lived or died. I had the right to make that decision."

Wisniewski had heard it. He'd heard it twice. Yet he had to make sure. "*You* decided Mr. Kohl should die? *And* you killed him?"

"Yes."

"Don't you think he should have had something to say about whether he lived or died?"

"No." She shook her head. "His mind had become diseased. He was like a mad dog that had to be put out of its misery."

"Did you *plan* to do it last night?"

"No. But when he and the Governor got into an argument, I listened to him, I heard how depraved he had become, threatening the Governor, blackmailing. I saw then it was my duty—to him. It was a mercy killing."

Oh God, Wisniewski thought, could I have gotten myself in trouble! The book was right about the argument—but was it wrong from there on! "How did it happen?" he asked Sophie.

"I was nearby, near enough to hear their voices, yet out of sight. He liked me nearby, you see." She paused, was staring straight at him, yet even as she confessed a murder, her eyes showed no interest in what she was saying. "I heard the Governor leave, go back to his room, then I heard *him* screaming my name. I went running to him. He was raving, almost foaming at the mouth, he started hissing at me. Finally he said, 'You are my trained ape, Sophie! Go! Go kill him! Go, Sophie! Kill! Kill!'

"Then I realized that this was the moment I must put him out of his misery. And he wanted it, too. He didn't struggle very long."

Sure, Wisniewski said to himself. How could that poor little guy struggle for long against a monster like Sophie? Then he asked, "And why me, Sophie? I never did anything to you."

"No," she replied, almost in a trance. "But I knew you were upstairs, and when I saw you take my diary out of your pocket, and the films, I knew that you could use those to keep *him* in disgrace. You could keep him dancing on the fires of hell. I had to stop you from disturbing his rest."

Wisniewski couldn't resist saying, "You came close. Now you're under arrest. You'll be charged with murder and attempted murder."

"Will I be put to death?"

"Nobody gets put to death in New York anymore."

"I want to die."

"That's not up to you."

"People should have some say over whether they live or die."

"What about Mr. Kohl? Did you give him any say?"

She clamped her mouth shut, but her eyes remained blank.

"Tell me, Sophie, did Mr. Kohl love you?"

"No. He didn't love anybody."

"Sophie, did you and Mr. Kohl ever . . . have sex?"

When he'd placed his chair near her, Wisniewski told himself he'd put himself too close to the edge of the pool. But he dismissed it; she was exhausted, her hands were tied. In the face of her fury at his question, he realized he should have listened to his feeling, but then it was too late. She lashed out with a powerful leg, toppled him and his chair into the pool.

He hit the water backwards, head first, did a flip that left him totally disoriented. Frantically, he tried to right himself—he'd never been any good at underwater somersaults—feeling the binding weight of his jacket, pants, shoes. He couldn't seem to get his head up and above water. It'd be funny—the thought flashed through his mind—if Sophie achieved with a stray kick what she'd been unable to do with a stranglehold.

Finally he got a hand on the side of the pool and used it to straighten himself and then to rise to the surface. Gulping air, he hauled himself out of the pool and looked around for Sophie. If she'd headed for a car, she'd be out of sight, around the house, by now. But her hands were bound. And he had the feeling she wouldn't be going that way. He thought he knew what she had in mind, and he started toward the dunes, trying to run, slowed by fatigue and sodden cloth-ing. He removed his jacket as he climbed the nearest dune, carried it with him as he ran, looking ahead at the sand and grass lit by the moon. Perhaps fifty yards away he could see Sophie, running, her arms twisting behind her as she tried to undo the belt binding them. But she was tied tightly, he knew, and she'd have a hell of a job freeing herself, especially while moving. He ran through the soft sand and the grass, happy to have his shoes and pants as protection against the brambles and the sawtooth edges of the dune cover.

Each time he reached a rise, he spotted her, then lost her as he dipped into a hollow. If he was gaining it was not by much. Then she dropped over the last dune onto the beach, and for several seconds, as he covered the distance to the beach, he couldn't see her. When he reached the lip of the last dune, he scanned the beach. The surf was high, the froth iridescent in the moonlight. He saw Sophie down on the hard sand, hands still bound behind her, headed straight for the water.

He raced down the slope, straining through the soft sand, his eyes on the woman's broad back.

"Hold it!" he screamed. "Sophie, wait!" His shoes were slowing him down, and he paused, dropped the jacket, pulled off the shoes without untying them, unzipped his trousers, stepped out of them and contin-ued his run. She was in the water, a retreating wave churning around her legs. What she was doing was clear; she was headed straight out into the ocean.

She wanted to die. She was a powerful swimmer and he was a splasher, yet he had to try to stop her. Why, he didn't know. But he had to. Now he gained on her rapidly as she tried to force her way through waves without the help of her arms. She was getting knocked around, pushed back, barely in as far as her waist when he felt the cool of the water on his stockinged feet.

He went right after her, wondering to himself how far he dared go in without drowning himself. He felt the pull of the undertow; then a towering wave headed for him. He ducked, it broke over him, its wash knocking him off his feet. He struggled to stand, and at the same time to see her. She was five yards to his right and about two body lengths farther out. He swam toward her; with the swell of a wave, the water was already over his head. How he could get her back to shore he had no idea; but he had to try.

He saw her kick her feet vigorously, realized she was moving just as fast with her kick as he was with the help of his arms. Just then a wave pushed her right at him, and with a lunge, he grabbed the belt holding her wrists.

"God, Sophie, come back!" It was half a gurgle, as his mouth filled with water.

Her response was to kick out powerfully with her left foot, catching him half on the thigh, half in the groin, breaking his hold. He groped for her, saw her feet churning in a flutter kick. Then a wave caught the two of them. For an instant, it brought her close enough for him to reach out, clutch her big calf. But he couldn't hold on. His hand slid to her ankle.

Then she was gone.

She got through the wave; he was caught by it, tumbled, shoved toward shore, back into water where he could stand. He was grateful, for he had no strength left. He looked for her, could see nothing. Then the undertow pulled at him and he felt himself being carried out. For an instant he was panicked—he'd always hated the goddamned surf, been scared to death by it. He told himself: don't fight the undertow, let it take you, then come back in on the wave.

He fought his fear, let himself get pulled a little, then swam in with a wave. It took him four waves before he could stagger out of the ocean's clutch and fall to the sand, gasping.

After a few seconds he sat up, got to his feet, scanned the ocean. There was no sign of Sophie. She'd done what she wanted.

Wisniewski turned, started back toward the house, barely able to drag himself across the sand. When he got to his pile of clothing, he first lifted his jacket, hefted the weight of it, then made a decision. He fished from the pockets the film cans and the diary, and headed back toward the ocean.

Now he knew who killed Kohl; what he'd read in Bea Fletcher's manuscript had been wrong and had come damned close to getting him in serious trouble—although having just missed being killed, he took the other trouble a little less seriously than he had an hour ago. Now he had no need for the film or the diary. He didn't know the secrets either contained, nor did he want to. He didn't know if they'd been ruined by his dip in the pool, nor did he want to.

Now he could do what he'd thought of earlier. He walked to the edge of the water, and in five separate throws, hurled the diary and the four cans as far out to sea as he could.

It was odd, he thought, that the literary set of the Hamptons was really untouched by all this. The two dead people were the outsiders, Friedrich Kohl and Sophie. Neither belonged. And both had lived without love, yet love had been the death of them.

Wisniewski walked back to his clothing. He was particularly worried about his shoes; he hoped they'd dry all right. They were his newest and he couldn't afford another pair until the January sales.

Labor Day Weekend, 1977;
Sunday (continued)

"THAT'S NOT Lady Sociability leaving a party early, is it?" Bea turned when she heard the voice. It was Harry and she knew it. Another two steps and she'd have been out of his sight, on her way to her car. She didn't know whether to be glad or not.

She smiled. "It surely is, and she's leavin' her title behind for you to award to someone else." He came toward her, drink in hand, glasses up on forehead just as he had on that summer day when they'd met.

"What's the matter, losing your zest for the fray?"

"Yes. Just frayed, and afraid."

"Oh dear, oh dear."

"You're responsible for my saying things like that, Harry. No use complaining."

He shook his head. "What I was complaining about was that you were leaving before we could have a drink."

"We just *had* a drink, at my place, remember?"

"I meant the two of us, alone together, so we could talk."

"We did *that* at the softball game, remember?"

"I meant 'neath the gauzy veil of eve, where moonlight touches up our blemishes and smooths our wrinkles—" He quickly corrected himself. "*My* blemishes, that is. *My* wrinkles."

"Oh no. Mine, too. And nothing hides them. The gauzy veil of eve just screws you up."

"I suppose," he said, "you're going on to another party, not bigger but better, where the likes of me would not be welcome."

"I'm going home. And if you'd like to come over for *one* drink, all right. But no funny stuff!"

"Romantic, or semantic?"

"Romantic. Semantic is hopeless."

"You're on."

"Who's going to look after Lolita?"

"Who?"

"Your date."

"They are waiting in line to look after Nellie."

"All right. One drink."

They walked to their cars and drove separately to her house. She got there first and let him in through the kitchen. As they walked together to the living room, she said, "There's a condition. I didn't tell you about it before."

"I agreed: no funny stuff."

"No, be serious. I'm working on an ending for the book and I want to try some things on you. Okay?"

"I thought you said no funny stuff."

"Stop it! Are you going to sit there and listen to me read?"

"Are you going to get me a drink first?"

She walked quickly to the bar, threw some ice in an old-fashioned glass and poured him a stiff vodka.

"Don't forget the twist!" he shouted at her.

She looked around, found a wizened piece of lemon peel, tossed it into the glass and carried it to Harry. Then she took his arm and led him to the den.

From her little clutch purse, she took her keys and began to open the desk. "There's something funny here, Harry."

"What's the matter?"

"I'm having trouble with this lock. It doesn't turn."

"Oh, women just don't know how to do little mechanical things like that." He didn't move as he said it. "Unfortunately, neither do I. Keep trying, you'll get it."

Now she could see something was wrong; the top of the drawer looked scratched. "Harry!" But then, stiff though the lock was, she managed to open it, and felt a little better . . . until she lifted the manuscript out of its drawer. The rubber band was off, and it started at page 509 instead of page 1. Somebody had been looking at the last few pages and had placed them on top instead of on the bottom.

"Harry . . ."

He could now see she was worried. "What's the matter?"

"Someone has broken into this desk, and has been . . ." She was reading page 509 as she spoke."Oh my God!"

Harry was up and standing near her. "What *is* it?"

Her eyes were wide. "Only one person . . ."

"Will you tell me what's the matter?" Harry stood right in front of her, grabbed both elbows.

"My God! He thinks . . . Harry, come with me, and I'll tell you while we're driving." She practically broke into a run as she headed for her car, and he loped after her. She started the engine, and had the car moving before he could slam his door shut.

"Okay, come on now!" he said.

"Only one person wanted to read that manuscript, was *desperate* to read it. The detective, Wisniewski."

"So?"

"He wanted to read it because he thought I knew who killed Freddie, and had written it into my ending!"

"Well, *do* you know who killed him?"

"No!"

Harry shifted his weight in the seat as he swiveled toward her. "So then why are you so upset?"

"Well, I thought I would try out a few endings. A novelist can take a certain license, you know."

"That's not the one you're going to lose if you keep driving this fast. By the way, where are we going?"

"To Freddie's."

"Maybe I'm supposed to understand all this. Maybe I'm dumb, but I don't. What the hell . . ."

"I tried out a *lot* of endings, Harry! The one that the manuscript was open to, that he'd been reading had . . . the Governor as the murderer!"

"Oh my God!"

"It had Mike Hughes and Freddie quarreling, it had Freddie telling Mike he'd shot film of him in bed with some of his bimboes, and if Mike didn't do what he wanted . . ." Bea was no longer even trying to use the fictitious names she'd given her characters.

"Oh my God! Did he actually shoot film like that?"

"Yes."

"Did they quarrel last night?"

"I think so. . . . Yes. They did."

"How do you know?"

"The way I usually know. Someone told me."

"Do you know that the Governor *didn't* kill Freddie?"

"No . . ." She turned briefly to glance at him. "No, I don't, but you don't accuse someone of murder just because you don't know he *didn't* do it."

Then Harry caught on. "Oh . . . so Polack Holmes reads it, he doesn't know it's made up, he goes straight over to Freddie's to confront the Governor . . ."

"No," she said firmly. "I think you're underrating him. I'm sure he was well aware of the problem of accusing a Governor—or anyone—based on a chapter of a novel. What he went for was to look for the film. The filming took place at Freddie's.

"What I'm afraid of," she went on, "is that the Governor might leave the party early, as we did, go back to Freddie's—and find the detective there. And Mike would ask, what are you doing here, and the detective might say, looking for film, and Mike would know what film, and get hot under the collar. And so would Wisniewski, and say: 'I know all about you from Mrs. Fletcher's book.' Do you see, Harry?"

"Yes, I see."

"What should I do?"

"Drive faster."

But when they arrived, the Rolls the Governor had been using for the weekend was already there. Bea's face turned white; she ran from the car, Harry following, out around the back of the house, saw Wisniewski standing with the Governor and Warren Daniels near the pool.

"Take it easy, take it easy," Harry said, for he could see she was close to panic.

Not knowing what to say, she just raced up to them, managed to blurt out, "Hello, I must talk to Detective Wisniewski about something extremely important."

Hughes was startled and a little put off. "It can't be more important than what Stan has been telling *me!*"

Bea feared she was going to faint, until Wisniewski said, in one sentence and with no pauses, "I was just telling the Governor that I know who killed Mr. Kohl—Sophie drowned Mr. Kohl and then she tried to drown me and then committed suicide by swimming out into the surf even though I had tied her hands behind her back."

"What?" It was all Bea could manage.

"Yes," the Governor said. "Stan was here doing a little snooping, when . . . hell, you tell her, Stan, it's your story, and a hell of a story, too."

"I'd been upstairs," Wisniewski began, and then went through the whole story. Except that he made no mention of Bea's manuscript, or any film, or Sophie's diary. When he was finished, the Governor added, "And the funny thing was, he'd found no evidence against her—at all!"

"She was crazy," the detective said. "At least she sounded it to me. And I think she wanted to die. Whether she loved Mr. Kohl or hated him, he was her only connection to life, I guess. Without him she had no life—that's only my opinion of course." As he spoke his eyes stayed fixed on Bea's, and she thought she read in them: I understand, don't worry.

For a moment no one had anything to say, then Wisniewski spoke. "If you folks will excuse me, I'm going to drive back to headquarters and do some paper work. And then get home. Tomorrow is not a day off for me."

"Listen, Stan," the Governor said, "you've done a hell of a job on this, and if you'd like me to call and tell them . . ."

Wisniewski smiled. "Thanks, Governor, but the truth is, I'd rather work tomorrow, and get the overtime. I can use the extra money. I don't have to tell you about a cop's salary."

Hughes was emphatic as he answered. "You sure don't. I've just been working on raises for the state troopers, and . . ." Then he gave up, shrugged, let his shoulders sag. "Yes, it's tough."

"It's been a pleasure, Governor," Wisniewski said. Hughes stuck out his hand, clasped the detective's.

"I'm going too, Mike," Bea said. "I'm glad the detective here has done such a great job. See you soon, I hope." And she turned. "Come on, Harry, let's have the drink I promised you."

"But Bea," Hughes said, "I thought you had something to tell Stan?"

"It doesn't matter now, does it? It was some amateur bit of detective work, but amateurs really should leave murder to professionals, shouldn't they?" As she spoke the last sentence her eyes shifted to Wisniewski, and he answered:

"We always appreciate help, Mrs. Fletcher."

Bea supposed she should be angry at him for breaking in and reading the manuscript, but she looked at him gratefully, said only, "Thanks."

Now Hughes had a hard, worried look on his face, "What about your book now, Bea? Does Freddie's death make any difference in your plans . . . ?"

She shrugged. "Oh yeah, I suppose. Yes . . . a lot. I'll have to think about it. Perhaps do some rewriting. I absolutely refuse to think about it any more tonight." Meanwhile, she noticed that the detective had walked off in the direction of his car. "All right then, Mike, see you. Shall we, Harry?"

Hughes, Daniels, Bea, Harry exchanged quick goodbyes, and Bea, with Harry close behind, managed to get to the parking area before Wisniewski left. She dashed to his car.

"Do you have time to talk for a while?"

He sighed.

"I know," she said. "But please."

"I'm just tired," he said. "That's all I meant. I do have some time. Why don't we drive to Georgica Beach? It's close by and it's a nice night."

She smiled gratefully. "That's fine, thank you. I'm going to bring Harry. He's very close and I told him all about this. If it's all right with you."

He shrugged. "Sure, why not? See you there."

They met at the beach, and walked down onto the sand. The storm they'd named "Shirley," which was the occasion of their first meeting with Wisniewski, had almost destroyed the beach, but it had built itself up.

They sat with their backs to the base of the dune.

"Sure is a beautiful place," the detective said.

"It sure is," Harry echoed. Bea waited for some kind of one-liner, but there was none.

"What really happened?" Bea asked.

"Everything that I said happened, plus some more. . . ." And the detective told her the whole story.

"You had no business breaking in and reading that manuscript," Bea said. She tried to keep her voice from getting shrill, and could hear she wasn't succeeding. "I told you you couldn't! I ought to . . ." Then she stopped; she just wasn't in the mood to threaten punishment.

"I know," Wisniewski said gently. "I shouldn't have, and it almost got me killed. I figure there's a lesson in it—about good police work, versus bad. Maybe they ought to use it as a case study in police academies—only I don't think I'll tell them about it, if it's all right with you."

Wisniewski looked down at the sand, scratched a meaningless hieroglyph in it. "You know," he said, "your ending was much better than the real one. Made more sense. And a lot more exciting. Scared the hell out of me when I thought it *was* real. It was a darned good ending."

"My ending?" Bea said. "You don't understand! It was only *one* of my endings! I had six, seven endings, and I was working on others. I had Buster kill him in a drunken fury; I had Johnny kill him to save the publishing business; I had Betsy Shore kill him while he was forcing her to commit an indecent act underwater; I had Irv kill him to save my literary honor; yes, and I had the Governor kill him because Freddie wanted to be Secretary of State; I had Warren Daniels kill him while the Governor stood there and cheered. I had the *group* throw him in and all swim around on top of him, shoving him under every time he tried to surface—that would have been a good one for a detective to solve!"

Bea looked over at Harry. "I even tried to make Harry the killer—only I couldn't work it out."

Harry smiled. "I take that as a compliment."

She touched the back of his hands, which were clasped around his knees. "I mean it as one."

"I don't know much about writing novels, Mrs. Fletcher," said the detective. "Heck, I don't know *anything* about writing novels. But it seems to me that any of those endings would be better than the real one. The real one must be disappointing to you. For your book, I mean."

Bea smiled, grimaced, said only, "I'll have to think about that too. But not tonight."

"Mr. Wisniewski," Harry said, and this time he got the name exactly right, "I don't know much about writing novels either, but I think Bea's endings are better only if you're looking for something snazzy, some fireworks, for your final chapter. If you want to tell the *truth* about the Hamptons, our part of it, anyway, you'd *have* to use the real ending."

Bea looked surprised. Harry went on. "Well, not that exact ending, but one like it. The killer would have to be an outsider. A burglar, any kind of intruder would do, as well as someone like Sophie. If there were a butler, he could have done it. Because if you really want to write *truth* about the people Bea is writing about, you have to say none of them would, none of them *could*, do anything as drastic, as absolute, as killing anybody.

"If you want to be a Hemingway about it, you can be contemptuous of it. You can call it impotence; you can say none of these book types can get it up, can come off, all they can do is talk about it, go round and round and round, pelting each other with words. You can say that even the macho types, Buster and Johnny, when they decided to join this group, checked their *cojones* at the door.

"Or you can look at it another way, and say, Lord be praised, here is a group that cannot, *will* not kill, unless you can *talk* somebody to death. That words are their deeds, and no matter how blustering or threatening, words are not lethal. That this group has reached the level of civilization where killing is not an acceptable weapon."

"Oh, I like that one better, Harry," Bea said. "That second one. After all, that is not a bad level of civilization to reach, is it?"

Harry looked as though he was thinking about an answer, when the detective spoke. "If the level of civilization is all that high, Mr. Majors, why is it that two people are dead?"

Harry shook his head. "Ah, Mr. Wisniewski, that is the best question that's been asked so far. Who killed these two people? Sure, it's easy to say Sophie killed Freddie and then herself. But couldn't you also say that this highly civilized community of literati pushed Freddie into a corner, literally drove him *crazy*, to the point where he provoked, *forced* Sophie to kill him—after which she *had* to kill herself?

"Now I know, Mr. Wisniewski, that's hardly grounds for a legal charge of murder. But let's suppose for a moment Freddie and Sophie had found themselves in another milieu, businessmen, let's say, bankers. Do you think this would have happened? I doubt it."

Bea didn't like that. "Harry," she said heatedly, "this group did not *ask* Freddie to become a member. *He* wanted that. He *pushed* his way in."

"True," Harry answered. "Nor did it reject him. It could have. After all, Southampton had the good manners to do it. The Maidenhead said to him: We do not want you. Go away. And he went away. But not us, we didn't say that. Why not? Because we *like* to have someone to sneer at? Of course! It's dangerous to sneer at another of the literary hotshots. After all, he's a *peer!* Besides, he might be too tough for you, you might end up taking more than you can dish out. So Freddie was just perfect as a scapegoat. But there's more than that. In a sense, we *wanted* him. We *wanted* his Dom Perignon and his Beluga caviar and his pool and tennis court and mansion as a kind of clubhouse. And we *wanted* his money, didn't we? Our collective tongue was hanging *out* at the thought of what he'd pay for a book, wasn't it?"

He turned to Bea, asked gently:

"Wasn't it?"

She nodded, answered softly but fiercely, "Yes, it was!"

"So those fingerprints on the back of his neck, that the detective told us about, maybe they were *ours*," Harry said. "While we kept staring at him, and saying Go away, our hand was on the back of his neck, clutching him close. Maybe it doesn't matter if you say we were impotent, that we couldn't come off in the explosion of fury needed to get rid of him, or you say we were too civilized, too *talky* to do anything physical—maybe it adds up to the same thing: we destroyed him in our own way. We *did* talk him to death."

"Do you really believe all that, Harry?" Bea asked.

He shrugged. "It's something to talk about."

Bea looked at the detective. "What do you think of his idea, Mr. Wisniewski?"

The detective looked at them and his broad face spread in a grin. "Don't take offense at this, but I think all you folks talk too much. You may *all* talk yourselves to death." He got to his feet. "I've got to get up real early tomorrow morning, but if I could stay, I'd just sit here and look at the ocean, and listen to those waves, and let the sand run through my fingers. It sure is pretty here."

"Mr. Wisniewski," Bea said, "I think you handled yourself very well, and I'm pleased to know you. You protected me at a time I was very vulnerable."

"Mrs. Fletcher, you wouldn't have been vulnerable if I hadn't done something I shouldn't have." He took her hand and shook it, then shook Harry's. "Mr. Majors, you've given me something to think about and I'm going to spend some time thinking about it." He smiled again. "But it won't keep me from sleeping tonight."

They watched the stocky detective walk up toward the parking area. Bea turned to Harry.

"Harry, let's not talk ourselves to death."

He nodded, put an arm around her shoulder. "It sure is pretty here," he said. Then he put a finger to his lips to signal silence.